Praise for *At Her Service*

"*At Her Service* is a charming, uplifting, and deeply relatable romance perfect for any reader who has ever dreamed of stepping into their own best life. I want to befriend Amy Spalding's characters and live in her quirky queer romantic world forever." —Susie Dumond, author of *Queerly Beloved*

"*At Her Service* is a painfully relatable story of finding the courage to reach for what you really want from inside the messy reality of your twenties. It made me snort with laughter more than once, and anyone who has ever taken comfort in a queer dive bar will be so invested in Johnny's—and its hot bartender—right along with Max. A wonderfully hopeful, queer, LA love story." —Anita Kelly, author of *Something Wild & Wonderful*

"*At Her Service* is an ingenious millennial coming-of-age story about trying to find yourself in the age of apps and a culture of grind. Highly relatable, laugh-out-loud funny, and full of hot-bartender sapphic swoon, Amy Spalding joyfully reminds us that growing up can happen at any age and that we're all works in progress." —Alison Cochrun, author of *Kiss Her Once for Me* and *The Charm Offensive*

"*At Her Service* offers a poignant and heartwarming look at modern love. With affirming themes of found family and self-belief, plus a sizzling romance that roars into a wildfire, prepare to fall hard for Max and Sadie! Amy Spalding is a powerhouse in romance, and *At Her Service* is a validating gift to the queer community." —Courtney Kae, author of *In the Event of Love* and *In the Case of Heartbreak*

"No one writes delightful heroines, fresh humor and dazzling portraits of the vibrance of Los Angeles like Amy Spalding. *At Her Service* is everything—a nuanced, deeply felt romance, a deft social-media send-up and an unforgettable story of finding your place and yourself."
—Emily Wibberley and Austin Siegemund-Broka, authors of *The Roughest Draft*

"Amy Spalding's writing will make you swoon, laugh, and fall in love with how outrageous Hollywood can be. I was rooting for Max and Sadie's achingly sweet romance, and found it hard to let go of them once I finished. *At Her Service* will stay with you in the best way possible!"
—Erin La Rosa, author of *For Butter or Worse* and *Plot Twist*

Praise for *For Her Consideration*

"I loved how joyful, how thoughtful, and how real *For Her Consideration* was. This book made me laugh out loud, smile big, and swoon hard. Amy Spalding made me adore Nina and her friends, fall in love with Nina and Ari, and want to live in their world forever."
—*New York Times* bestselling author Jasmine Guillory

"With vibrant prose, a setting that is both upscale glam and homey comfort, and a thrumming, pounding, romantic heart, *For Her Consideration* is pure romance magic."
—Christina Lauren, *New York Times* bestselling author of *The Unhoneymooners*

"*For Your Consideration* is so many things I want in a book: funny, sexy, and super queer. Spending time in Nina and Ari's world was a joy. Amy Spalding has written a warm celebration of Los Angeles, chosen family, and learning how to love and be loved."
—Cameron Esposito, bestselling author of *Save Yourself*

"*For Her Consideration* is a heartening, dishy, celebratory novel that features true-to-life queer characters—the exact kind of book I've longed to see flourish on bookstore and library shelves. It is an absolute delight to read and a worthy addition to the modern romantic-comedy genre."
—Camille Perri, author of *When Katie Met Cassidy*

"*For Her Consideration* is the perfect kind of romance— it sucks you in, makes you swoon, and leaves you utterly satisfied AND wanting more. Amy Spalding has created an authentic Hollywood love story between two wonderfully relatable women both striving to find themselves while also falling for each other."
—Kate Spencer, author of *In a New York Minute*

"Flirty and fun, with romance and laughs on every page, *For Her Consideration* is a rom-com that truly embodies the term. I loved every moment of this book, from Nina and Ari's love match, to their found families, to the Los Angeles-local backdrop. Spalding's singular sense of humor and lovable characters make for a perfect escape. I tore through this with a smile on my face!"
—Sarah Skilton, author of *Fame Adjacent*

"*For Her Consideration* by Amy Spalding is a charming romantic comedy with two winning heroines. I especially enjoyed the strong family bonds, including a truly delightful group of friends. My heart ached at the emotional moments and I giggled aloud at all the funny parts. I loved watching Ari and Nina learn to trust themselves and each other and follow their dreams. Cute and heartfelt, *For Her Consideration* is a highly recommended read."
—Erica Ridley, *New York Times* bestselling author of *The Perks of Loving a Wallflower*

"A fiercely funny, super sexy story about believing in your dreams, finding your chosen family, and letting yourself be loved. After reading *For Her Consideration*, I'm in love with both Los Angeles and Ari Fox. Amy Spalding has such a gift for snappy dialogue and loving, quirky friend groups, and I'll read everything she writes."
—Kerry Winfrey, author of *Just Another Love Song*

"*For Her Consideration* is incredibly funny, queer, sweet, and sexy. Anyone with a toxic ex or a serious celebrity crush will be able to relate! It's about learning to trust yourself and the people in your life, and it's guaranteed to leave you smiling and wanting to hug your chosen family very hard."
—Celia Laskey, author of *So Happy for You* and *Under the Rainbow*

"Brimming with passion and tenderness, this book proves that unexpected love can last." —*Stamford Magazine*

AT HER
SERVICE

Books by Amy Spalding

For Her Consideration

At Her Service

AT HER SERVICE

AMY SPALDING

KENSINGTON
PUBLISHING CORP.

www.kensingtonbooks.com

KENSINGTON BOOKS are published by
Kensington Publishing Corp.
119 West 40th Street
New York, NY 10018

All Kensington titles, imprints, and distributed lines are available at special quantity discounts for bulk purchases for sales promotion, premiums, fund-raising, educational, or institutional use.

This book is a work of fiction. Names, characters, businesses, organizations, places, events, and incidents either are the product of the author's imagination or are used fictitiously. Any resemblance to actual persons, living or dead, events, or locales is entirely coincidental.

To the extent that the image or images on the cover of this book depict a person or persons, such person or persons are merely models, and are not intended to portray any character or characters featured in the book.

Special book excerpts or customized printings can also be created to fit specific needs. For details, write or phone the office of the Kensington Sales Manager: Kensington Publishing Corp., 119 West 40th Street, New York, NY 10018. Attn. Sales Department. Phone: 1-800-221-2647.

The K with book logo Reg US Pat. & TM Off.

ISBN: 978-1-4967-3954-4 (ebook)

ISBN: 978-1-4967-3953-7

First Kensington Trade Paperback Printing: March 2024

10 9 8 7 6 5 4 3 2 1

Printed in the United States of America

*To anyone who's ever felt like a child
cosplaying as an adult*

Chapter 1
Not a Day for Salads

Before I worked at Exemplar, I had no idea how quickly an hour could pass. If anything, time had gone too slowly my whole life. As a kid, I'd spent a lot of time willing myself to be older and more grown-up, like if that old movie *Big* was about a teen lesbian instead of Tom Hanks. Unfortunately, the years inched by without a magical instant adulthood.

I'd been twenty-five years old with very little to show for it when I'd started this job. And now it felt like I'd just blinked a few times and I was twenty-six. All of it was less magical than I'd hoped for. Today, in particular, was anything but magical, unless there was a fairy tale I'd missed in which an extremely hungover girl toiled away, unseen and overlooked, with the previous night's mistakes pounding in her head in sync with the tequila, and then died alone.

I checked the time on my Apple Watch—I guess I couldn't get away with saying that I was unseen and overlooked while wearing a birthday gift from my very generous boss—and tried not to curse. My watch glowed *8:52*, but my Full Focus Planner laid out half a dozen tasks—written in my tidiest, least hung-over penmanship—still unchecked.

Everyone said in job interviews for assistant positions that they excelled at multitasking and prioritizing, but the thing was that *I truly excelled at multitasking and prioritizing!* Normally speaking. At the moment, the tasks I was juggling were trying not to throw up and also trying not to think about what I'd said last night—and, worse—to whom. It definitely wasn't the time to dwell on the fact that I'd, in my only truly safe place in LA, blurted out something incredibly horrifying to the woman I'd had the biggest crush on. Which meant that, in one fell swoop, I had neither a safe place nor a crush.

I wouldn't let this stop me. "Focus," I whispered to myself in my sternest tone, which unfortunately was not very stern. Talking to myself, regardless of my tone, was probably one of the factors that contributed to having no work friends. But as usual, I was the first assistant to arrive in my little section of cubicles, so no one witnessed this particular incident.

I decided to take that as as good an omen as I was getting this morning and got back to my checklist. Assistants at Exemplar Talent Agency weren't actually expected to show up to work as early as I did, but I was determined not to stay an assistant forever. There were so many tasks to be completed before my boss, Joyce, arrived that it just made sense to give myself extra time so that I could look as polished and professional and achieving as possible. Normally that worked out fine.

Still, despite last night's terrible choices thudding in my head, the tasks got checked off. Headlines on *Deadline*, *THR*, and *Variety* were reviewed, my summary of the entertainment trades' morning news was in Joyce's inbox, the agency-specific client email inboxes were checked, the intra-agency grid was updated with the casting information that was my responsibility to input, and a K-Cup was loaded and waiting in Joyce's Keurig. By the time Joyce's number flashed on my phone, I practically felt like myself again.

"Good morning," I greeted her.

"Can you get Peter at the studio on for me?" Joyce asked in lieu of a greeting. Actually, since I'd been working for Joyce for over a year now, I knew that it *was* her greeting.

"Of course, just a moment," I said, placing Joyce on hold while I pulled up Peter's information. When I'd started, I was overwhelmed by the shorthand—why not tell me Peter's last name or what freaking studio he worked for? Now, though, I knew the players as well as Joyce did. I knew their names, at least.

After I got Peter on the line, I patched him through to Joyce but stayed muted so I could take notes since she was in her car on the way in. When I was first hired, I couldn't believe that part of my job was to listen in on calls between Hollywood bigwigs. I imagined the A-list gossip I'd get would be *ridiculous*. Now I knew that the first half to two-thirds of the call would be about a vacation someone just took or some industry event someone else didn't get invited to or a new restaurant that was impossible to get into which would be the expected setting of Joyce's next business lunch. I'd yet to overhear anything that could be described as even approaching *salacious*.

By the time I was jotting down notes from the call with Peter and preparing to connect Joyce with whomever she wanted to speak with next, I realized the full-body jangle of panic had shrunk down to a mere pounding headache. Considering last night's massive rounds of alcohol and humiliation, a headache? That I could manage. This job? I wouldn't only *manage* it, I would keep proving my immense skills to Joyce every single day until I was officially on the junior agent track. Sadie? OK, no, the future where Sadie and I fell into each other's arms was dead, but that future had never actually ever started. It was fine. I was fine.

After Joyce's second call wrapped up, she let me know she was about to pull into the garage, so we said goodbye before her signal dropped off. I dashed into her office, pushed the Keurig's

brew button, and grabbed the oat milk creamer while the organic San Francisco Bay Fog Chaser blend dripped into Joyce's
YETI mug. I stirred in half a packet of stevia and walked carefully to the elevator bay; there were tales told of assistants fired
for dripping beverages on Exemplar's pristine white flooring—
and, true or not—I vowed that I would never become an urban
legend.

"Thank god for you," Joyce said as the elevator doors parted
and she stepped off. It was a pretty great morning greeting, even
if it was potentially directed at the contents of the mug and not
actually me. "I assume if there was any interesting news in the
trades this morning you would have already told me."

"Correct. And no new messages since the summary I sent
earlier."

We walked together down the main corridor, and my headache nudged me again, pounding in time with my feet hitting
the floor. I tried not to wince because I already felt like such a
disaster walking next to my boss. Joyce was inches taller than
me to begin with. Her daily footwear was four-inch heels that
cost roughly the same as my monthly rent, while mine was one
solo pair of black Dr. Martens oxfords that I'd had since college, so the height difference looked even more extreme. On
top of that, Joyce was the most stylish person I'd ever met. Today she wore a patterned yellow jumpsuit that contrasted really
beautifully against her dark brown skin. Her black hair was up
in a topknot that seemed to defy gravity—and make me look
even shrimpier. Between the shoes and the hair, I probably appeared about a full foot shorter than Joyce. I felt lucky that
she never seemed embarrassed that a tiny weirdo was always
scrambling to keep up with her around the office.

When I was hired last year, Joyce was already on the path to
becoming Exemplar's top talent agent. She would have already
been there, I knew, if she had narrowed her client list to A-list
stars and Oscar winners only. Joyce, though, was savvy enough

to spot rising talent early on, and so her list was an interesting mix. It was still kind of shocking that I was the person who assisted her.

Even though every article on the internet insisted that workplaces were getting so much more diverse these days, especially in the entertainment industry, I was pretty sure I was the only visibly queer woman in the whole building. One time I thought I spotted another, but she turned out to be a delivery person, like I was literally living out "Ring of Keys" from *Fun Home*. (I waved to her anyway. She was confused I didn't have any packages to be sent.) Not that my queerness was an issue here— it was just that Exemplar seemed to have an unspoken dress code of dresses and super femme jumpsuits and very tall heels and those sandals that kind of looked like boots or maybe the other way around but regardless I had never understood, exactly, what weather they were good for.

So I still couldn't believe that I'd showed up in my nicest patterned Peau de Loup button-down and my only pair of pants that wasn't jeans with my frantically polished Docs and then got the job. But since that was exactly what happened, I tried not to dwell on how out of place I still felt every day. I had twenty-six years of feeling out of place, after all. It was just a different kind of out of place in the entertainment industry.

"Today's call with Paul is confirmed?" Joyce asked as I followed her into her office. We started every day this way, going over upcoming meetings and any breaking news. Since Joyce already had her coffee, this is when I usually made myself a cup, because she was generous enough to let me use her fancy organic brew and creamer. It went down a lot smoother than the cup I guzzled during my daily morning commute, but I couldn't wait that long for the good stuff (especially this morning). After all, even cheap coffee got the job done.

Joyce's office, like Joyce, was stylish and intimidating beyond what I could have imagined before landing this job. (I'd interviewed in Joyce's favorite meeting room, and therefore wasn't prepared to walk into this stunning space on my first day of employment.) Exemplar's overall vibe was of bright whiteness, like an Apple store that sold talent and intimidation instead of phones and computers, but Joyce's office, like Joyce herself, was vibrant and warm . . . and intensely intimidating. Paintings and prints in bold colors hung on the walls, and color had been injected wherever possible—the yellow sofa, the cobalt blue desk lamp, even the file cabinets were Tiffany blue.

I, a person without one ounce of interior decorating ability, didn't understand how all the competing vivid hues didn't clash or look like a nightmare circus, but it was the exact opposite. Joyce's office was striking and anything but quiet, but it was also harmonious and beautiful. I was still a little amazed that I'd become comfortable here in this room. As comfortable as I was anywhere, at least. Anywhere except—oh my god. I couldn't think about that.

"Your call's confirmed," I told Joyce, ignoring that while my headache had dulled, there was still a sensation of someone hammering around in my skull. Who needed to feel a hundred percent to do her job? Not me. When I'd started at Exemplar, I'd lived in constant fear of saying the wrong thing, dropping the wrong call, making a reservation at the wrong restaurant. So even though this would never be a stress-free gig, I liked feeling how much fear had fallen away since then.

"And Meeting Room 2 is reserved for you for your three p.m. with Tess's team."

"Wonderful," Joyce said, and an Outlook reminder chimed on her computer and my watch at the same moment. "It's just the weekly meeting. I assume you've already grabbed my chair for me."

Oh, no. I should have known I couldn't just *power through* my stupid headache and my stupid heartbreak. Somehow, even with my multiple systems set up to keep something exactly like this from happening, I'd let a task slip anyway. I'd not only forgotten that Joyce was due for the Exemplar executive meeting but—so much worse—I hadn't reserved her seat at the conference room table.

"What?" Joyce asked, watching me, and I knew my face must have given me away.

"I'm so—let me see what I can—"

Joyce's gaze was so intense that I stopped as if she'd actually interrupted me. The seat thing was actually the story I told the most on first dates when people asked me if it was as ridiculous working at a talent agency as it seemed. *Not always*, I'd say. *But there's this thing about "the good seats" for the executive meetings though, where the only way to hold your spot in advance is that your assistant has to write down your name on a buck slip—Do you even know what that is? Why would you? It's like this old timey slip of heavy-duty paper—and put it on the chair in advance of the meeting. Otherwise they'll get stuck with a shitty spot and also everyone knows your assistant sucks.* I loved telling the story because Hollywood was indeed often very silly, but also because I never messed that up.

Never before today, at least.

I took a deep breath and tried again. "I know how important it is to—"

"It's fine," she said in a tone that made it clear it was anything but, and I tried very hard not to burst into tears. It was bad enough being tiny and weird—weird for this world, at least. I couldn't also be *a crier.*

Joyce's phone rang, and even though in more casual moments, I might have just reached over and answered it from her desk, I knew to carefully transport my fancy coffee out of there and back to the relative safety of my cubicle. An easy call would be great right now, honestly. I could solve some small problem, Joyce would witness how great I was at literally almost every single part of my job, and I'd be distracted enough to forget everything I'd messed up in the last twenty-four hours.

"Max, it's Karissa. Looks like we still haven't received Dan's payment for *Last Year's War.* I know you were looking into this, did you have an answer for us yet?"

"Yes—no, I mean, I don't have an answer, but I am looking into it and—"

I realized Joyce was standing right in front of me. I shook my head to let her know she didn't need to concern herself with the call, but considering she was on her way into the meeting that I'd messed up for her, I didn't feel as competent and irreplaceable as I'd aimed for. I didn't even feel mildly useful, *and* I was definitely destined to be alone forever. That didn't really have anything to do specifically with my job here, but somehow it all felt tied together right now, not just the boring work parts or the exciting romantic parts, just *all of it.*

Joyce headed into the meeting and I handled the call, and by the time I was off there were a dozen new emails to sort through, and on any other day all of this would be a great distraction. No matter how much I had to do, though, my head kept pounding. The hangover turned into a constant murmur, as if I could hear someone talking from a room or two away. All I could hear was *Sadie, Sadie, Sadie,* over and over, like my headache and my heartache had a little chat and were now sharing information freely. I'd been in this business way too long not to have made them sign NDAs.

After all, I wasn't built for hangovers and regretful mornings. While everyone else I knew had spent the tail end of their teens and their early twenties off at college, getting these experiences out of their system—or at least learning how to mess up and move on—I'd commuted all four years. I had stayed up too late sometimes, sure, but I was usually reading *Supergirl* fanfic in bed and working on homework assignments, not drinking at cute bars while even cuter bartenders—

The phone rang again, and now I had to figure out a "more inventive" location for a client dinner tomorrow night. Apparently, Horses had fallen out of favor since I made the reservation one week ago. I pulled up The Infatuation in my browser but also texted my roommate who was objectively cooler than me, as well as my former coworker who was not only also objectively cooler but in a relationship with an actor so would know where talent liked to eat these days. Hollywood really was silly and stupid, but for some reason I loved all of it. OK, most of it, the thing with the buck slips on chairs was beyond.

Joyce stopped by my desk on her way back from the meeting, smiling broadly. "I forgot Andrew's out this week. Didn't have to sit in the worst chair after all."

"Oh, good," I said, hit with a rush of relief that sort of washed over my anxiety but didn't clear it out all the way. Obviously, it was great that Joyce was in a good mood, but my screw-up was still fresh and I didn't like rehashing any part of it.

"I think it's going to be one of those days," Joyce said, and I felt a note of sympathy for my probably-very-obvious state of slight disaster. While I hated that she'd picked up on something, I also knew I was lucky to have a boss who actually saw me as a person. That wasn't something taken for granted in this town—or even in this building.

"I'm afraid so," I said, which made Joyce chuckle.

"Since I'm fairly sure I'm going to be stuck at my desk for the next however many hours, will you order over a salad for me? Get yourself one, too, all right?"

"Will do," I said, even though I could think of no worse hangover food than crisp greens and a delicate vinaigrette. Today called for pancakes for lunch, or one of those burritos that they doused like an enchilada, or just a trough of mac and cheese. But it always felt so lucky when Joyce treated me, when Joyce assumed that someone like me fit into her world of expensive salads. I would never dare upset that balance.

Joyce was right about the afternoon; it stayed as busy as the morning, though for me it was less painfully so because my headache gradually faded, and the work was steady and just complicated enough that I wasn't thinking nearly as much about Sadie. Obviously, I knew that it was impossible to notice you weren't thinking about someone without actually thinking about them quite a lot, but I was pretending that I wasn't. I was pretending I was already over her. I was pretending I hadn't ruined the one true thing I'd found here, in Los Angeles, all by myself.

A DM popped up on my monitor around six, as I was compiling my end-of-day summaries and getting my task list ready for the next morning. I clicked on the message from Aidy, the assistant who sat at the far end of my row of cubicles.

Need your advice on something, she messaged.

Of course!! I tried not to feel too pleased at this. People gave and got advice all of the time. But if I was truly just a tiny-voiced oddball, people wouldn't come to me, right? Definitely not Aidy, who'd been here a year longer and was one of two assistants assigned to Gary Kirchoff, one of the top agents at all of Exemplar.

Need to make dinner res for talent plus a producer way outside of Vancouver since that's the filming location. I know I could hit up Yelp but since you're Canadian maybe you have better ideas??

Oh, sorry, I'm not Canadian?? I typed.

"I'm on my way out," Joyce said, appearing at my desk with her bag over her shoulder. "I believe I have another nine-thirty tomorrow, so let's make sure everything's set up, please and thank you."

"Of course," I said, while wondering if it was bad to seem like someone from Canada. It obviously wasn't, people could be from anywhere. I'd just wanted an advice request on a topic I excelled at, that proved someone like Aidy saw me as an expert in an area. It was too bad that area was outer Vancouver.

A notification popped up on my screen. **Oh, no problem, you just seem so polite and Canadian!**

"Joyce," I said, as she stepped back from my desk, "I really am sorry about—"

"I'll see you in the morning."

For some reason, I then gave her a thumbs-up instead of a normal goodbye. It was a minor miracle that it was very nearly time to go home because I was pretty sure I was only going to find a way to make my entire life more awkward than it already was.

Chapter 2

Dumb Hollywood Job

My roommate Chelsey texted as I walked through the parking garage to my beat-up Yaris. Unlike my clothes and my whole general aesthetic, the car didn't set me apart at Exemplar. The parking garage was cleanly split between agents and assistants; you could see where the border of Teslas and Alfa Romeos ended and the clump of old, rusty, or dinged-up moderately priced cars began.

Having people over for snacks and bevs before going out, Chelsey messaged. **Mainly the usual suspects. Both a heads-up and an invite!**

I navigated out of the garage and onto Wilshire Boulevard into a very still sea of cars. When I'd moved here, I'd hoped that traffic in LA was one of those unfair stereotypes that locals poked holes through, but unfortunately the rumors were true. Some of my coworkers dealt with this by living closer, but I couldn't do it, even knowing I could sleep a little later and get home a little sooner. The Eastside was the only part of the city I could imagine living in, so I accepted my fate. There was also something about being in my car to and from with a Tegan and

Sara album blasting that reminded me of commuting to college, back when all of life seemed to be ahead of me. I knew that twenty-six was technically not old, not even middle-aged, but, oh my god, if this was the life that had been ahead of me, sometimes I wished I could time-travel back and tell my younger self to lower her expectations, at least a little.

Normally when I got a heads-up text from Chelsey, I headed to Johnny's, even when I'd already gone the night before. A heads-up text from Chelsey was how I discovered Johnny's in the first place. Tonight, though, it was out of the question. It was out of the question from now on! But I knew that a heads-up-slash-invitation from Chelsey was never actually an invitation, only a heads-up. And considering that I had two scripts to read before tomorrow morning, even if I wanted to hang out in the apartment while Chelsey and her friends snacked and bevved, I was in need of a quieter locale.

Mom called while I was still midway through my drive as well as my decision on where to go, and I reflexively tapped *answer* even though I didn't want to. I just wasn't the kind of person who knew how to send her mother to voicemail.

"Hi, honey, big day out there in Hollywood?"

"The guy dressed like Spider-Man was standing in the crosswalk at Sunset and Highland, clogging traffic, but I feel like that's not what you mean."

"It's so great you get to have all these exciting adventures while you're young," she said.

"I feel like you're not believing me here," I said. "He's emphatically *not* a very good Spider-Man. His boots are Uggs."

Mom laughed. "You know what I mean. Not everyone gets to live and work in Hollywood. No matter what happens in life, no one can ever take that away from you."

Mom said a lot of things like this, that later on I'd look back and enjoy this time of life so much, or that tales of buck slips and fancy salads would be hilarious fodder to share when I got back home. Because I knew that Mom loved me, I tried my best not to think about the fact that she clearly didn't think I could make it out here.

"Today I was told we had to find a more 'inventive' restaurant for a client dinner," I told Mom, as this was usually the closest kind of thing I had to industry gossip.

"Inventive?" She laughed, and I was relieved. I'd done my daughterly duty, a little entertainment and an anecdote I knew she'd tell her coworkers. Maybe a longer reprieve before she made me feel my days in LA were already numbered. "What does that even mean? I feel like the idea of inventing food already got covered a long time ago."

"Or at least when Molly put Hot Pockets on a bed of lettuce and called it a microwave salad," I said, which made Mom laugh even harder at the memory.

"I forgot all about that. Your sister was ahead of her time! Think they serve that at any of your fancy Hollywood restaurants?"

"Speaking of that, I need to figure out where I'm headed to get some work done," I said. "Talk to you later this week?"

"You know that I don't think it's fair how often you're working at night," Mom said. "I know they pay you plenty, but that's not a sustainable work-life balance."

"I have enough of a life," I said, which was even less true than Exemplar paying me plenty, but she already clearly thought I was bound to fail out here. I wasn't giving her any additional ammunition.

"Remember," she said, and I braced myself, "it gets too tough and unreasonable, you've always got a place here."

"I know, Mom," I said, even though the thought of my childhood bedroom felt like nothing but failure to me. "Love you."

"I love you too, Max."

My music roared back into the speakers, and I scrolled through a mental list of the easiest and cheapest spots where I could get dinner, escape my apartment for a while, and make my way through at least one of the scripts I'd brought home with me. It would be nice, I knew, if I had the kind of friend I could text for help. A quiet apartment to work from for the evening. A recommendation for the unknown-but-perfect spot. But that was something else I hadn't figured out here yet, the whole chosen-family best-friends thing, so I ended up doing the easiest thing I could think of once I'd parked behind my apartment. Me, the scripts, and a big order of chips and queso at the taco stand down the block. It was kind of in view of Johnny's, but only just barely, and I knew I could get away with holing away in a booth here until they closed. Plus, even though that salad had actually been delicious, grease and carbs were both long overdue.

By the time my order was up, I'd already checked my work email, dealt with a couple of issues that had popped up during my commute home, *and* gotten started reading the first script. I picked up my tray at the counter and, inhaling the warm cheesy goodness of the bubbling queso, let myself relax a little. I'd gotten through today. I was nailing my job again—or at least remembering its basic functions. And what couldn't be fixed with cheese and chips?

"Hey, number 72, watch out there!"

I turned to see if the guy at the counter meant me, but it was too late. My foot slid through a greasy patch on the tiled floor, and I teetered in what felt like a few thousand directions before slamming into a nearby, blessedly unoccupied, booth. I was inwardly congratulating myself for my catlike reflexes when I realized my hands were empty, which meant that my chips and vat of cheese were—

Oh my god. The plastic cup of queso had, defying more laws of gravity than Elphaba at the end of act I of *Wicked*, taken flight. That would be bad enough, but it was flying toward another customer who was on their way to the counter, and my reflexes were not fast enough to stop what was about to happen. Because the cheese was flying exactly toward that person's backside.

I almost managed to shout a warning, even though I wasn't sure if the speed of sound was faster than the speed of flying queso. But the words jammed up in my throat because I realized that the backside looked very familiar. I had, truth be told, checked out that ass many, many times.

"Sadie!" I called, but it was too late. The queso splattered against her before she spun around and made eye contact with me.

It would have been extremely helpful if I could have suddenly learned to disappear, but instead I had to stand right there and figure out what expression was appropriate when you'd just inadvertently thrown a hot cup of melted cheese at the ass of the woman you were sort of in love with, with whom you had absolutely zero chance.

I settled on a weak smile and a weaker wave. It was, I knew, only faintly better than my earlier thumbs-up.

"Max," Sadie said, her expression changing into a smile. I could have swooned watching Sadie smile, especially at me, even now, after the last twenty-four hours. "Did someone trip and dump a side of beans on my ass?"

"It was queso," I said, unhelpfully. Or maybe it was helpful, I'd never been in this situation before. "And, yes. Also, the someone was me."

Sadie laughed as she tried peering over her own shoulder. "How bad is it?"

"It's . . . it's not great." I tried not to stare at her (extremely good) ass, even with the question out there. "I'm so sorry, I can pay to have them dry-cleaned—"

"Max, I'm a bartender," she said, shoving her brown hair back from her face. She wore it a little longer than mine, like Leonardo DiCaprio in the 1990s *Romeo + Juliet*, and I loved how it always looked slightly disheveled, how you could trace the paths her fingertips took through it. "This is far from the worst liquid someone's spilled on me."

I couldn't believe how *normal* she was acting, as if I hadn't blurted out a horrifyingly embarrassing secret to her the night before. As if we ran into each other outside of Johnny's all of the time. As if I wasn't just a regular customer and she wasn't the dreamiest bartender in all of Southern California. And as if I hadn't just *spilled hot melted cheese on her ass.*

"I'm so sorry about your jeans," I said. "Let me—"

"Come with me," she said, and did not need to say it twice. I would go wherever Sadie asked. Which ended up being the one-stall all-gender bathroom.

Sadie efficiently tore off a few paper towels and soaked them with hot water before handing them off to me. "Do your best."

I froze, water dripping everywhere. "Like . . . ?"

"Like exactly what you're thinking, yeah," Sadie said, and before long we were both laughing. How was I in this situation right now? Maybe I'd actually hit my head on the tile floor when I fell and this was what I was dreaming about in a coma. Or maybe this was heaven. I wasn't sure I believed in the afterlife, but it had to at least be considered.

I tentatively scrubbed at Sadie's jeans, but it was hard to work effectively before I sort of gripped her waist with my other hand. It took my breath away, horrifyingly, embarrassingly, humiliatingly. I had to pause my cheese-removal because nothing about today had prepared me for physical contact with the person I worried I'd scared off forever.

If cheese-removal counted as physical contact.

Still, no matter the situation, there was no way I could ignore the curve of her ass in these beat-up Levi's, the softness of her waist underneath my hand. When I once described Sadie, Mom said that she sounded like a Bruce Springsteen song. Sadie dressed like my idea of a 1990s heartthrob, vintage denim and faded T-shirts, and so the curves of her body weren't always visible. Right now, though, I felt like I knew everything.

"How's it going back there?" Sadie asked, and I let go of her waist like I'd been caught red-handed.

"I guess it's better, though—well, I'm sure you can tell that it's really wet now. So it's not ideal."

She laughed again and turned around to face me. We'd never been so close before. At Johnny's, the bar was always between us. In the bright light of the bathroom, I noticed how long her lashes were, how her cheeks and the bridge of her nose were dotted with freckles. Up until now I'd thought her eyes were brown, but they were more like a hazel, with some greenish tint sloshed in there.

I knew that it was embarrassing and immature to think I was in love with someone when I didn't even know what color her eyes were or what her last name was. Even though I'd moved away and (sort of) grown up, had an ex-girlfriend and approximately a million first dates under my belt, was this any different than middle school when I wrote countless diary entries about cute girls out of my league? It was really annoying how adult life didn't feel separate and defined at all. I thought it would feel like its own new thing, but here I was, still. Same old Max.

"I told Billy I'd be back in twenty," Sadie said, "so I should head out and order."

"It's on me," I said, even though my bank account did not exactly agree with spontaneous bursts of generosity. Luckily, despite that Los Tacos was a newish hipster restaurant, their prices were low enough that it was one of my regular spots for cheap meals. "It's the least I can do."

We left the bathroom and got into line, where the cashier waved us ahead like we were VIP customers and not two people who'd just handled a queso-and-pants-related emergency in the bathroom together.

"We're so sorry about the floor, number 72," he told me.

"We'll get more queso going for you, and whatever else you'd like."

I knew that he was probably only offering so that I didn't try and sue him for the greasy floor, but I was too broke and not nearly proud enough to turn down free food. Would that look bad in front of Sadie? Was I, somehow, still trying to impress Sadie?

"Split your queso with me and let's get some tacos?" Sadie asked, and I quickly agreed. There was nothing I wouldn't have agreed to, obviously. I was a very lost cause.

"You don't have to sit with me," I told Sadie as she slid in across from me in the booth I'd abandoned.

"It'd be hard to split the queso if I didn't, number 72," she said, and I laughed. "Sorry, is it weird hanging out with your bartender outside of the bar? Like when you'd run into your teacher at Rite Aid and you'd be hit with the knowledge that she was also a person who bought tampons and aspirin?"

"I know that you're a person," I said, smiling, and then it felt so outrageously flirtatious that I stopped smiling. Then I reconsidered, because it probably only sounded flirtatious if you were inside my head and knew all of my goopy embarrassing feelings for Sadie—the same consistency as the queso, honestly—so I smiled again.

It was truly no wonder I was single.

"I'm barely a person, if it makes you feel better." Sadie's eyes locked onto my pile of scripts that I swept off the table. Agents and other assistants read them on iPads, but I liked being able to handwrite notes in the margins. "God, I'm sorry, you have work to do, and here I am distracting you."

"I live for distraction," I said, feeling accidentally flirtatious again. "You said you only had twenty minutes anyway, that gives me lots of time to read."

"And it's quiet tonight," she said. "I assume you're coming by the bar after."

"Oh, I—" I wished the food was already here so I had something to stare at besides the stainless-steel table. "Last night, I feel like—"

"Number 72! Your order is ready!"

I hopped up to grab the tray and then walked as carefully as I ever had back to the booth. The booth with Sadie. I started to wonder again if maybe I really had conked my head and this was the great beyond. Honestly, nothing sounded nicer than heaven being a taco stand.

"Are the scripts for your dumb Hollywood job?" Sadie asked, and before I could even fully reel from her question, she jumped right back in. "You called it that once, I'm sorry. I sound like an asshole."

I shook my head, relieved that she hadn't meant it and full of something bigger—that she'd held on to something I said, my exact wording, even. Again, there was nothing real about falling for a bartender. I couldn't imagine how many people had fallen for Sadie. But it had to at least mean that I was more than a generic customer to her, that she was here, that she remembered what I'd said about what I did.

We were quiet as we ate. I kept my eye on the time, even though Sadie didn't seem concerned by it. I'd never been a bartender, but I'd been a barista all through college, and back then my lunches and dinners were always eaten in at least a mild panic, ready to jump back into action at any given moment. Sadie, though, calmly dipped chips into queso and unwrapped tacos at no extraordinary speed.

"I've been worried this place is going to siphon off business from us," Sadie said, looking around. "Billy's not worried, says they don't serve alcohol so it can't affect us, but I don't know if it's that simple."

"Well, if it was more of a hangout, maybe," I said. "It just sort of looks like a slightly fancier Chipotle, though."

Sadie burst into laughter. "Yeah, there's no hangout vibe. I'm still worried about business but every time I come here, I'm less convinced this place is going to put us under."

"Is business bad?" I asked, though the question felt silly and uninformed once it was out of my mouth. I didn't only like hanging out at Johnny's because of Sadie, it was low-key and easy to catch up on script coverage or other work. Successful bars probably didn't have that much in common with coworking spaces and libraries, though.

"Not terrible, not great," Sadie said with a shrug. "I guess it had always been enough, but expenses keep going up while business doesn't. And the property's worth millions. Anyway." She crumpled up the wrappers from her tacos and dipped a chip into the diminishing pool of queso. "I should get back. Thanks for letting me crash your work time and benefit from your lawsuit-avoiding free food."

"Anytime," I said, hearing that I said the word with way too much meaning, and trying to fix my expression into something far less dreamy.

Sadie stood up and took a step toward the door. "See you in a few?"

"Oh, I . . ." I looked down at the tray of food, the last few chips and probably not enough cheese for all of them. "Maybe not. I feel like last night I got too drunk and acted way too stupid and—"

"Max," Sadie said, in a very kind tone. "It's a bar. Who hasn't? And, also, I have no idea what you're talking about."

My heart leapt. Was it possible my drunken ramblings had stayed inside my own brain and not been uttered right at the face of the woman I—

I mean, there was no escaping the fact that today I'd spilled melted cheese on her backside, and obviously I knew that whatever I felt would never be more than unrequited. But if I hadn't completely humiliated myself and Sadie didn't look at me with embarrassed sympathy, maybe things weren't nearly as terrible as I'd thought.

Sadie smiled right at me. Her mouth was a little crooked, I'd noticed over the months I'd known her, tipping a little higher on the right side. At first, I assumed she smirked more than she gave anything an earnest full smile, which felt expected. The hot bartender who was always a little dubious, always keeping something to herself. And then another regular had made this terrible corny dad-type joke, and when it'd somehow struck us all as hilarious, I'd seen that Sadie's grin was a real one. It had been a real one all along.

"So I'll see you soon?" she asked, still smiling.

"OK," I said, returning her smile. "You'll see me soon."

Chapter 3
Where Some People
Know Your Name

I always felt better when I walked into Johnny's, but I'd never felt as good as I did walking in that night about a half hour after Sadie left my booth at Los Tacos. Giving up a crush had sounded bad enough; giving up my hangout was somehow even worse. My crush, I was happy to admit, was far fetched and impossible. This bar? Anything but.

Johnny's was the first place I'd found in LA that felt like mine. I wasn't sure if that was because it was emphatically un-cool, or if that was an unrelated fact, but besides Sadie's presence, there was absolutely nothing cool about Johnny's. The walls featured little décor besides promotional beer and liquor neon signs, and the bar menu had been designed in the baffling font choice of Comic Sans with clip art of cocktails and beer mugs clinking.

There was no rhyme or reason to the crowd. Akbar down the street had a cooler, younger, and queerer vibe, but Johnny's wasn't quite a dive bar either. It just sort of *was*. I was usually the youngest of the regulars, and tonight was no exception. The others sitting around the counter ranged probably from in their thirties to sixties, but trended toward that upper number, like the owner, Billy—not that I had a very specific idea of how old Billy was, besides *old*. Most customers, like me, came alone, but not everyone. A straight couple who seemed to be around Billy's age were usually here when I was, and a polite group of middle-aged gay guys often commandeered one of the back booths.

Billy waved me over to my regular seat at the bar. Obviously I preferred it when I walked in and Sadie was standing near it, but I loved being a regular. At a bar like this one, it felt like I'd earned something.

"The usual, Maxine?" Billy asked, and I nodded. Besides my late grandmother, he was the only person who called me Maxine, since my full name was printed on my credit card. I found it weirdly comforting. I'd moved to LA without knowing a soul and hadn't realized that, besides the inherent freedom in it, there could be loneliness too. At Johnny's, though, I didn't feel it. I wasn't the assistant who didn't fit in with the other assistants, and I wasn't the less-cool roommate, I was Maxine who had a regular seat and a regular drink and people who always looked happy to see me. It was the one place in LA where I was having the exact experience I'd hoped for.

"The usual," I said, and fished out my credit card as soon as I was settled on my regular stool. The booths were more comfortable—especially when you were only five-foot-even—but since I was almost always at Johnny's alone, I liked the company at the bar. I liked random conversations with other customers, and finding out what Billy was cranky about that day, and of course watching Sadie work.

"I got it," Sadie called to Billy, already reaching for the cheap tequila that was good enough as far as I was concerned. "And this one's on me because of dinner."

Billy looked between us, and for a moment I wondered what he thought. Even just a misunderstanding that Sadie and I had been out together let my ego take flight, but before I could get too far down the road with that fantasy, I caught myself. Billy, Sadie had mentioned once, was notoriously cheap. He wasn't tracking anything about Sadie and me and any potential co-mingling outside of the bar. He just hated drinks on the house.

"If Sadie says it's on her, I guess it's on her," he muttered, sliding my card back toward me. I made eye contact with Sadie, and I saw the strain in her neutral expression that she was doing her best not to laugh.

"Here you go, number 72," she said, depositing my Paloma in front of me. "Yell if you need anything else. I know you have a lot of work to get through."

I nodded and hesitated in taking out a dollar bill to tip her. I always tipped, of course, it was never the wrong thing to do. Except was it weird when you'd just had a semi-friendly dinner immediately after spilling queso—

"Don't worry about it," Sadie said, and I realized she'd caught me staring into my messenger bag and probably had no idea I'd fallen into some kind of existential crisis. Well, could it be an existential crisis if it also felt extremely horny? Somehow I felt like philosophers hadn't had thirst in mind with all of that.

"I feel like I should still tip you," I said, enjoying this moment where I could be sort of honest without admitting all the paths my brain had just taken. Sadie, I was sure, had no idea that it wasn't just the relatively cheap drinks or the familiar stool or the easy walk back to my apartment.

"Nah, you're good." She headed off to grab someone else's order, and I took a couple of sips before flipping back to my place in the first script I had to read tonight. The good thing, I'd been told, about agency assistant jobs these days is that it had become frowned-upon to have us stay late until all hours of the night. The work, though, was still expected. I kept an eye on emails until I went to bed and carried home a script or two almost every night. Some of my coworkers complained that it wasn't actually any different than the old days, but for the most part I liked the work, and reading scripts at my favorite bar or in my cozy bed was way better than sitting in my Exemplar cubicle. But I also knew that I was lucky to report to Joyce, who seemed like an actual human with empathy and other important emotions that didn't always seem present in the entertainment industry.

"So I'm going to rephrase my question from before," Sadie said, across from me behind the bar again. "Are the scripts for your not-dumb-at-all Hollywood job?"

I smiled and tried not to make eye contact so intensely that all my feelings were evident. "Yes. The thing is that I know it's kind of a dumb job, but secretly I really love it, and I feel like I'm not supposed to feel that way."

"I get it," she said, and I wanted to write that off as bartenders knowing exactly how to empathize with customers as part of the job, but there was something in her expression, still locked right on mine, that felt like more.

Sadie took a step closer, glanced at Billy and then looked back to me. "A lot of people make me feel like I shouldn't like this gig, that I should be embarrassed about how my life turned out. But I love this place. What's the worst thing that happens, I turn out like him? Seems OK."

I followed her sight line to Billy, who was arguing with a guy around his age about something to do with New York baseball. "Definitely OK."

"I know you might be sarcastic," Sadie said, leaning even closer, her tilted smile stretching even wider, "but I mean it."

"I'm not very good at sarcasm." I hoped my face wasn't as flushed as it felt, with Sadie only inches away. "I'm basically always sincere out of necessity."

Sadie turned to greet a customer as they walked in, and so I turned back to my script with as much focus as I could manage.

I could still feel her standing nearby, could sense the motion of her arm shoving her hair into place and the way she could keep an eye on the entire bar with a quick turn of her head.

It was six months ago when I'd first come to Johnny's. Things had been harder then. My breakup with Daniela was still super fresh, work was newer and therefore much scarier, and I'd never felt so alone in my whole life—which felt like a feat for a queer kid from Kentucky. Chelsey had been having one of her extremely cool parties for extremely cool people, and the thought of walking through that to get to my bedroom had been too much to bear, even once I'd parked behind the apartment complex. It had sounded so good to be in for the night, but I'd walked down the block to Sunset instead. Akbar had seemed too noisy and fun for the day I'd been having, so I'd walked into the other nearby bar instead, behind a couple of silver-haired men who'd looked too dapper to be leading me somewhere unseemly. Billy hadn't greeted me so much as shot me a look that doubled as a shrug, and even though I'd wanted to leave, immediately, that felt too awkward. The booths had been taken so I'd climbed onto one of the barstools. I'd been working up the nerve to ask the snarly bartender for a drink, but then someone else was right in front of me, wearing a faded black T-shirt and jeans ripped from, I could tell, wear and not fashion. She'd mixed me a very good Paloma and asked politely about my day and I'd mumbled something noncommittal because I wasn't very good with girls in general but absolutely not hot girls in unexpected places. And then I'd settled in with my phone and my work and an old Prince song started up on the jukebox. I'd felt the room buzz softly around me and also how I fit right into that quiet buzz.

And, OK, it wasn't untrue that just the possibility of seeing said hot bartender girl again would have been enough to bring me back to Johnny's. But Sadie wasn't why I came back. Johnny's was. Johnny's, in all its uncool glory.

Sadie was just a very nice bonus.

"So where do you work?" Sadie asked, wiping down the countertop. "Can I ask?"

"Oh yeah, of course," I said, as if it was an imposition I was graciously tolerating and not an exciting chance to share information with the girl of my dreams, one small step for man but one giant leap forward for this unrequited lesbian. "I work at Exemplar. It's a talent agency."

She nodded. It was like I was the only person there for how focused she was on me. This was the thing about Sadie; she always found a way to maintain eye contact, even when the bar was crowded, and she always sounded genuinely interested in what I had to say, even when it was normally as generic as how my day had been or what traffic was like. I knew that it was bartender magic, how they could look into your eyes and make you feel better with a well-mixed cocktail or a wry remark, but magic was magic. I loved it just the same.

"So are you making deals for celebrities all day?" she asked.

"That's what everyone thinks. It's way more admin stuff than that, like keeping schedules and making sure actors have updated passports if they're shooting in other countries, and chasing down payments. But I also get to read scripts and sometimes listen in on interesting calls."

"And you like it," she said. "The job."

"I do like it."

"People make you feel like shit about it?" she asked, leaning forward, her forearms flexing as she held on to the bar's edge. Was it possible to get lost in someone's forearms? "You were really quick with that whole *I know it's a dumb job* and all."

I shrugged, flipping the script over so she wouldn't notice it was for a film currently titled *Dinosaur Block Party.* "I think if I were just paying bills it would be fine. But a dream career should be something less superficial that ends war or cures cancer or helps injured cats."

A grin slid back across Sadie's face. "Are those the three approved dream careers? War-ending, cancer-curing, and cat-helping?"

"*Injured* cat-helping," I corrected, laughing. "I don't know. All the time I wish I wanted something different."

I said it casually—well, as casually as I said anything—but it was something like a confession. I didn't go around telling people I wished my dreams were different, wished my wants and needs matched who I wanted to be. Everything would be so much easier, but also it felt big to say. If I admitted how much I wanted this career that people didn't think I was cut out for, it would hurt more when I didn't get it.

"Isn't everyone supposed to be a shark in that world?" Billy asked. "You don't seem much like a shark, Maxine."

"Those were the old days," I said, trying again to sound casual instead of panicked that even someone outside of the industry was convinced I wasn't cut out for it. "My boss says it's been over ten years since she's heard of anyone getting a phone thrown at their head."

"Hmmm," Billy said, furrowing his brow and heading off to take an order. Sadie glanced in his direction and then leaned in even closer to me.

"You look at contracts too, right?" she asked. "Paperwork, I guess I should say. Sorry, I feel like I've seen—sorry, how fucking nosy do I sound?"

"You don't sound nosy," I said. "You sound like you pay attention to people."

Oh, god, could I sound any more adoring? But it felt special, of course, being paid attention to by Sadie.

"It's part of the job," she said, and whatever had just washed over me, well, it washed right away. I was a customer, not an object of Sadie's affections, and it was really only in my weakest moments when I let go of that for a fleeting second or two.

Sadie got back to work—though I guess talking to me was

work, too—and I got back to the script. Writing coverage—basically a book report for a script—was part of my job, because agents like my boss didn't have time to read every single script that came in for a client or that was floating buzzily around Hollywood. It was my job to give Joyce the gist as well as some key takeaways about potential casting.

If I was actually lucky enough someday to ascend to Joyce's ranks, I wouldn't miss picking out inventive restaurants or dropping pieces of paper onto important chairs, but this part I'd miss. I loved how a script could be so spare, just action lines and dialogue, and still paint a whole picture in my head of what that finished film or TV pilot would feel like. But it wasn't just the imagination part of it. It was the aspect that was even more relevant to what we did at Exemplar that made me feel that I had more to offer. When a script had buzz, it was easy for me to see which of Joyce's clients might be perfect in a role. I could see when a role that looked small on paper would land big on-screen. When Gregory Hart finally landed an Oscar earlier this year, I knew that I'd been the one to send along the script coverage to Joyce with more exclamation points and excitement than I usually allowed myself. No one knew that in some ways that Best Actor Academy Award had started with me, but in a small way, it had. Not that I was looking for glory and recognition! I just really liked being good at something, and I liked when other people succeeded because of me.

The bar got a little busier, and I got more absorbed in *Dinosaur Block Party*—well, absorbed enough to finish my coverage for Joyce. I was midway through my second script of the night when Sadie walked back to me. Even though I could feel her move close with her hands on the bar and her hips snug against the edge, I kept my eyes on the pages in front of me. I was nothing but work to Sadie, and I had my own work to worry about. The script was for a pilot episode of a prestige cable golden-age-of-television show that would be packed wall-to-wall with talent but hit all the clichés possible.

I couldn't believe I found myself missing the dinosaurs of the titular block party.

"Hey," Sadie said, and I let myself look up at her. Her face was a little flushed, and she'd clearly just run her hands through her hair because it swooped up at a pretty unnatural angle. The hem of her T-shirt, I noticed, had caught on the edge of the countertop, so a sliver of pale pink skin was—

"Oh, hey," I said, forcing my eyes upward to meet hers. "Hi."

She grinned, but the smile wasn't in her eyes, and it didn't hold long. "So, contracts, paperwork, that kind of stuff. That's something you look at for work, yeah?"

I had no idea why she'd now brought this up twice, but I just nodded.

"I have to review this—it's a whole long story with a lot of documents. But I don't know what I'm doing, so I thought— no, sorry, this is so presumptuous."

"It's not presumptuous," I said quickly, because wondering what that sliver of skin would taste like, *that* was presumptuous. This was just a conversation about documents or something. "Do you need help?"

I'd had fantasies like this before, of course. Me sweeping in to save the day, suddenly having summoned the strength to carry Sadie out of a burning building or something. Looking over the terms of a contract was basically the same thing and luckily didn't require any additional upper body strength I'd had yet to build.

"You're the best," she said, and glanced again at Billy. "This is not the best time to talk about it, though. Would it be weird if I . . ."

I watched as she took a phone out of her back pocket. Well— kind of a phone. "What is that?"

Sadie grinned and *flipped it open*. I might've actually gasped.

"Are you a time traveler?" I asked, and she burst into laughter.

"I'm off the grid," she said. "Nah, I just like it like this. I can get calls and texts and that's all I need. I don't feel like it's good for me to be as connected as everything makes you these days."

My phone chose that moment to buzz with an incoming text, followed by my watch alerting me with a *ding* to the same message.

"Oh, sure," I said, trying to look like I had any authority on this topic.

"You seem very well-adjusted," Sadie said, leaning forward more, her shirt sliding up further. I hated how much I could practically feel her soft skin, how clearly I could imagine slipping my fingertips past the waistband of her jeans and—

"I'm not that well-adjusted," I said.

"Well, you probably never found yourself in a screaming match in the middle of the night throwing your old iPhone into a dumpster," Sadie said.

"OK, if that's the baseline for well-adjusted, sure." I pictured my last breakup. My *only* real breakup. Civilized and private, so quiet that the next morning I'd had to explain to my roommate what had happened and why Daniela was gone. Somehow I felt like I'd even managed to do a breakup the wrong way.

Sadie handed me her phone, but I actually had no idea how to input my name and phone number, so she laughed and swiped it back from me before sliding a pencil and a slip of paper to me across the bar top. I wrote carefully before sliding it back to her, pretending for just a moment that this was exactly what it looked like and not something about legal documents and being a regular customer.

"You have very nice handwriting," Sadie said as she tapped a whole bunch of buttons on her tiny ancient phone.

"Thanks," I said, smiling up at her. "I won an award once."

"In grade school?" Sadie asked, still tapping.

"Well, sure, but it still counts, doesn't it?"

My phone buzzed again, followed by my watch's *ding*. It was from a 323 number I didn't recognize.

Yes it still counts.

I grinned up at her. "It would be different if there were more awards in adulthood. You have to be super successful to win awards past the age of seventeen or whatever. It was nice to only need to have the best penmanship, you know? An achievable goal."

Sadie nodded emphatically. "Max, believe it or not, I do know."

"Sadie," Billy called. I knew very little about Billy, but I had the feeling he was on to me and my big dumb crush. It was funny how someone could make you feel seen in a good way and a way-too-real way all at once. "Can you bring out some pint glasses? We're running low."

"Got it, boss," she called, but she looked right back to me. "I'll hit you up soon, OK?"

"OK," I said, and tried to smile like a regular customer and not a lovestruck fool. It was too bad that I was both.

Chapter 4
The Roommate

There were no warnings the next night from Chelsey, via text or DMs or any of the multiple methods she used to reach me, about hangouts or *Yellowjackets* watch parties or pregaming before dancing at the Verdugo, so after driving across town and pulling into my parking spot, I walked right up the stairs to our third-floor apartment.

"Oh good, you're home," Chelsey called as I walked inside and pulled the door behind me. There was not really a sense of coming *home* because this apartment hardly felt like mine, even after over two years in LA.

Chelsey had really embraced maximalism, even before it was trendy. The spacious apartment was decorated to its every inch. There wasn't one but *three* gallery walls of pop-culture-related prints, fabric wall hangings, a tall ceramic pink cheetah that was the same hue as the living room sectional, and an accent wall featuring brightly colored wallpaper. My ex-girlfriend had remarked once that it looked like Lizzie McGuire but grown-up, to which I'd said, *Elizabeth* McGuire, and it had stuck. Considering that I still thought of the apartment that way, it had stuck even longer than my relationship.

"Yep, I'm home," I called, hoping that counted as conversation. I never knew what to say to Chelsey, so I aimed for as little as possible.

She walked into the room, her blond hair blown out into perfect waves. Before I met Chelsey, I honestly didn't know anyone's hair could just look that good all the time.

"Do you have plans tonight?" she asked.

"Um, no, I know, pathetic, ha ha," I said, not because I believed it but because I knew that girls like Chelsey didn't fantasize about putting on pajamas and watching old sitcoms for comfort. Chelsey, after all, was wearing a bright orange cropped tee over mom jeans and platform sneakers. Meanwhile I was in pants and one of my ten good-enough-for-the-office buttondowns. I rotated them on an every-other-week schedule.

Chelsey kind of cocked her head at me, like she was still learning to interpret and speak the language of nerds. I gestured at my messenger bag, still on my shoulder.

"I should probably—"

"I know you always have a ton of work, but you have to eat, right? I was going to Postmates some Pine and Crane, sound good?"

I immediately did the math on my checking account balance.

"My treat," Chelsey said, apparently already having learned my *Do I have enough money for this?* face. "I still have a million gift cards from that campaign I did the other month."

"Well, OK," I said.

"Yay!" Chelsey whipped out her phone. "Any requests?"

"Whatever you want is fine," I said, because she was treating, and also because it was true. Before I moved to LA, I was such a boring eater. It wasn't entirely Kentucky's fault, though of course the Kentucky of it all didn't help. My mom raised me and my younger sister on a pretty consistently boring diet, and I'd never minded. I'd never even noticed it was boring! Not until I arrived here and realized all that I'd missed out on.

"OK, I'm comfortable with that arrangement," she said, tapping away on her phone. "I feel like gift cards bring out something unrestrained in me, the true core Chelsey or something, who wants ten sides with her dinner."

"I know what you mean, whenever there's free food at work I always sneak back in for more," I said, even though I really did try to interact with Chelsey as little as possible. Normally, she didn't say things I related to so much, though.

"I do miss a good old-fashioned corporate lunch spread," she said with a dramatic sigh. "OK, twenty minutes."

"Meet you back here in comfy home clothes then?" I asked.

"Max, these *are* my comfy home clothes," Chelsey said. "But, yes. It's a date."

When I'd decided to go for it and move to Los Angeles, a year after finishing college, I'd been overwhelmed by the reality of the situation. I'd managed to save money from all the various coffee shop and retail and data entry jobs I'd juggled since high school, but rents in LA were so much higher than my budget would allow for. I'd thought of spending another year in Louisville, living with Mom and working jobs I hated. It would have been one more year of waiting for my life to begin. Louisville wasn't my life. It was like a purgatory in between childhood and adulthood, and I'd known adulthood wouldn't hit until I was ensconced in Los Angeles.

Amazingly, though, a post had shown up in the LGBTQ+ alumni Facebook group I'd completely forgotten I'd joined. How was I even still on Facebook, like a boomer?

Hey y'all! This is a long shot but I'm looking to find a roommate for my sweet little Silver Lake (yes that's Los Angeles) 2-bedroom. It's rent-controlled, comes with

*parking, and I'm a very good roomie. If you're looking
or you know someone, message me! Xo Chelsey*

I'd dashed off the fastest message of my life, and Chelsey
had pinged back almost immediately. The rent was near the top
of my budget, but it was doable. And Chelsey! She'd been so
friendly and so full of helpful moving-in information. How
lucky was I to find another queer girl from Kentucky who'd
gone to the same university? I couldn't imagine how much we'd
have in common.

We wouldn't only be roommates, I'd determined, we might
end up best friends. Best friends were something I'd never
managed, probably due to my denial over my sexuality that
made me panic whenever girls got too close. Now, I'd thought,
in Los Angeles it would all be different. I'd be completely out,
I'd get a really gay haircut, I'd have a best friend and a whole
queer friends group, and I'd fall in love or at least finally lose
my virginity a million years after everyone already had, but
hopefully both.

As soon as I'd arrived at the apartment on Manzanita Street,
though, I'd immediately crossed off that goal of Chelsey as a
best friend. It had been so naïve to think our locations, alma
maters, and identities had set us up for something magical. She
was beautiful and confident and just about every single thing
I wasn't. Having a best friend, period, had suddenly felt like
a childish goal anyway, so I focused on everything else. Two
years later, I was a completely out non-virgin with a really gay
haircut, but I still felt like the same Max who'd driven away
from Kentucky. I was still waiting for my life to begin.

I headed to the living room once I heard the doorbell ring.
Chelsey was dashing around, setting out plates, chopsticks,
and cans of beer. My roommate did not do things halfway.

"Do you need any help?"

She waved me off. "I've got everything. I ran out earlier to get Taiwanese beer to go with dinner. I figured I could talk you into Pine and Crane, and if I couldn't, it's not like I mind having extra beers in the fridge."

I sat down at one corner of the pale pink sectional. Its delicate color and texture normally kept me far away from it, even when food and beverages weren't involved. Mom told me once never to buy furniture that wouldn't hide food stains; I had a feeling Chelsey had never gotten that particular lecture from her family.

"Is it OK to eat?" I eyed the spread in front of me. Chelsey really had gone all-out; there were shrimp wontons tossed in chili oil, potstickers, heaping rice bowls and noodle dishes, small plates and sides from the Taiwanese restaurant just up the block and down the street from us. LA offered so much, so close. Even if I felt like the same Max, I did love it here.

"Oh, yeah, of course it's OK to eat," Chelsey said, grabbing an eggroll with a neon-green-manicured hand. "I would have warned you if this was content."

When I'd arrived in LA, Chelsey was also an assistant, and had even gotten me the interview for my first talent agency job. But her Instagram, then her TikTok, blew up, and before long she was producing so much content and fielding so many spon-con opportunities that she was now a full-time influencer specializing in plus-size fashion and queer lifestyle stuff.

"How's work?" Chelsey asked as I was digging into a pile of three-cup mushrooms and rice. "Feeling like you're going to move up anytime soon?"

"I have no idea," I said, instead of the *no* that felt more honest. "I know that I do a really good job"—Joyce's chair reserved for the meeting notwithstanding—"but I know it isn't enough to just do a good job. The other stuff . . ."

I trailed off because I didn't always know how much to say to Chelsey, who'd been so successful *just being herself.* Obviously, Chelsey was savvy enough to see that I was not bold, confident, *shark* agency material. I didn't want to sit here and spell that out for her, though; it was insulting to both of us.

"It can be such a ridiculous industry sometimes, right?" Chelsey smiled like we were in it together, which wasn't true literally or figuratively. "I did have an idea for you, though."

If I were the kind of person who narrowed their eyes when they were suspicious, I would have narrowed my eyes. Instead, though, I just blinked. Immediately I worried that I looked like a very small, very nervous fish. Finding Nemo's dad or something. "You do?"

"Yes!" Chelsey was the first person I'd ever met who seemed to speak in actual exclamation points. "Have you ever heard of You Point Oh?"

I shook my head while snagging several strands from the container of dan dan noodles. Chelsey was so good at everything, including ordering feasts.

"It's pretty new," she said, before grabbing noodles for her own plate. "God, I love this place."

"Me too," I said. "Thanks for treating."

She waved me off again. "It's barely treating when it's a gift card."

"You could have done something nice for Ava," I pointed out. Chelsey, of course, had a girlfriend who was as beautiful and accomplished as she was. More accomplished? Ava was the in-house legal counsel for a national advocacy group for transgender people of color, and in her spare time—how did she even *have* spare time?—designed custom hats. I knew very little about fashion but the hats were bright and bold, and Ava sold out immediately whenever she announced a drop on Etsy.

Chelsey laughed. "I feel like you can only use so many gift cards on your girlfriend, you know?"

"I don't know," I said. "I mean, Ava's glamorous, but sometimes I think my love language is a good bargain, so—"

Chelsey cracked up, nearly spilling her lychee-flavored beer.

"I mean this with all the affection in the world, Max, but you sound like my mother right now."

"I sound like my own, too," I said. "It's concerning."

"But this is great, actually! So, You Point Oh is this pretty new self-actualization app. They just went through their soft launch, and it went really well, so they reached out to me to partner up for a big campaign."

I nodded, even though I had no idea why she was telling me this much about one of her campaigns. Normally I only picked up context clues from products piled up in random places in the apartment that made more sense once I eventually saw her sponcon after she posted it for the world to see. It was probably the same vague sense of familiarity she had with the scripts I sometimes left piled in our shared spaces.

"The thing is," Chelsey said, "I really would love to do this campaign. Not to be gross and capitalistic, but I could use the money, of course. But I also actually think it's a cool app that could help a lot of people, which is more exciting to me than, you know, another fair-trade lip gloss."

"Sure," I said, still—perhaps naïvely—having no idea where this was going or why she was still talking about it.

"But on our kickoff Zoom call, their team was just a bit worried—even though they were the ones to reach out to me!— that I'm a little too . . ." Chelsey shrugged, but it was clear to me that she knew exactly what she wanted to say, just not how to say it to me.

". . . self-actualized?" I supplied, and she covered her face in what I assumed was mock embarrassment.

"That's exactly what their director of marketing said, yes," she said with an eye roll. "Which was so flattering I didn't want to fight them on it."

I shrugged an actual shrug and focused on eating another dumpling.

"So we came up with this idea together, that I could use my account and expertise to bring on someone who still has a lot of goals left to meet, and I could sort of be the You Point Oh cheerleader and use my platform to . . ."

Chelsey kept talking, but I realized I was no longer listening because suddenly I knew exactly where this was going and why there was so much free food and why she was treating me like a person she confided in.

"Before you say anything else," I said, but of course my voice came out squeaky and small, and since Chelsey didn't hear me, she was still going.

". . . and they partner with related vendors, so, for example, since you have goals about your career, you'd get complimentary career coaching, or if you set a goal to—"

"I really don't want to do this," I said, finally loud enough that Chelsey heard me and stopped talking. "I'm sorry. I know it would help you out, but . . . it all sounds terrible to me. You know I have like forty-seven followers on my Instagram, most of whom I'm related to. I don't like a lot of people watching me."

Also, yes, of course I wished my boss took me more seriously and that I had a girlfriend and it felt like my adult life had already begun, but I wasn't going to fix all of that like this. Not for other people. Not *in front of* other people. Not where I had to confess everything I lacked just so people could watch me stumble around trying to improve myself or whatever. I couldn't imagine anything that sounded more embarrassing.

"Sure, I know, it's a lot to consider," Chelsey said, nodding as if she understood, when someone like Chelsey would never understand someone like me. I hated that I'd gotten a little pulled in to her orbit instead of seeing this meal for what it was. "Think it over for a few days, and if you have any questions at all, just let me know."

I watched her bite into another eggroll as if everything was going exactly according to plan. Who knows, maybe it was, maybe she had a flowchart in her bullet journal for the initial resistance I'd put up and how she'd overcome it.

"Thanks for dinner." I stood up, even though I could have

eaten more. Not here, not after what had just happened. "I should go get some work done tonight."

"Oh, OK." Chelsey glanced up at me. "Max, whatever you're thinking, I didn't mean—"

"No, sure, of course," I said, backing out of the beautiful room and down the hallway to the safety of my bedroom. It wasn't fancy or Insta-ready like the rest of the apartment, but it felt like mine and that was more than enough. I'd moved here with just a few suitcases' worth of a past, but I'd gotten really good at scouring Goodwill and Out of the Closet locations for the best used furniture and home décor (and button-downs to rotate into my work looks). Throw in a few Target sales and Ikea runs, and I really loved my little room. Bookshelf full of favorites, dresser that I'd managed not to overstuff or pile clothes on top of, framed prints and photos on the walls that hopefully struck the balance between generic and trying way too hard, and a bed big enough for girls to comfortably sleep over, not that any girls besides Daniela had slept here. I'd hardly given up on this, even if I was convinced no one in LA had gone on more terrible first dates than I had. If I didn't think love was still possible for me, I'd really fall apart.

I curled up on my bed and fought the urge to text my mom. It was three hours later in Louisville, but she'd be up and willing to listen. But I was ostensibly an adult, and I didn't want to give her any more material for *maybe you should just move home* chats. Still, though, at least she'd be on my side.

With Chelsey's offer, though, *would* Mom be on my side? I could hear her initial comforting, practically a reflex for her, followed up by, *But, honey, it does seem like you could use some help getting ahead.* What if she thought You Point Oh sounded like a good idea?

I changed into sweats and flipped open my MacBook to watch an episode of *Frasier* while I swiped through all my dating apps. Sometimes, when I still lived in Kentucky but was spending my evenings in an almost identical manner, I'd type a random Los Angeles zip code into Tinder or HER and feel like a very hungry person eyeing a faraway feast. There were *so many girls* out west, and I knew if I could just get myself there that I was destined to fall in love with at least one of them.

Now, after years here, everyone was starting to look a little familiar, and I prayed for influxes of new matches into the area. (That felt better, karmically speaking, than praying for break-ups and other disasters that led to available girls.) It wasn't that LA wasn't what I'd expected; it was that I was still me, even after relocating over two thousand miles away.

Before I'd arrived, I'd imagined it all: nights out, a diverse and fun crew of friends who loved me, a job where I got to prove how freaking competent I was, and of course a girl I loved who believed in me who was also very skilled at providing earth-shattering orgasms. But here I was, watching Frasier and Niles plan a dinner party in my staying-home clothes, like I hadn't changed anything at all.

Chelsey wasn't wrong; I was far from self-actualized. OK, I was absolutely *not* doing this whole You Point Oh thing, but I could do *something*.

My phone dinged with a text, and even though I hoped it was Sadie from her ancient phone, it was my old coworker Nina. I knew that keeping my sound on was a real boomer vibe, but I never wanted to miss an after-hours work message. When we weren't in the office we were expected to keep a vague eye on things, and I liked my eye to be more than vague.

Did you get the inventive restaurant thing taken care of or do you need more ideas? Nina texted. **I forgot we went to Mother Wolf the other week and it might fit the bill. Also, it's been a while! Do you want to grab drinks soon? Would love to hear how work (and Joyce!) are going. And of course anything else!**

I paused the TV episode even though I'd seen it multiple times before. Good comfort TV still required a little attention even when the details were familiar, and so did texting acquaintances you wished were actual friends. This felt like a good opportunity to lean into these goals that seemed so far away.

Thanks, I will bring that one up to Joyce as well. Drinks sound great! I'm free the rest of this week if that isn't too soon or too pathetic? I included a spectacularly unoriginal SpongeBob meme because tired outdated memes always cheered me up and it would let Nina know I wasn't actually that self-pitying.

Nina had been in charge of the communications coming in and out of the agency to and from the talent, and even though she'd worked remotely, she'd been my very favorite coworker. She'd been super good at her job and yet only a little less afraid of Joyce, and I'd been slowly figuring out how to become her friend when she fell in love with one of Joyce's clients and, obviously, had to quit. I figured that would be the last I ever heard from her, but her new job was just down Sunset from my apartment, so we grabbed drinks occasionally and texted a little more often than that. I still wasn't sure we qualified as friends, per se, but Nina always gave really smart advice and made me feel less hopeless. Getting to see her soon would be perfect timing.

It's definitely not too soon or too pathetic! Tomorrow?

I finalized our plans and unpaused the episode, where the doomed dinner party was in full swing. Things always went disastrously for Frasier and Niles, but they just kept planning dinner parties. Maybe that was exactly the energy I should harness moving forward.

I pulled up the text from Sadie and added her to my contacts. Since I didn't know her last name, she went in as Sadie Bartender. And instead of overthinking it or flashing back to that stupid drunken night earlier this week, I typed.

Hi Sadie, it's Max. Let me know when you want to meet up to go over contracts. I'm not sure how much help I'll be but I'm happy to try!

My phone dinged again, and of course it wasn't Sadie. Would her phone even allow her to text so quickly? But at least I now had plans tomorrow with Nina, so I felt a little better turning back to my comfort TV. One set of plans hardly meant self-actualization, but it had to bring me a little closer, right?

Chapter 5

Self-Actualization for One

The next morning unfolded like it was choreographed. I got up five minutes early, wore my favorite Wildfang button-down and best jeans—so grateful that jeans were acceptable office wear in the industry after suffering through many terrible business-casual settings during high school and college—and hit almost all green lights on my way across town to the Exemplar office.

At my desk I flew through my inbox, checked the trades, dashed through the talent's inboxes, scanned Joyce's schedule for the day, and was waiting with her coffee when she arrived. I knew that I was actually very good at my entire job, but overall I was proudest of the aspects that involved my actual skills and talent. Still, it felt satisfying to be in the right place with the right coffee at the right time.

"I don't want to jinx anything, but it looks like a light day," Joyce said as she settled at her desk and I made my own cup of coffee. "Relatively speaking, of course. Are you current on all of your admin duties? Might be a good day to tackle whatever's outstanding."

"I think everything is up-to-date, but I'll triple-check."

I knew that everything was up-to-date, but I'd learned that bosses weren't comforted by that certainty. They wanted a support staff who was always willing to check again and make certain.

I could tell that Joyce's eyes were about to fully settle on her iMac. I knew every beat of our morning routine in my bones by now, and it was just about my time to head out to my cubicle, but it also meant that I knew that there was a split second where I could talk. I could bring up the future I wanted here—or elsewhere, a smaller agency, where I could get my start as a junior agent. It wasn't something I needed immediately, but I did want to be on the path. Right now it felt more like I was on a cul-de-sac, going around the same area indefinitely.

Joyce's phone rang, and she glanced over at its display. "Gordon over at Three Cities. Could you take a message? It's too early for his whole . . . thing."

I laughed and agreed, as I felt the moment slip past me. Sure, I didn't even really have to double-check that I was caught up on receivables. Yes, I had the coffee ready at the right time. Of course, I'd take a message from Gordon York and relay it appropriately. The harder stuff, too! The parts of my job that made me proud! I wasn't only good at script coverage, I knew what kind of news to relay to Joyce from the trades and why it mattered. But if I couldn't even get my thoughts together quickly enough to ask her about my future in this industry—

No, I told myself. I was self-actualizing! I'd get another opportunity with Joyce again, soon, and I'd speak up more quickly next time. I wasn't doomed. Not even close.

The day proceeded as I rehearsed versions of my speech to Joyce. *I've been here for close to two years and I think it's fair to say that I've solidly contributed with my expertise in communications, script coverage, and grasp of the nuances of this industry. I know that there's still so much to learn, and that's exactly why I'd love to mentor under you with the expectation of being on the junior agent track. Yes, I'm little and maybe too quiet at times but I think if anything that only leads people to underestimate what I can bring, and could perhaps even be an asset.*

Was that true? Did I even believe it? I wanted to believe it; maybe that was good enough for now.

My watch dinged with a notification, and, miraculously, it was not Chelsey warning me of another cool-person apartment happening. The tiny display showed *Sadie Bartender: MESSAGES.*

I'd never grabbed for my phone so quickly in my life. Unfortunately, Joyce chose that exact moment to stop by my desk.

"Is this a bad time?" she asked, as if you could answer that question from your boss honestly!

"No, of course not, I—" I stopped when I saw that Joyce was barely holding in a laugh. "What?"

"Who's on your phone?" she asked, though she didn't look annoyed or concerned that I was clearly not doing my job at that moment. "She must be something, yes?"

"Oh my god, no—" I said, then burst into laughter myself because I was so obvious that even I smelled the lie on myself. "Sorry. She is, yes, but I'm at work."

"Max, I've been married for twelve years." Joyce leaned against my cubicle, her eyebrows high with expectation. "Let me live vicariously."

"Oh, no, there's nothing to live through," I said quickly. "I mean, she's in my phone as *Sadie Bartender* so . . ."

"Oh, a bartender?" Joyce laughed. "There's some trouble."

I started to say that Sadie wasn't like that, but then I remembered the old flip phone, the tossed-out comment, the iPhone thrown in a dumpster in the middle of the night. Maybe Sadie was exactly like that. I didn't really know Sadie at all.

"Though they're hard to resist," Joyce continued. "All that Sam Malone energy."

I really only thought about Sam Malone as, of course, a guest role on *Frasier*, but I didn't think that was helpful information to add. I was generally very good at keeping my scattered thoughts to myself. It was too bad my expression had given away as much as it had.

"So what's the story?" Joyce asked.

"Sorry, there's really no story," I said. "Obviously, I wish there was a story."

"She's texting you, though," Joyce pointed out.

"I think she wants me to look at some contracts for her," I said, covering my face in embarrassment as Joyce cackled.

"Oh, Max, you're in too deep already."

I mean, that much I knew.

"Did you need something?" I asked, doing my best to seem like the picture of professionalism despite this entire conversation.

"Can you touch base with Jeffrey's team to see if we can push my three o'clock back to four?"

"Of course," I said, jotting down the note to myself. It was, like my promise earlier to triple-check, productivity theater. I tended never to forget things—barring extremely hungover mornings—but I knew I looked the picture of the perfect employee when I took good notes. I wondered if it was normal to spend as much effort making sure I looked like a good assistant as I did actually being a good assistant.

In the entertainment industry, probably yes.

"Wonderful," Joyce said. "You're the best, Max."

It would have been, potentially, a great moment to start the conversation that could change my life and push me toward being self-actualized, but my phone rang and my inbox chimed and Joyce took off down the hallway and this moment was gone, too.

But, of course, my professional concern lasted only until a split-second later when I remembered that a text from Sadie was waiting on my phone. I scrambled to pick it up again, and somehow—oh my god. I lost hold of it and it flung itself down the sleek row of cubicles. I tried not to take it as a sign that my phone was bailing on me.

"Sorry about that," I said, dashing to the last cubicle in the row. Exemplar had been designed with an eye on every detail, so this was not like the depressing cube farms I'd worked in at past jobs. Our clients required discretion, and so there was plenty of space between each workstation, except in the case where multiple assistants managed the desks of top agents. In general, I loved the setup, but with everyone's eyes on me, it felt like a very long way to walk.

"No problem." Gillian, the assistant who had the last desk in the row, smiled and handed me my phone. "While you're here, I just wanted to let you know before you hear from the rumor mill or whatever that Friday's my last day."

"Oh, wow," I said, uselessly, though I wasn't sure what to say. I wasn't close to any of the other assistants, had never felt included by them. It had never seemed intentional, just like an unspoken vibe that everyone else appeared to fit into this world effortlessly while I was still finding my way. Obviously, this was yet another thing on my list of concerns about succeeding in this industry, but I didn't want to dwell on that right now.

"Yeah, I'm sure you know how it is, right?" She smiled as she smoothed a curl into place in her super casual updo. "You burn through a job like this and you're thinking, there's got to be more out there, right?"

"Oh, sure," I said, nodding, even though I desperately wanted to get back to my cube with my phone, and also the only *more* I hoped was out there was more responsibility in the exact same industry. "Where are you going next? If you don't mind me asking."

"Max, you're so polite, no wonder Joyce loves you so much," she said, and I knew it was a throwaway remark but at least a very nice one. "Honestly, it's a pretty generic gig in tech, but I'll have more control over my hours and make more money, and I'll never have to beg a restaurant to open early so that everyone can get a salad that the Kardashians are supposedly eating, fingers crossed."

I laughed. "Yeah, there's such dumb stuff sometimes, I know. Plus there are way better salads than that one."

"Way better salads!" said Javier, the assistant in the next cubicle. Every day, he wore button-downs and pants that looked like they cost a million dollars or so, so obviously I was a little terrified of him. "You'll miss 'em, though, Gill. These are literally your salad days."

"Hmm, doubtful," she said. "Anyway, Max, Aidy's organizing a happy hour for my last day, so—"

"So even though you never come to anything," Javier said, "you should join us."

"I'll Slack you the details," Aidy called over from her cube. "Ignore Javier. Work happy hours are all he has."

I let out a burst of shocked laughter, and Aidy, Gillian, and even Javier joined in. Then Elise, the assistant closest to my desk, yelled that Joyce's line was ringing, and so I dashed down and managed to catch it before it went to voicemail. Was the universe trying to tell me something? I was never going to see Sadie's text at this rate.

The phone call was about a finance issue I'd just managed to clear up, and by the time I was off and settled in at my desk again, I saw that there were two new scripts in my inbox I'd need to read within the next few days, if not sooner. I jotted everything into my planner, checked my inbox again, and felt that it was finally time to check my phone for whatever Sadie had sent.

thx i assume u work weekdays, what about coffee sat morn 10 am alfred?

OK, I still of course thought she was very hot, that she emitted kindness on a regular basis, and that she made the best Paloma in Los Angeles. But this? It was the least sexy text I'd ever received. Was that how old phones messaged? If so, how did anyone get laid before smartphones?

Still, I jotted this into my planner, this set of plans with Sadie the bartender, and tried not to smile too much at the thought of seeing her again outside of the bar. After all, as long as I managed not to throw queso on her ass, there was no way it could go worse than last time.

I absolutely didn't need Chelsey and her sponcon influencer campaign and a public attempt to self-actualize. I was figuring everything out at my own pace and—with maybe just a little pressure applied—I could get to where I was headed at exactly the right time.

I usually called Mom on my Thursday commutes home, but—despite my newly applied pressure—the Chelsey conversation was still so fresh in my mind and I was so, so bad at keeping things to myself, at least where Mom was concerned. So I bailed with a **Working late, sorry, catch you this weekend?** text before getting into my car for the trek across town. Obviously, I felt guilty, because lying to your very supportive mother felt like it should be one of the seven deadly sins, but sometimes it was for her own good.

I was five minutes late by the time I parked in my spot and dashed up to Sunset. Nina had already gotten us a table in the back of the Black Cat, which had been a queer bar in the 1960s but was just an everyone bar now. I'd been thrilled to land in such a historically queer neighborhood. West Hollywood got all the credit, but Silver Lake had so much queer cred, too.

As always, Nina looked amazing—like Joyce, she was a full-fledged grown-up, though in a cooler Eastside way that somehow combined maximum comfort with some femme glam. Her glossy brown hair rested on her shoulders like a Disney princess, and her brightly patterned sleeveless dress showed off her curves and just a little cleavage. I would have probably ended up with an inappropriate crush on Nina if I hadn't basically been shipping her with Joyce's client Ari Fox from the first time I saw them together. I could take only a teeny bit of credit for them actually ending up together, but that was more than enough. Except—

"Nina, oh my god, what are you doing?" I asked, stricken, watching her fingers swiping left and right on the app open on her phone.

She looked up at me and lit up. I loved that someone in this city was that happy to see me. "Max, hi! You look great."

"So do you," I said, sitting down across from her. "And sorry I'm late, but . . . ?"

She glanced at her phone and burst out laughing. "Did you think I was on Tinder? It's just PuppyCupid."

"Wait, what?"

She laughed even harder. "Sorry, we've been calling it that. Or DogHarmony. It's just an app to match with rescue dogs and I've become *obsessed*."

"You're getting a dog?"

"I wish. Do you know the lengths these rescue places want you to go through? I swear that my friends who adopted a baby—a human baby—only did slightly more paperwork."

"Do you have to have, like, a hot profile that makes all the dogs want you?" I asked, and she laughed again.

"I know you're kidding, but *yes*. It's so embarrasing." She tapped an icon on her phone before handing it over to me. Candid, sun-kissed photos of Nina and Ari stacked on top of details about how responsible and committed they were.

"This is . . . a lot," I said, and it was, but I was also jealous. It would be so nice to be in a candid photo next to Sadie while we laughed about something only we knew, with a love so visible that someone would let us take in a homeless cat.

"Right? Sorry, though, obviously I didn't make plans with

you so I could tell you all about three-legged dogs I've fallen for and lost. But, for the record, four of them."

A waiter swung by to get our drinks order, and I let myself sit back in my seat and relax, a little, in the low lighting and extremely chill vibe. Neither Nina nor I had very chill vibes ourselves, and it did help to see that it hadn't held her back in life. She had a perfect relationship, a good job at an entertainment marketing firm, and a life that was super enviable. If she'd managed all of that with zero chill, there had to be hope for me.

"Any bad dates lately?" Nina asked, once we had cocktails and a few appetizers between us on the table. "Or good ones, of course, but the bad stories are always so much more fun, sorry-not-sorry."

"No, I've had a lull," I said. "I feel like there's only so many girls on the apps and what if I've met all the good ones already? And most of the bad ones too?"

"I'm not sure that's possible," she said. "I know this is such an old-person thing to say, but I think sometimes it just takes time. Dating, finding the right person, feeling the right stuff at the right time."

"I do still have stupid feelings for that bartender," I said, and Nina's eyes lit up. "No, please don't look excited, I feel like it's the opposite of—seriously, it's nothing."

I filled her in on the most recent happenings, from a highly edited version of my very dumb and drunken night, to the queso on Sadie's Levi's, to the cold shower of a text I'd received a few hours ago.

"I actually have a good feeling about this," Nina said, studying Sadie's text. "Do you know what a hassle it is to text on a flip phone? She made an effort for you."

"She made an effort for *contracts*," I pointed out before shoving a few french fries into my mouth. "I'm just cheaper than a lawyer."

"Yeah, but she didn't bring these supposed contracts to the

bar and have you look over them there. She's plotting out time together."

"No," I said. "I think it's something she's hiding from the owner. I don't know. I can't tell if she's mysterious or I just don't know her very well."

"It's the bar just down the block on the other side of Sunset?" Nina asked, gesturing.

I nodded without thinking. "Oh, Nina, no, we can't—"

"We are *so going* after we eat," she said, rubbing her hands together. I couldn't tell if her glee was at this plan or the fried chicken that just arrived at the table. "I'll be very cool, don't worry."

"That seems unlikely," I said, but it was so good to laugh with someone that I didn't mind too much, and once our snacks had been eaten, we headed over to Johnny's. I couldn't decide if I was more nervous that Sadie would or wouldn't be there, but I didn't get a chance to land on an answer because she grinned at me as soon as we walked in.

"Hey, Max," she said, and while I felt that I should elbow Nina or indicate in some other manner, I realized that was completely unnecessary. The only other bartender was Billy, and no one would confuse him for a dreamy lesbian.

"Hi." I sat down at my regular barstool and tried to avoid eye contact with Nina as she pulled up the stool to my left. I would have been completely unaware not to notice the very cute blond girl already sitting to my right, and I wondered if magically Johnny's had gotten cooler and I just hadn't realized it.

"You're a regular," the blond girl said, and I flushed because I really was that awkward around surprise interactions with cute girls. "I just moved to the Eastside."

"Welcome," Nina said, leaning around me. "I'm Nina and this is Max."

I waved, and the blond girl grinned at us, but mainly at me.

Was this what happened when you gave self-actualization a try? Girls at bars wearing cute rompers just smiled at you even when you were with a hot friend?

"I'm Paige," she said. "Do you guys live around here?"

"Max lives really close," Nina said. "My girlfriend and I are over in Echo Park."

I loved that Nina got her relationship status out there so there was no confusion whether or not we were together. I knew we were ostensibly here so Nina could give me her opinion of Sadie, but having her as my wingwoman was pretty good too, and felt way more hopeful than my chances with a distractingly hot bartender. Bartenders were barely real; they had more of a magical fantastical existence.

"I'm glad you're here," Sadie said, doing that thing where she drew near to me but didn't cut off Nina or Paige in the process. Her ability to keep people included was high on my list of reasons I could fall seriously in love with her. "My neighbor gave me a box of grapefruits and you were the first person I thought of. Hang on."

Nina nudged me, hard, as Sadie disappeared into the back room. I ignored her because I felt Paige's eyes on me, even as Sadie returned with a grapefruit and a citrus squeezer.

"Where did you move from?" I asked Paige.

"Brentwood," she said, playing with a piece of her long blond hair. "Just took a job downtown, though, so I wanted a better commute. Plus I love this neighborhood."

"Me too," I said. "I have to drive to Beverly Hills every day but it's worth it. I mean, usually."

"Sometimes nothing is worth the 10," she said, and I loved that in LA you could flirt about freeways.

"Here you go," Sadie said, setting down a tumbler in front of me. "Don't get used to it, as soon as we run out of these grapefruits we're back to Jarritos."

"I *like* Jarritos," I said, but as I took a sip of the cocktail made with freshly-squeezed-by-Sadie's-hands grapefruit juice, I actually let out a little gasp.

"Yeah, right? I knew you'd love it." Sadie turned to Nina to get her order, and then checked on Paige. My watch dinged, and I dug out my phone to check the text I'd just received from Nina.

MAX NO WONDER THIS IS YOUR FAVORITE BAR IT'S LIKE A MAGICAL WORLD WHERE EVERY HOT WOMAN IS TRYING TO GET INTO YOUR PANTS

I shoved my phone back into my pocket as quickly as possible, as Nina laughed beside me.

"So is this the best bar in the neighborhood?" Paige asked me.

"It's not even close," Sadie told her. "So don't feel the need to lie on our behalf, Max."

"This is my favorite bar in the neighborhood," I said, looking down at my drink. "It's always cozy here and it never feels scene-y or exclusive."

"Max is generous," Sadie said before moving on to a group of regulars who had settled in on the other side of the bar.

"I actually have to go," Paige said, glancing at a delicate gold watch on her wrist. "My sister and I always do a weekly phone call and it's—sorry, why am I telling you this?"

I grinned at her as she stood up and grabbed a brown leather bag from the hook underneath the bar top. I loved how classic all of her accessories were, how put-together a cute girl in a romper could be. "That sounds nice. My sister's at NYU and is way too cool to set aside prime evening time to talk to me."

"The key is to have a less cool sister," Paige said. "But it was really nice to meet you, Max. Maybe you can show me around the neighborhood sometime?"

Nina nudged even harder, so hard that between her elbow

and a badly timed swig of my drink, I coughed in a definitively unsexy manner.

"Yeah, sorry, of course, I'd love that."

We both got out our phones—matching iPhone models in similar cases—and exchanged numbers. I could still feel that Sadie's presence was opposite us, looking away as she tended to the other side of the bar, and I was grateful for that. Was that a messed-up thing to feel, though?

Paige left, calling a goodbye over her shoulder at Nina and me on her way out, and I stared at my phone like it contained something magic. Maybe it did.

"Have you ever tried to self-actualize?" I asked Nina, who cracked up.

"Is that a euphemism?"

"Oh my god, Nina, *no*," I said, but then I couldn't stop laughing either, and I realized I didn't want to talk about anything serious. Maybe everything really could be as simple as putting myself out there a little more and being a little less afraid of how people saw me. Maybe people were seeing me the right way after all.

"I'll just say that my girlfriend goes out of town a lot for work, so I am *very familiar* with self-actualization," Nina continued, and I realized I was actually laughing so hard I was *crying*. "Oh my god, a notification!"

"From Dog Tinder?" I asked, right as Sadie showed up again.

"They make Tinder for dogs, and you wonder why I got rid of my iPhone," Sadie said, which made Nina and I laugh even more. It was exactly the kind of night, in so many ways, that I'd once dreamed about having in LA. When I crawled into bed a couple of hours later, I didn't do my normal routine of over-thinking the events of the entire day. I fell right asleep.

Chapter 6

You'll Never Forget to Eat Lunch in This Town Again

I took my surging confidence to work the next morning and flew through my inbox, made some updates to the agency grid, and had every trade reviewed before Joyce's first call in. I managed to wave to Gillian, Aidy, and Javier as they each arrived, and felt like this new life where I didn't sit and wait to be noticed was absolutely on track.

After all, I'd already accomplished a half-day's worth of work in less than an hour, and I had two very cute texts from Paige to prove last night had gone pretty amazingly, and a date planned tonight—tonight!—at Café Stella. Yesterday felt like proof that when I put myself out there and didn't overthink things, they went OK. They went more than OK!

"Hey, Max." Gillian popped up in front of my desk, holding out a box of Sprinkles cupcakes. They were not the best cupcakes, but the industry had decided they were our standard, and so they were pretty ubiquitous around here. "Jeff got me cupcakes for my last day, but you can't have one unless you're coming out to my goodbye drinks tonight after work."

I decided that a red velvet cupcake was not legally binding, so I took one even though I wasn't positive I could make it—or wanted to.

"Two years of my life and I'm rewarded with these dry-ass cupcakes," she said. "I guess I should just be grateful it's not nothing."

"No one cares about assistants," I said, though I felt guilty as soon as the words were out of my mouth. It was true, in general, but I did feel pretty cared about by Joyce. She'd do better than cupcakes if I left, at least.

"Truly," Gillian said. "OK, gonna keep making the rounds, but I'll see you tonight."

When Joyce arrived, we went over her day's schedule, and I was about to take my fancy coffee and head back to my desk when she stopped me with a look. I wondered if that was something you were born knowing how to do or it developed over time. I couldn't imagine anyone being frozen into place by anything I could do with my eyes.

"I wanted to mention that your script coverage this week was really great work," Joyce said, and I felt my cheeks warm. "You have a real eye for projects, and somehow your work just keeps getting stronger."

"Thank you," I said.

"It's probably good timing to discuss something," Joyce said, nodding to the chairs facing her desk. They tended to be for talent and executives; I normally just sort of hovered around the perimeter, and I tried not to beam as I sat down in the cushy bright blue chair across from her. All this time spent worrying about how to bring this up, and Joyce was going to handle it for me. My talents hadn't gone unnoticed, and maybe everything was about to change.

"It feels a bit . . ." Joyce seemed to be considering the right word. ". . . tacky to say this, but my position at Exemplar has shifted quite a bit in the last—well, honestly, it's been rising for years now. But with the two Oscars this past season on top of

all the success my clients have been seeing across the board . . .
let's just say that I'm at a very good place in my career and that
it hasn't gone unnoticed."

"Of course not," I said. In fact, I'd thought it was pretty common knowledge that despite that there were agents at Exemplar
who'd been here longer or had a client list that was A-list only,
Joyce was the one everyone buzzed about—sometimes quietly,
sometimes not so quietly. I was thrilled for her—not just as her
assistant, but as someone who knew that this agency and most
of the rest of them had been started by old white men. Watching a Black woman become the most respected agent here was
really wonderful.

"You've been such a huge part of my team, Max, so I didn't
want to enter this next sort of deliberation without discussing
it with you first."

I nodded. "Thank you for saying that."

"As you probably know, the top tier of agents here tend to
have at least a couple people working their desks," Joyce said,
and that heavy feeling from earlier dropped even lower. This
wasn't about me and my strengths; I could feel that already.

"Right," I said, doing my best to keep my voice light and
pleasant and not squeaky with fear.

"And so I've been offered that opportunity to bring in
someone else to work alongside you," Joyce said. "I've obviously rarely felt that you weren't handling everything—"

I wished she'd said *never* and not *rarely,* but that Tuesday
morning meeting incident was probably still as fresh in her
head as it was mine.

"—but I also know that we're not supposed to work all of you
the way assistants used to," Joyce said, and laughed brusquely.
"I know you put in a lot of after-hours work, but I always just
thought of that as part of the job. Maybe I shouldn't."

I shrugged, partially to cover my shaking shoulders. "I've
never minded."

"And it's very appreciated. But do me a favor and think about it."

"Think about it?"

"If I were to bring on a second assistant, how it might make sense to split the work. Is it by client, or sets of duties, what makes sense to you?" Joyce paused. "You're so good at all of the administrative tasks, maybe it would be wisest to bring in someone who's more interested in my side of the business, who's a year or two out from mentoring with me to advance to junior agent."

Me! I wanted to say. I was the one who was already here, and interested in her side of the business, and was maybe even closer to mentoring with her! But my shoulders were still shaking, and my voice felt tight and locked up in my chest. If I focused on holding myself still, I wouldn't cry and I wouldn't visibly tremble.

"Anyway, I obviously very much like how things are, so I'd rather keep them as-is than blow up a perfectly functional system," Joyce continued. "But think about it, would you? I'd really value your input on this."

"Oh, sure," I managed, and then luckily Joyce's line rang and I was able to excuse myself to answer it outside of her office, back at the safety of my desk. Tess Gardner was scheduled to start shooting in Germany next week, but the production company hadn't been able to confirm her passport. It was the kind of task that used to inspire me with panic—production deadlines combined with government bureaucracy were a terrible mix—but I'd sorted out something like this at least a half-dozen times before. I *was* good at the administrative side of things, which never felt like a ding against me, but now I wondered. Had I given the impression that was *all* I was good for? What about my skill with coverage that Joyce had just mentioned? What about all the shitty clauses I'd caught in contracts before we had to even call in the legal department? Was that all just admin stuff too?

Before I could stew on it any longer, our internal finance team sent over a payment they'd flagged with an incorrect agency fee, and I knew from the studio involved that it was going to take me the rest of my morning to get it sorted out. I needed the distraction, sure, but it was tough staying completely focused. My brain had plenty of spare energy to wonder if I should have done something differently and declared my intentions sooner, or if there was something intrinsic to how Joyce saw me that labeled me as admin forever.

Aidy actually stopped by my desk and invited me to a lunch with her and Gillian and a few other assistants, but I was still stuck on an endless loop of holds and was afraid to give up my position in the queue, plus I was still kind of close to tears and worried if I talked too much that I'd start crying.

I wanted to gather myself and all my feelings and that whole speech I'd been writing in my head for Joyce, but the longer I stayed on hold, the less possible it seemed. Hold music did nothing to quell my tears, and maybe it riled up something else too. Was I angry? Sometimes I felt like anger was an emotion for tougher people, not someone like me who everyone saw as tiny and harmless. Suddenly, I didn't exactly wish to cause harm, but I knew that if there was something about me that felt intimidating, like a threat, I might have been seen as a contender for a mentee to Joyce, instead of a girl who just sat on the phone.

"Oh no," Joyce said, approaching my desk. "Don't tell me there's another billing issue."

"Don't worry, I've got it," I said, practically a knee-jerk response.

"Of course you do," Joyce said. "You always do. Anyway, after this lunch with Sarah from Netflix, I think I'm just going to head out for the weekend. I'll give you a call when I'm driving home to review any loose threads."

"Oh—OK."

"Talk then," Joyce said, heading off without a look back at me, while the tinny hold music blared in my ear.

I'd hoped to be off hold shortly and building my speech. I saw myself back in Joyce's office by the end of the day with an impassioned plea for the future of my career. By now, though, I could take a hint from the universe that today was not the day.

Still, I wanted to stay as late as possible to knock out as much extra work as I could to prove—well, *something*, but Gillian called to me on her way out, and I remembered I'd promised via cupcake that I'd be at her happy hour, so I guessed I would have to overachieve on Monday morning instead. Was it even *over*achieving? Maybe it was just achieving. I had no idea what Joyce expected of me, only that we obviously saw my role in two very different ways. Since she'd already checked out for the week, I knew that it didn't really matter if I was here or not, even if the thought was a little depressing.

I consulted Waze and did the math, and it looked like I'd be able to spend forty-five minutes at the happy hour with enough time to comfortably get to Café Stella by eight. It was good to remember these plans, remember how Paige had smiled at me, remember that I had more going on than this job. Maybe Joyce saw me one way, and maybe my roommate saw me in another even less flattering way, but that didn't have to mean anything if I was doing OK in all these ways that mattered.

Traffic was light on my way to Honor Bar, and I even found free street parking only a block and a half away—which basically counted as a miracle in Beverly Hills. I scanned the dimly lit space as I walked inside. So far I'd done a pretty good job of only going out on the Eastside, even after nearly three years of living in LA and working on this side of town. Heading west, though, things got slicker and more intimidating, like the glossy blond Erewhon stereotype Los Angeles was to people outside of it.

"You actually made it!" Aidy waved me over to the small group of Exemplar employees crowded at one end of the narrow wooden bar. It was nothing like Johnny's, but of course, what else was?

"I said I'd make it, I'm here," I said, trying to be nice, but it came out a little salty. Still, Aidy laughed and gave me a hug. I surveilled the group that had gathered here: besides Aidy and, of course, Gillian, it was Javier, Elise, Teddy, and Stephen. Basically, most of the assistants on our floor.

"I can't believe Max is actually out with us," said Javier, and I wanted to have some kind of justified big reaction to that, but the truth was that I hadn't responded to any of the handful of happy hour invites over the last year. There'd always been a reason, and a good one at that: a call I was stuck late on, a stack of scripts higher than usual, a checking account so dangerously low that even a Diet Coke felt impossible to buy.

I did my best to make eye contact with the bartender so I could get a drink for both something to do with my hands and also to take a little bit of the edge off.

"Could I get a Paloma?" I asked, and he laughed.

"That's a good one."

What did that even mean? "Do you . . . not have grapefruit juice?" I asked.

"I'm gonna need to see some ID," he said, still laughing. I had no idea what was going on as I handed it over, but I did feel correct in my typical avoidance of going out in this general area.

"Oh, sorry," he said, sliding my driver's license back to me. "I thought you were twelve or something. Coming right up."

Twelve? Getting carded was normal, but this felt like a new low. Literally. Luckily, my drink was ready fairly quickly, and it appeared that none of my coworkers had overheard the interaction.

"Should I ask to switch to Jeff's desk?" Elise asked Gillian. "I hate working for Nicole, but would it be any better?"

"Well, it's higher profile," Gillian said. "And I do think Nicole is specifically unpleasant, but I'm not sure how much less unpleasant it would be."

"Maybe just get out instead," Aidy said with a laugh. "It's what all the cool kids are doing, right?"

"If we were smart, we'd all do that," Teddy said, downing his drink. "Unless you're trying to level up to junior agent, we do too much and get paid too badly to stick around."

"We do get free salads sometimes," I said, which made everyone laugh. It wasn't just that it was true—yes, free salads seemed plentiful in our industry, but also I felt the need to say *something*. I understood the complaints, of course. This was not the nicest business, not even close. It wasn't just a joke I'd told to Sadie; Joyce really had said *with a laugh* that the days of agents throwing phones at their assistants had mostly ended by the late nineties. I'd laughed along and pretended that I was lucky. I guessed that I was, but not having a phone thrown at your head seemed like a really low bar to clear.

"I stopped asking for salads," Elise said, tucking her thick black hair behind one of her ears. "Just started getting myself burgers, or a big vat of pasta."

"Oh my god, you're brave," I caught myself murmuring earnestly, and then everyone was laughing even harder. I could tell that everyone agreed with me, too; we were within a very silly industry that expected ridiculously silly things from all of us. Now that I was in the middle of this conversation, it didn't seem like I was some kind of odd guy out; maybe all the assistants were on more equal ground than I'd realized. Maybe, even mistaken for a tween, I should have ventured out sooner than this.

"So are you going to be moving on soon?" Aidy asked, and even though she was looking right at me, I looked to Teddy and Elise, on either side of me, because she couldn't mean *me*, Max Van Doren, who cared about this job as much as she cared about anything.

"I'm talking to you, Max," she said with a laugh that sounded kind and not mocking. But in my best-case scenarios, it wasn't a kind question. It didn't make any sense at all.

"Oh, no, I mean, I don't think so," I said, and since everyone was still looking at me and, apparently, expecting me to say more, I took a big gulp of my cocktail to indicate that I didn't have anything else to say on this topic.

"Well, get out before too long," Javier said. "Except for those of us who are trying to move upwards in this godforsaken world for whatever cursed reason, you don't want to be seen anywhere as an assistant for too long. Makes landing the next gig harder and harder. Anyone like you who's clearly never going to be an agent, get the hell out."

I nodded a whole bunch and forced myself not to chug the rest of my drink, both because I needed to be driving across town in less than an hour and even if I wasn't a lightweight, I really couldn't afford another anyway. But, wow, I needed something—anything—to do that wasn't dwelling on Javier's words.

"I love how you talk with so much authority," Gillian said to Javier with a roll of her eyes. "I had no trouble landing my new job, thank you. Max'll be fine too when she's done with agency life."

Gillian, I knew, was being kind, but I couldn't will myself to take it that way.

Teddy asked Gillian for résumé advice, while Aidy and Javier talked about all the ways they were making sure they were seen as candidates to be mentored, to be promoted, to be given their very own clients. *Work hard, put in the hours, don't just be invaluable but be* smart *about it.* Hadn't I done all of that? Wasn't I doing all of that as often as I could? Wasn't I the best at coverage that Joyce had seen, smart with client opportunities, eagle-eyed on contracts? But if my peers couldn't see it and my boss couldn't see it, I wasn't sure what else I was supposed to do.

Conversation continued at the same pace but instead of attempting to be part of things, I stared into my nearly empty glass and focused on not panicking, not crying, not being completely obvious how hurt I was. That was the whole game of this business, keeping that stuff to yourself. And then suddenly it was exactly the time I was supposed to head back to my side of town, and I still had to say goodbye to everyone and walk that block and a half to my car.

Normally I was not an aggressive driver, but today that felt like just one more LA failing instead of proof of patience. I passed every car I could, even cutting off others to honks and raised middle fingers as I swerved back and forth between lanes down Wilshire Boulevard, desperate to shave off time from my ETA that kept, somehow, ticking upward.

I finally gave in and yelled to Siri to text Paige, and was just about to compose the nicest, flirtiest version of *I am running very late like the Los Angeles flake I promise I am not* when my phone rang with a call from my mother.

"Shit," I said, then felt terrible and took the call. "Hi, Mom. Everything OK?"

"Well, honey, I know that Thursdays are our normal night to chat, but you seemed so busy and stressed out when you texted yesterday that I wanted to touch base and see how you were. You're not still at the office, are you?"

"No, I'm on my way home—well, not home, I have a date, but I—"

"Oh, how exciting. Tell me everything about her. Did you meet on Tinder? Or HER? What's that other one, Lez?"

"It's Lex," I said, though even with my correction, I felt like my mom knew more about the app dating habits of queer women than most straight boomer moms. "And, no. I met her at Johnny's."

"At *Johnny's*?" Mom's tone was horrified. "Not in front of Sadie!"

"Mom, no, Sadie was on the other side of the—also, you understand I'm really stupid about Sadie, right? She's a bartender, she's nice to everyone, it's stupid I'm hung up on her. I'm trying not to be. This is progress or whatever."

"Aw, don't be so sure about that," Mom said. "I remember when you said how it felt so easy and comfortable to talk to her. That's exactly how I felt when I met your dad."

"Mom, this isn't helping." I heard the irritation in my voice and tried to tame it back. "I'm sorry, it's just been a rough day and I'm running late and I should probably let you go before I yell at you even more."

"You know I never mind if you yell at me," she said, because my mom was a saint. "What happened? Bad day at work?"

My stomach growled loudly and it hit me that I'd completely forgotten to eat lunch, which surely wasn't helping my mood. Or the way that drink had hit my system.

"I really don't want to talk about it, OK? Can I promise to call you this weekend and catch up when I'm not stuck in traffic?"

"Max, of course. Good luck on your date. I can't wait to hear how it goes."

"Thank you," I told her, trying to sound sincere and grateful and in no way impatient. "Talk to you soon, OK?"

"Of course, honey. I love you, kiddo."

I squeezed my eyes shut for just a second to keep from bursting into tears. "I love you too, Mom."

By the time I'd hung up, I saw that Waze had knocked a couple of minutes off my ETA, and as traffic continued to lighten I flew the rest of the way east. It wasn't until after I'd parked my car at my apartment and taken off on foot toward the restaurant that I remembered that I'd been about to text Paige when Mom called. Paige had texted that she was early and had grabbed a table on the patio, but now I saw that she'd also sent a polite and very cute **Just wanted to make sure we're still on and that I didn't get the restaurant wrong, classic eastside newbie mistake!** and then, as I ran into the restaurant and out onto the patio, an **Is everything OK?**

"I'm so sorry," I said as I reached the table. She was wearing a short pink dress, and her blond hair was piled on top of her head in one of those styles that looked perfect and messy all at the same time. A beautiful date look, for me, and here I was running through this beautiful space like a sweaty nervous coyote. "I thought I texted you that I was late but my mom called and I know that's not a sexy excuse but—"

"But you're here now," Paige said with a smile. "Remember, I just had a bad commute before I moved. I understand."

"I'm not normally like this. Today's just been a lot." I eyed the bottle of wine on the table, and Paige laughed.

"Yes, that's to split. I took the liberty and got a rosé, hopefully that's OK."

"Anything would be OK right now," I said, which felt rude out of my mouth but hopefully she understood that it wasn't. It was just that I was still somehow moving a million miles an hour in panic, even if I was now sitting across from my very cute and patient and interested date.

"So what job keeps you going to Beverly Hills and back?" Paige asked, leaning forward.

"I'm an assistant at Exemplar," I said, and none of the pride that I normally felt accompany my role was there. Before I'd felt on the way up. Now? Maybe it was just embarrassing. "It's a shitty job, whatever."

"Oh, sorry to hear that," she said.

I knew that it was my turn to ask her about her job downtown, but it hit me that if I'd forgotten to text her because I'd been so distracted, it was possible I'd forgotten other tasks too.

"I'm sorry," I said. "Can you give me just a minute? I should check my email on something . . ."

"Sure," she said.

I tried to hurry through my inbox and my Outlook calendar and my task list and my Notes app, but since a waiter stopped by twice while I was doing so, I wasn't sure that I'd been very good at hurrying.

"Sorry," I said, finally, shoving my phone in my pocket. "Should we order? I guess I should look at the menu."

"I guess you should," Paige said, and even though it had felt like I'd lost a little of her patience, her tone still had a flirty edge to it, and I tried to focus solely on her. She was so radiantly pretty, sitting here in the patio lit by twinkle lights and the setting sun. Meeting her had been like something out of a dream, and it felt like all I had to do was not screw it up.

"Everything OK?" she asked, as I looked at the menu.

Apparently I had not done a good job hiding the *yikes* I felt when I saw the prices. Last night in a fog of confidence—and three freshly squeezed Palomas, of course—I'd simply googled *best date spots in silver lake* and offered the first choice to Paige. But I was too broke not to know better than that!

"No, everything's fine," I said, as my watch dinged. "Sorry, I should check that. Work . . ."

It wasn't work, though. My watch said I had a message from Sadie Bartender. I should have let it go, but I found myself taking out my phone so I could read her text on the bigger screen.

just making sure ur still on 4 2morrow c u there

Yes, I'll see you then! I texted and then turned back to the menu. Maybe I should have turned back to Paige, but I was worried I had some kind of lovesick expression on my face and oh my god why was this going so badly?

"Maybe we should—"

I could tell Paige was going to attempt a getaway, so it felt like a miracle that the waiter was back yet again. I ordered a salad because it was cheaper than anything I actually wanted, and clocked that Paige's steak frites was one of the most expensive items on the menu. Of course I was going to pay, because I'd picked the restaurant and because I'd been late and because I probably made a regrettable expression while texting Sadie. It was time to get it together. Maybe my career ambitions *were* doomed, but I knew that if I could focus on Paige that we could have a really good evening together, and maybe even a very good night together. And then a whole happily ever after. All I had to do was get through this dinner.

"I'm sorry," I said again, once the waiter was off with our orders. "Today has been a lot. Boss stuff, really boring, I don't want to make you suffer through it. Tell me about your new job downtown."

"Oh no, it's so boring and now I feel like you expect me to be interesting," Paige said with a laugh. "I'm a project manager at a creative agency. Basically I just make sure everyone does their work and sends it to the right people or places in the right formats."

"That sounds important, though," I said, drinking from my wineglass like it was water. Rosé was so refreshing. "I mean, you're a *manager*."

"As I tell my friends, I feel more like a PDF babysitter," she said with a laugh, and it was very cute and one side of me really wanted to lean forward and take down her hair from that updo so I could run my fingers through it, so I could pull her to me and kiss her.

But the other side of me was humiliated she already knew that I was only an assistant, and an assistant with no future at that. Not that she could know that much, the no future bit, but we'd learned while texting last night that we were the same age. Was it humiliating that I was so far below her?

"So do you do any volunteering or anything on the weekend?" Paige asked, and I realized I'd been draining my wineglass instead of holding up my end of the conversation. "I'd love to look for some opportunities, but I feel like the organizations I like always have their volunteer gigs during the week when I'm at work."

"I feel like I should clarify," I said, pouring myself another glass even though a voice in my head was screaming in a very shrill tone not to. "Like, I really am just an assistant, super low level. But my plans are to move up, you know, not just get coffees and throw buck slips into chairs forever."

"Well, sure," Paige said, and from her tone I gathered that

maybe I had not exactly made myself look less pathetic with this pronouncement. The voice in my head screamed even more loudly.

"I know being a twenty-six-year-old assistant is really pathetic," I said. "Like no one wants to show off a girlfriend who's an aging assistant, I get it. It really is a temporary thing for me."

"I . . . don't really care about things like that," Paige said. "To me, a job is a thing that lets me pay for my life, and I guess in a lot of ways, that's it. It's not some big part of my identity."

"It's really easy to say that when you're not like an abject failure," I said.

"OK," she said softly, and it was like my brain finally listened to the screaming voice and I was able to get myself under control and back to safe topics like upcoming concerts and movies and the last season of *Generation Q*. Paige's meal was huge so she offered to split it with me, and as I gratefully took bites of the savory steak, I felt my soberness slip back in and nudge me.

"You're being really nice," I said to Paige, who laughed.

"Max, we've all had bad days."

It felt like maybe I'd managed to redeem it—or that Paige was so kind that it didn't matter that I was still an unmitigated disaster—but then the bill came and I panicked and pulled up my checking balance on my banking app. I was too drunk and sloppy not to do it but not enough drunk and sloppy to miss that it was obvious and embarrassing. Paige clearly noticed and grabbed the check.

"You don't have to do that," I said.

"Max, it's fine."

"I just wanted to check. I was the one who picked this place. It's embarrassing if I—"

She sighed. "Just let me, all right?"

"Fine," I snapped, because I was mad at myself but that wasn't how it sounded, and I knew it. The waiter grabbed the check and Paige's credit card before I could attempt another fix, and then suddenly the check was back, Paige was signing the receipt, and we were walking out onto Sunset with, most likely, our fates sealed.

"Would you, um, like to come over?" I asked, gesturing down the block. "I live just off Manzanita."

"Max, are you seriously asking me if, after you show up late, barely make conversation with me, and then get mad at me *for paying*, if I'll go back to your place and fuck you?"

"No, I just thought . . ." I hated that of course I was.

She sighed loudly and shook her head. A strand of her hair came loose, and I longed to lean forward and tuck it behind her ear. "I'll see you, Max."

The shrill voice told me to say something nice and apologetic and grateful. "Can I Venmo you for my half at least?"

She just turned and walked away. By the time I got back to the apartment, I was in full-on tears, and couldn't stop even when I saw that Chelsey and Ava were in the living room watching *Real Housewives of New York*.

"Max," Ava said, looking up at me with objective concern in her dark brown eyes.

Chelsey jumped up and made her way over to me. "Are you OK?"

"I changed my mind," I said, realizing it as the words left my mouth. "I'll do your self-actualization thing. When do we start?"

Chapter 7
Commit to the Bit

My internal clock had me up in a wild panic early the next morning before realizing two things: that it was Saturday, and that even after the detoxifying smoothie Chelsey had Postmates'd for me last night, I was extremely wine-hungover.

My date flashed back to me as I got up and headed down the hallway for a shower I hoped would make me feel refreshed and also way less guilty about how things had gone with Paige. Not that I didn't deserve to feel guilty. I'd been such an inattentive asshole and then tried to sleep with her? It wasn't even *like me.* I could feel that this was how people turned bad, how they let unrelated resentments and disappointments eat at them until they morphed into something ugly and mean. I just didn't think it happened in one traffic-snarled Friday night drive from Beverly Hills to Silver Lake.

The hot shower did leave me feeling—well, not exactly *better*, but less shitty. I blow-dried my hair into place—people always said my cut must be so easy, but short hair required so much upkeep. If I didn't style it every day, I'd look less like a Silver Lake lesbian and more like a homosexual Q-tip.

I picked out a button-down I hadn't worn to Johnny's in a while, and paired it with jeans that were too ragged for work but soft and broken-in, and my old too-beat-up-for-Exemplar boots that made me feel bad-ass even though I was—clearly—anything but. Maybe it was shitty of me to make an attempt to look cute for Sadie mere hours after my disastrous evening with Paige, but the stupid heart wanted what the stupid heart wanted.

I was pretty sure that was how the saying went, at least.

Sadie was just *right there* when I turned from my little side street to Sunset, and it hit me that I'd never seen her outside in the sunshine. Her brown hair glowed a little golden under the morning sun, and her skin looked tan against her worn-out vintage Dodgers T-shirt.

"Do you live just down the street?" Sadie asked, and I nodded. "I figured you were close, but that's really close. No wonder you tolerate the bar. It's the nearest one."

I grinned and fell into step beside her. She was wearing jeans cut off just above the knees with a ratty pair of black Converse Chuck Taylors, and a beat-up brown leather messenger bag was slung over one of her shoulders. I knew that plenty of people had strict taste in the people they dated, but I loved how worn-in and vintage Sadie looked, and I'd loved how glamorous and chic Daniela had been, and—even though thinking about her made me feel like shit—I loved how soft and classic and girly Paige was.

"I really do love the bar," I said. "After all, Akbar is technically closer to me. But it doesn't feel the same way. Is that weird to say? I always just feel cozy at Johnny's."

"It's not weird," Sadie said. "It's actually really nice to hear. Makes me feel like that thing that was at the heart of it is still there. Though maybe we should wait on this until after we've got coffee."

"Sure," I said. "Does this have something to do with the contracts?"

"Paperwork, and, yeah. It's a whole thing, and I really appreciate you helping me out."

"Again, I'm not sure how much help I'll be," I said, feeling her hand brush mine as we paused at the light at Micheltorena Street so we could cross Sunset. "So don't thank me yet."

I held open the door to Alfred Coffee for Sadie and followed her up to the counter of the tiny coffee shop. We were both regular drip coffee drinkers, and Sadie tipped in splashes of oat milk for both of us at the self-serve counter once she'd paid for our drinks.

"Sorry, my job puts me on autopilot whenever and wherever drinks are concerned," she told me, carrying our coffees as we walked outside to a table next to the sidewalk. "Obviously, you could have poured your own oat milk, but I can't turn it off."

"I didn't say you should turn it off." I grinned as we sat down across from one another. Our knees bumped under the table and I felt jolted by the physical contact, especially when Sadie didn't make an effort to pull away.

"So I'm sure you're like, why is this bartender asking me to a top-secret contracts meeting," Sadie said, as I practically chugged my coffee. "Wow, rough night?"

"Kind of, yeah," I said. "But I'm here for the top-secret contracts, so how can I help?"

"I realized as I was thinking about this that it might involve a lot of backstory," Sadie said, tapping one of her hands against the edge of the table. "This already feels like more than you bargained for, I'm sure, so feel free to bail."

I shook my head, trying to understand that someone like Sadie appeared to be nervous right now. "I don't want to bail."

"Well, remember that consent can be revoked at any time," Sadie said, which shot images through my brain that were completely inappropriate for—well, for whatever this coffee date was. It was certainly not the kind of activity that was going to lead to us naked together later, so I did my very best to shut out those images as quickly as they'd arrived.

"So I've been—" Sadie cut herself off and took a sip of coffee. "Wow, it's really fucking weird saying this out loud."

"Take your time," I said, and she smiled.

"I've been saving up to buy Johnny's from Billy," she said. "I don't make a ton, but my expenses are even lower, and I have a little chunk of savings from my parents' life insurance."

"I'm sorry about your parents," I said.

"It was a long time ago," Sadie said. "But thank you."

"My dad died when I was little," I said. "So I . . ."

I didn't know where I was going with the statement. So I understood? I just didn't want Sadie to feel awkward about it, the way having a dead parent could really lead-balloon a lot of casual conversations, I'd learned. People with two living parents rarely knew what to say.

"I'm sorry, too," Sadie said, lightly touching my hand before picking up her coffee again. "It puts you in another world, huh."

I felt weird smiling, but Sadie was smiling too. "The Dead Parent world?"

"Exactly. People treat you all gingerly and tiptoe around it, and I can just tell they've never lost anyone like that yet."

I nodded in recognition. "Everyone always thought I was so fragile because of my dad, but . . . I'm just small."

Sadie studied me for what felt like more than a moment. "You've never seemed fragile to me."

Could you blush over your entire body? I felt the blood rush to my—well, my *everywhere.*

"Anyway. Dead parent stuff aside. I am not all the way there to having the money for the down payment, but my goal's been to do it before I turn thirty, and that felt so far away but now it's getting closer and—well, it's not certain but it's possible."

"That's amazing," I said. "And Billy wants to sell?"

"To paraphrase Billy, he wants to take his Social Security and the profits from the bar and ride into the sunset never to be heard from again. Which I think means live near his sister in Fresno."

"OK, so . . . are the contracts for the sale? Did he have them drawn up in advance?"

"I wish." She sighed and opened up her bag. "Billy's been getting offers from developers basically since my uncle—Johnny—died and he took over. And—well, you know Billy."

"Well, kind of."

Sadie set a couple of manila folders on the table. "You know him well enough, I think, that you're not surprised that he refers to most developers and such as money-grubbing gentrifiers trying to turn the neighborhood into Epcot Center: Silver Lake."

"Yeah, OK, I guess I know him that well," I said, and we laughed.

"The offers just . . . keep getting better," Sadie said, the fun zapped away from her tone. "And I'm staring down the barrel of thirty with this tiny pile of money and Billy's not going to wait forever."

"So . . . someone would buy it and make it—like a fancy bar?"

"That's not even what scares me," Sadie said, and it hit me that I didn't think someone like Sadie could be afraid of—well, anything. "Luxury condos, a multilevel parking garage, soulless corporations, that's the shit that keeps me up at night."

"Oh," I said, feeling naïve and young to the ways of the world, even though Sadie was only three years older. "Yeah, that would be terrible. Johnny's feels like an institution."

"OK, well, it sort of is, so that's my plan." She finally opened the manila folder. "I know Johnny's isn't as old and was never as historically recognized as the Black Cat or wherever, but Johnny opened it in the seventies. It's not *not* part of history here, you know? I feel like if I can get it designated somehow then there are protections involved and—maybe I'm just making things up. But it feels like I should be able to secure it as a historic landmark or something, and then no one can knock it down so people can park cars or tech bros can disrupt something. It feels like there should be a way for me to buy this place for an amount that—shit, it feels so stupid saying it aloud to you."

I shook my head. "It doesn't sound stupid at all."

"I dunno, it just feels like a queer person should be able to buy her uncle's semi-historic queer bar for a sum that's not impossible. But all of real estate in LA is impossible, you probably think I'm living in some kind of fantasyland."

"I feel like we already determined that we live in Dead Parent world, not fantasyland," I said, which made Sadie laugh. "Just because the prices here are so high that I can hardly comprehend them doesn't make your plan stupid. Also, I guess I didn't realize there was a titular Johnny. Or that he was your uncle."

"He was my dad's oldest brother," she said. "And the coolest person I'd ever met. Even now, he still holds that title. He was one of those people who could just command a whole room, you know? He bought this building dirt cheap and made it this really warm neighborhood place. He taught me how you can make strangers feel welcome and how to make well drinks taste like top-shelf. Also he was out even when it was really tough to live that way, and so I got to grow up with this actual gay role model in my life."

My watch, obviously unaware I was having this kind of conversation, dinged three times in succession.

"I'm so sorry," I said. "Though I should—I'm sorry, I'm being terrible."

"Check your robot watch, don't worry about me," Sadie said.

Are you going to be home soon? I figured we could start working on You Point Oh this morning!

I'm honestly impressed you're already out and about. I was going to make you one of my hangover-cure smoothies. It might be a fun video to film if you still want to make them when you get home??

One thing you can start doing now is to list out your goals! Big life goals! Career, love, finance, social life, all the big things! Remember that my followers love when I'm VULNERABLE so don't be afraid to reveal yourself! I can't wait to dive into all of this with you!

"Oh, god," I mumbled. What had I gotten myself into? I'd been way too panicked and susceptible last night. Not only did this seem like my worst decision ever in the bright light of the morning, but those dings had ruined whatever moment I'd been in with Sadie.

"I'll just say," Sadie said, "this is why I'm off the grid."

"You're not really off the grid," I pointed out. "I could text you three times in a row, if I wanted."

"Go ahead and try. My phone will freak out, truncate all your messages, and buzz politely *once.*"

"It's weird you're so proud of that," I said, and she grinned.

"I'm not proud. I just think it's good to get some distance sometimes, not be so reachable."

I wondered if that were true.

Sadie took a sip of her coffee. "Do you ever walk the Lake Hollywood Reservoir?"

I shook my head. "I don't even know what that is."

"It's this completely flat walking path, a few miles around. Even with a phone and a robot watch like yours, your signal mostly drops out there. It's just you and nature. Feels like another world."

"That seems dangerous," I said. "What if someone needs to get in touch with you?"

"It's barely more than an hour to walk around." Her gaze seemed to intensify, as if I was being evaluated. "Not to be nosy, but whatever texts you just got, would anything have changed if they'd arrived an hour later? Would your life have gotten worse?"

I started to answer (*Yes, obviously something would have changed, Sadie, we would have kept our amazing talk going!*), but she shook her head.

"Sorry, I'm getting all old-man-yelling-to-stay-off-his-lawn at you. Too much time with Billy, maybe. You have a whole life and an important job and you being reachable is valuable to people."

"Yeah, that tracks," I said, which made her laugh. I really, really liked making Sadie laugh. "Also these really are unimportant texts. Your point stands."

"Are you always off Saturday mornings?" she asked. "From your dumb Hollywood job?"

I nodded.

"Next Saturday, let's go on a walk," she said. "Let your signal drop out. See what happens."

"OK," I said, more quickly than I've ever said those two syllables before. "I can look at the historic paperwork and contracts and whatever in the meantime."

She glanced at the envelope, biting her lower lip. I knew that this was hard for her, but for me it was very hard not to think about her teeth, her lips, the parts of my body I longed for them to make contact with.

"Can we talk more about it?" she finally asked. "Next week. Some of this is really Billy's paperwork and—it's not that I don't trust you, Max. I just know I'm not just sharing my own financial shit, but someone else's and—"

"I understand," I said, even though I knew that I didn't, not fully. The truth was that I rarely felt unready for anything. I was ready for *so much* to finally happen, always.

"Thank you," she said, her tone soft and sincere. "Your next drink's on me."

"I'm not sure Billy would like that," I said, and we grinned at each other again. Was it naïve to think we had some kind of connection? Were we just two women sharing jokes and experiences? I worried I didn't know enough about life and love to tell the difference.

"When Billy's off in Fresno, he'll be grateful for you, too."

At the apartment I escaped the hangover smoothie video session, but Chelsey did sternly send me to my room with a notepad, pen, and the command to emerge only when I had my list of goals. I reminded myself that no one had to see my work-in-progress, so I took a deep breath and started to write. Just for me.

Goal #1: Get a Promotion or At Least a Mentorship Offer. Make Joyce see the value I could bring to a bigger role here. Get her to take me seriously!!

Goal #2: Fall in Love, Ideally with Sadie. Figure out a way to not just have a crush but to pursue something for real with her, or at least find out if something real is worth pursuing, and if not with her, with someone. I want to be in fall-over, swooning, out-of-control, deeply connected love. I want someone to see me for everything I know I can be, and I want that for her too.

Goal #3: Get Strong. Since I can't wish to be big like in the Tom Hanks movie, could I at least not feel like such a tiny wimp? Sometimes I worry that if there was an emergency, like a building caught on fire, I should be able to carry a girl out of it, like a big hero. Right now I'm not sure I could even carry out a medium-size dog from a fire.

Goal #4: Get a Group of Friends. I watched The L Word *a lot when it was still on Netflix and I thought for sure that when I arrived in LA I'd find my queer chosen family. Instead I found out the original series was mainly shot in Canada and it is much harder to connect with people than I thought.*

Goal #5: Get Mom to Stop Keeping My Childhood Bedroom Ready for Me. Probably if I can achieve the other four goals, she will (???), but I want her to see that I'm out here for real. Even if it's hard and I'm a nearly-thirty-year-old who's not great at (I really hate this word, but) adulting, this isn't a fun thing I'm doing while I'm relatively young, this is my life.

This was not a list I saw myself handing over to Chelsey. And it was kind of scary seeing it all laid out like that, how far away I felt from the things I needed. I was careening into my late twenties and sometimes I worried I hadn't accomplished *anything*. And it was hardly for lack of trying! I tried very hard, all the time. Though obviously I worried that maybe that was part of the problem.

I reminded myself that if I had already achieved my goals, I'd be like Chelsey: self-actualized and confident. Needing help and being far away from my goals was the whole point!

I tore out the way-too-honest list and started over. When I was done, I marched down the hallway to the kitchen, where Chelsey was setting up some content about irregularly shaped vegetables or something. She was wearing overalls over a T-shirt with her blond hair in thick Heidi braids, a very farmers-market look. I honestly loved how much she always committed to the bit.

"... taste just as good, even though they look like a—oh, yay, did you finish your list?"

"I didn't mean to interrupt," I said, even though it was impossible not to walk in on Chelsey's sponcons and organic content shoots. The apartment was only so big and the content was just *so much*.

She waved her hand. "I was about to mess up anyway because this cucumber looks so phallic."

I snorted. "Don't they all?"

"*Extra* phallic," she said, holding it aloft.

"I'm pretty sure I saw that exact shape at the Pleasure Chest," I said, which made her dissolve into giggles. "Anyway, yes, I finished my list. You're not going to make me read it right now, are you?"

"No, Max, do you think I do anything that spontaneously?" She all but ripped the sheet of paper out of my hand. "Oh, this is good. This is *so good*."

"Is this enough?" I'd taken off the thing about Mom. I figured if I could achieve the rest, she'd stop counting on my imminent return. "Four items doesn't seem like a lot, but ..."

"No, these are big items! You did great."

"So ... what's next?" I asked. "I have to be on camera and embarrass myself? Do I have to put on makeup? I don't own makeup, so ..."

Chelsey laughed and shook her head, braids whipping back and forth. She looked like an American Girl doll with a very modern agenda. "Next I'll chat with my team, and we'll come up with a whole strategy. At this moment you don't have to do anything at all."

"Shouldn't I be involved in the strategy?" I asked. "I mean, it's ... literally about me."

"Don't worry about it," she said with a smile that scared me, more than a little. "I'll take care of everything."

Max's You Point Oh Goals

#1. Stand out in my job and work my way toward the next level of my career.

#2. Seriously pursue a long-term relationship.

#3. Become physically stronger.

#4. Cultivate a larger social circle and find real connections.

Chapter 8
Some Sloppy Paraphrasing

"Hey, y'all, I can't wait to introduce you to one of my favorite people in my life." Chelsey spoke in a confident but casual tone, and she exuded a vibe that read as chill and fun and not way-too-intense even though she appeared in tight close-up.

The picture zoomed out and there we were together. My tall and beautiful roommate dressed in a wildly patterned Nooworks dress with her hair cascading down in harmonious waves, and me in a faded button-down and jeans with my light brown hair in place with the seven styling products that short hair required. For all my fears, Chelsey hadn't touched my hair or my face at all. For good or bad, I looked exactly like myself.

"This is my roommate Max, she/her pronouns," Chelsey continued. I looked a little stunned in the warm glow of multiple ring lights, but not as bad as I'd feared. I'd begged Chelsey to let me watch the video before she posted, but that, I learned, was not how Chelsey operated. "Max shares my taste for Taiwanese takeout and nineties sitcoms and always does her half of the chores. In other words, she's the perfect roommate."

I saw the surprise flash in my eyes, that my cool roommate had such nice things to say about me—that she'd even noticed, really. Maybe I was a little embarrassed about the sitcoms thing, but did we actually have something in common? I might have asked, had we not been on camera.

"I guess Max has bigger goals in life than that, though, so she's going to try out You Point Oh and let me share how it goes with you all," Chelsey said, professional and natural at the same time. How did she do it so effortlessly? "Max, how do you feel about achieving all your goals?"

"Um, nervous?" I hated how my voice sounded so squeaky, but Chelsey grinned like it was charming. Was my voice charming? I didn't think so, but it was very sweet of her to pretend. Was Chelsey actually sweet and I hadn't noticed, or was this all artifice for her audience? Watching the edited video made it impossible for me to tell.

"Which part makes you nervous?" Chelsey asked, sounding very interested in my plight. "The work ahead of you to accomplish your goals, or the thought of having them actually achieved? Like, that whole fear of success thing?"

"Chelsey, I am not *afraid of success*." I hadn't said it to be funny, but she'd giggled, and I could see that maybe it was. There were already several comments on the video that said "CHELSEY I AM NOT AFRAID OF SUCCESS omg dying" or some variation.

"OK, then what makes you nervous?"

Everything, I'd wanted to say in that moment, and it was weird to watch myself very clearly not say that.

"Doing it on camera," I said after what felt like a very long pause. I kind of appreciated, on an artistic level, that Chelsey hadn't edited it out. There was an honesty there; her content videos weren't just highly curated depictions of real events.

"I guess that's where we are very different people," she said with a sly grin, and that was that. We had actually filmed a few days of content in one go, just switching out outfits in between so it wouldn't look like we'd filmed everything in a couple of hours on one Sunday afternoon.

I stowed my phone away and got back to my inbox. It was a typical Monday morning, which meant that watching Chelsey's one-minute video was enough time for twelve new emails to hit my Outlook. I filed everything I could and started on the this-should-only-take-five-minutes tasks when Javier and Aidy popped up in front of me.

"Chelsey Sullivan is your roommate?" Aidy asked.

"Oh, um, yeah, she—" I cut myself off because I knew immediately how she knew. "You saw the video? You follow Chelsey on social?"

"Like a half-million people follow Chelsey Sullivan on Insta," Javier said. "It's weird you never said anything."

I shrugged, still trying to keep up with my inbox. "What would I say? Hi, I'm Max, I'm Joyce's assistant and my roommate is an influencer?"

"Well, maybe," Javier said.

"It's LA," I offered. "I figured everyone had an influencer roommate."

"That's fair," Aidy said. "So are you excited about this whole You Point Oh thing?"

I shrugged. "It feels like a last resort. And also I said yes to Chelsey when I was crying and kind of drunk, so I may not have been using my best decision-making brain cells."

Immediately I regretted so much honesty; why was that my default so often? Just nervousness and truly awkward confessions, the Max Van Doren conversation method.

Javier and Aidy laughed, though, and not rudely at that.

"Been there," Javier said.

"Haven't we all," Aidy said with a sigh, just as my phone rang with HARRIS, JOYCE flashing across the display.

"Joyce time," I said, which made them laugh more, even

though I didn't think it was that funny. Was I actually funny? Why did life feel so confusing these days?

Javier and Aidy headed off, and I rolled a bunch of calls for Joyce—traffic was apparently at a standstill, even though she lived much closer to the office than I did. Taking notes kept my brain busy, so it wasn't until Joyce was on her way up and I was standing in position with her coffee that it hit me that my coworkers were going to see me talk about needing more respect at work.

Obviously, I knew that my roommate was successful. But a half million random people was one thing—and a scary thing at that, sure! But a half million people *that included at least two of my coworkers* was another thing completely. Not just scary, maybe a full-blown horror movie.

"Everything OK?" Joyce asked as she stepped off the elevator and hoisted the coffee out of my hand. "You look nervous. Should I be nervous? Who's been acting up lately? Is Gregory still annoyed about his latest offer? Did Ari back out of another interview?"

"Everyone's behaving," I said. "Sorry about my face, just a weird morning. For me personally, not client-related."

I thought she'd look relieved at that, but Joyce raised an eyebrow.

"Everything OK with you then? Problems with that bartender?"

I laughed and shook my head, feeling my cheeks warm. "Nothing's up with that bartender at all." Except a non-date to walk somewhere without cell reception? Everything about Sadie was a little confounding.

"Did you look at her contracts?" Joyce asked, bursting into laughter.

"Oh my god, no, she got all weird and private about the contracts," I said, which just made Joyce laugh harder. "Can we please talk about work now?"

"I suppose we can," Joyce said, but I could see that the

laughter still danced behind her eyes. I imagined her reaction if I told her about the non-date and the flip phone. "Thanks for getting through all the coverage that came in at the end of the week. Very smart notes, as usual."

I told myself to find a way to segue that into—I knew it would help if I actually knew what to segue into. Yes, Joyce knew I was good at *this* job. What did I need to say for her to see I could be good doing so much more? Why could brutal honesty fly out of my mouth at the silliest times when the big and important moments left me all clammed up?

Chelsey was waiting when I walked in that evening. Literally standing practically in the doorway so that when I stepped in with an armful of scripts, I only barely managed not to scream and throw all those pilots and features into the air.

"Max!" she shrieked, making it—well, far from *better.*

"Why are you trying to give me at least two heart attacks?" I tried to breeze past her, but I wasn't really a breezy kind of person. "What's up?"

"Want to go out and celebrate? We can hit up that depressing bar you like so much."

"It's not *depressing*," I said. "What are we celebrating?"

"Are you not seeing your notifications?"

"The only notifications I have pushed are texts, Slack, and work emails." I pulled my phone out of my pocket and tapped to Instagram, where— "Oh my god."

"People *love you*," she said, grabbing me by the elbow and steering me out of the apartment. In her platform sneakers, she was a solid foot taller than me, so I hurried to keep up. "I can't wait until we unveil your goals list tomorrow!"

"Ugh," I said.

"'Ugh'?"

I scrambled down the sidewalk next to her, feeling like a miniature Chihuahua trying to keep up with a pack of Huskies.

"I didn't know my coworkers follow you," I said as we

rounded the corner onto Sunset. I couldn't believe I was going to my favorite place to hopefully see one of my favorite people while I had my beautiful and hot and confident roommate with me. This couldn't have been a good plan, none of it. "So I'm kind of embarrassed that I'll be talking about how no one re-spects me at work but—"

"Aw, Max," Chelsey said. "It's so *relatable*. You'd be sur-prised how many people feel exactly like you do. Why do you think I was so happy to leave my assistant gig behind?"

Chelsea had been the publicity assistant for a high-profile gallery in the Arts District up until her influencer success had grown to full-time job status.

"I dunno, you had enough money and sleeping in is better than . . . not?"

"Well, sure," she said. "But I didn't feel like my bosses took me that seriously either. I worked my ass off and still. I'd pro-pose these amazing social media ideas and they kind of waved me off, like, oh, you Gen Z kids and your TikToks."

"Meanwhile you're getting rich on your TikToks," I said, as we reached Johnny's. "Do you feel super validated?"

She held open the door for me. "You have no idea. I love it when people underestimate me."

"Hey, Maxine," Billy said, and gestured to my usual spot at the bar.

I quickly scanned the room and determined Sadie was nowhere to be found. With Chelsey here, that was probably safest.

"I'll get your drink started," Billy said, already grabbing a bottle of grapefruit Jarritos from under the bar. "What can I get your companion here?"

Companion?

"Vodka and soda with a lime wedge for the companion, thanks," Chelsey said.

"Oh my god, I'm sorry, that was weird," I whispered.

"You're the one who thinks this place is cool," she whispered back. "I expected nothing less than weird."

Billy had our drinks ready in a flash, and Chelsey raised her glass to me.

"Here's to the success of our You Point Oh campaign," she said. "The *continued* success."

I clinked my glass against hers and downed a sip. It didn't compare to last week's fresh-squeezed cocktail, but it was obvious that Billy had been doing this for a very long time. The drink was still somehow perfect.

"Oh, hey," a familiar voice said, and I looked up to see Sadie walking out from the back room. She was in a white tank over a pair of Levi's, and I felt extremely weak at seeing her shoulders.

"Oh, hey," I echoed back.

"I'm Chelsey," my roommate said, all smiles and charm. "Max's roommate."

"Sadie," she said with a nod. "I'd say I'm Max's bartender, but I think Billy would argue that I'm stealing his title."

Billy gave us a look as if he could not physically care less about any of this, and Sadie and I exchanged a grin.

"Are you excited about Saturday?" she asked me. I had no idea how to answer, because *of course* I was excited. Time with Sadie, just us, three miles that we were supposedly walking to get away from screens and the evils of modern life. Three miles to make Sadie see me and—

"What's Saturday?" Chelsey asked, leaning in as if this were a fascinating conversation.

"I found out Max has never walked the Hollywood Reservoir," Sadie said as she put away a tray of shiny clean glasses. "I feel like she'll like it. I was gonna say that it'd be good for her, but it sounds more patronizing than I mean it."

"Good for her how?" Chelsey asked.

"Sadie says there's like no cell signal so my robot watch won't bother me as much or whatever," I said.

"That's some pretty sloppy paraphrasing," Sadie said.

"I get the gist, don't worry," Chelsey said. "It's nice of you to worry about Max's screen time. Really above and beyond for a bartender. No wonder Max loves this place."

I shot her a look that I hoped, very badly, Sadie would not notice. Luckily the door chimed and a couple of regulars walked in and took their seats down from me, and Sadie's attention was on them and some news about a Dodgers pitcher, and no longer us.

"What are you doing?" I hissed at Chelsey, who giggled into her cocktail.

"I can't believe I wondered why this was your favorite bar."

"Please don't," I said.

"Please don't what? Talk about the forearms on that bartender? Or how she's very concerned about you unplugging from your hectic life? Or—"

I breathed a sigh of relief that the bar was filling up and I knew Sadie wouldn't overhear us. "Right, all of those topics."

"Max, it's obvious that *you like her*. Why not just—"

"Can we not talk about this here? Please?"

"Of course, of course," Chelsey said, and switched seamlessly back to engagement numbers and other markers of success. But as soon as we'd finished our drinks and were on our way back to the apartment, I saw a gleam in Chelsey's eyes that seemed dangerous.

"We can reshoot your goals," she said. "If there's someone specific you're pursuing, you should talk about that! That's also relatable as hell, Max. People will eat it up."

"I don't want to be eaten up," I said, groaning as it came out of my mouth. Chelsey cracked up and gestured wildly in the direction of Johnny's.

"I'd say you do very much want to be *eaten up*," she said.

"OK, yes, of course," I said. "I have a big, stupid, very obvious crush on the very attractive bartender. I think about her forearms *all of the time*. I am more than *mildly curious* what her shoulders would taste like. But I am also not a complete idiot, I know that she flirts with me because it's part of the job, and that she's doing nice things for me because I'm going to help her with some contracts or forms or whatever legal documents are confusing her."

"Wait, what?"

"It's a long story," I said. "And I like her—I mean, besides all of that. She's funny and interesting and I don't have many friends here and I want to help. But falling in love, finding a partner, all of that stuff, I know I'm silly to even think it could be Sadie, you know? This is the same kind of crush I've had my whole life, cute waitresses and baristas and gym teachers and English professors."

"OK," Chelsey said. "But I don't think it's as hopeless as you do."

"This would hardly be the first time we've disagreed about something, Chelsey," I snapped, but she cracked up again, and it hit me that I kind of liked this dynamic we'd developed. And then I remembered my goals were going up the next morning and that at least two of my coworkers would see it, and I couldn't believe I'd gotten myself into any of this.

Chapter 9
Saying Yes

Big night tonight! Your first official You Point Oh task! Will need you camera-ready by 8. Does that work?

Chelsey texted while I was trying to both schedule a meeting for Joyce and a streaming service exec as well as read a dark comedy script for a competing streamer. This job had probably been a lot easier back when only a finite number of companies made movies and TV shows.

As the rest of my intro videos rolled out over the past few days, I'd done my best to stay invisible at work. I had no desire to make eye contact with Javier or Aidy, knowing they'd probably seen me confess to Chelsey that "I have huge career goals for myself but it's like no one takes me seriously," with all the earnestness in the galaxy drenching every word. Would anyone take that girl seriously?

I'd never been so relieved that Sadie only had a flip phone. Yes, it was disappointing she didn't possess even one social media account I could pore through. A typical stage of a crush was the time I spent scrolling through profiles, searching for details in photos, captions, and comments that would tell me even more about someone I was falling for. As much as I wanted those glimpses of Sadie, it felt freeing she had no idea I'd become involved in the You Point Oh campaign. My goals and dreams were still secrets as far as she was concerned.

And work was busy anyway, with an influx of potential projects for clients. Actors were, of course, sent scripts by studios and production companies, hoping to woo them, but Joyce also stayed on top of buzzy projects that could be potential fits for her clients. It was my favorite part of the job, but the work could stack up fast. Even if I wasn't desperately avoiding thinking about certain topics like my earnestness, every spare minute of my workday had to go into the stack of scripts, pitches, and treatments. The last thing we needed was for a client to miss out on a career-altering role because I hadn't read it quickly enough.

I have a ton of script coverage to work on, I texted back. **So I'll be home but busy. As long as it doesn't take too long I guess I can't say no, right?**

Love your enthusiasm! See ya tonight!

I actually laughed before shoving my phone back into my pocket and managed not to spend every single spare moment before eight p.m. dreading it. Chelsey somehow did the impossible: made me less scared of a thing that really scared me.

"OK, so I got it set up with the You Point Oh team that you'll get your first task alert tonight," Chelsey said as she dusted powder on my face to make me less shiny on camera. I was worried that she'd been working up to slathering me with a bunch of products, but it was, luckily, the only makeup she made me wear, other than some clear lip gloss that smelled like roses, which I kind of liked.

"So we'll just start recording and then get your reaction in real time," she continued.

"Sure," I said with a shrug.

"Save your saltiness for the camera," Chelsey said, as our front door made a noise and then, terrifyingly, swung open.

"Are you recording?" I asked softly. "Will it capture the identity of our murderer?"

"Oh my god, what are you two on about?" Ava closed the door behind her and shook her head. "I've texted, called, and sent you DMs on two platforms, Chels. I had to break out that emergency key."

"Babe, I'm so sorry, just getting this whole shoot set up," Chelsey said. "Though I'm glad you're not a murderer."

"Me too," I said. "What an embarrassing way to go."

"Dead on TikTok?" Chelsey asked.

"Dead at the beginning of a self-actualization program! Everyone'll immediately know I never achieved any of my goals."

We both cracked up, but Ava still looked annoyed.

"It won't take long, I promise," Chelsey told her. "Everything's already set up, and as soon as we're done with the shoot, we can go out."

"It's fine," Ava said with a sigh, but she leaned in and kissed Chelsey's cheek. "I have a whole bunch of work I could be doing, so take your time."

Ava headed off down the hallway, and I glanced at Chelsey, who was somehow fiddling with her phone tripod and one of her ring lights at the same time.

"If you had plans with Ava, we can just . . . not do this," I said.

"This is my job, Max," Chelsey said, apparently happy with everything's placement. "It's almost eight, pick up your phone so we can start."

I did, while she tapped hers to start filming.

"Ava gets it," Chelsey said. "She's the most understanding ever. I just get real ADHD-overfocused and can be a very bad girlfriend sometimes."

"Maybe we should talk about something less personal while my phone's about to ding with a terrifying command," I said.

"Oh, absolutely. How are things going with your hot bartender?"

"She's not *my* bartender," I said. "She's the world's bartender, I guess."

"Uh-huh. What are you wearing on your big hike?"

"Wait, is it a big hike?" I asked. "I googled and it said it was flat. I don't need special shoes or anything, do I?"

"Why are you asking me, do I look like some kind of hike expert? The only thing I do outside is brunch," Chelsey said, right as my phone chimed ominously.

"Sonically, that's a weird choice for trying to become my You Point Oh self," I said, as Chelsey cracked up.

"Hey, y'all, I'm here with Max, who has just gotten her very first You Point Oh notification. Max, how are you feeling?"

"I mean, not amazing, to be honest," I said.

"Cool, cool, as always, love your honesty. So the thing I love about You Point Oh—no, Max, don't look at your phone yet—is they pair up sort of big-picture life advice, the stuff we all hear but aren't always good at actually following, with super specific customized help. Max's first notification is going to contain the first of two things: one of those big-picture statements that she can apply to her goals. Later tasks will have that as well as appointments with experts in the areas where she's looking for improvement. Sound good, Max?"

It, emphatically, did not, but I wanted to be positive, so I gave her a thumbs-up.

"So, are you ready to check out your first task?" Chelsey asked.

"Obviously I am, you practically just smacked my phone out of my hand." I held my phone in front of me and tapped to the You Point Oh app.

Hi Max, it's time to start achieving with You Point Oh! We know that for a lot of us, it's easy to keep doing things the way we've been doing things. It can feel impossible go-

ing outside of your lane or fighting inertia. So, with that, your first task is to SAY YES. Go to that networking event you were going to skip! Have lunch with that acquaintance! Show up at that party you RSVP'd a dishonest MAYBE to.

Good luck, Max! We can't wait for you to upgrade into You Point Oh!

"How are you feeling right now?" Chelsey asked. "Good, bad, excited, nervous, nau—"

"No, I understand what adjectives are," I said. "I guess good, actually. It's not as scary as I thought. I can say yes to some stuff."

"Amazing! I'm so excited to hear all about you saying yes," she said, and then that gleam from the other night was back in her eyes. "Why don't you go out tonight with me and Ava and some of our friends? Hadley Six is supposed to do a surprise DJ set at the Verdugo."

I opened my mouth to deter, and then realized I was trapped.

"Did you know the task was going to be *Say Yes*?" I asked, thirty minutes later, from the front seat of the Lyft that the three of us were taking up the 2 freeway to Glassell Park. "Is that how you tricked me into this?"

"No, I can think on my feet," Chelsey said. "And I would have invited you anyway! Normally you just would have said something about all the work you had to do and gotten out of it."

I couldn't argue with that, and it didn't cease to be true because an app was now in charge of my life. But when our Lyft driver pulled up to the Verdugo Bar and the beat spilled into the night air, I realized that maybe I could forget about that pile of scripts for a while.

Chelsey treated to drinks, and I followed her and Ava out to the twinkle-light-lit patio where a crowd was already moving to the music played by Hadley Six, who was famous in queer circles as a DJ and mixologist and also occasional significant-other of celebrity lesbians. I'd never seen her in person before, and I wanted to hang back and observe, how a DJ worked a crowd, how a crowd moved to a DJ, what a big group of queer people dancing their asses off looked like in real life. But Chelsey and Ava herded me into the crowd, and suddenly I was dancing awkwardly in this little sea of people—and then I was just dancing. I forgot to worry about any of it, just moved to the beat and with the crowd. It hit me that when I'd dreamt about moving to LA, nights like this were exactly the life I'd pictured for myself.

I was exhausted and behind at work the next morning, but it didn't feel regrettable. Not without the hangover and the bad decisions made. I just felt tired, and I could remedy that with an extra cup of coffee.

My inbox was halfway organized when a Slack DM popped up from Elise on the all-assistants-on-this-floor thread. **Friday happy hour after work, who's in? And I mean WHO'S ACTUALLY IN, not who says they are but are gonna flake later!**

I'd always ignored this conversation; it had been made clear ages ago that this wasn't my crowd. And Gillian's happy hour last week had been pretty terrible—well, it had actually been a lot of fun until I was mistaken for a twelve-year-old and then realized that none of my coworkers took me seriously. It honestly, I'd realized, would have been better if they'd been mean about it. Then I could cry about them being jerks and do my best to forget about it. But it was clear that they *hadn't* set out to be mean. Javier and Aidy and everyone else saw two paths for Exemplar assistants, and to them I was clearly on the path that headed away from careers like the one I wanted.

Normally I typed out a quick **Sounds fun but can't make it, have a good time everyone!** but I had promised very publicly that I was saying yes, so instead of going home after work to obsess over my non-date with Sadie tomorrow morning, I stopped by instead. It wasn't any different than I'd really expected; the same general crowd as last week, which meant that I didn't magically fit in better or discover some heretofore unknown coworker who was exactly my vibe. But it was *fine*. I drank a Diet Coke to save money and answered plenty of questions about Chelsey and You Point Oh, and suddenly people were headed out and it felt safe to do the same. And once I was cozy in my bedroom in my pajamas with my laptop and leftovers and laid-out clothes for my walk tomorrow with Sadie, I could admit it hadn't been that bad to *say yes* today, or last night either.

Maybe it had even been for the best.

Chapter 10
Off the Grid

Even after our conversation at the bar the other night and our texts confirming logistics, it was still like a miracle when I walked out of my apartment on Saturday morning and saw Sadie standing at the corner. She was wearing a vintage Stanford University T-shirt over the same jean shorts as last week. It still felt like a scandalous amount of leg to take in, and I did my very best not to stare.

"What?" Sadie asked.

"Did you go to Stanford?" I asked, eyes up-top, nowhere near the curve of her thighs disappearing into faded denim.

"I didn't," she said. "Johnny did. You OK with driving?"

"Yeah, of course." I gestured around the corner and led her to the apartment's parking garage. Last night on the way home, I'd swung through a drive-thru car wash and paid extra to vacuum out all the dirt and dust that accumulated no matter what when you lived in Los Angeles. I was pretty sure this was the nicest a slightly dented Toyota Yaris had ever looked.

Sadie the bartender is in my car, I thought as we sat down, but calmly put on my seat belt and started the car instead of letting on how surreal this felt. I noticed that Sadie had this particular scent that I'd taken for granted as maybe a part of Johnny's, but now it was right next to me, changing the air in my car to something soft and musky. Like the way she looked and dressed, Sadie smelled classic, of some other time.

"Are you nervous?" Sadie asked, clicking her seat belt into place.

"About walking? No," I said quickly, even though I was. I wasn't sure I'd ever walked over three miles at once and had no real gauge for it. Would I fall apart? Were my Converse inadequate? And then, of course, there was the Sadie of it all. Would we run out of things to talk about? Would I panic and confess my feelings? Would she start telling me about some girlfriend I didn't know she had, which could lead to me—oh my god, *crying*?

"I meant about being off the grid," she said with a laugh as I backed out of my parking spot and swung the car out onto the street. "But you actually *do* sound nervous."

"Sadie, I don't know if you've somehow not noticed this, but I'm nervous about everything."

"Everything?"

I could hear the smile in her voice.

"Will I know where to park, did I wear the right shoes, do people think I'm a loser, can I pay my rent next month, does my roommate pity me, does my mom think I'm destined to fail, that's some of it. *Everything*."

"Your shoes seem OK and I don't think you're a loser," Sadie said. "And I'll tell you where to park. The rest I can't help you with. Your roommate seems cool, though."

"Well, sure, that's the whole problem."

Sadie laughed. "I meant cool as in, I don't think she's sitting around pitying you. It feels like y'all have a good vibe."

I shrugged. Did we?

"Also, you don't seem that nervous to me," Sadie said. "And

I'm a pretty good judge of character. Not much of anything else, but that I tend to get right."

"You're good at lots of things, what are you talking about," I said in a breathless manner I hoped Sadie did not read too much into.

"Like?" she asked. "Oh, man, I love this song."

Sadie leaned forward and turned up the King Princess track, and I silently thanked Spotify's shuffle for this moment. Plus I loved how Sadie just did it, spun up the dial like she was comfortable here in my car next to me. I felt like I wasn't that comfortable anywhere, but I guessed at this moment I *was*, singing along to "House Burn Down" with my favorite bartender. No, I pushed myself, Sadie wasn't just a bartender, and even if my crush was embarrassing and naïve, there was something real about us, too. Not romantic, but real anyway.

"Did you forget my question?" Sadie asked, and even though my eyes were responsibly on the road, I could feel that she was grinning at me.

"I didn't. You're very good at listening, and making people feel welcome, and of course you're amazing at making Palomas, if that counts."

Sadie was quiet, and—even if she'd been the one to ask—I worried I shouldn't have just said all that. Earnestness was such a burden.

"That's really kind of you," Sadie said.

She didn't say more, and I managed not to list every other single thing I liked about her, and before long we were singing along to my playlist as I drove us up the 101 freeway. We ended up in a residential neighborhood that felt squeezed in between Burbank and Hollywood, and I was nervous I'd typed in the wrong destination, but also nervous about—well, appearing too nervous. And then suddenly the houses gave way to a hill leading down to nothing but a view of trees and the Hollywood sign, and we were there.

"I love that this is nature in Los Angeles," I said, swinging the car into a parking spot. It was a benefit of having a tiny car; there was almost always somewhere it fit. "A bunch of greenery but the Hollywood sign is still within view."

"I know, right? It's almost too on-the-nose to be real. Come on."

I followed Sadie down the hill to a paved loop we had to share with cars, which also felt so freaking Los Angeles. There was nothing about it that looked special, and if I weren't with Sadie, I probably would have turned back.

"This is only the first stretch," Sadie said, as if she could read my mind. Which would have been wildly inconvenient and humiliating. "Then the street dead-ends and it's just us. People, not cars, I mean."

"Oh," I said, as we walked together. Sadie was probably about six inches taller, so her casual, steady gait required a rush from me so that our feet were hitting the concrete in unison. That was what most of life felt like, when I thought about it: everyone else moving through it naturally while I was in a wild panic just to keep up.

We were quiet as we walked, cars and runners whizzing past, and then—just as Sadie had promised—a metal gate dead-ended the road, and we slipped past it and kept walking.

"This is nice," I said, as the noise of traffic fell behind us, and all I could see up ahead was green. "Sometimes I forget LA can look like this, too."

"It's easy to lose track," Sadie said, glancing over at me. "Sorry, I forget that you're shorter than me. Let's slow down so this is actually nice for both of us."

I tried to act neutral about this and not as if I could have literally swooned over this moment of thoughtfulness. And then we rounded a turn and something shifted even more in the setting. The cars were so far behind us it was as if they no longer existed. To our left side were hills and wildflowers and, of course, that ever-present Hollywood sign. On our right was a fence separating us from lush trees overlooking a lake. It wasn't really that I forgot LA could look like this; up until this moment, I hadn't even known that it was possible here at all.

"This is . . ."

Sadie chuckled. "I told you so."

"Don't be so smug," I said. "You told me it was nice to get off the grid for a little bit. You didn't tell me it looked like Jurassic freaking Park back here."

"Is that a selling point?"

"I dunno, I love nineties stuff, all my mom's favorites, watching old VHS tapes when I was little and everything felt really safe and easy." I shook my head and wished I'd thought to bring my sunglasses. It wasn't too bright, but I felt they helped me hide some of my rampant earnestness. The only way, I was sure, I had a shot with anyone was to tamp that down as much as possible. In some ways it was probably good that Sadie was an impossibility already, because it seemed I could only hammer that home further now that we were actually spending time together.

"That's sweet," Sadie said. "I remember being *terrified* by that movie, so it's nice it's some kind of wholesome childhood memory for you."

"Wait, are you scared of dinosaurs?" I asked, and a giggle slipped out.

"Max, people *got eaten* in that movie. I wasn't good with shit like that when I was a kid. Honestly, I'm not very good at it now."

"So no scary movies for you?"

"It's not that hard to avoid movies where terrifying things happen, you know. I do OK." Sadie ran a hand through her hair, but it all kind of fell right back into her eyes anyway. "I'm nervous to talk to you about Johnny's, if you couldn't tell. Like I've been wanting to, but I also keep delaying bringing it up."

"Honestly, I had no idea," I said. "Like, I seem like a nervous person. I can barely picture you scared of dinosaurs and nervous about conversations."

"The other month, I tried to do this meeting at a bank and it was like all my hopes and dreams and goals for my whole life turned into this printout of numbers showing how inadequate I was. Like I'd been playing pretend this whole time, and why was I there wasting their time."

"But you're saving up," I said. "It sounds like you're on your way to making it happen."

"I'm saving up because I, as I am right now, can't borrow enough money to buy out Billy and make Johnny's what I know it could be." She sighed loudly. "And at a certain point, Billy's going to stop waiting around on me and not be able to resist some asshole developer who's backing up a truck of millions."

"Imagine what millions could get him in Fresno," I said, hoping to make her smile, and it worked. "Sorry. I wish I knew how I could help. *Is* there a way I could help?"

"I'm trying to learn about historical preservation," she said. "To see if it could—I don't know. Help? And Billy's got some offers, not ironed-out contracts yet or anything, but paperwork he's willing to let me look at but—I'm just not good at stuff like this. Research and legal shit."

"Not to brag," I said. "But I am very good at research and legal shit."

"Well, yeah. You have that air about you."

"I can look into historical preservation," I said. "What do you want me to check on the contracts? I mean, I can't promise I'll be helpful at all. Normally I'm making sure actors are getting paid enough and that everything discussed beforehand is present."

"I guess I just want to know the reality of the situation," Sadie said with a heavy sigh. "I honestly hate admitting this,

but when I try to get an honest view of what Billy's being offered and how I could do anything about it, I feel like I start to
shut down. It's like I need someone smarter and less emotionally involved to look at the facts for me."

"I'll do my best," I said. "Though I'm not smarter than
you." And, sadly, probably not much less emotionally involved
either.

"How do you propose we settle that?" Sadie asked. "IQ
test? SAT scores?"

"Both, as soon as possible, sure," I said, laughing. "Seriously, I'll do my best to take a look at everything and see if
there's some kind of game plan to formulate."

"Do me a solid and don't say anything about this in front of
Billy," she said. "If this could just be between me and you for
now . . ."

"Yeah, of course." I caught movement out of the corner of
my eye and glanced over. "Oh my god."

"What?" Sadie asked, but then I could feel her following my
sightline as two young deer quietly munched leaves, just behind the wire fence. "Oh, yeah. I love whenever I see wildlife
in here."

"Will you kill me if I take a photo?" I asked.

"No, go for it. Your life's safe in my hands."

I slipped my phone out of my pocket. It didn't have a signal,
but of course I could still snap a few photos of the deer surrounded by greenery. It was something I could send later to
Mom to prove that I had plenty here: wildlife and someone to
spend time with, at least.

"I hope this doesn't violate your off-the-grid thing," I told
Sadie, tucking my phone back into my pocket and setting off
walking again. I couldn't believe, actually, that this was here,
just this beautiful loop of nature in this little pocket of Hollywood. LA wasn't new to me anymore, not really, but sometimes it could still surprise me.

"It's not *my* off-the-grid thing," Sadie said with a grin. "This is about you, if you haven't noticed."

I thought back on the poorly timed dings right when it felt like maybe Sadie was opening up, and the truth was that of course I was glad that wasn't a possibility this morning. "Thank you."

"Though maybe it's rude I decided you needed this and yanked you into the wilderness."

"Sadie, I know I called it Jurassic Park," I said, "but it's not exactly the wilderness. I'm from Kentucky; I know wilderness."

"My point stands!"

I laughed. "Sure. But I let you yank me. It's all good. Anyway, I don't think I realized I actually needed something like this. To be honest, I didn't even know something like this existed here."

"How long have you lived here now?" Sadie asked.

"Over two years," I said. "But sometimes it feels like all I really know is like my immediate neighborhood and the path from work to home. Did you grow up here?"

"I did," she said. "Well, the Valley, close enough. Maybe I take it all for granted. I feel bad for you that you don't know more of the city by now, but I get you've got one of those jobs that takes a lot of your time and attention."

"Yeah, I also pictured it really differently," I said, and laughed to myself because strolling through this hidden pocket of nature was also something I'd pictured differently about Los Angeles. "Not to sound stupid, but I guess I thought I'd get here and have like some big friend group and have a girlfriend and then I'd do all this exploring with her and with them. I've been, like, holding off."

It was somehow so much honesty and also a little bit like a lie at the exact same time. Because in some ways, I'd been holding off my whole life. It wasn't just that I didn't come out to my family until college—I hardly even dealt with it in my own head until then. And that year I lived at home before moving here, I probably looked at app results in LA zip codes more than I looked at my own. I didn't swipe right on anyone local because I was bound for somewhere else. Now, though, I didn't know how I felt about always having lived one foot out the door, ready for the next phase to start. I had no experience living in the right now.

"Well, I know a lot about LA," Sadie said. "I can't always keep you off the grid, but if you're helping me out so much with Johnny's, I can try to return the favor by making sure you're not missing stuff. If you're off next Saturday, we could do something that's not your job or your apartment or Johnny's."

"Deal," I said very quickly, then laughed. "I should probably learn to agree to deals less quickly if I'm going to become an agent someday."

"This was clearly a good one," Sadie said, knocking her hip into mine softly. Unfortunately I was not expecting Sadie contact in that general area of my body, and the surprise combined with our height difference sent me toppling over.

"Wait, what the hell just happened?" Sadie asked, and I could tell from her strained eyebrows that she was trying very hard not to laugh at me. She leaned over and pulled me up, and I kept my hands in hers for maybe one moment longer than anyone else would have.

"You OK?" she asked, and I nodded. I was so, so OK right then. Maybe I could learn to live in the moment after all.

"I'll give you all my paperwork next time we do this," she said, as we set off walking again. "Or if I can get Billy to take a night off, I'll text you if I'm at the bar alone. Sound good?"

I—of course—agreed, glowing a little at the thought of *next time we do this*—and then we were both quiet for a bit. Our view shifted again, denser greenery giving way to a view of the lake and the bridge up ahead over it. It really felt like a whole world back here, and even though there were other walkers and runners around, it also somehow felt like it was just for us.

"I can't believe this is here," I said. "Like, right up from Hollywood."

"I know," Sadie said. "No one's cleared it all down to put up shitty condos or coworking spaces."

I knew that it reminded both of us of Johnny's, but neither of us said anything. I could tell it wasn't the time.

"I really appreciate you," Sadie said, and at first I thought I must have misheard, that of course she'd said *I really appreciate it.* "That someone like you would take the time to help me with this probably hopeless project . . ."

I didn't know how to interpret *someone like you,* but I'd have plenty of time to roll that around in my brain later. For now, something else was more important. "I swear, there's nothing hopeless about this. We'll figure it out."

Chelsey banged on my door on Sunday morning, the only morning this whole week I'd had to sleep in. I was *this close* to yelling for her to leave me alone, but it sounded ruder than I wanted to be, and also there was that whole *saying yes* matter which now sort of held me captive. So instead of dozing longer while replaying all of yesterday's best moments in my head, I dragged myself out from under my quilt and opened the door. I was extra grateful I'd done so because it was Ava and not Chelsey, and she definitely didn't deserve my morning grouchiness.

"Chelsey wants to give you a heads-up that she's having people over for brunch," Ava said. "Also that attendance is mandatory."

"Ugh, I feel like a prisoner," I said, and Ava's laugh pealed out.

"Yes, this is exactly why we should fight for prison reform. It's always a brunch or a queer dance party or a—"

"OK, I get the point and really feel like a jerk now, thank you."

Ava was still laughing. "Get ready, Max, to suffer your meal of avocado toast and tofu scramble, the same thing they serve inmates at—"

"Hilarious!" I said, but Ava was hard to resist, and I was laughing too by the time I closed my door and dug through my closet for whatever constituted a cute brunch outfit. Chelsey and Ava were so fashion-forward and so femme that it was hard to take cues from them, but when I emerged from my room in my brightest patterned button-down over khaki shorts and my favorite boots, Chelsey nodded approvingly.

"You look like a scoutmaster," she said.

"Thank you?"

"Definitely a compliment. Who didn't want to kiss their scoutmaster? Can you help squeeze more oranges?"

I agreed and was happy I had a task as the doorbell rang, and Chelsey and Ava's crowd assembled. They looked like the kind of group I'd pictured in my fantasies before I moved here, stylish and bursting with chat about culture and TV and stupid memes, all the stuff I loved. In my fantasies, though, I'd somehow not been myself, I'd been the cooler version who fit right in. It was such a bummer that I'd made it all the way out here without becoming that cooler Max. So at least I had a pile of oranges to squeeze and no immediate concerns on how to actually socialize.

Once there was enough orange juice, I helped Ava finish slicing melons for the fruit salad, and suddenly our apartment was full of people and the food was ready to eat, and I squeezed onto one end of the sofa with a plate in my lap like this was what I did all of the time. I could feel that I wasn't a part of this group, but things were fast and loud enough that it didn't matter that I just sat there, eating my toast and tofu and melon, soaking it all in. I was *saying yes*. And the truth was that I didn't feel like a prisoner at all. (And not just because that had been an incredibly thoughtless metaphor to make in the first place.)

I wasn't naïve enough—despite that I knew I could come off

that way to others—to think that *saying yes* alone was going to fix my entire life. But I couldn't deny I'd had fun this week, including at times I would not have suspected. It could only take me so far, though, because unless the right people were asking, I might not ever get a chance to say yes to the things that mattered most to me.

But I guessed even if I never leveled up at work or fell in love, I might have a really good time not achieving my goals. Which didn't actually sound too bad.

Chapter 11

The Next Task

My typical Monday morning panic at work had just subsided when my watch thumped with a notification. I hoped, even though it wasn't likely, for a text from Sadie, maybe a confession that after our walk together she was too in love with me to live another minute without speaking up.

It was only Chelsey, though. **Don't freak out but you're about to get a You Point Oh notification with your next task. Don't worry about me! We'll film later! First some more content about your last task (think about all the stuff you've SAID YES to!!) and then we'll discuss the new one. How exciting is this?**

I rolled my eyes but also I was a little excited, if I were being completely honest. Eager and uncomfortable all at once. Excited and scared, like Little Red in *Into the Woods*. And since I couldn't get out of it even if I'd wanted to—and I guessed I was starting to *not* want to get out of it—I texted back an affirmative. After all, even though *say yes* was pretty generic advice, it would actually be great if You Point Oh could solve all of my life problems. So far, so good.

My phone buzzed while I was still holding it, but it was Nina and not the app. **We need to catch up! Drinks this week at your fave bar?**

I replied to Nina right away—even if having her and Sadie near each other again seemed a little risky—and we were still in the middle of setting up plans for the next night when my phone buzzed again with the You Point Oh notification. It was easy to ignore it for a second and finish up with Nina while gathering my courage to see what was in store for me next.

Hi Max, we hope you've been having a great time SAYING YES with You Point Oh! And even though your next task is here, we want you to keep SAYING YES, too!

We hope you've seen how your life can really open up when you take on the possibility of doing the unexpected, but we think that even more goals get achieved when you're proactive. So for your next task, we'd like you to BE BOLD & ASK FOR IT!

Maybe you're after a promotion! Maybe there's someone you have your eye on you'd like to ask out! Maybe there's a friend you've been meaning to spend more time with! Don't wait around to be asked . . . SAYING YES is great but asking for what you want can be even more powerful!

We know this is a lot, so there's no way we'd have you go it alone. To make sure you've got support, and so that you can get some specialized advice about your career, we're also including the contact information of a career coach, Judy Wax. Judy's already heard lots about you, and is ready to help you level up in your field.

My email chimed about four times in a row, so I managed to tear myself away from the You Point Oh app and back to my job—which was, by comparison, far less scary. For now, at least. Until I, Max Van Doren, the mildest person in the world, had to become bold.

Driving home that night, I felt a growing bubble of dread in my stomach, toward Chelsey and her ring lights and her iPhone tripod. It was undeniable that this whole thing was going well, in general—Chelsey and You Point Oh seemed happy with the numbers of engagements and signups and all of that—but I hadn't had to get *too* personal yet. With people like my coworkers watching, it was more treacherous. Of course there was a promotion—or at least a path to it—I wanted to ask for. Obviously there was a woman I very much wanted to ask out for real. None of this seemed possible, though, just because I'd spent a few days saying yes.

At home, though, there was such a frenzy so I could get on-camera that I forgot to keep getting nervous until Chelsey's phone was aimed at me and she was already addressing her followers.

"Wait, what?" I asked, and she laughed.

"I said it seemed like saying yes went well for you. Obviously some things are private," she said with a cheeky look to her phone, "but what were some of the things you said yes to since you got your first task from You Point Oh?"

"Well, you know I went out to dance with you," I said. "Even though I'm a very awkward dancer. And I went to a social thing I normally don't, and it was pretty fun. Sorry, this doesn't sound very life-changing."

"Well, it doesn't *sound* very life-changing," Chelsey said. "But I know you! It's a big deal you did all of that, right? Would you say that you switched up your typical routine? Talked to some new people? Tried some new stuff?"

"That's true, normally I would have just gone to bed and watched like three and a half episodes of *Frasier*," I said. "Maybe I shouldn't admit that."

"No, people need to know what we're working with here,"

Chelsey said, and I let out a laugh, even if it was at my own expense. "Are you happy you said yes to going out more and therefore no to the Crane brothers?"

"A little, sure."

Chelsey cracked up and leaned forward to stop recording. "OK, go change into another shirt so we can pretend it's another day and I'll ask you a little more about going out, if you're game."

"Going out with you and your friends, yes," I said. "I don't want to be awkward about going out with my coworkers for a normal happy hour thing that they do all the time. It turns out they all follow you, and it might be too embarrassing."

She eyed me for a moment, blinking her long lashes (spon-con with Jenna Lyons's fake lash company). It felt like a very long moment.

"I totally understand—well, I don't, clearly, I live my whole life on camera. But I get that it's awkward for you. But you know that your next task has so much to do with your job—after all, that's one of your big goals. So you won't be able to completely avoid work topics. Work topics are kind of why you're here, aren't they?"

My stomach twisted. Sure, I knew this, but I didn't love dwelling on it.

"It's going to be *great*," Chelsey said with a wild gleam in her eyes. "Go get changed! I promise that you'll get used to revealing all your feelings on video. It's a little addicting."

"Chelsey," I said, "usually things described as *addicting* are not exactly good for you."

Even though I ended up talking way more about work than I'd wanted to, I allowed myself at least a day off from stressing out about it because Chelsey was releasing the videos on a schedule, and my *say yes* videos were up next. For at least twenty-four more hours, my coworkers would have no idea that little Max Van Doren had wild career ambitions. It was so annoying how often it could be embarrassing just to be yourself.

After work, I headed across town to meet Nina for drinks. Traffic was blissfully light—grading on a scale, of course—so I took a few minutes once I parked to watch Chelsey's latest videos. I was getting used to how I looked and sounded on camera; it wasn't so much that I *loved it* but I could at least see why people enjoyed watching us. Our curated-for-social-media roommate relationship was pretty cute. It was too bad we weren't actually that close IRL.

"The usual, Maxine?" Billy asked me as I walked into Johnny's, and I nodded and tried not to look like I was desperate for a glimpse of Sadie. Plus I liked the ritual of it, even when my bartender wasn't Sadie. Billy was an old pro; I could tell from his ease with the bottle of tequila, the careful way he dropped ice into the waiting tumbler, that he'd been doing this a very long time. Mixing good cocktails wasn't just about following a recipe, I could tell, there was a whole art to it.

"Busy day at your big office?" he asked.

"It always is," I said, and I saw something that I could have sworn looked like *envy* flash in his eyes. "Did you ever work in an office? I mean, if that's OK to ask you."

He chuckled, though it was low and growly so even his laughter sounded a little cranky. "I sure did. Put in a lot of years in buildings with fluorescent lighting."

"Is that why this place is so dark?" I asked, and a genuine laugh erupted from him.

"Nah, it's always been this dark here. Sadie complains about it too, says it looks like some sad grandpa's forgotten basement. But I like keeping things. You're young, I know, but someday you'll realize not everything has to be improved or updated all the time."

"Oh, god, what are you two talking about?" Sadie asked, walking out from the back and standing next to Billy, facing me. Her hair flopped into her face, but I still saw a flash of panic in her eyes. She was wondering, I could tell, if I'd said something to Billy about the sale of the building and her plans for it, not that she'd given me many details about either thing. How was it possible that she thought I'd betray her confidence like that? I couldn't tell if I should be hurt or if I'd done a bad job conveying how seriously I took anything and everything I'd promised to her.

"Your little friend here also seems to think the bar's too dark," Billy said, and Sadie cracked up. I, of course, was too busy mulling over *little friend* to join in the fun. Was that a euphemism? Honestly, I worried it wasn't. It didn't sound sexy to be a little friend.

"Hey," Sadie said with her standard regular-customer head-nod, and I smiled as Nina took the barstool next to me. Her hair was up in a casual bun, and her red-and-orange-patterned dress stood out in the dim lighting.

"Hi," Nina greeted Sadie, before fixing her smile on me. "We have so much to talk about."

"Did you and a dog both swipe right?" I asked, and she burst into laughter.

"Not yet, don't even get me started, Max."

Sadie raised her eyebrow at us, and then Nina was laughing again, which set me off. "What can I get you, Max's friend?"

"Let me get a Paloma, too. Max always makes them look so good."

"Got it, another Paloma for Maxine's friend," Billy called out, which was so much better than when he'd referred to Chelsey as my *companion*. Part of me was desperate to know what Billy thought of me, but mostly I was relieved that he kept so much to himself.

"I can't believe you didn't tell me," Nina said. I truly had no idea what she was talking about and said as much. "Your whole thing with Chelsey Sullivan."

"Blargh." I buried my head in my hands. "I know this sounds

dumb, but even though Chelsey has literally a half-million followers, I really didn't think people I knew would see all these videos. It's so weird."

"It's weird you think I wouldn't know about cool queer influencers," Nina said. "I'm not *that* much older than you, you know."

"That's not what I meant! I just—I was in a vulnerable state and I said yes and I maybe shouldn't have but also . . ."

Nina grinned, as Billy deposited our drinks in front of us. "But also?"

I shrugged, feeling exposed with all those goals sitting out in the open between us. Nina knew more about me than most people, like how desperate I was to fall in love and how terrified I could be at work. This still felt like opening another door, though, and I guess I hadn't realized just how much I liked my doors closed. In some ways, I hadn't realized I had doors at all.

"Well, I am definitely not self-actualized, Nina," I said, once Sadie was at the other end of the bar, serving beer to a couple of men around Billy's age.

"Who's self-actualized these days?" Nina asked.

"Oh, come on," I said. "You have this whole perfect life."

"I have a very good life, yes," Nina said. "But, lest you forget, I'm also really just a glorified assistant at my day job, and maybe that's all I'm ever going to be. Which is OK and all, but I assume you know I have bigger dreams than that, don't you?"

I hadn't really thought about it, actually. Nina was so glamorous and in such a good relationship and seemed to have a million friends. The thought of her wanting more in exactly the same way I wanted more was difficult for me to wrap my head around.

"Any good dates lately?" Nina asked me. "Or very bad ones?"

"Oh my god, one of my worst," I said. "Probably second only to that time that girl tried to get me to join her cult."

Nina cracked up. "Please tell me."

And so I told her about Paige, and then because the story was out there—and because Sadie was still all the way at the other end of the bar—I explained how the night led to me giving in to Chelsey's demands and doing the whole You Point Oh thing in the first place. It had only been a couple of weeks, but it also kind of felt like a lifetime ago. I also let Nina know about my still unreleased next task on the lineup.

"So when do you meet with the career coach?" Nina asked.

"Tomorrow after work," I said. Judy Wax had been easy to schedule with, and I hoped she'd have some sort of secret code for unlocking the next phase of my career. Could it really be that easy?

"Let me know how it goes," Nina said, her tone so encouraging. "I can't wait to hear what you want to do with your life."

I knew I could have just said it. *You know what I want to do with my life, Nina! I want to be like Joyce! I want to make killer deals and savvy choices and wear intimidating outfits and prove everyone wrong who's ever underestimated me.*

But I couldn't get the words out, and was relieved when Sadie stopped back by so I could let myself off the hook.

"I was wondering," she said, wiping the bar area clean while she held eye contact with me. "Are you married to taking a walk on Saturday? I can't promise your signal would drop all the way out, but there are other things we could do."

I could see Nina's expression shift into wide-eyed, and I kicked her to qualm any inappropriate reactions. "You're the one who wanted my signal to drop. I'm fine with anything."

"Good, good," she said with a smile. "I'll think of something."

The door opened, and a guy I recognized as a regular stepped in, which meant that Sadie began mixing his drink immediately and Nina and I were left alone again.

"Max, it seems like there are a large number of details about your life you haven't shared with me yet," she said.

"It's nothing," I said. "I'm helping her out, she's helping me out."

"Uh-huh," she said. "The last person I did a bunch of mutual helping out with is now my girlfriend, but I'm sure it means nothing and you're right."

I glanced over at Sadie and inadvertently caught her eye. *You good?* she mouthed, and I nodded and looked away. Still, I could feel her gaze follow me, and I wondered what it would be like if I could actually be bold and ask for what, in that moment, I wanted most of all.

I expected the career coach's office to look like all the generic office buildings I'd worked in before landing at Exemplar, but once I was past the shared office lobby, the tiny front room was warm and inviting, even if it looked a little LA woo-woo with plants, candles, and bowls of crystals and polished gems decorating the counter and coffee table. I'd lived here long enough that I was hardly immune to a little woo-woo.

A woman around Mom's age leaned into the room, as I was about to sit down on the turquoise sofa. Her dark hair was pulled back into a low ponytail, and her business suit had loose, laid-back lines.

"You must be Max," she said. "I'm Judy. Sorry, my assistant had to head home early tonight, so I hope you weren't sitting here long."

I shook my head and followed her into her office, which was even smaller and yet just as crystal- and candle-filled.

"So I've watched all your You Point Oh videos so far—how fun, by the way, you must be having the time of your life—but I'd love to hear from you what it is you're looking for."

"At work?" I asked.

"Well, sure, but . . ." She kind of waved her hand at me. "In general, too. What's the life you're after, Max?"

I gulped. I'd spent the drive down Wilshire planning out

what I'd say about my job, about Exemplar, about Joyce, about where I wanted to be in five years. But my whole life? I hadn't prepared that at all.

"Can I start with work stuff?" I asked.

"Of course! Tell me about work. You're currently a talent agent assistant?"

I nodded. "And I know I'm supposed to hate it, but, honestly, I don't. I mean, it's stressful and I'm probably underpaid, but I still love it. I want to be like my boss someday, which was like . . . *not* a dream I had growing up. I could never figure out what I wanted to be, you know, I got a communications degree so it could be kind of vague and I assumed I'd sort it out later. And then that's what happened, I got here and I got this job and it all clicked for me."

Judy nodded, and I could see in her direct gaze that she was really listening. I expected her to say or ask something, but since she seemed to be waiting for more, I kept going.

"It was totally just a job to me at first, like I had to make rent and pay for stuff, but it was like . . . it wasn't that I just liked the job a lot."

"You were good at it," Judy said.

"*Yes.* It feels weird to say that, but I am. I know I'm not perfect or anything, but—I don't know. The really admin stuff is where sometimes I'm not perfect. But I think that the other stuff . . ." I wondered what she thought of me, *Finding Nemo*'s dad in a sea of sharks. "Maybe it sounds like I'm delusional or I'm bragging—"

"Max, none of this will work if you can't assess yourself," she said with a warm smile. "It's great that you know where your strengths lie. In fact, I'd love to hear more."

I told her about my script coverage, contract review, the light negotiation I managed before Joyce was set up for the bigger stuff. I tried to find words for the more ephemeral stuff like the good gut feelings I had about scripts that should get passed on and scripts that should get passed by, next steps for careers that felt instinctual in me, and of course how to present ideas to talent so they saw it from our angle—for me that was more about how I presented ideas to Joyce, but I saw how her eventual communication sometimes echoed my words and ideas.

"It really sounds like you're doing great," Judy said, after jotting a few notes into the notepad open in front of her. It felt a lot more like therapy than I'd expected. "But of course, you're here because you don't necessarily feel like you're doing great, so tell me more about that, and what you wish was different."

"I just feel like no one takes me seriously," I said. "Like, that's the whole thing in one sentence. I found out that no one at work—like the other assistants *and* my boss—thinks I'm serious about this as a career. Even though I know people think I'm good at my job. And I know some of it is just that I'm—I don't know, I don't have a very confident exterior or whatever, and my voice comes out squeaky sometimes, and I'm shorter than everyone but—look, I don't think this is it completely. It would be an easy answer that people stereotyped, but there must be more to it."

"I don't think your voice or your height count you out as an agent, no," Judy said with a smile. "And, again, it really does sound like you excel at plenty of what could make you a very good agent. So let me ask you—is there anything you think you need, to take that next step? Besides putting in the time and being recognized by others?"

I didn't, even though I worried it was obvious.

"Have you talked to your boss?" Judy asked. "I know that many agencies have mentorship programs in place. Have you looked into it?"

"I've looked into it a little, and I've tried to talk to my boss but—"

"Sure," she said, looking up from her notepad and meeting my eyes again. "It can be tough. Especially when you don't feel seen to begin with. But I encourage you to look at all the skills and tasks you're aware you're good at. Let that build some confidence in yourself."

"Oh," I said, that word vibrating at a frantic pace in my chest. "That's what you think I'm missing, right? Confidence?"

Judy smiled faintly. "Is that what *you* think you're missing?"

"I think I'm missing a lot, Judy," I said, and we both kind of laughed as I held back tears, too. "It's hard to be confident when no one believes in you."

"Absolutely," she said. "But you believe in yourself, don't you? What if you let yourself broadcast that idea a little?"

I tried to imagine that, hold it in my brain, Max Point Oh or whoever, striding boldly into Joyce's office, asking for what I wanted. It felt like science fiction but also it sounded *great*.

"OK, that's all the touchy-feely stuff for now, I promise," Judy said, and I laughed and wiped my eyes as covertly as I could. It was nice that it felt safe to cry in public here; at work I felt like that would have set me back another year or two from possible promotion. "Let's talk about actionable steps. Are you ready?"

I was. But once I was in my car driving home, toward Chelsey and her ring light and her six figures' worth of followers— including Nina and my coworkers—I had no idea how I was going to talk about any of this.

Chapter 12
Zesty at Best

Even though Chelsey recorded what felt like hours of testimony after my meeting with Judy, her content schedule meant that I got through the entire workweek without my coworkers seeing my very well-lit face explain that Judy Wax and I both thought that I needed to work on my confidence and to have a very serious talk with my very intimidating boss. I imagined that information buzzing around the office, getting to Joyce before I could get it there myself.

This potential situation buzzed in my head as I finalized my Friday tasks, very aware that Joyce was still in her office but might not be for much longer—executives here rarely stopped working, but they tended to disappear from the building as early as they could on Friday afternoons. All I wanted to dwell on was getting through my itemized list—and wondering what Sadie might have planned for us tomorrow—but between Chelsey's forthcoming content about my secret career goals and humiliating lack of confidence coupled with my latest You Point Oh task—somehow even double-checking client payments was nearly unimaginably difficult.

"Max," said Aidy, appearing a little out of nowhere at my desk. "Do you have an email address for Zach at Weekend Productions?"

"I do," I said, keeping my ears open for the pattern of sounds coming from Joyce's office—computer locked, purse grabbed, empty desk chair pushed in—that meant she was on her way out. "I'll Slack it over to you."

"Great," she said, as it hit me that she could have just asked that on Slack to begin with. "So how's the whole You Point Oh thing going? Did you get your new task yet? Can you say?"

"I did," I said. "Do you want spoilers? To be fair, I think Chelsey's posting it any minute now."

Aidy's eyes lit up as if this were seriously exciting. "Ooh, yes!"

"It's about being bold," I said, hoping I wouldn't accidentally go into more detail. "I know, I'm like mild salsa. Not even. Hummus, at best."

Aidy burst into laughter. "I think you're too white to be salsa or hummus, Max. Maybe ranch dressing. But that's zesty sometimes, right? Maybe you should aim for that."

"Zesty?" I buried my head in my hands, while Aidy cackled. "Thanks a lot."

"Come on, ranch dressing is delicious and revered. You could do way worse."

I heard a rustling from Joyce's office and jumped to my feet. "I should—"

"Of course," she said, walking back to her cubicle. One easy thing about work was that every assistant knew how chained we were to our desks and our phones and our bosses. Explanations were never required.

Joyce was, miraculously, still seated when I popped my head into the doorway. Asking one of Exemplar's top agents to stick around just for a conversation with the ranch dressing of assistants seemed like a fairly bananas situation.

"Yes?" she asked without looking up. Could she actually hear the sound of my head in the doorway?

"Do you have a moment?" I asked, and she gestured to come in. And then I was inside her office and I guessed it was happening. I sat down in the chair across from her as if I'd fully been invited, which I knew I had technically *not*.

Joyce kept working, which made it hard to know the exact right moment to start talking. I knew, though, that someone *bold* would not run through scenarios in her head of ideal times to speak and would just speak.

So, finally, I spoke.

"I've been thinking about our talk the other week," I said. "The second assistant. And I think you should do it. You'll look like a bigger player with two people on your desk, so if it's being offered, you should take the offer."

I now had Joyce's full attention.

"And also," I continued, "I don't want to be the more admin assistant."

Joyce raised her eyebrows as I tried to accept that those words had indeed left my lips. "Oh?"

"I understand that you see me a certain way, which is, obviously, not someone who wants to move up into a role like yours eventually, but . . . I do. I really love working here, and—" I somehow choked on *my own spit*, and Joyce handed me one of the fancy little bottles of water she kept on hand just in case a client stopped in for an impromptu visit. "Sorry. I mean, thank you. I mean, I guess, both. Anyway, I think I'm good at this job and I think I could actually be good in a role like yours someday, so this is me saying it to you."

Joyce was silent for way longer than I would have liked. I knew there was power in being comfortable with silence and not feeling the urge to immediately fill it, but also I knew I had no power anyway, so why not keep going?

"Obviously this is all up to you and you can hire whoever you want for whatever duties you think they should do but also since I'd never said this to you before I thought that I should."

"I'm glad you did, Max," Joyce said. It'd never been such a

relief to hear her voice. "For the record, I also think that you're good at your job."

"Thank you," I said, even though of course that wasn't really the part up for debate. It was still nice to hear.

"And I'll keep the rest in mind," she said, her expression so neutral that I had no idea what she was thinking. The ability to sit through silence combined with a neutral expression, I thought, could really take you anywhere. And at present, I possessed neither.

"Thank you," I said. "I'll let you . . ."

I didn't know how to end the sentence, so I just sort of ran out of the office. Which, to be fair, *was* a bold choice. Just probably not what You Point Oh had in mind.

Back at my desk, I'd somehow gotten eleven emails while I was in Joyce's office, so I dealt with them, printed out a couple of scripts that had just arrived, and tried not to think about the last several minutes. Unless I should? I had, technically, done what I'd been advised to do, by Judy Wax and by the app. This was as bold as I got!

My watch dinged with a text, and even though emails were coming in at the brisk pace that sometimes happened on a Friday afternoon when executives started getting panicky about the fast-approaching weekend, I was grateful for a distraction.

do u like thai food

Unbelievably, Sadie's texting style was starting to grow on me. Though I guess it really wasn't that unbelievable. The unbelievable part was that we were texting at all.

I do like Thai food.

gr8 bring $

I laughed again as I typed a message back to her. **Do you mean, bring cash? And when? What time do you want to meet?**

yes cash and what about noon

I agreed to that before getting back to my accumulating pile of emails or dwelling on it too long. After all, I didn't think I knew Sadie well enough to guess what parts of LA she thought I needed to be exposed to. I also probably didn't know enough about LA to guess in the first place. It felt embarrassing to be on the later side of my midtwenties and still not know so many things.

Joyce stopped by my desk, her laptop-sized yellow Loewe bag over her shoulder. I'd stopped monitoring her office for the sound of her leaving once that talk was behind us, and I was absolutely not prepared to see her again before I'd entirely mentally processed our conversation. I wanted to fixate longer on Thai food that required cash.

"I'll be in my car if you need me," Joyce said. "Have a good weekend."

"Oh," I said, surprised and also not surprised she was acting as if I hadn't just bared my soul to her. "OK, you too."

She headed toward the elevator bay without a look back, any indication at all that what I'd said had resonated, or that it hadn't, or that it had happened at all. Somehow in all of my panic to be bold before someone else did it for me, I'd kind of forgotten to picture how it might go. Even so, I knew that this specific situation where Joyce perhaps pretended it never happened would never have been one of my hypothetical scenarios. I supposed it was better than her outright rejecting the idea . . . but how much better?

I wished I had someone to talk it out with—talk *all* of this out, really. I drove home thinking about how much easier things would be if I could text someone to meet up so I could discuss it, but I just didn't have that person. The closest I had, really, was *my mom*, and I couldn't imagine how she'd react to hearing this story. At her job, there were annual reviews with very set expectations, and whenever I was ready to give up my outrageous Hollywood dreams I could just come home where things were so much more straightforward. She'd snag me a job in the cubicle next to hers and I'd be set forever.

At home I headed into my room with a pile of scripts but was intercepted by Chelsey, who stood in the hallway dressed in a hot pink minidress and chunky white sneakers, her hair in an updo that was somehow complicated and messy-casual at the same time.

"You look cool," I said because that was the kind of thing nerds said to their very hip roommates.

"Thanks, the dress arrived shorter than I imagined, but that's shopping on Instagram for you," she said. "We're going out to the Semi-Tropic for a queer dance party, and you're coming."

"I think you need tickets to that and it's sold out," I said, because even though I didn't actually go to queer dance parties, I followed all the queer dance party organizers on social media in case I ever became the kind of person who attended.

"Ava's friends with one of the planners so it doesn't matter," Chelsey said. "Go change, we're going to Thunderbolt first for food."

"I have work," I said, gesturing to my tote bag. "So many scripts for so many actors."

"The actors will survive, you deserve a night out," Chelsey said. "Also you have to say yes. You promised You Point Oh and all our followers."

Ava stepped out of Chelsey's room into the hallway, dressed in a bold printed dress that would look like a shapeless muu-muu on most people but hung beautifully on her. Her black hair was in tiny braids, and she was makeup-free except for a deep fuchsia lipstick that looked striking against her dark brown skin.

"Y'all look so good," I said, honestly awed. It blew me away that people could put together looks like theirs.

"Thank you," Ava said, bowing dramatically. "I always dress so seriously for work, it's nice to mix it up and actually compete with this one for once."

"Oh please," Chelsey said, but her cheeks flushed. "Go change, Max."

"I guess you can make me go," I said as the realization dawned on me. Goodbye, night in with everything that made me feel cozy and not like someone who was in way over her head in a city that would never be home to her. Hello to . . . well, maybe that feeling exactly. "But I don't have anything to change into. You've seen everything I own."

Somehow Chelsey and Ava charged into my room and invaded my closet, and I watched helplessly as they tossed items of clothing at each other as options. It was the saddest makeover sequence ever.

"Wait," Ava said, and I realized a moment too late what was about to happen. She pulled out a pair of bright blue sleeveless coveralls I'd thrifted before I'd even moved here, when I thought I might become the kind of person who went out wearing bright blue sleeveless coveralls. "This."

"No, those are so not me, it was silly I even bought them, they were just super cheap and—"

"You're supposed to *be bold*!" Chelsey shouted. "Try them on."

I made a sound that sounded like *blargh* and they both laughed in a way that was somehow kind of warm.

"We would never let you go out looking less than amazing," Ava said. "If you look ridiculous in it, we'll tell you."

So I stripped down to my sports bra and briefs and stepped

into the coveralls. It wasn't even buttoned all the way when Chelsey and Ava started making excited sounds.

"It's really good," Chelsey said. "Super bold."

I looked into the mirror and didn't hate what I saw. In this outfit I didn't look so mousy. Maybe I even looked a little tough, like the person I still wanted to be someday.

"OK, fine," I said, while Ava and Chelsey cheered.

"Put your boots on fast, because I already ordered the Lyft," Chelsey said, heading out of my room.

Ava stayed put, handing me my shoes as I tied them as quickly as possible. "While I personally don't believe you actually legally owe it to that app to say yes or be bold, you look incredible."

"Oh—thanks." It sounded a little like a question because Ava's statement didn't fully sound like a compliment.

"She can be very persuasive," Ava said with a smile. "Trust me. But this is still your life, your face and name—your username, at least—publicly across social media. Obviously, I think you should wear the hot-mechanic suit and go out dancing more often, but you still have a say in your own life."

"No, of course," I said quickly. I was prepared to defend myself more, but Ava just nodded and headed out, and then Chelsey yelled that our Lyft was pulling up, and before long we were out of the building and on our way to whatever intimidating place Thunderbolt was.

The Lyft dropped us off just a few miles away, near Echo Park, at a bar that looked very normal and not overly cool from the outside. Inside, there was a ton of natural light—I couldn't deny that the late-day sunshine made the bar seem a little nicer and more welcoming than Johnny's—and all sorts of seating options, from a beautiful natural wood bar to smaller tables and communal-style ones in the same wood, to leather couches that looked like they were straight out of a sophisticated person's study. The whole look felt modern but also classic, and I wondered if this was the kind of makeover Sadie had in mind for Johnny's.

Chelsey and Ava grabbed one of the high tables, the most awkward seating option for anyone of my height, but I was determined to be the person wearing this outfit, so I managed to climb into a chair without looking too much like a toddler en route to their high chair.

"Have you been here?" Chelsey asked, passing me the menu. "I know we're both, like, hybrid South, not like *deep* South, but I still love this place. It makes me miss my mom."

"I haven't been here," I said, scanning down and seeing biscuits and pimento cheese and a fried green tomato sandwich—which of course reminded me equally of home and of a very gay book I'd read multiple times in high school. Was Chelsey actually thoughtful? Had she picked out this place for both of us? Years into being her roommate, I really wasn't sure what was her and what was content.

Still, the bar menu was incredible—we all ordered a drink called the Echo Park Trash Can purely for the name—and the food reminded me of back home in a way that felt cozy and not homesick.

"It's weird you two didn't know each other in college," Ava said, which I supposed meant that she and Chelsey sometimes discussed me when I wasn't around. "You're from such a small city."

"OK, Brooklyn," Chelsey said in an overly affected New York accent that made Ava and I howl in laughter. "Sure, compared to your hometown, ours is small. But whatever you're picturing in your head, let it go. We went to a giant state school. It's not at all strange that we didn't know each other."

"I commuted," I said. "So I was never on campus except for my classes. Which now feels like I really missed out but at the time I just thought made sense, since we lived so close."

"You didn't miss out on much," Chelsey said. "My freshman

year roommate was always hooking up with the weirdest guys and I got sexiled all the time. My sophomore year roommate always burned these super intense candles from Bath and Body Works that smelled like pumpkin waffles? I still hate pumpkin and waffles. Junior year was OK, did you know Becky Gaad?"

I shook my head.

"Well, she was this very hot, very butch finance major, and let's just say it was very convenient sharing a room with her. But then she cheated on me and so I cheated on her to prove a point and the last two months of sharing that room were *intense.*"

"See, but that's the thing," I said. "I feel like I'd be better at grown-up life if I'd had an intense two months like that in college! I got here with, like, nothing."

Ava raised an eyebrow. "You think you'd be better adjusted if you'd slept with a roommate and then revenge-cheated on them?"

"When you say it like that, I don't know," I said, spreading more pimento cheese on a cracker, and we all laughed. "I just still feel like a kid sometimes."

I probably shouldn't have admitted that, right here, to Chelsey—Ava seemed way more trustworthy—but I wasn't great at keeping that stuff to myself when I had any opportunity not to. Confessions just flew out of my mouth.

"I thought I'd feel like an adult when I passed the bar exam," Ava said. "Nope. First job? This job—my dream job? Still waiting."

Chelsey shrugged. "Yesterday I spent two hours recording content about glow-in-the-dark underpants. When my mom was my age, she had two kids and a union job."

"See, I don't think revenge-cheating would have helped you," Ava said to me, and we all cracked up.

"You know what I mean, though," I said.

"Sure," Ava said. "But that just means you had different

kinds of experiences. Just because you weren't avoiding waffle candles or hooking up with your roommate doesn't mean you didn't live."

Chelsey was tapping on her phone. "Ooh, you'll never believe what Becky Gaad's doing now. She's running for mayor of some small-ass town."

Ava looked down at Chelsey's phone. "Are you *donating to her campaign?*"

I practically did a spit take on my cocktail.

"I still feel a little bad about how junior year went down," Chelsey said with a shrug. "And she probably has a strong platform."

Ava watched Chelsey for a moment and smiled. "I think that might be weirdly sweet."

"Maybe I'm an adult after all," Chelsey said. "Another round of Echo Park Trash Cans before we head out?"

At the Semi-Tropic, packed with queer people of so many types and shapes and styles, I no longer worried I looked too bright or too bold for who I really was. Somehow I just fit into this crowded and colorful world. Chelsey and Ava's friends found us in the mass of people, and before long I was caught up in a Hayley Kiyoko track and forgetting I was not actually very good at dancing. What was dancing, anyway? Just an excuse to be around people listening to music you all loved? Knowing how to move was overrated. Any way we moved, I realized, was more than good enough.

Chapter 13
Metaphorical Double Dutch

The night before had seemed so successful that I let Chelsey pick out my outfit for my Thai-food-related plans with Sadie the next afternoon. I didn't think I had a good conversation with my roommate and her girlfriend or a good time dancing because I'd worn an outfit I normally wouldn't have, but I did probably need a little help being bold. And maybe boldness wasn't as ill-fitting on me as I'd assumed. This was why I was in the outfit Chelsey had deemed my scoutmaster look with a pair of neon-orange socks and an honest-to-god bolo tie she'd pulled from her own jewelry collection.

It *was* bold. I'd give her that.

Sadie, of course, met me on the corner in vintage Faded Glory jeans and a gray T-shirt that must have been black at one point, Docs even more worn than mine.

"You look—"

"My roommate's idea," I said, tugging at the bolo tie.

"I was going to say *cute*," Sadie said, and my heart went into double-time. "I guess pass that along to your roommate instead."

"No, I mean, I'll take the compliment," I said, and we both laughed. "Do you want me to drive again?"

"I don't have a car, you realize," Sadie said.

"I didn't realize," I said. "You seem like you'd have some old muscle car that you're always working on or whatever."

Oh my god, I thought I was only bad at letting out *low-stakes* confessions.

"That's fucking flattering," Sadie said. "Sometimes Billy lets me borrow his Mazda3. Probably not what you're picturing."

"I don't picture it a lot," I said, though that wasn't entirely true, as we walked to my parking garage. "Is it hard not to have a car in LA?"

Sadie shrugged. "It's been OK for me, but I also basically live my whole life on this block. When you live over your job, the commute doesn't really require wheels."

"Wait, you live over Johnny's?" I asked, letting us into my car.

"Yeah, there's a huge apartment above it. Billy's an OK roommate and I don't pay any rent, so it could be a lot worse."

"Oh," I said, because this also didn't fit any of my fantasies.

Sadie burst into laughter. "I can tell you think this is pathetic that I live with my dead uncle's partner. Which is fine. Lots of people think it's pathetic. It's kind of pathetic!"

"I don't think it's pathetic," I said, backing the car out of my parking spot and pulling onto the street. "You just have . . . I don't know. The vibe I thought you had maybe isn't your actual vibe."

"You always say the nicest stuff," Sadie said. "It makes me forget I'm such a loser. Not that it's the only reason I like spending time with you. But it's a perk."

"Sadie, what are you talking about?" I asked, as my brain hung on to *I like spending time with you.* "You're like the farthest thing from a loser. Also, where are we going? Do you want to type it into Waze? Or do you even know how to use an iPhone?"

"Hilarious, of course," she said, removing my phone from its dashboard mount. "The thing is, I had lots of plans and all of that. But after Johnny died . . ."

"I'm so sorry," I said, trying to glance over at her meaningfully while still keeping my eyes safely on the road.

"It always felt like this miracle he was still around, you know," she said. "Since he'd been HIV-positive back when that meant a death sentence. And then things changed and he survived. A fucking miracle. He got through it when a lot of his friends didn't. So for this random heart attack to take him when he was only fifty-four, I don't know. I should have been grateful for all the years I had with him. But I was just mad at the universe anyway."

"I would have been too," I said. "I try really hard to be one of those gratitude type people, but I'm not sure I'm very good at it. It's not that I'm not—grateful, I mean. It's that I'm always worried about the next thing so it's hard to dwell on the thing in front of me."

"Yeah, me, I think I just have a bad attitude," Sadie said with a laugh, and it felt safe to join in. "Also, that thing you said about your job, how maybe you're not supposed to like it but you do, that's *exactly* how I feel."

It was tough to grasp that things I said resonated with Sadie as much as things she said resonated with me. I guessed I didn't even know I could be that for someone else.

"I know this wasn't how things were supposed to end up," Sadie said. "First of all, dead parents, that really puts a spin on things."

"Well, sure, it's a real plot twist," I said, and we both laughed in that way only people with dead parents could, the laugh that came from the darkest grief and all the healing that came after.

"Johnny was real determined I was still going to achieve whatever I wanted," Sadie said. "But after he died and Billy quit his job to take over the bar, I figured I should do the same—well, drop out of school and learn how to mix drinks—and . . . obviously, Billy hates it a little. But I don't."

"I feel like whatever Billy did, he would hate it a little, to be fair."

Sadie laughed. "That's for sure. He does his best. He didn't know he was going to end up with his dead partner's kid and a bar instead of making partner at some prestigious law firm."

"It's weirdly sweet," I said. "I mean, for Billy. I can see why you want to keep the bar open. I mean, I got it anyway, but I really get it now. It's like your legacy or something."

"Yeah, I don't know about that," Sadie said. "Feels like *legacy* is for bigger stuff than me, just a dirtbag who wants to keep a queer bar open."

"Why do you keep doing that?" I found myself asking. "Running the bar already is—I don't know, Sadie, it feels really important. And the fact that you want to make sure it doesn't get bought out by terrible real estate investors or whatever, it's really special. You don't have to keep saying everything you've done or want to do isn't a big deal."

She was silent next to me, and I kept my eyes straight ahead, definitely worried I'd said too much to someone who was just my—what even *was* Sadie? Not only my bartender, but . . . what?

"You're really kind," she said, finally, softly, tracing a couple of fingers down my arm. When they moved past my sleeve to my bare skin, I nearly gasped. *Please*, I hoped, let Sadie have no idea how much her touch affected me.

When I pulled the car off the freeway, I realized I was further north in the general LA area than I'd ever been. From here, even though Waze was still directing me, Sadie pointed me in the direction of what looked like a church and told me to find street parking behind.

"What are we doing?" I asked as we got out of the car. "Is this like the church of Thai food?"

"Yeah, kind of?" She grinned at me as we took off down the sidewalk. "It's a Thai temple, and they do a food court on the weekends, and it's *so good*. I used to go a lot—"

"Like back in the days before you threw your phone in a dumpster?" I asked.

"It wasn't just any dumpster, it was the dumpster out back behind Johnny's," she said. "But, yeah. I was kind of an asshole back then. I think I was angry about how everything turned out but since I hadn't gotten any therapy yet, I just yelled at people."

"I can't imagine you yelling at anyone," I said.

She grabbed my arm and pulled me into a short line of people. "We have to trade our cash for tokens. No, I don't know why, but I do feel like paying for authentic Thai food with plastic tokens lines up with this whole off-the-grid thing I was going to cultivate for you."

"And I haven't looked into historical preservation yet," I said with a realization. "Sorry, work's been—"

And You Point Oh *had been*, too, though I still wanted to keep Sadie shielded from all of that. I wanted to get through these thirty days, thrive, and get on with it—Sadie none the wiser.

"Well, I haven't given you any of my paperwork yet, either," she said. "Don't worry about it. I know you're not going to flake on me."

We turned in our cash for a pile of purple and orange tokens, and I followed Sadie over to the sprawling line of booths. Savory aromas drifted in all directions, and I had no idea where to start.

"I probably shouldn't admit this, but I never even had Thai food before I moved here," I said as Sadie examined the posted menu at a crowded stand. "And then I moved here and it was like this whole world opened up. My first month here I got pad see ew like five times."

"Don't you have Thai food in Kentucky?" she asked in a horrified voice, and I burst into laughter.

"No, of course we do. I was just never—my family didn't go out a ton, and when we did, we tended to stick to what we already knew."

"I guess there's a lot I take for granted because I grew up here," Sadie said, pulling me into line. It did not escape my attention that I felt like she was touching me more. Even if it was casual and in no way romantic, it was very hard not to notice Sadie's hand on me.

Once we reached the front of the line, Sadie ordered boat noodles, pad see ew, and pork belly skewers, plus Thai iced teas to drink in exchange for a chunk of our tokens, and we carried our huge tray of food to a picnic table.

"This place is magical," Sadie said, expertly winding noodles around chopsticks while I stuck with my fork. "It was a lot of pressure when I realized I offered to give you some secret-spots-of-Los-Angeles tour, considering I barely go anywhere these days."

"You should feel, like, zero pressure," I said, feeling just bold enough to snag some noodles from Sadie's plate. "I'm happy to help you with everything, with nothing in return."

Sadie nudged my knee with hers. "Maybe I needed some pressure."

"Do you feel like all you do is work and sleep?" I asked. "Because that was sort of me. Well, work, sleep, watching *Frasier*."

"Yeah, Max, for sure," she said, using her chopsticks to slide pork off a skewer and onto a Styrofoam plate. "Not always literally *Frasier*, but metaphorically *Frasier*. A hundred percent."

"I'm trying to do more," I said.

"Well, yeah," Sadie said, gesturing around her. "Obviously me too."

"Sometimes I just feel like—you know when people do that fancy jump rope?" I asked, and Sadie laughed.

"Like double Dutch?"

"Yeah, that! And someone's like off on the side, watching the ropes and planning that perfect moment to jump in? Whenever I'd get a chance—you know, back on the playground, when I was a kid—I'd just watch the ropes forever. I never knew when to jump in."

Sadie just watched me, her expression serious. My face flushed at the attention, at her rapt gaze.

"Anyway, I just sort of still feel like that. Like I'm watching the ropes but I have no idea when to jump in. And other people, clearly they know, they can see something I don't. But it's like, even if I stare, I have no clue."

Sadie's gaze shifted into the distance, and she took a sip of her iced tea. "Yeah, at least you're waiting to jump in. I feel like I'm somewhere out there playing some other game entirely and everyone's too embarrassed to tell me that everyone else stopped playing marbles or whatever a million years ago."

"Well, it's a pretty old-timey game," I said. "Which would make sense for you."

Her attention snapped away from that far-off serious look, and the corners of her mouth tugged up into her crooked grin. "Wait, because I don't have an iPhone and a robot watch I'm *old-timey*?"

"Your shirts are all vintage," I pointed out. "You work at kind of a retro bar."

"You're the one always talking about shit from the nineties and dressing like Zack Morris," she said, and my mouth fell open. "Sorry, lesbian Zack Morris, if that helps."

"Well, it helps a little, but it wasn't really the vibe I was going for."

We both cracked up and turned our attention back to the spread of food in front of us. I couldn't decide what I liked best so I kept switching between dishes.

"I do like thrifting," Sadie said. "Old T-shirts feel so much better than new ones. I started wearing all of Johnny's stuff after he died, and then I'd find similar stuff in shops near the bar."

"I like thrifting too," I said. "It's the only way I can afford to decorate my room well, and to have enough outfits for work. And of course to play with my band the Zack Attack."

Sadie let out a shriek of laughter, and I marveled that it was me who'd gotten that sound out of her. Maybe we were just two people who were maybe not the best at life, eating Thai food on a bench in the upper Valley, but I allowed myself a moment to think that maybe something beyond that was happening, too.

"How're you doing?" Sadie asked as she scooped up the rest of the boat noodles. "I know we've already accomplished a lot here, but they have these awesome tiny coconut pancakes they make in this giant griddle. I wouldn't feel like I'd truly done my duty unless you got to try those too."

"I can't let you not do your duty," I said, and we threw out our trash on our way to getting into another line. Standing together in the bright sunshine, debating exactly how many snacks we could get to use up all of our tokens, it hit me that now that I'd told Sadie about the metaphorical double Dutch of my life, in this moment I didn't feel like I was waiting for anything. Right now, I just *was*.

I came into work on Monday morning like usual, even though I was still reeling a little from my day with Sadie and the way it seemed her hands kept turning up reasons to find me. On social media I followed plenty of queer meme accounts and tapped *like* on probably every single Useless Lesbian meme. Every date I'd gone on had happened thanks to a dating app—no matter how many bartenders I'd smiled at over the years—

and so my romantic situations had all been as straightforward as possible. The thought of being completely oblivious to feelings or intent didn't seem like a trap I could fall into.

Except here I was, feeling potentially like a very Useless Lesbian.

To be fair, I hadn't been in a situation like this—like whatever I was in with Sadie—before now, even if that was kind of unbelievable. Of course I'd pined over girls who had no idea! That was basically my whole closeted college life. But to wonder if someone felt the same way I did was new. If only I'd met Sadie on Tinder or something; we could have gone on something that we'd both clearly labeled a date and I could have kissed her at the end of it and—well, who knows. In that scenario we hadn't spent all this time getting to know each other. In that scenario would I even know exactly how special she was?

Not that I should have been thinking about any of that, definitely not how it felt for Sadie to slide two fingers down my bare arm, because my Monday morning inbox felt more Monday-morning-y than usual. Though I also welcomed as many distractions as possible because by this point Chelsey had posted significant content about my agenting dreams and the advice from the career coach and me being generally earnest about work-specific things. By now, I knew, people had seen the videos, including probably Javier and Aidy and who knew who else. I couldn't imagine that Joyce was on TikTok, but I did lurk on her Instagram sometimes, where she infrequently posted beautifully shot photos of her home and her husband and the backyard space where she occasionally hosted wine tastings for her intimidatingly rich-seeming friends. It seemed impossible that Joyce and Chelsey's online worlds overlapped, but—could they? Way better to think again (and again and again) about Sadie and her hands.

Everyone greeted me normally on their way in, but a Slack DM popped up almost as soon as Javier was at his desk. **Why didn't you say you were angling for jr agent job?**

I sent back a shrug emoji and tried to get focused and back to work before Joyce called, on her drive in.

Was that your big power move, letting me and aidy talk about it while not saying anything??

I actually laughed aloud at the thought of Max Van Doren, big Hollywood player. **Seriously? I'm on my roommate's Instagram whining about my promotion prospects and you think I was playing some kind of long game?**

Fair point, he typed, which made me laugh too. I probably should have been as nervous as I was when I walked in this morning, but it was just hard to stay that way. Yeah, Javier and Aidy both seemed—well, *bolder* than me, the kind of people others would expect to move ahead here. But if there was anything about me that could seem even vaguely calculated, maybe I wasn't quite as mousy as I'd thought.

Or maybe, impossible as it seemed, You Point Oh was working, and all the saying yes and being bold was shifting something vital in my life. It hit me that up until now, I hadn't *really* thought that would happen. Chelsey would fulfill whatever terms of her contract with the app, I would make myself vulnerable and, at times, apparently likable in front of a huge audience, and then the whole thing would wrap up and we'd all get back to how things were. Right now, though, it was easy to see that I wouldn't have talked to Joyce last week without this campaign, and Javier wouldn't see me as some kind of potential threat either.

It made me wonder, if all of this was going so well, what would have happened Saturday if I'd been a little bolder and told Sadie how I felt? You Point Oh wasn't magic, obviously; it didn't make all my goals just happen. There was no guarantee that if I'd covered her hand with mine and told her—

Maybe I couldn't be bold until I knew what I'd say. I wasn't actually in love with her, because that was something bigger and realer and more mutual. And when I thought of looking deeply into Sadie's eyes and saying something like *I like* like *you*, it didn't sound very bold. It sounded like someone catching up from experiences she didn't have in junior high. Which, to be fair, was accurate.

Joyce's morning call was the same as always, though knowing at any moment she could mention Friday's conversation kept my heart racing as I did low-key tasks like rolling calls and updating her on a few key pieces of news reported on *Deadline* that morning.

"I'm about to pull into the building, but we should take some time today to discuss something a little confidential," Joyce said. "Is anyone standing near your desk right now?"

"Nope," I said, not my most professional response. Still, maybe something was happening for me, or was just about to.

"I've heard rumblings Meghan Ramos could be in the market for new representation," Joyce said. "So I'd like to get a couple of gifts sent her way. Find out if she's still shooting that HBO thing overseas or if she's back home, and get a list going of potential gift ideas."

"Absolutely," I said, jotting the information down in my planner. A-list actors didn't necessarily *decide* to get new agents; the truth was that agents were swooping in all the time to snag talent from competing agencies. The process often started with gift baskets, or pricey bottles of wine—literally the cost of my monthly rent, sometimes more—or whatever trendy bag or skincare product was in at the moment. There were agents at Exemplar who did this constantly; I saw other assistants scrambling to confirm the trendiest expensive candle or gluten-free muffin company. Joyce was more selective and, I thought, seemed surer and less desperate in her maneuvers.

So right now I'd focus on being the very best at my job and find out anything I needed to know about restricted-diet baked goods and the year's hottest scents, instead of obsessing over if it was a bad sign that Joyce didn't say anything about our conversation last Friday. After all, if everything You Point Oh had told me so far was going so well, it was hard not to feel hopeful about this too. Nail the tasks, nail the opportunities to come.

And then my watch chimed with that ominous You Point Oh noise, which didn't sound optimistic at all. My new task was already here.

Chapter 14

All Endorphin'd Up

I tiptoed into the gym like the imposter I was. The space was full of people on various workout machines that I couldn't even identify. OK, some were just treadmills, but almost everything else was some complicated contraption that looked designed for torture.

"Can I help you?" asked the girl sitting at the front desk. She was Asian, with dark hair up in a thick ponytail and dressed in brightly colored athleisure, and despite that she was very cute and very stylish, her smile was warm and welcoming. I could see why she was stationed here to greet people and, hopefully, guide them.

"I'm, um, supposed to have a personal training session," I said. "Max Van Doren. Not *with* Max Van Doren, that's me, it's with someone else."

The girl smiled. "Hi, Max, I'm Rose, and I see that we've got you on the schedule. You're training with Landon. I think they're in the back, but I'll let them know you're here."

She walked off after I thanked her, and I tried to stand as normally as I could, even if my surroundings terrified me and

the hour ahead of me terrified me even more. Was that overreacting? Maybe. When You Point Oh had given me my third task
to *level up*, I'd expected some kind of career seminar or perhaps
an introduction to an agent who was more excited about mentoring me than Joyce seemed to be. Instead it matched me with
a personal trainer so I could start getting strong. Yes, that had
been one of my goals, but somehow I hadn't imagined trying to
accomplish it in this clichéd Los Angeles setting surrounded by
buff and swole types—

Actually, now that I was surveying the room, it didn't look
like an LA house of horrors. The people here looked how they
did everywhere I went. All body types and sizes and ages and,
at least on the surface, I fit in fine. Except obviously that they
were dallying with these torture devices and I was standing
awkwardly just staring at people.

"Hi, Max?"

I turned around to see a person around my age with a golden
mullet, clad in silver workout clothes. "Are you Landon? I
mean, yes, I'm Max. Sorry, I feel like I'm bad at peopling today."

They laughed and held out their hand to shake mine. "Yes,
I'm Landon, they/them pronouns."

"Max, she/her," I said. "Sorry, I didn't think you'd look that
cool. I'm kind of intimidated by gyms and was just like getting
acclimated."

"A lot of people feel that way about gyms," Landon said,
nodding. "Especially, I think, for us queer folks who didn't
always see locker rooms and whatever in school as a super affirming and safe time. That's why I love training here at All
Bodies; it's such an inclusive space."

"Yeah, I guess that's true," I said. "Also I'm just small and a
wimp and for a lot of sporty stuff that's not ideal."

"Wow, you just came out and insulted yourself so quickly,"
Landon said, concern in their blue eyes. "Yes, it's true, you're
small, but *a wimp*? I'm sure you're capable of plenty. My con-

tact said your goal was getting strong, so that's definitely what we're going to work on. But let's start out by not underestimating yourself, OK?"

"Oh no, this sounds like therapy," I said, and Landon laughed.

"Yeah, all my clients say that. Come on. I'm going to welcome you to the world of weightlifting."

I started to protest because I couldn't think of a worse-suited activity, but I had a feeling Landon would just pull out more therapy-speak. Once I tried, they'd surely see my wimp talk wasn't self-hate but just accuracy, and hopefully we could do something better suited to my little spaghetti-noodle arms.

Landon walked me over to the section of the gym containing a wide array of different kinds of weights. In the mirror I could see that my eyes were round like a scared cartoon cat, so I tried to fake a neutral expression. Landon caught my reflection and we both laughed.

"I promise, you're going to like this, Max," they said. "Do you have your phone on you? If so, can I see it?"

I handed it over because I already felt like I was there to do whatever Landon said, and they quickly tapped through to purchase an app from the app store.

"Don't worry," they said, "I'm entering a discount code that You Point Oh set up for you so you get this for free. It's just so you can keep track of your current lifting ability, and all the progress you're going to make. It's really cool to see it laid out in tangible results."

I knew that You Point Oh had set up ongoing sessions for me that would extend past the thirty days of the campaign, but it was hard to imagine I'd keep doing this once I didn't have to. There was something nice about Landon's belief in these tangible results, though.

"So I'm going to teach you four different kinds of lifts," Landon said, walking to the wall of weights. "Squats, dead lifts, presses, and bench presses. I'll do them along with you, and I'll start you out nice and light so we can get an idea of your existing strength. From there I can come up with an idea of your workset weight—that's the goal weight you'll be lifting today—and you'll build toward it."

"Oh cool, a bunch of words I don't really understand," I said, and as we both laughed, I remembered my first day of work as an agency assistant and how the vocabulary seemed like another language entirely. Trades, book outs, back ends. And then before long I was speaking it along with everyone else. This much, I knew, I could accomplish.

Landon approached the empty bar on the weight rack and demonstrated as they talked through it. "You'll want to duck your head under the bar and line it up like this, so it rests across your shoulders, not your neck. Then you can slowly move up so now it's fully resting on you, not the rack, and step backwards so you can start the squat."

"Are you showing me on an empty bar because I said I'm a wimp?" I asked.

"Everyone starts with the empty bar without weights," they told me. "It's forty-five pounds, so that's not nothing."

That was actually heavier than I'd realized, so I felt a little less pathetic as Landon helped me move correctly and repeat an entire set before moving on to dead lifts. Before long, I was sweaty and a little breathless, but it seemed like ages ago that I'd thought I was too weak for this. Maybe I was weaker than a lot of people, but I was able to keep going the entire hour I spent today with Landon.

"So I'll see you on Thursday?" Landon asked as our session drew to a close and we exchanged contact information. "Same time, et cetera?"

"Perfect. Thank you. That was a lot less terrifying than I'd predicted."

Landon cracked up. "Please put that in my Yelp review."

I checked my phone as I walked through the parking lot to my car—no less than thirty-five work emails, but all of them could be dealt with in the morning—and I saw that something much more exciting had arrived: a new text from Sadie.

If ur around billy is taking off early tonight

I sped home, swapped my sweaty gym clothes for, after only a moment's hesitation, the blue jumpsuit, grabbed my bag, and hurried down the block to the bar.

"Hey!" Sadie greeted me, straining a cocktail into a martini glass. "I'll get your usual in a second. I'm shorthanded, as you know."

"I'm super patient," I said, climbing onto my regular stool and getting out my phone. Chelsey had somehow texted six times since I'd last checked.

How did lifting go?? I'm sure you're buff already.

I thought I heard you come home—but you're not here?

We should really film content while you're still post-workout and all endorphin'd up!

Not to be annoying but I feel like on new task or new appointment days it's kind of taken for granted that we'll film content, so just let me know when you'll be available.

Ava says I'm being annoying and you're allowed to have a life, which is very on-brand for her but I feel only partially correct.

Max! I was kidding! Now I'm afraid you think I've lost my mind. Just text back and let me know your schedule.

"Oh my god," I murmured. **Sorry, maybe I should have checked? I have plans after nearby, so I came home to change. I will probably be home too late to film content. Tomorrow?**

"Here you go," Sadie said, and I tucked my phone away and looked up at her as she deposited a drink in front of me. "Try this."

"Not my usual?"

"Sometimes I pretend I'm a real bartender and I invent new cocktails," she said with a grin.

"Where's Billy?" asked Marty, the old guy who often sat a few stools over from me. "Now that guy, he's a real bartender."

Sadie laughed. "Only barely. He's allowed a night off occasionally, Marty. You not happy with your beer or your frosty mug? I let you down in some other way?"

Marty grumbled something, and Sadie and I both laughed.

"Tell me what you think," she said, her eyes back on me and the cocktail. I took a small sip and coughed.

"Oh, shit," she said. "Not the best review."

"I didn't expect the rim would be spicy," I said, and took another sip. Now that I was ready for it, I actually couldn't believe how good the spiciness was in contrast to the grapefruit and— "Is it mezcal instead of tequila?"

"You're good," Sadie said with a nod.

"I love it. Are you adding it to the menu?"

Sadie laughed, and I joined in, because "the menu" at Johnny's was one small laminated sheet of paper that listed three things in Comic Sans: **Cocktails, Beer, Wine**. Those weren't categories. Those were literally the three words on the sheet of paper.

"Maybe someday," she said with a shrug. "I'm really just messing around."

I hated how she looked in that moment and was determined to find the magic key that unlocked the solution to her buying this bar and changing every single thing she wanted to.

"I actually do have a complaint about this mug," Marty called, and Sadie shot me another grin before heading over to him.

It felt like maybe I was going to be there for a while—even on weeknights, Johnny's was open late—so I got out my pile of scripts and flipped open the top one. I loved the mild buzz around me and the way I could feel Sadie's presence as she manned the bar. It felt like a preview of her dream come true, the version of Johnny's that was hers.

I stayed focused on my work, though, and only vaguely noticed the dwindling crowd and the lateness of the hour when Sadie walked past me and flipped off the neon Open sign before locking the door.

"I've never been here this late before," I said, and she laughed.

"You've been here *almost* this late," she said. "You're just really polite and you're always gone with at least one minute to spare, even on your latest nights."

"That's my goal," I said. "Good manners."

"Swoon," she said, walking into the back. *Swoon?* I didn't have time to finish turning that over in my head before she had returned with a pile of papers. "OK, here's some paperwork. I have no idea what's useful. I printed off some stuff from the historical preservation site but it was pretty overwhelming and I already knew we probably didn't qualify. Plus everyone in LA seems so happy to knock shit down and build smoothie shops, I don't know why I'm—"

I put my hand on her forearm. "You do know why you're pursuing this. You want to save this bar, and also you're *good* here. You have all these plans—or at least it feels like you have all these plans, not that you've told me much. Stop telling yourself it's stupid and impossible before you've fully even tried. If it was stupid and impossible, would I be here?"

She blinked a few times, and I was shocked she might be holding back tears.

"Sadie—"

She waved me off. "Sorry. I'm just not used to people believing in me, it threw me. I'll get back to work and leave you alone."

The very last thing I wanted was to be left alone, but I dove into the stack of papers, making neat piles and turning to a blank page in my notepad to jot down information and questions I had. Sadie's afterhours work had a rhythm to it too, and I loved the gentle sounds of the counters being wiped down, the bottles being organized, the *clink* of the clean glasses fresh from the dishwasher getting stacked under the bar.

"Hey," I said, as I got through the pages and made as many notes as I felt like I needed to research on my own. "Will you tell me your plans for the bar?"

Sadie covered her face with her hands. "It sounds so goddamn cheesy when I say it aloud."

I flipped to another empty page in my notepad. "Write it down then?"

Sadie rolled her eyes, but walked around the bar and sat down at the stool next to me. She was silent as she wrote, and I tried not to stare even though we'd never sat together like this at Johnny's. The bar had always separated us before now.

"Here," she said after a few minutes, pushing the notepad back my way. "Don't read it aloud or, I'm sorry, Max, I'll be forced to murder you."

"That's fair, sure," I said, and looked down at her writing, which was plain but very neat. Classic and got the job done, just like her.

- *Better lighting, more seating, less "trapped in the late 1970s but not in a cool way" vibes. Clean up weird back outdoor space to make tiny patio*
- *Specialty drink menu with non-alcoholic options for cocktails because participating in queer community*

> *shouldn't have to revolve around alcohol, add stuff*
> *on tap like seltzers and kombuchas because it's LA*
> *after all*
> - *Agreement with nearby restaurant or something so*
>   *people can at least order food even if we're not the*
>   *ones to make it*
> - *Low-key events or something? Johnny's is never*
>   *gonna host a dance party, but chill live music or*
>   *game nights maybe. Mainly I really want it to feel*
>   *like a community space, which I think queer folks*
>   *still need even in this day and age*
> - *I know this is all really basic shit but I'm not trying*
>   *to reinvent any wheels, just make Johnny's more*
>   *modern and the kind of place I'd go to even if it*
>   *wasn't mine*

I looked up and saw that she was watching me intently, her bottom lip caught in her teeth. "Don't look so terrified."

"Watching you read this was probably worse than if I'd just said it out loud," she said. "I have no clue what I was thinking."

"This is all really good," I said. "Like it's normal stuff but together it would be—I don't know, it would make a big difference! Bringing Johnny's into this decade."

Sadie grinned. "More like this century."

"Well, sure, that's fair," I said. "You know I actually love it here, but if all of this happened?"

She watched me, her golden-green eyes through those long lashes. "Yeah?"

"Just—can you believe me that I wouldn't lie to you? It would be incredible, and I know that you're capable of being the person who makes this happen. I know there's a lot of money for you to figure out, but the rest of it, you've got."

She was still sitting so close, still watching me as if I was the most interesting person she'd ever known. *Be bold*, I told myself, and then *level up*, and then I stared at Sadie and thought, *say yes*.

"What?" she asked, which was funny because she'd been staring longer than I had. So I laughed and she joined in and, in the dim light of the bar like we were the only two people left in the world, I leaned in to kiss her.

There wasn't even a moment to worry I'd followed terrible instincts, because Sadie kissed back immediately, almost as if it had been her idea too. The kiss was soft and somehow familiar, and I realized it was the first time I'd kissed someone I already knew so well. It was like coming home.

We kept kissing, though it didn't stay soft for much longer than that first perfect kiss. My lips kept snagging in her teeth, and her hands were in my hair pulling me impossibly, perfectly tight against her. It was if we'd always meant to be kissing.

Even so, sitting side-by-side on barstools was not necessarily the easiest place to do this, and I wrapped my arms around her shoulders to keep us closer to the same height. There was no reason to waste any moment not kissing.

Sadie's tongue was swirling a lazy but constant rhythm in my mouth, but I imagined its movements elsewhere. A low moan came from the back of my throat as I throbbed between my legs with the thought of her and the night still to come. It felt beyond freeing to let go, for my body to tell Sadie what I wanted.

"You like that?" she murmured, and I nodded frantically and leaned in again for more. It could be fun, I realized, to ache so badly for someone, when the release was in plain sight. Not that I wanted to wait forever. I was so ready for her.

We tried to continue negotiating the barstools, but as our kissing intensified it grew harder to literally leverage ourselves. I forced myself back from Sadie only to hop up and wait what felt like a million years for her to do the same. There was another long moment as we studied each other, but something felt opened wide for me. I grabbed Sadie around her waist, finding her soft bare skin with my fingertips, and pushed her back against the bar, something I'd thought about doing just about every time I was here.

The fantasy usually ended as it began, the bold movement and my lips on Sadie's. In real life, though, she hooked her thigh against my hip and pushed up against me in a move that made me groan. The truth was that I was still fairly inexperienced, and I'd never known these sounds slipping out of me. Maybe they'd been waiting for Sadie too.

I cupped a hand around one of Sadie's breasts as our hips continued the push-and-pull rhythm we'd found. The curve of Sadie's thigh was tight between my legs and every little shift in movement made my ache deeper. Her breath hitched in her throat as I rubbed my thumb over her T-shirt and bra, and I felt practically mad with power and lust as her nipple hardened under my touch. I wanted it all at once, dizzy with the possibilities swimming in my head.

Sadie deftly unbuttoned my jumpsuit, and I pushed up her T-shirt and tried not to gape at the sheer fabric only barely restraining her breasts. Sadie, yes, was a little curvy in her vintage tees and beat-up jeans. Underneath, though, Sadie was a fucking pinup model.

"I know," she said. "My ex always said I wear the wrong bra size."

"That is . . . very not much what I was thinking," I said with a laugh. "I knew you were beautiful, but—your body's kind of bananas."

"I like keeping it under wraps," she said, her eyes fluttering shut as I resumed touching her, teasing her through the filmy black material of her bra. "Most of the time."

"I'm glad tonight's an exception."

She moaned into my ear, and I realized with delight that her bra clasped in front. After a simple twist, her soft round breasts were fully revealed, dusky pink nipples hard and, it seemed, ready for more of me. I kissed down her collarbone, between her breasts, and sucked one of her nipples into my mouth as my fingertips toyed with the other. Her hips rocked harder now against mine, and I could take a hint. Right now I didn't feel like a Useless Lesbian at all.

I managed to shrug off the top part of my jumpsuit as I un-buttoned Sadie's jeans and slid down the zipper, but as I slipped my fingers underneath the waistband of her underwear, I felt something in her body language shift.

"I'm sorry," I said, pulling back from her. "Should I have not—"

"No, you didn't do anything wrong," Sadie said, but she was fastening her bra and buttoning her jeans.

"It kind of feels like I did."

She shook her head, pulling her T-shirt into place. There was no non-awkward way to get myself back into the top of my jumpsuit, and Sadie ended up having to help me, just to add to whatever awkwardness had already unfolded here.

"We shouldn't have gotten so carried away," Sadie said.

"I . . . wanted to get carried away," I said. "With you."

"Sure," she said. "People think that. You think that right now. Because here I seem all hot-bartender-who-knows-what-she's-doing. Girls think they know what they're getting into."

"I don't know what you mean," I said. "What girls?"

"Girls like *you*," she said. "Girls with jobs and plans. Girls who think I'll grow out of who I am."

"You also have a job and a plan," I said, but she was already walking back behind the counter. "Sadie—"

"You've been a really good friend to me, Max," she said. "Especially with everything I'm trying to figure out with the bar. And I don't want to mess that up."

"OK," I said, feeling the exact opposite of *OK*. "I don't want to mess anything up either."

"You should probably go," she said. "I need to lock up and get some rest."

"Sure." I waited for her, but she was still behind the counter. So I walked to the door and let myself out into the cool night air.

Chapter 15
No Gallant

Joyce called me into her office early the next morning. I hoped it wasn't because she'd noticed that the bandanna I'd worn as, hopefully, a jaunty scarf, had slipped and given anything away. Because even if Sadie wanted to act like nothing had happened last night, her teeth had scraped the pale skin of my neck and left indelible proof that something, indeed, had.

"You look very cute," Joyce said, so I assumed I was in the clear there. "Scoutmaster chic."

I found myself laughing, despite that maybe my soul had died last night. If I even had a soul left, working in the industry. I'd spent a lot of business hours this week scheming the best gift baskets to steal a client from another agent, after all. "My roommate said basically the same thing."

"So, as you know, Tess Gardner is in with the rest of her team on Monday," she said.

"Yes. I already have those boxed waters in your mini fridge," I said, and Joyce made an expression very close to rolling her eyes. "They *are* more environmentally sound."

"Sure. Glad she's being flown around in private jets but

making sure there's no one-time-use plastics anywhere near her. Anyway, why don't you sit in on the meeting with me."

"Oh, sure, I can take notes," I said. "I'll look less like a scoutmaster, promise."

"You can look as much like a scoutmaster as you'd like," Joyce said with a smile. "It's good for talent to know that young people work on their account, too. And, of course, take whatever notes you'd like, but mainly I'd like you to get more chances to watch me one-on-one with clients."

I nodded, trying not to smile. "Of course. Thank you."

"It can be a long road," Joyce said. "And there are a lot of internal politics here, as you must know."

I nodded again, my face still neutral. "Yes, obviously."

"The truth is that there are a lot of assistants in your shoes," Joyce said. "But I do think you're very savvy, and it's no secret you put in more hours than others. I'd love to at least give you the chance to learn more, even if that next opportunity isn't going to be here."

"Thank you," I said. "That's all I wanted. Just—the chance. I'm happy to prove myself however I need to."

"Sounds good," Joyce said, and since I could tell the conversation was finished, I headed back to my cubicle without another word. On any other day, it would have been time to secretly rejoice. I had said yes, I had been bold, and now, it seemed, I was leveling up.

So then why had last night gone the way it had? I couldn't understand what Sadie thought; it seemed clear to me that her goals were real and that I believed in them. I believed *in her.* Sure, yeah, of course I was disappointed that our night ended when it did. I'd been full with desire for her, and things couldn't have felt more mutual. But I'd had plenty of sexually disappointing nights! What felt new—and so much worse—was that a person I cared about somehow couldn't see that. And even with my new arsenal of You Point Oh tips, I didn't see how I could convince her otherwise.

* * *

I was already home after work and settling into a make-shift pillow-and-blanket fort with a pile of scripts and a semi-freezer-burnt microwave burrito when Chelsey banged on the door like an angry mom.

"You said we could film content tonight," she said. "Get out of whatever sad hole you've constructed for yourself in there, and please do something about the fact that your room smells like a Taco Bell."

"Can we not? I had a humiliating night and I need to be alone with my feelings and also a bunch of work and this burrito."

Chelsey dove into my carefully constructed fort, which meant my pile of pillows tumbled toward my half-eaten burrito.

"I'm going to murder you," I said, but my squeaky voice kept it from sounding very threatening, something clearly confirmed by Chelsey's laughter.

"What happened?" she asked, and there was a note of what sounded like genuine sympathy in her voice. Maybe Chelsey had originally only dragged me into this because she wanted the You Point Oh contract and also she'd seen me as pathetic, but it felt like we were somewhere else now.

"Just between us," I said as sternly as possible, and she nodded. "Sadie and I hooked up last night—or we started to—"

"Ooh, say more."

"There's no more to say. She cut things off and said it was a bad idea and I had no idea what I was getting into and we should stay friends."

"God, I hated it whenever girls wanted to be friends," Chelsey said. "Like I'm not even one of those queer girls who wants to stay friends with her exes."

"No, same," I agreed. "It's way too painful and awkward. Which makes me feel like whatever's been going on with Sadie is over. I'm not sure I can help someone with historical preservation after I took off their bra or whatever."

Chelsey cracked up. "OK, if I give you the night off from

content, will you let me make you a non-goblin dinner and loan you my essential oil diffuser to get rid of the essence of ennui?"

I agreed to that, and she made us salads from a meal kit and let me quietly read a script while she filmed a bunch of videos of herself talking about the meal kit company. It was, I realized, a vibe that was starting to feel comfortable. Maybe it *was* healthier to hang out with my roommate than hide in a pile of bedding with an old burrito.

"Hey," Chelsey said, and I ignored her because I assumed she'd gone on live to say more things about salads or meal prep services. "Max. Don't give up on Sadie yet."

I looked up from the script I was reading about a man getting stalked by a bear who might or might not be a symbol for his own toxic masculinity. "I think that's pretty hopeless and the healthiest thing I can do is stop pining. You're not on live, are you?"

"Obviously no," she said, though I didn't see what was so obvious about it. "I was really intimidated when I started dating Ava. We'd met at this event and had hit it off super well and gotten each other's numbers, and then while I was schmoozing with everyone hoping for some networking opportunities, this girl I'd just hit on is welcomed to the stage to accept an award for activist of the year! Between our first and second dates she said she had to pop out of town for a work thing, and then I saw on Instagram that it was to DC to *meet the president to discuss trans rights*. I make money by getting people to try organic boxed mac and cheeses and, like, lotions to make their butts smoother. I absolutely tried to end things with Ava because I felt like a Goofus to her Gallant."

"Chelsey," I said, "I am no Gallant."

"Yeah, well, that hot bartender thinks you are," she said. "Just be a little patient. Or don't! It's your life! I'm just trying to tell you that sometimes people need time. What if instead of going on that second date with Ava, I'd hidden in a burrito cave?"

"What if it was a sponsored burrito cave?" I asked. "Organic burrito, fair trade cotton blankets?"

Chelsey smiled, but it faded. "Take me at least a little seriously, OK? I understand that the president isn't flying you out for summits, but your bartender clearly thinks you're pretty great. That doesn't sound hopeless to me."

I wanted to take Chelsey's words to heart—and I did believe she meant every word she said, which was a new way for me to think about my influencer roommate—but when I got my next You Point Oh task a couple of days later, it felt like a sign.

Hi Max! We hope you've been enjoying leveling up—and pumping some serious iron, too! Speaking of serious . . . it's time for your next task. And that's for you to GET SERIOUS ABOUT IT.

What's "it"? In some ways, that's up to you. But since you mentioned finding love in your initial goals, this seems like the perfect time to connect you to a dating coach who will hopefully help you make a little magic happen.

Max, we know these tasks are coming fast and furious, but we want to give you as much of these 30 days as possible to actually tackle them. This will actually be your last new task for a bit: we hope you are digging into all your new opportunities and enjoying the process to become You Point Oh!

The dating coach messaged me almost immediately, and I took the first appointment slot she offered me, the very next day—on Saturday afternoon. Just days ago I assumed my Saturdays would all be held for Sadie, for walks and out-of-the-way meals and getting to know each other more and more. But here we were, two weeks of that and I felt—

I actually didn't fully know how I felt. Was I heartbroken?

I knew that I wasn't, not really, because Sadie hadn't actually been my girlfriend and we hadn't been in an actual relationship. I felt heartbroken over what could have been, but there was no denying that it hadn't been. Did I feel foolish and naïve for pining away over someone unavailable? That didn't feel accurate, given the events of Tuesday night. Was Sadie what people meant when they talked about others being emotionally unavailable? Maybe it didn't matter how eagerly someone kissed you back if they'd already constructed a wall between you in their mind.

My phone buzzed almost as soon as I set it down after getting the alert as well as the coach's message. Work was too busy for me to fixate over my romantic troubles for too much longer, and I assumed it was only Chelsey demanding content-filming time. But when I glanced over, I saw a different name lit up on my screen and—against all my better instincts—I grabbed for my phone.

have u been 2 the huntington

I sighed and tossed my phone down. I had tasks to complete and lunches to schedule and a boss to impress and I did not want to think about the fact that I had not been to the Huntington Gardens but I'd seen them and their beauty all over Instagram. Of course I'd imagined strolling through bright flowers and lush greenery, hand-in-hand, with someone I loved, who definitely wouldn't have sent me an unpunctuated request from a flip phone.

It wasn't like me, though, to ignore a text, so I picked up my phone again. **I have plans on Saturday.**

And I guessed I'd hoped she would fight me on that at least a little. Because as satisfied as I was sending the message, I only had one emotion rattling around in me at the end of the workday when Sadie hadn't responded: disappointment.

The dating coach really had her work cut out for her.

* * *

I expected another office building, but our appointment was at a Starbucks just up the 2 freeway from me. As I walked up to the giant patio, I wondered how I'd figure out who I was supposed to meet up with. On dating apps we'd at least seen each other's faces.

"Max?" A woman just a little older than me waved me over, and I remembered that I was heavily featured in at least half of Chelsey's content these days. And since I only owned a very finite amount of clothing, Isabella Morales had probably seen me looking exactly like this already.

"Hi," I said, shaking her hand and taking the seat across from her. Isabella's hair was cut similar to mine, and while her button-down shirt was obviously *nicer* than mine and probably not pilfered from an Out of the Closet for seven dollars, I felt immediately at ease. You Point Oh had not told me they were putting a queer dating coach in charge of my love life, and yet they did that for me anyway—just like with my new personal trainer.

"Let me get you a drink before we dive into things," Isabella said with a huge smile. "I know it's a lot, to talk about your dating history and all your romantic dreams with a complete stranger, so we can warm up this way."

"To be honest I'm constantly blurting out embarrassing things, so it might not be that tough for me," I said. "Not that I wouldn't take a caramel Frappuccino, I mean, when in Rome."

"Ooh, that sounds perfect, I'm going to do the same," she said, opening the app on her phone and tapping through to order. "So how's this You Point Oh thing been? You're the first client it's connected me with and I'm so curious."

"Honestly, I only did it because my roommate made me and also I was temporarily falling apart, but it's been kind of great." I shrugged. "Some of the advice is pretty basic—like there are *a lot* of self-help things about saying yes or whatever—but it did force me out of my comfort zone. I mean, I'm not sure if it would work as well if Chelsey wasn't also broadcasting my progress to all her followers, so—oh my god, do I actually think this? I guess it's good that she is. It's holding me accountable."

"That's so wonderful to hear," Isabella said. "I'm impressed that you can put yourself out there. A lot of my clients really struggle with that, so I can see in some ways you're already doing great."

"I would not go that far," I said, and we both laughed.

"Well, let me see if our drinks are ready, and we'll get into all of that," she said, hopping up and returning moments later with our Frappuccinos. "These always remind me of being a teenager. I thought I was so mature getting this might-as-well-be-a-milkshake from a coffee place."

"Oh, cool, this is a thing I drink normally if I go to Starbucks," I said, and we both laughed. "I'm always worried I seem twelve, so this isn't helping."

"I said *teenager*, so I at the least made you thirteen," Isabella said with a grin. "OK, let's get into it."

I groaned, but I really was almost always ready to talk about my pathetic love life. The details were always just *there*—closeted, including to myself, through high school, closeted to everyone except myself and strangers on the internet in college, and then the big gay life I tried to have once I arrived in Los Angeles, which so far included one girlfriend and a few other assorted hookups.

"I can tell from how you're telling me all of this that you think you're uniquely pathetic or something, Max, but you do understand that you aren't, right?" Isabella asked.

"Oh, and also I'm hung up on someone who is one of those hookups—well, attempted hookups—who I've just realized is probably completely emotionally unavailable, or at least she might be to me."

"Still not that pathetic," Isabella said. "Dating's hard! Though

I guess I'm lucky it is, or I'd have a much more boring job. So tell me, first of all, what do you want right now, Max? I watched your videos so I know that you've said you want to fall in love and be in a serious relationship. And if that's what you're after, I have plenty of advice. But if it's not, being honest about those real goals is important. I meet so many women who, deep down, really want to hook up and have fun, and that's more than OK, too, even when society is pushing all of us to couple up seriously."

"I mean, I wouldn't mind hooking up and having fun," I said. "If that happens along the way, great! But I really do want to fall in love. I want to have big feelings for someone and for her to have them for me. I wish I could explain more why I want that—"

"It's a very normal thing to want," she said. "Lots of people do. So let's talk about it. How have you usually met people? In person? Through friends? On the apps?"

"The apps," I said. "I have no idea how anyone meets in person. That feels like the cool persona of people way better at stuff than I am."

A little voice in the back of my head reminded me that I'd met Sadie in person, but I hardly thought she counted in this particular conversation. Paige either.

"Are you on the apps a lot?" she asked.

"I mean, I open them a lot. It's been a while since I've met anyone there, though. I feel like there's only so many girls and everyone's starting to look familiar or something?"

"When you say that you're on them a lot, do you mean at least once a day?"

I shrugged. "If I'm bored and holding my phone, I usually at least pull them up. After Instagram, but before I see what my mom and my older cousins are posting on Facebook."

"So I've found that when people are using it like that—you know, swiping like it's Candy Crush or something—you're not going to have the best results. What if instead you set aside a time once a week to look, swipe, connect, all of that."

I stared at her. "Once a week?"

"How about twice to start? See how it goes. I bet you won't take it for granted, won't just feel like you've seen everyone already and there's no one new for you."

"OK, fine, I will at least try that," I said. "Maybe three times a week to start. Do you want to see my profile to see if it's terrible?"

Isabella laughed. "Yes! I also want to talk to you about your community and your other connections. Not only can queer community, of course, be a wonderful way to meet potential partners, it can be really fulfilling in other ways, too. I know you spoke in your goals about wanting that, so let's find something that's a good fit for you."

"What do you mean, *something*?" I asked.

She opened her bag and took out a folder. "I printed out some ideas. Want to take a look?"

"Thanks to that whole *say yes* thing, I don't really have a choice."

We switched; Isabella got my phone and access to my apps, and I got the envelope of community ideas. I wasn't sure what to expect, but Isabella's options were surprisingly thoughtful considering that all she knew of me were the videos I'd filmed with Chelsey. Volunteering at the Los Angeles LGBT Center, a queer hiking group, a book club that only read LGBTQ+ titles, and—

"Oh my god, I used to be really good at kickball in grade school," I said, reading the details of the noncompetitive queer kickball league. "No one expected it from me, because I was so little."

Isabella looked up from my phone and grinned. "They have openings! I can have you on a team by tomorrow. How's that sound?"

"Um, kind of fast?" I laughed and shook my head. "No, I'm saying yes. It sounds weird and potentially like a not-well-thought-out idea, but—I mean, you're right. I thought I would get here and just get this like instant group of friends, the whole chosen family thing, but . . . I haven't."

"Making friends as an adult is hard," Isabella said. "Sometimes harder than dating. But also, I've found, just as rewarding. Maybe you'll find one—or both—playing kickball. Maybe you might try one of these other ideas in the future. Community isn't something you receive; it's something you build."

"This *also* feels like therapy," I said, because I could feel how true it was that I hadn't tried to build anything for myself like this. I'd been so hopeful it would just happen.

"Speaking of therapy, a little, one more thing before we get to your app profiles," she said. "And maybe this isn't something that's relevant to you, and if so, you can completely ignore it. But I talk to so many people who think they have to really work on themselves before they get into a serious relationship. Obviously, yes, work on yourself! Go to therapy and build good habits and strive for whatever you're after in your career, but for some people there's this myth that you have to be a perfect person to find someone. And it's just not true."

I nodded, but I wasn't sure how to fully hold on to her words. In theory, sure. But it was hard not to wonder what my romantic prospects would be like if everything else in my life was going the way I wanted. It was basically impossible not to assume I'd be happier in that aspect too.

"I mean it," she said, like she could read my thoughts. There was actually something comforting that maybe they were just really basic common thoughts. "There is no wrong version of you who isn't good enough for a relationship."

"Thank you," I said, because even though she obviously said that to everyone, there still felt like something pointed and personal about it. "OK, tell me everything wrong with my profile."

Isabella laughed and showed me some screenshots of potential updates she suggested. The changes weren't very big, and it made me think that maybe not *all* of my instincts were terrible. And once I was home—and pointedly *not* scrolling through any apps until one of my new scheduled times—I thought about community and building things myself.

So even though friendship had not been the goal with Sadie, I tapped on her text anyway. **I have some free time tomorrow and I have always wanted to check out the Huntington, if the offer is still good.**

Chapter 16
Max on Purpose

Even though I had early afternoon plans with Sadie, my community-building activity first thing on Sunday was, unbelievably, kickball practice. I'd thought Isabella was doing some kind of bit when she said she'd have me on a team this quickly, but here I was, making my way across Rio de Los Angeles State Park in a mildly unflattering T-shirt-and-shorts combo, just as she'd promised. Well, not the part about the unflattering shorts, but everything else.

I worried I'd never figure out how to find the team, but then I saw a small group gathered and knew I'd found the right place. Undercuts, asymmetrical haircuts, a Rockford Peaches T-shirt, an *Autostraddle* A-Camp hoodie, and—oh, shit. Paige.

We accidentally made eye contact, and I started to literally back away, but I was mildly awkward at best, and walking backwards on wet grass meant I slipped and then somehow stumbled *forward*.

"Hi," I said with a wave. "I'm Max. I'm supposed to join the team today? I promise that's not indicative of my kickball skills. Not that I've played since grade school but—"

"Nice to meet you, Max, I'm Tonya, they/them pronouns," said the person at the center of the circle. Their blond hair was buzzed short, and they were wearing a faded Wellesley T-shirt. "My team nickname is Captain, since I'm the team captain of the But I'm a Kickballers, which means I'm the one in charge of all these folks."

"Also because they're bossy as fuck," said the person standing to Tonya's right, and the rest of the team burst into laughter. "If that wasn't obvious."

The group went around introducing themselves, and I tried to act like Paige's presence was no big deal at all. And before long, once we were running drills, it kind of wasn't. Staying focused meant I didn't have time to dwell on past humiliating romantic situations. And once we were playing a modified game against one another, I was too relieved that my elementary school skills were still intact. Every time I went up to kick, the ball soared effortlessly while I had ample time to get to first or second base. Even though no one knew me—well, no one minus Paige—the whole team—well, the whole team minus Paige—cheered for me each time.

"Look, Max," Tonya said, "we just lost a player. If we're going to play our scheduled game this week, even in a noncompetitive league like this one, we needed another body on the field to qualify. So I wasn't that nervous when you slid on over here this morning. But I have a feeling you're going to be our secret weapon in our game against the U-Haulers."

"Team nickname," another player shouted. "Secret Weapon!"

"That's too long," Tonya said with a shake of their head. "Max, your team nickname's Weapon."

"Wait, really?" I stared around at this team—my team? "I get a nickname *already*? A really cool nickname?"

"We don't go around giving shitty nicknames," Tonya said incredulously, and everyone laughed even though I thought Tonya was serious. "OK, practice over. Brunch at Delia's Restaurant?"

It sounded like everyone was in agreement, but I shrugged.

"What could you possibly have to do that's more fun than this?" Tonya asked, and I felt my cheeks redden.

"Go to the Huntington with a girl I'm trying to get over," I said, which made everyone crack up in a way that didn't feel terrible. It felt knowing, like who hadn't reserved a chunk of time to see beautiful wildlife and make potentially regrettable personal choices?

"You're right, definitely more important," Tonya said. "Go make smart decisions, Weapon. Everyone else, I'll see you over there."

I said goodbye to the team—*my* team—and hurried to my car, where I texted Sadie before taking off to pick her up. Since I was now only trying to build community with her, I didn't go upstairs to change. I met her on the corner in my kickball clothes.

"Hey," she said, leaning forward to hug me. I wasn't at all ready for it; as her arms slid around me, it was impossible not to remember our bodies pushed back against the bar together. "Sorry, maybe I shouldn't have—"

"It's fine," I said in my work tone, the one that kept my emotions safely stowed away. "I'm probably gross from practice."

"What practice?" Sadie asked, and I told her about the team as we headed to my parking garage and got into my car. I couldn't believe that we were talking as if we hadn't almost had sex only five nights ago, but I guessed we'd gotten really good at just talking.

Though it seemed like we might be really good at having sex, too, if the other night had been any indication, not that I was thinking about that anymore. My pining days were through! I had a set appointment in my Outlook calendar to look seriously at all my apps later! I was going to fall in love, or at least make a very earnest attempt!

"I can't believe you're making me take you all around to interesting shit in Los Angeles, when you're the one who joined a queer kickball league, which is apparently something that exists," Sadie said.

"I didn't *make* you do anything," I said, and even though I didn't mean something by it, out of my mouth there was bite to my words. We stayed silent, for the entire half-hour drive to the Huntington. And maybe I preferred that to whatever Sadie was doing, where it was like Tuesday night had never happened.

Sadie had free passes for admission, and when I thanked her, she shot me one of her grins. Without even a word from her, the silence felt lifted.

"Tell me more about the kickball league," Sadie said as we walked past the entrance buildings and toward the gardens. "Sorry, did you want to see the art gallery or anything? I'm taking us straight to some plants otherwise."

"I'm good with plants," I said. *I would be good with anything.* "And there's not much to say about kickball yet. I just joined literally this morning. A girl I went on a terrible date with is on the team so we're pretending nothing ever happened between us."

Sadie laughed, as I realized what I'd said. I mean, it was true, but it also sounded remarkably like I might be commenting on the other night.

"Hey," Sadie said, as we swung right on a path. There was greenery as far as the eye could see, so it didn't seem like there was a wrong way to go. "I really do appreciate all your support about Johnny's. You make me feel less ridiculous for wanting it."

"Do you mind if I . . . ?" The question came to me basically as I asked it, somehow. "Did someone make you feel like you were ridiculous? Because, like . . . it just *isn't*? Real estate money in Los Angeles is stupid and we've covered that, but other than that it feels like you have a solid plan."

Sadie shrugged, and I decided not to push. The path turned,

and my breath caught in my throat as the view turned to nothing but brightly colored roses in practically every color of the rainbow.

"People post this place on Instagram all the time, but I wasn't expecting it to look so . . ." I shook my head. "It's just really beautiful. I wish I had something smarter to say."

"I think that's more than adequate," Sadie said, pausing near an enormous red flower. I thought about getting out my phone, taking a photo, two beautiful images together. But I kept it in my pocket. I already knew the beauty of this place couldn't be translated into a photograph, so why not just stay right here in the moment?

"I started working at the bar in college," Sadie said, as we slowly moved between rosebushes. I marveled how, close-up, they could be so different from one another and also, together, be part of something big and united. I guess I marveled, too, that Sadie hadn't forgotten my question and had been waiting to answer. "Just after class at first, and then the semester ended and I just . . . kept working. Billy made a few halfhearted attempts to get me back into school, but we both knew I was staying put. But then a few years later I started dating Allison, and I let it slip that at one point I'd been following Billy's old path, poli sci undergrad and then law school, and—I don't know. Something shifted."

I tried to imagine Sadie as a lawyer, and even though I knew that she was smart and good with people, I couldn't stop picturing her arguing in front of a judge in a faded old T-shirt and ripped jeans.

"She got obsessed with this idea, sent me links to degree programs I could transfer into, sent me shit on how I could start back at USC, just—she couldn't let it go that this was my chance to get the life I was supposed to have. She couldn't see that the life I was supposed to have had been completely different, once upon a time. It was all new now, and my big plans weren't going to law school, they were making sure the bar survived."

"Yeah, understandable," I said. "Also, the bar fits you. Or you fit the bar. I don't know. I can't imagine one without the other. Is that weird? I'm sorry, maybe—"

"No, I love that you think that," she said, pausing at a canary-yellow blossom. "I keep trying to pick my favorite one, but it turns out maybe I like every rose I see."

"Ugh, that sounds like some kind of beautiful metaphor. I fully love the bright red ones the most, like some clichéd Valentine's Day fetish."

Sadie laughed so hard that the group of well-dressed people nearest us shot us a glare. "What about candy hearts and bears holding boxes of chocolate?"

"That stuff's all objectively great, isn't it?"

"It's OK to like obvious things," Sadie said. "Sometimes that's why they're so obvious."

We let the group who hated our noise get a little further down the rose garden from us and wound slowly through the bushes, pausing to read about the different varieties. When I'd googled the gardens yesterday, I'd read that they spanned 120 acres. That obviously sounded big, but reading that number in the Wikipedia article was nothing like seeing it spread out around me. We could have probably lost hours of time spent only with the roses—not that anything about today felt like a loss. It was all gain—friendship gain, of course! Later I'd be swiping right on women who could actually fall for me in return.

"Anyway, we should have figured out sooner it wasn't going to work," Sadie said. "Allison kept introducing me to her friends and family and always managing to shoehorn in *Sadie's going back to law school as soon as her uncle's estate is worked out*, like it was so shameful I might just be the girl she loved who happened not to have a college degree."

"Also, *estate*?"

"Right? It was like a pile of menus in Comic Sans, his T-shirt collection, and a bunch of show tunes on vinyl."

We collapsed into giggles, and somehow even though that group of older people, two women and two men, was practically out of the rose garden by now, they still managed to give us a look. It only made us laugh harder.

"I wish I could have met him," I said, even though maybe it was a weird thing to wish. "I mean, I love show tunes."

"Yeah, you two would have loved each other," she said. "Anyway. Allison and I should have broken up, but we were both convinced we were in love and we'd get through it. I thought she'd accept me and she obviously thought I was going to give up the bar and head back to school to become a respectable member of society. I was halfway living with her even though it was always easier to just collapse upstairs in my room over Johnny's, and so most of our communications were just series of passive-aggressive texts. Sometimes tweets, Allison loved vague-tweeting about her dirtbag girlfriend."

"I can't believe you know what vague-tweeting is," I said, and she laughed again.

"Max, I'm not actually a time-traveler. I understand apps and shit. I just gave them up."

"After the dumpster incident," I said. "Which I assume was with Allison."

"Wouldn't you be terrified to learn I had a terrible breakup with *a different* woman who was that disappointed in me? Yeah, it was Allison."

I watched Sadie, her back to me as she stood on her tiptoes to smell a pale pink rose. "She sounds terrible."

"You know, I bet when she tells the story, I sound pretty terrible too. And it wasn't only her. My friends expected more from me and it was like I didn't fit into their lives anymore. Anytime it'd start to get serious with someone I was dating, some version of that happened. And at least half the time, it was my own fault, maybe more."

"This is going to sound weird, but I'm kind of jealous," I said. "I've only had, like, one girlfriend, and it wasn't even that serious. She was . . ."

I pictured Daniela, who'd been so funny and kind and, well, *hot*. It had felt miraculous our first date went so well, and then our second, and then after our third we ended up in her bed and I'd finally had sex, and a girlfriend, somehow all in one go.

"I don't know," I said. "It didn't end with anyone screaming or throwing anything. Which I know sounds healthier, but also at least when there's yelling there are strong feelings. The whole thing just felt . . . anemic."

"It's all hard," Sadie said with a nod that felt understanding and not dismissive.

"Maybe so," I said. "It just all adds to how I feel about life in general, you know? Do you feel that way about stuff? Sorry, that's so vague. But I already worry that no one takes me seriously, and having a breakup that felt like a candle dying just feels like more of that."

We walked toward another grouping of rose varieties, but I could feel that Sadie's eyes were only on me.

"What?" I asked.

"Just can't imagine anyone not taking you seriously," she said. "That's all."

It turned out that even if Sadie was never going to fall in love with me, her words still settled somewhere in my metaphorical heart. There were a lot of ways, I knew, that people could be important in your life, and if Sadie was someone who understood and accepted me, maybe it didn't matter that we weren't going to be anything else. Whatever we were, right now, felt like way more than enough.

Downstairs reception buzzed me the next afternoon to let me know that Tess and her team had arrived. We had to move quickly; talent was never supposed to wait on our behalf.

"Joyce," I said into the phone's intercom setting, "Tess and team are downstairs."

"Why don't you greet them and bring them to the meeting room?" she said. "I'll meet you there. Sound good?"

It sounded very good indeed. Joyce rarely let me greet talent; that was the job of a full-blooded agent, not an anemic assistant. Normally it only happened if Joyce was either stuck in another meeting herself or some other extenuating circumstance. This, Max on purpose, was completely new.

I checked my hair in my phone's front-facing camera and dashed downstairs, until the last several steps when I knew I'd be visible to the reception area below. Tess and I made eye contact right away, and she beamed her million-dollar Pantheon Cinematic Universe smile.

"Hi," I said, trying my best to strike that halfway casual and halfway deferential tone that professionals like Joyce were so good at. Also, the truth was that Tess, with her wavy light brown hair and dazzling green eyes and brightly patterned low-cut jumpsuit, was extremely hot and I needed that to not show on my face at all. Tess had only publicly dated men, but she had a certain vibe that made me wonder if she was bi or pan. A girl could dream, as long as she kept that dream off her face.

"I'm Max," I said, even though I'd met some of them in person before. Executives tended not to remember assistants. "I work with Joyce, and I can take y'all to our meeting space."

Tess was still beaming at me. "Hi, Max, it's good to see you."

The rest of her team—manager, manager's assistant, lead publicist, and lawyer—shook my hand and followed me up the staircase to Joyce's favorite meeting room that I always snagged for top talent. Tess had been turning in solid performances since her early twenties, but ever since she was cast as a minor superhero in a comic book franchise, everything had changed.

Joyce walked into the room, and I hung back while everyone schmoozed and did their standard amount of industry small-talk about trips to the Maldives and dinner reservations at Ana-jak Thai for their multicourse tasting menu. This part, I knew, would be tough for me if I got to break in to the next level. My last real vacation was to Disney World and Epcot Center when I was eleven, and the last Thai food I'd eaten had been paid for with plastic tokens.

Tess's manager segued the room into actual career talk, and I jotted down notes while trying not to look too subservient— even if I wasn't really supposed to participate otherwise. The gist was that Tess loved the money and fun of her Pantheon films, but she'd studied at Juilliard and was ready for Acting-with-a-capital-A opportunities moving forward. It was her manager's job, mainly, to guide her career, but Joyce was the one keeping her eyes out for the right projects to fit that career trajectory. And I guessed that I was, too; now that I had this in-formation, I'd approach my script coverage with Tess in mind for the kind of projects I might have ignored before.

The meat of the actual meeting was slim; soon small talk crept in again, and I could see from Joyce's expression that she would have rather gotten back to her desk and her inbox and voicemails instead of weighing in her opinion on what was go-ing to happen on this season's *White Lotus* finale, but she was good at participating and then standing up so slowly that the rest of the room ended up beating her to it. I was pretty good at keeping up on premium cable, but I had a feeling if I tried that standing move I would slide off the office sofa and end up on the floor.

Back in Joyce's office, I checked my emails on my phone while Joyce did the same at her iMac. My phone had buzzed an improbable number of times during the meeting, and I had as-sumed Chelsey had sent me ninety-nine reminders to film con-tent later or something. Chelsey had actually only texted once, requesting my measurements—a weirder text from her than usual—and the others were all from numbers I didn't know. I'd apparently been added to the But I'm a Kickballer group text, and it was *lively*.

"Something wrong?" Joyce asked, and I quickly turned my screen off and shoved my phone into my pocket. "Uh-oh, the bartender?"

"Oh my god, Joyce, why do you remember that?" I asked, and we both laughed. "Just got added to a group text that went a little wild while we were in the meeting."

"Oh, god, don't get me started on those. My sister-in-law has the tendency to—anyway. What did you think about the meeting?"

I knew that it was a test, and I knew even more assuredly that I didn't want to fail it. "I personally am excited for the kinds of roles Tess wants, but I have a feeling you don't love that she doesn't want the more lucrative path of more superhero stuff or things in that vein. IP projects and such."

Joyce smiled at me. "I've trained you well. So keep an eye out for meaty Oscar-bait-y roles for her, but let's not let her go down some kind of indie hole where she's making next to nothing."

"Got it," I said. "Thanks for including me. It's definitely helpful getting to see things directly."

"I'm glad," she said, and seemed to be waiting for something.

"I'm sorry, did I forget to schedule a meeting? The information for tomorrow's lunch is in your inbox and your Outlook calendar."

Joyce raised an eyebrow. "How *is* that bartender?"

"Oh, Joyce," I said. "Please don't ask."

The truth was, though, that I liked that bartender in my life. No matter what role she played there.

Chapter 17

Good Version of
Getting Punk'd

It seemed impossible that I had only joined the team on Sunday morning and had a game on Wednesday night, but there I was, frantically changing into my team jersey in the public restroom at the park while Tonya yelled into my stall. I didn't think they were technically yelling; Tonya just had one of those booming voices that really filled up a space. I felt like my voice had a crush on theirs.

"I know we're really throwing you in there," they continued as I emerged from the stall wearing my jersey with shorts and my sneakers. "But I believe in you, Weapon. You're gonna kill it out there."

"Isn't this a noncompetitive league?" I asked, following them out of the restroom and toward the rest of our team, Paige included. I hated it for us that we'd probably both joined up to find community and instead found evidence of an awkward night best left forgotten. "Is it super important we win?"

The rest of the team stared at Tonya, obviously ready for their reaction. Tonya merely sighed loudly, as if we'd already lost.

"Technically, yes, it's a noncompetitive league," they said.

"You'll do great," said a player I only knew as her team nickname, BBQ, the woman who'd worn the Rockford Peaches T-shirt at our first practice. Obviously I had questions, but I guess I also liked being in a world where someone was named BBQ and no one felt the need to explain it. "We hardly ever win and that's fine."

Tonya sighed even more dramatically, but everyone else was smiling and high-fiving, and before I had too much time to worry, a ref took the field and called the team captains over. The U-Haulers had basic T-shirts in comparison to our custom jerseys (it turned out that BBQ's wife worked at a print shop) but there was no one shrimpy like me on their team. Everyone kind of looked like Tonya. Some made Tonya look kind of shrimpy, actually.

Still, we won the coin toss and were up to kick first. Even with the danger implied by my team nickname, I was last in the roster, and I honestly felt good about that. My performance had been strong in practice, but I was still an untested and unknown quantity. It made sense to send out the guaranteed players first. I wasn't even sure that I had been that *good* on Sunday; I was just better than people expected.

We were out after our first five kickers, so we headed out to the field before I had a chance to prove myself. Or humiliate myself, whichever happened. There weren't many people in the crowd—apparently Wednesday night queer adult kickball games weren't a huge draw—but I knew that Chelsey and her phone were out there, so I wanted to turn in at least a semi respectable performance.

The U-Haulers scored a run against us in the next inning, but we evened it up at our next time kicking, though I still hadn't had my turn. By the time that finally arrived, an inning later, I'd spent so much time thinking how ridiculous it was that I was here and that I'd purposefully chosen something athletic to find community when I was still only using the empty bar when I lifted with Landon. My kick was weak and nearly fouled out, and I hoped Chelsey's giant iPhone wasn't actually good enough to film the particulars of my play. Somehow, though, I still got on base, so ultimately it didn't matter how pathetic my kick had been.

I wondered if that was a metaphor for life.

BBQ kicked after me, a beautiful soaring arc that passed above the heads of the U-Haulers outfield, and I incredulously rounded the bases to home, where Tonya was waiting to high-five me.

"That was the saddest kick I've seen in a while," they said, as BBQ made it to home base right behind me. We were up two! "But you did it anyway! You really are our secret weapon."

"Thank you?" I said, and the three of us laughed as we walked back to the bench, where I received even more high fives. This, I realized, was why I'd felt myself pulled to the lure of adult kickball. Community was hard to build, I knew, but teamwork like this happened faster. I didn't even know all of my teammates' names yet, and I still already belonged.

Ultimately, we lost, because there was really no getting around it that the U-Haulers were better. Our tiny group of supporters ambled over to join us after Tonya gave us a surprisingly kind post-game pep talk, and I stared because Chelsey wasn't alone. Well—Ava was with Chelsey, which was a surprise but not unexpected. But on Chelsey's other side was Sadie.

"Why are you here?" I asked, and immediately regretted my wording.

"Hey, it's a public park," she said with a grin. "You said you had a game tonight. Your first game. I'd want my friends here for my first game."

I had done a good job of not doing a mental highlights reel of my dorkiest moments in the seven innings I'd just played, but now that Sadie was standing here it was tempting to go through them.

"You looked so good out there!" Chelsey said. "Not that I know anything about sports. Ava and Sadie kept having to explain things to me."

"Didn't you play kickball in gym class?" I asked. "Also it's basically the same rules as baseball, just less innings."

"Max, if you think I'm all warmed up cozily to my grade school PE memories and not repressing the shit out of them, it's like you don't even know me."

"My trainer says a lot of queer people have trauma about gym class and it's good to reclaim physical fitness," I told her.

"I love that," Ava said. "You seem like you're thriving, Max."

"I wouldn't go that far," I said, but it wasn't as if I didn't know what she meant. It sounded ridiculous that an app could actually change my life, but I wasn't even a month in and my life was almost unrecognizable already.

"Weapon!" Tonya yelled over in my direction. "We're all going to drink at the Roost. Bring your friends."

"*Weapon*?" Chelsey asked.

"It's a long story. Will y'all come? I don't really know anyone yet."

"You should get to know your teammates," Ava said. "But, hell *yeah* we'll come. I love that bar."

"I should get back to work," Sadie said, touching my arm. "Billy didn't complain too much but—"

"I get it," I said. "Thank you for coming. It was really nice of you."

"Wouldn't have missed it," she said, giving me a gentle hug. "See you soon?"

"Definitely," I said, and tried to look completely platonic and casual as she said goodbye to Chelsey and Ava and headed off from us.

"She's got it *bad*," Chelsey said, and I shot her a glare.

"I'm working on getting over that, thank you."

Ava laughed. "She wasn't talking about you, Max."

We piled into Ava's Subaru Crosstrek, along with a couple

of my teammates who hadn't driven. Ava drove us one neighborhood over to Atwater Village and managed to find parking right outside of the bar. I loved how all the Eastside neighborhoods were packed in so cozily next to each other; that part at least was a lot like the LA I'd pictured before I'd moved here. Tonight, crammed into a dim and tiny dive bar with a dozen or so queer folks, I could see how maybe my life was turning into that vision after all.

I tried to follow Ava's advice, even though I would have been happier sticking near her and Chelsey all night. I talked to my teammates and I looked at photos of people's pets and partners on their phones and I even tried to give Paige neutral-but-kind looks to convey that I was a safe person who wouldn't act like a complete asshole to her ever again. She stayed clear of me so I wasn't sure how effective those neutral looks were, but at least when we were headed out at last call I didn't feel like a jerk who'd learned nothing. Lately, it was like all I did was learn.

When I got up for work a couple of days later, a huge box was right outside my bedroom door. A pink Post-it with Chelsey's swirly handwriting on it was stuck to the side.

Local all-gender clothing company loves your videos,
sent you a bunch of clothes! We'll film content later on
with you wearing some looks so we can give them a
(required) shout-out. Enjoy!

I pulled open the box and wondered if there was some equivalent of a good version of getting Punk'd. I'd gotten ads for some of these exact button-downs and wished I'd had the money to buy stuff new and full-price. Now here was a whole box, just for me, just for—well, revealing my deepest wants to six figures' worth of people.

When I looked at it that way, a box of free clothes didn't sound that over-the-top.

I didn't have the time—nor the mental wherewithal pre-caffeine—to go through everything, but I grabbed one of the button downs dark blue with a subtle pale blue paisley print—and threw the shirt I'd grabbed from my closet only minutes earlier back into my bedroom. I knew that You Point Oh had wanted me to *level up* in my attitude and effort, but once I was out of the shower and in this perfectly cut, brand-new shirt, I felt I was leveling up in other ways too.

At work, I knew that people weren't probably logging the ten looks I typically wore, but I still felt better walking in with something brand-new and pricier than I normally could have afforded. Better still: in my inbox were two scripts that had already seen some buzz in the industry, and I was excited about both for Tess Gardner. Actually, I was only excited about one, *The Only One*, which had big indie buzz for the female screenwriter and director who'd had a small hit a couple of years ago and took home a few trophies at the Gothams and Indie Spirit Awards. The other script was by Eric Sorensen, who'd won approximately a million Emmys and Oscars and wrote the kind of talky, in-your-face scripts that the industry loved. To me his scripts were kind of nearly-two-hundred-pages-of-mansplaining, but if Tess nabbed the lead in his latest film, an Oscar nomination was all but guaranteed. This was, I knew, exactly the kind of script Joyce wanted for her, and I promised myself I'd try to weigh it carefully.

Javier DM'd me on Slack while I was still getting through my pre-Joyce morning routine. **That Sorensen script hit your inbox this morning? Also Aidy and I were gonna order non-shitty lunch today if you wanna get in on that.**

Yes to lunch, maybe on the script. You?

Will treat to a healthy burrito if you forward that on to me.

I laughed to myself. **Sure, Joyce murdering me is absolutely worth $14.99 plus tax and tip!**

It's $17.99 and don't forget delivery fees!

I do still want in on the order, unless you were only including me for script access, in which case I'll figure out my own overpriced burrito situation.

Look, Max, I had to try. Let me know what burrito you want before noon-thirty.

I smiled over in Javier's direction and gave him a thumbs-up, and he rolled his eyes and then we both cracked up. Even if my only change in status at work was that I sat in on the occasional extra meeting with Joyce, everything felt different anyway. None of it was exactly what I'd hoped, but I supposed that was some kind of life lesson I was supposed to learn.

Once Joyce was in and I felt semi-caught-up for the moment, I checked my phone to see if any of the dings that had sounded earlier were important. Chelsey was begging for selfies in my new shirt to show to the brand, which is exactly what I'd assumed those notifications had been. But then, right below that in my texts (and right above the never-quiet But I'm a Kickballer group chat) was Sadie Bartender.

the other nite was rly fun. hope u feel good even w a loss bc u were great out there. r u free tomorrow for something i haven't figured out yet?

It hit me that given all my new life stuff, like Tuesdays and Thursdays with Landon and this brand-new team that was taking up at least one practice and one game per week—and a lot of my texting time—I hadn't really gotten around to researching much at all about historical preservation in Los Angeles. And I was genuinely determined to; it hadn't just been a ploy to save the day and make Sadie fall in love with me.

I googled for the website, but then Joyce was buzzing me to get a Hulu executive on the phone, and suddenly I was frantically DMing my burrito order (wild-caught salmon) to Javier and Aidy, and after I set up two meetings, finagled reservations to Mother Wolf, and sent flowers to the actress Joyce was wooing under the guise of her having just won a very inconsequential award, I finally accepted defeat and closed the tab. I'd figure it out later.

After work my plans were to grab a drink at Johnny's and start work on my script coverage, but the Kickballers chat had talked me into hanging out on BBQ's back patio while she— well, it seemed her team nickname was hangout-related and not game-related. We drank cans of White Claw and La Croix while BBQ did as her name said and I tried to figure out what people's actual names were and chat with everyone. Everyone except Paige, who managed to keep at least five feet of distance between us at all times. I worried that the right thing to do was quit the team, but less than one full week in and I didn't want to. All the queer-girl Instagram meme accounts I followed talked about drama, and so maybe it had just finally found me.

I stayed out late enough that I was too tired for Johnny's and then, of course, too tired to read scripts in bed, but at least I had Sadie to look forward to the next morning. Except, *fuck*, I realized my day had gotten away from me and I'd never responded to her. Was it too late now? I knew she was working mere yards from me, but I couldn't figure out if it was ruder to respond late than to not respond at all. Wait, what was I thinking? Obviously it would have been worse to ignore Sadie, *my friend*. Which was fine! Having her as a friend was not some sad substitute for romance; having her in my life, period, was what mattered.

And maybe I wasn't doomed on the romance front anyway. On the apps I was chatting with a few different people, trying to take things at this new speed. Nothing could move fast when I only checked in once a week, but I could see how that was the point.

Sorry, today got away from me but if this isn't too late, I am free tomorrow. Also you don't have to think of anything! We could just do something boring.

it's never 2 late 4 u max. and boring is good 4 me 2. walk and then food? food and then walk?

We decided to take a walk around Silver Lake Reservoir, which I'd driven by a bunch but never actually stopped and explored. It wasn't like our first walk; the path looped around two man-made lakes, a rec center, and a dog park, so it didn't feel anything like Jurassic Park, and my phone kept up a signal the entire time. Also, Sadie didn't feel like all but a stranger now. In some ways, Sadie was the first true friend I'd made for myself in LA.

After we'd looped back to the spot where I'd parked, we debated brunch spots. Sadie pointed to LAMILL, which was walkable from there, but I shook my head.

"I went on a date there once and accidentally ordered a twelve-dollar latte. No thank you."

Sadie laughed, pushing her hair back out of her eyes. "Were you paying or was she?"

"She'd already offered so I felt like such a jerk. There just shouldn't be a risk something like that could even happen!"

"Dude, you're telling me," she said. "Breakfast sandwiches at All Day Baby?"

"I haven't gone there yet," I said. "No surprise, I know, I'm boring and haven't been anywhere in my two years here."

"What are you talking about," Sadie said as we got back into my car. I didn't set Waze to the restaurant because it was just a few blocks down the street from home. "You've been to the twelve-dollar latte place. You've lived plenty."

"Shut up," I said, as we both laughed. "Maybe it just feels like this forever. LA is so big and I have no idea if I can ever actually explore all of it."

"I grew up here and there's plenty I haven't seen," she said. "Though some of that's my job, kind of keeps me occupied when everyone else is out."

"Do you hate that?" I ask. "It seems like you basically work every night."

"Yeah, I dunno, as I've said, I really love being there. But I know it keeps me from shit too. It would have been cool to go out with everyone after your game the other night, but instead I was hurrying back and feeling guilty. If it was my bar—"

"*When* it's your bar," I said, and she grinned.

"Sure. I'll just have to figure it out that it isn't like that. I can love the place and love the gig and still want more out of life. Travel and friends and nights out at other places. Nights in, too, doing nothing at all. Johnny's on my own terms in my own name is not my only goal."

"Yeah, I hear you, but finding a balance or whatever really is hard. I'm doing all this . . ." I thought about how to say it, because I was *not* going to tell Sadie about You Point Oh. It was bad enough that seemingly everyone I knew was watching my progress. Sadie was my off-the-grid safe space.

Sadie also, I suspected, wouldn't think highly of any of it: sponcon, my baring my soul on social media, gamification of life goals.

"Self-improvement stuff, you know? The team and the gym and whatever, and suddenly it's harder finding time for all my work, which is still just as important to me. I don't know how, like, self-evolved people balance it all."

I found parking only a block from All Day Baby, and even though the café and tables out front were packed, we snagged seats at the bar. Sadie talked me into ordering the breakfast sandwich, which was a bacon, egg, and cheese biscuit sandwich also slathered with strawberry jam. I was dubious about the jam, but was not at the point in my relationship with Sadie where I wanted to say no to things. In general, after all, I'd learned that a lot of good came out of saying yes.

And also, the jam was perfect.

Chapter 18
The Big Move

Even without a warning from Chelsey, I was ready when I got a notification on Day 30 of You Point Oh. I knew that leveling up wouldn't be the peak of this improvement effort, and as time passed without another task, I assumed there would be some kind of grand finale. I was not nearly close enough to self-actualization yet.

Hi, Max! Time sure flies when you self-actualize, huh? Your 30-day program is nearly complete! We hope that you've been having a blast—but more importantly, we hope you're thrilled by the changes in your life!

Before we say goodbye, we've got one last task. Before you reevaluate where you are in life: do the thing that scares you. MAKE THE BIG MOVE.

We'll see you on the other side!

I wasn't surprised; in normal life, a month wasn't long, but I was living on You Point Oh's timeline. And this is where it had been leading the whole time.

After a quick shower, I styled my hair with four new products sent to me by a queer-owned hair styling company, stepped into one of my new, more casual suits—dark gray—with a new maroon and white button-down, both of which had arrived recently from another clothing label that wanted to see me in their clothes on Chelsey's social media, and laced my Docs. If people were supposed to dress like the job they wanted to have, this was probably the closest I'd ever come. I very much looked like a boss—or at the least, very cool middle management.

"Oh my god, you look perfect," Chelsey said as I walked into the kitchen in search of coffee and a morning smoothie. Chelsey had offered me one the morning after a particularly rough Kickballers practice, and it turned out some extra nutrients in my life made me feel even more awake than coffee alone. "I need your reaction to your new task. Your final task!"

"I need to be out the door in four minutes, can it be before four minutes?" Normally I would have asked for way more time to prepare, but there was a benefit in wearing a perfect outfit and finally having near-absolute confidence in your hair. Thank you, You Point Oh.

"Absolutely." Chelsey grabbed my arm and pulled me next to her and in front of her already-rigged-up phone. "So, y'all, this is the day we've all been waiting for. Max's final You Point Oh task. Max, how do you feel?"

"Like I'm going to be late to work, Chelsey," I said, and not only because it seemed like Chelsey's followers—and mine too—liked it when I was a little salty. How was I going to make the big move at the office if I was late?

"Very funny, Max. So then, without further ado, why don't you tell us your final task."

"It's *Make the big move*," I said.

"Wow, so it all comes down to this. Do you already know what the big move is?"

I waited for something to pop into my head, but I hadn't

even had my improved coffee yet—sent last week by a local brewery who'd seen me snark about my subpar blend I chugged on the way to work—or the stupid smoothie I was honestly already kind of hooked on.

"I have thoughts," I said, instead of, *Chelsey, I am utterly clueless and in need of caffeination and whatever chia seeds do for you.*

"Ooh, some mystery, I don't hate it," Chelsey said. "So, no plans of action yet, just vibes?"

"Yep," I said. "Just vibes."

"OK, so we'll check back in soon. But even before this final step, how're you feeling? Like the last twenty-nine days were an amazing journey? Like you're just trudging to the end? What are *those* vibes?"

"I dunno, not to jinx anything, but a bunch feels like it's going OK," I said. "Not to be too earnest and optimistic."

"In this house, we welcome earnestness and optimism," Chelsey said. "Though I love that you think 'a bunch feels like it's going OK' is some kind of burst of sappiness."

"Anyway, I should get to work," I said.

"Maybe you'll make the big move there," Chelsey said.

"Maybe," I said, hoping to sound a little mysterious, but from Chelsey's look it probably just sounded like a tiny ghost. I threw a premeasured smoothie into the blender while I brewed my coffee, and it wasn't even five minutes later that I was out the door.

I thought hard on my entire drive to work, but despite everything that had happened in the last month—and all the things I still hoped would happen—I had no idea what big move was next for me. I'd already basically marched into Joyce's office and told her what I wanted. In some ways, I just had to stay the course. I'd said yes, been bold(ish), leveled up, and gotten serious about—well, I was at least trying. And maybe I was just excited about new shirts and better coffee and nights out with my new team, but I actually thought I could feel how my life seemed to be all pointing up now, on the precipice of something. Was the big move the thing that could push me fully up and over? That felt like a lot of pressure for a task from an app.

Though I guess the truth was that it turned out I kind of liked pressure.

Traffic magically went my way, and despite my late start, I was still second to arrive, behind Aidy. These days, she or Javier often beat me there. I knocked out all my admin tasks and was already reading the trades when Javier walked in. I expected him to rush to his desk, as always, but he paused at my desk and whistled.

"Are you cat-calling me?" I asked, and we both burst into laughter.

"Nice suit, Van Doren," he said. "Big meeting today?"

"Just wanted to look like a boss," I said, even if that felt like a lot of information. By now I wasn't worried about what Javier would do with anything that made me look vulnerable. We were in pretty similar boats, after all.

"Goal achieved, then," he said, and headed to his cube. It was almost *funny* to me how less than thirty days ago I'd been slightly terrified of him and all his confidence. Now here he was, twenty minutes earlier to work because of, I assumed, potential competition *from me*. Was You Point Oh actually that good? Originally the app had seemed insulting and also no fuller of wisdom than the smooth butt cream Chelsey also did sponcon for. There was no denying that things had changed, though. *I* had changed.

I met Joyce by the elevator bay, as always, and her eyes swept over my outfit. Would I eventually get used to this?

"Great look," she said, taking her coffee from my hand.

"Thanks. It's been quiet this morning so far. I mean, relatively speaking, of course."

"I noticed, which always makes me suspicious."

We stepped into her office, and I got my own coffee started while she settled in at her desk. These routines were often the best part of my workday, after the morning rush had passed, and the rest of the day hadn't gotten out of control yet.

"Ooh," Joyce said, scrolling her email. "We're supposed to get the official offer for Tess today."

"Oh, exciting," I said. "I loved that script so much. I hope they can scrape together the money to make it—"

"Oh, Max, no," Joyce said, giving me an expression like I'd just announced I was dying. "Not that little indie film. The Eric Sorensen one."

I rolled my eyes without meaning to. "Oh, sure. That's exciting, too."

Joyce raised an eyebrow. "I'm well aware you preferred *The Only One* script, but you must understand it isn't that simple."

"Obviously I do, but, I dunno, I just feel like everyone still talks about Sorensen like he's this amazing writer, but he had like one good TV show and then the rest was all just a bunch of good actors mansplaining. Tess is *so* talented and wanting to break out as this award-winning acclaimed actor, and I think she deserves better. The script for *The Only One*—"

Joyce sighed. "Max, you understand that there's going to be so little money for that film, don't you? Tess is trying to make a big leap up."

"I think if she took it that it would be like Ari and *Treading Water*," I said, even though Ari Fox had filmed her Oscar-winning role before I took the job at Exemplar. I still knew I would have spotted the potential in that script had I been the one to read it. I could feel it now for Tess.

"Tess is at a very different point in her career than Ari was," Joyce said. "Last year she had a supporting role in the biggest box office title of the year."

"No, I understand," I said. And I *did*. But I also felt like— naïve or not—careers weren't just about big box-office numbers. I knew from that meeting with Tess that she wanted *more* than being a relatively minor superhero, even if that alone would have been the ultimate dream for a million other actors.

"But?" Joyce asked, her eyes twinkling a little.

"I know you're just humoring me, but I think that the script for *The Only One* is extraordinary, and it's Argon Films and that distributor usually really knows how to put out a movie, and I just think it could be big in a different way for her. It wouldn't be her and some actor and Sorensen sharing all the press, it'd be her and this incredible female filmmaker."

"I promise that I take your opinions into consideration," Joyce said. "Really. I'm glad you're willing to say things that sound objectively wrong."

"Oh my god, Joyce," I said, and we both laughed.

"I actually wanted to discuss something with you," she said. "Take a seat."

I doubted she'd be joking with me if anything truly terrible was about to be revealed, so I sat down across from her, feeling a sense of déjà vu for that day somehow less than a month ago when I'd finally told her what I actually wanted out of my role.

"I ran into Riley Howe—you know, Tess's manager—last night after my drinks with Bobby from Sony. We ended up grabbing a bite—I'm warning you, Max, in twenty years you're going to have to immediately have a meal if you attempt drinking multiple cocktails after eight p.m.—and got to talking, and it sounds like her group might be in need of a new junior manager."

I felt my eyes widen so much that I probably looked like an overdrawn cartoon owl.

"I talked you up a little, even though the thought of you leaving stresses me out more than I'm comfortable with, and she asked me to ask you to send over your résumé."

"Oh," I said. Was this a compliment or an insult? I literally had no idea.

"I know that you were hoping for a junior agent opportunity, and ideally a junior agent opportunity *here*, but I think management could ultimately be a better fit for you."

"Is that . . ." I took a deep breath, as something that felt like disappointment clanged in my head. "Is that bad? Like I'm . . . not enough something important to be an agent?"

Joyce laughed her throaty, brusque laugh. "Not at all. I just see the passion you have in, for example, choosing a beautiful project for Tess instead of working out a deal that's going to make any of us rich and on top here at Exemplar. I think that you could work side by side with someone like me and lead talent to some very smart projects."

Everything she said resonated somewhere within me, and I couldn't ignore that. But I also couldn't ignore that my goal since I'd arrived had been to eventually get to her level, and this felt like I was maybe being taken out of the game before getting a chance to go onto the field.

Kickball had really changed my metaphors.

"I'll be honest with you," she continued, "I don't know if it's the right opportunity for you. While I do think that management is a great fit, Spring Hope Management as a company is a lot smaller than Exemplar, and you'd probably have to manage all your duties for yourself. Basically, not even shared assistants for the lower-level managers. And I'm not sure how much more money you'd stand to earn right away. Hard to believe their benefits package is as good as the one over here. Et cetera."

"Wow, Joyce, you really know how to sell me."

She laughed again. "It's a step up, and I know you want that. I can't guarantee there'll be an opening here anytime soon, and I also can see a very good future for you as a talent manager, so I think it's at least worth pursuing. Think it over this weekend, do some research, and I believe you should already have Riley's contact information. And make your résumé look impressive; I don't want Riley to think I'm sending over someone green and inexperienced."

"Will do," I said, and despite that it wasn't the job I'd

thought I wanted, I couldn't deny that this possibility had potential. I tried to keep from smiling or squeaking or anything else that could be seen as unprofessional. Any over-the-top enthusiasm could be saved for another push for *The Only One* script. "Thank you, Joyce."

Back at my desk, I took it as a sign that my inbox was quiet, Joyce's line wasn't ringing, and You Point Oh had literally told me to make the big move! I'd taken notes back at my meeting with the career coach, and so in my downtime I tuned up my résumé and found myself looking more and more impressive. I finally had time to actually think about it, not just get caught up in the moment with Joyce and a shiny new possibility glittering in front of me. Was I actually ready to guide someone's career without the wisdom and experience of Joyce? Maybe turning down high-paying mansplaining scripts was actually a terrible move. Would anyone take me seriously, even if I wore a suit and had a title that didn't contain the word *assistant* anywhere (though *junior* was pretty close)?

I dug around on Spring Hope's website, and noticed almost immediately that their office was in Downtown LA. It would shave my commute down to very little, but I didn't want to make a choice solely on that. Not that sending in my résumé was making a choice.

Still, it felt a lot like *the big move* and the timing couldn't have been better. I wouldn't be able to fully share it for the campaign—though I knew Chelsey would do her best to make me—but it would be something good to hint at. Maybe we'd do a follow-up series, once I had proven to self-actualize in some way. So many people seemed to be rooting for me; I loved the thought of not letting them down.

After work, I felt too charged up on possibilities to head home, so I stopped by the assistant happy-hour and got into a pretend fight with Javier about the best places to order for work lunches, which turned mildly contentious when he went to bat for boring salads instead of overpriced burritos. My watch and phone erupted with a series of buzzes as I was shouting *Carbs are what people respond to even when they say they don't want them*, which I wasn't even sure was true. I couldn't believe I used to be *scared* of these outings when it was just drinking overpriced cocktails and yelling our opinions back and forth, two things I was pretty great at actually.

I took a second, while Javier defended the glory of the lunchtime salad, to check my messages. The Kickballers group chat had exploded with meetup plans, and so I settled my tab, said goodbye, and headed across town to join up with the team at the Hermosillo in Highland Park.

"Weapon!" Tonya shouted as I walked in, which made everyone surrounding the team look around in alarm until they realized I was the weapon in question and hardly a threat to the safety of their evening.

"Maybe we should work on that nickname," I said, as my teammates greeted me with hugs. "It feels like yelling *fire* in a theater, you know?"

"Once Tonya gives you a nickname, that's it," BBQ said, laughing. "Do you know how much effort I spend making sure most of my non-kickball friends have no idea y'all call me BBQ?"

"But your smoked meats are so good!" I laughed and accidentally caught Paige's gaze, and then somehow ended up at the bar at the exact time she got into line to order, too. For all that I'd improved since our terrible date, when I was around her it was easy to forget.

"Don't run off," she said sharply, then grimaced. "Sorry, that came out bitchy. But I see how you dart away from me whenever you can. And you don't have to, if you don't want to. I'm fine."

"I've been trying to give you space and act really neutral," I said, running through Kickballers practices and games and hangouts in my head. I'd been so convinced Paige had been avoiding me that maybe I should have considered I was inadvertently the one actually doing that.

"No offense, Max," she said, "but you are extremely bad at acting 'neutral.'"

"I feel really, really shitty," I admitted. "You're like the nicest girl I've met in ages, and I just . . . I acted like a huge jerk that night."

Her gaze softened. "Yeah. You did. But it felt like you had a bad day and—I don't know. I don't think I owed you anything, but there was probably a version of the night where I was a little more understanding."

"I still can't believe I asked you to go home with me," I said. "Like, what an embarrassing thirsty fool I was."

Paige laughed. "If I had a dollar for every time I'd acted like an embarrassing thirsty fool . . ." She gestured to the bartender. "What do you want? My treat."

"No way, after you had to buy me dinner? This is completely on me."

"Yeah, that seems fair," Paige said with a grin, and we each ordered a beer. "I'm glad you didn't run away tonight, Max."

"I'm glad you're really understanding," I said, grabbing our drinks from the bartender. "And that apparently there's a small enough number of kickball-playing queer people in Los Angeles that we ended up on this team together."

She snickered, leading me back to our little group. "Your face when you first showed up. You were *not happy* to see me."

"Just humiliated. That night was like my personal low point. It made me take some pretty drastic steps to get my shit together."

"Oh, like a huge social media campaign?" Paige grinned at me. "Yeah, I saw. You're really cute on camera, Max."

The knowledge hit me with a panicky rush. "It's so weird how everyone's seen it. It's like people have read my diaries or something."

"Maybe more people should let strangers read their diaries then," Paige said. "It's really relatable to know so many of us are flailing. I keep thinking how when I graduated high school I made this big list of things to accomplish by the time I turned twenty-five, and I have done *none* of them."

"Why didn't anyone tell us that twenty-five is *so young*?"

"If it makes you feel better, it wasn't a great night for me either," Paige said. "I replayed it a lot in my head, thinking of ways I could have shown you a little more grace. But I think it's easy when situations are stressful or surprising to have kind of big reactions you reconsider later."

I was still rolling that around in my head when our teammate Megan, known as The Janitor ("She's always jumping in and cleaning up messes," per Tonya), jumped in to ask me where I'd gotten my suit, and before long we were out on the patio, discussing last week's practice and putting in food orders to split. Paige stayed within my peripheral, though, and I wondered if this was a sign. Asking out the girl who'd inspired my whole journey with You Point Oh would be a big move, wouldn't it?

I couldn't stop thinking, though, about my chat with Isabella the dating coach. Because, yes, Paige was cute, and we clearly had things in common, and it felt like if I asked we could probably try another date again. But I knew that the whole point of You Point Oh—and my attempted self-actualization—wasn't just about a good story. It was about actual growth—or, at least, it was supposed to be. And the truth was that if I was supposed to approach dating with an eye on what I actually wanted for myself, right now that wasn't Paige.

And I'd grown enough to know exactly what I wanted—even if it was big and risky. When I thought about situations like Paige had said, surprising and stressful, I didn't think of our terrible date at all. The disappointing night in my head was that night when I kissed Sadie, and when Sadie told me I only wanted the idea of her. Why hadn't I told her that I wanted way more than the idea of her? I could beat myself up, but I honestly had been so surprised at her reaction—and maybe a bit stressed as well. And maybe, I realized, Sadie had been too.

So I said goodnight to the team and headed toward home, toward Sadie. It was late when I walked into Johnny's, and Sadie called out a *Just so you know, we're already at last call* when I walked in. And then she saw that it was me.

"Sorry," I said with a grin, as if it was just dawning on me what I was about to attempt. "Do you want me to go? Just a warning that I really don't want to go."

"Good, because I don't want you to go either," she said, opening a couple of beers for the guys sitting near my usual spot at the bar. "Give me just a minute while I close out a couple of tabs, OK?"

"Take as long as you want," I told her, my voice shockingly steady for the whirlwind of emotions swirling through me. Was this the big move? There was nothing else that was bigger. There was nothing I wanted more.

Sadie was back as promised with my drink and her crooked grin. "You wear that suit well, Max."

"Thanks, I'm really glad you like it." I looked right into her hazel eyes, kept her gaze right on me as the flurry of bar activity continued around us. "Is it OK if I stay until I finish this?"

"You can stay as long as you want," she said, but another customer needed her tab closed, and the moment passed.

It was ultimately a good thing, of course, that Billy was already off for the night, but this also meant that Sadie didn't return to me until the bar was officially closed. I thought about the last time that I sat here as she flipped the sign from *open* to *closed* and tried not to blush. If everything went as I hoped, last time would be nothing in comparison to tonight.

"Business seemed good tonight," I told her as she wiped down the bar top.

"It's OK. I'm not sure it's fighting-off-the-gentrifiers good, but, yeah. It's not nothing." She paused her cleaning and glanced over her shoulder at me. "What's up with you tonight? You seem—"

"Yeah?" I asked.

"Honestly, I don't know. But I like your energy."

"Sadie, I have a question for you," I said, and it didn't come out smooth at all. It was a squeaky, jumbled pile of words now figuratively lying between us.

"Sure," she said, and turned to face me. "Shoot."

"Will you go home with me?"

Sadie stared at me, and I couldn't read her expression at all.

"I know that you're about to say that you can't, that you don't want to mess up our friendship, that girls don't know what they're getting into." I took a deep breath, steadied my tone and my gaze and my breathing. I steadied everything. "Sadie, I know exactly what I'm getting into."

Sadie blinked. I still had no idea what she was thinking about any of this. I wanted to apologize, to pretend I was kidding, to run away like I'd basically done to Paige the past couple of weeks. But I made myself sit still. I made myself wait for her.

"I have to lock up the register," Sadie said, walking behind the counter.

My heart thudded with so much force I wondered if it was possible it could have collapsed in on itself. "OK. I'll let myself out and—"

"No, Max, I meant, before I can go," Sadie said with a laugh. "I'll just never hear the end of it from Billy if the money's not in the safe when he gets in tomorrow."

"Oh," I said. *Oh.*

"Yeah, Max," she said softly. "Of course I'll go home with you."

Chapter 19

Boss Lady Fantasies

My heart raced as I unlocked my apartment door with trembling hands. Yes, this was it, without a doubt, the big move. Yes, Sadie just said *of course*. Yes, Sadie had come home with me. Yes, this was everything I'd wanted.

It felt like make-believe, though. It felt impossible.

Still, I laced my fingers through Sadie's. I led her to my bedroom. I closed the door behind me. And I waited to summon the courage to take the next step. But it all still felt impossible.

"What are you waiting for?" Sadie asked, her voice soft and a little playful, right into my ear. I could have melted at her warm breath, her tone, the implication that she wanted what was next, too. That she wanted me.

So I told myself to stop overthinking, and I rose on my tiptoes to kiss her. The last time we'd kissed had been thrilling, shocking, abrupt; I had barely kept my thoughts together. But I didn't want tonight to be anything like last time. Tonight was on purpose. Tonight we knew what we were doing. Tonight, I hoped, would be for good.

Sadie kissed back eagerly, gripping the back of my neck with her hand and slipping her tongue past my lips with an urgency that sent a shock through my body. Even if Sadie was my dream girl, even if this was the real-life version of a fantasy I'd had many times before, I was still surprised at the magnitude of want throbbing within me already. One kiss and already I felt practically undone.

"You're so much shorter than me," Sadie murmured, leaning over past my mouth to brush her lips against my neck.

"I'm sorry," I said, shivering at her touch. And I heard her *laugh*. Had this already somehow gone sideways? *Again?*

"Why are you apologizing?" she asked, kissing me again. "For your *height*? I only meant that this might be easier in your bed."

A moan escaped my lips at just the thought—though her lips back on my neck probably weren't helping any with my lack of control. Was my lack of control ridiculous? Right when I started worrying that I should have been embarrassed, Sadie grabbed my hand and tugged me forward.

"I'll take that as a yes," she said, pulling me further into the room, closer to my bed. "Your bedroom's so cozy. It must be so nice to curl up at night."

"Yeah, it's one of my favorite places," I confided, shaking again as we lay down in bed facing one another. If it were a dream, I only hoped that I'd never wake up.

Sadie was right; it was easier kissing this way. We settled in next to one another, kissing gently because now it felt so easy and there was no reason not to kiss in every way possible. Tonight, I decided, could go on forever. Taking our time felt like the only reasonable option. We kissed soft and we kissed rougher with teeth snagged on lips. We used more pressure, then less. We kissed deep, and Sadie kissed lightly down my neck to my shirt collar.

"Maybe it's time for this to go," she said with a smile, and it really wasn't until she slid her fingers down my jacket's lapels that I realized I'd been making out in bed this whole time *wearing a suit.* "Though honestly this is satisfying some boss lady fantasies I didn't even know I had."

I laughed and yanked off the jacket. Sadie's fingers nimbly undid my button-down, and then her lips were back on me. She slid up the band of my sports bra as she made her way down my clavicle so that there was no pause, just her lips on one of my nipples and her fingertips lightly tugging at the other.

"Fuck," I said, focusing hard on—well, anything that wasn't Sadie's lips and tongue and fingertips. A warming pulse danced throughout my body, its tempo ratcheting up at a maddening pace. It didn't feel possible that I was still mostly dressed and yet I felt so dangerously close to release. It felt too soon to give in, though; I wanted this to last.

Sadie looked up at me, her lips parted, her hands still. "Max. Can I ask you something?"

"Um, yeah," I said, trying to sound chill and not at all panicked that Sadie had a question in the middle of hooking up with me.

"I wanted to ask if that thing you said that night at Johnny's a while back was true."

Oh my god. Enough time had passed, and Sadie had acted so unaware. I'd convinced myself that I'd never said it aloud, only thought it, and the embarrassment once powerful enough to change the entire direction of my love life had receded. It was almost as if it had never happened.

I'd firmly believed that it had never happened.

Except that it had. Because it turned out that, about a month ago, not only had I actually drunkenly confessed to Sadie that I'd never actually ever had great sex, but she remembered.

"I feel so—"

Sadie laughed softly and shook her head from side to side. "Shit, no, I only wanted to . . ."

"Figure out what was wrong with me?" I asked. Because it wasn't just that I hated that I'd gotten to be twenty-six years old without a great love story. It was that even in the intimate moments I'd waited for what had felt like my entire life, I hadn't felt what I'd wanted. And I definitely hadn't felt like I'd been that for anyone else either.

"No, Max, the goal is to change that for you." Sadie's voice was low and right in my ear again. Her breath was warm, but I shivered. "After tonight, I don't want you to ever have to say you haven't had good sex yet. How does that sound?"

It sounded like the best question I'd ever been asked. But—

"It might be me," I said softly. "Statistically speaking—"

"Then let's just find out," she murmured, as her fingertips found my nipples again. "How's this for you?"

"Um, good," I said, trying to get back to the moment and out of my head. I was almost positive that was why my sex life had so far been less than thrilling. It hadn't been anyone else's fault, that much was for sure. No, it had been my brain's refusal to be quiet and play along. Instead of moments of passion climbing toward climax, it was like I could see myself too clearly. Were my actions hot enough? Were the sounds that came out of me sexy or just awkward? Was there something I didn't know that showed I was embarrassingly inexperienced? Tonight I wanted to lose myself in Sadie, but now that I knew my experience was a goal for her, could I think about anything other than making sure her mission succeeded?

"Let's try something else," Sadie said gently. "Will you show me how you touch yourself?"

My cheeks reddened, though it felt a little silly being embarrassed when we were in my bed, when it seemed clear what tonight's activities at least vaguely held in store for us. Somehow, it still felt more intimate than anything that had happened so far between us.

"C'mon," she said, her crooked grin sliding across her face, reminding me this wasn't some girl I barely knew. This was *Sadie*. "Can you trust me?"

I didn't want to say no to her. So I wordlessly unbuttoned my pants, opened my nightstand drawer, and took out my vibrator. It was hard plastic and battery-operated, nothing fancy, but in the many years it had been part of my life, it'd always gotten the job done. Plus Sadie had a flip phone! She'd have to appreciate classic hardware.

I lied on my back and slipped the vibrator into my underwear before flicking on the power. I hadn't managed to make eye contact with Sadie, but I felt her next to me as I slid the buzzing cylinder up and down in slow movements. My underwear kept the hard length tight against me, and I was already so wet that I found I could increase my rhythm and pressure almost right away.

Sadie lay down at my side, and now it was impossible to forget she was here. She kissed me as I maintained stroking myself, and already I couldn't remember why I hadn't wanted to do this. My vibrator and I had never had this good of a time before.

"Can I?" she asked, her hand on top of my hand. I let go as an answer, and now it was Sadie in charge, Sadie's rhythm sliding back and forth against me as I rocked my hips upward with increasing need.

"You're so fucking sexy," she said, and I blushed again because no one had ever said those words about me before. Much less my dream girl in my bed next to me.

"How's this?" she asked, increasing her speed and pressure. I marveled that my body followed her instinctually, that when I let go I knew what to do.

"Everything you're doing is very good," I said, which made her laugh as her hand stroked faster still. I felt so full with— whatever the conclusion of longing was. I hadn't come yet but I already felt ripe with satisfaction. My hips matched Sadie's rhythm, and this time when I felt it coming, I didn't try to hold it off. I let the heat wash over me until it exploded into a glittering release.

"That was—" I stopped myself because Sadie was still going. "Did you notice that I—"

"Yeah, obviously I noticed," she said. "But I can be an over-achiever, and I want to hear that sound you make when you come again."

"Right now?" I sort of squeaked, and we both laughed.

"Right fucking now," she said. It seemed unlikely her goal would be achieved, but soon her lips were on my nipple again as she increased both her speed with the vibrator and its actual speed setting, and only a few moments later I felt it all go again, writhing against her as I came undone.

"Told you so," she said as I tried to breathe normally again, though it seemed a small price to pay if I never could.

"It's never been like that for me before," I admitted.

"Yeah, well, it's not always like that for me, either," she said. "I've had bad sex too. It's normal."

"For the record, though, that was not bad," I said, and she laughed.

"No, for the official record books, that was fucking great."

Her tone was teasing, but I knew it wasn't at my expense. Nothing about Sadie ever felt at anyone else's expense.

"Thank you," I said. "For making it really good for me."

"Well, sure," Sadie said. "It wasn't some kind of charitable act, though. Tonight's not exactly the first time I've thought about making you come."

"Seriously?"

She kissed me gently. "A sexy girl hangs out at my bar all the time, yeah, I have thoughts."

I kissed her in return, deeper and slower, and pulled myself on top of her. She was still fully dressed, though her nipples showed hard through her T-shirt. "What about you?"

I wasn't sure that I could push Sadie over the edge the way she had with me—twice! It wasn't only that she deserved to feel as good as I did in this moment; I was desperate for it. I wanted, very badly, to make Sadie come.

"What about me?" She raised her eyebrows in a manner that might pass for innocent if she hadn't just gotten me off *twice*. "What do you want to do with me?"

I moved aside so that I could slip her T-shirt over her head. She tugged off my unbuttoned pants and I followed by unbuttoning her Levi's and sliding them past her hips and the curve of her thighs. In the bar she'd been a vision, but lying in my bed in a sheer black bra and briefs and what felt like miles and miles of creamy soft skin, I practically felt like I might black out.

"What?" she asked me, lying back against my pillows. It was, somehow, all very casual. Also surreal.

"I can't believe you're here," I said, lying down next to her. "I mean, I'm really glad that you're here."

"I'm really glad I'm here too," she said, and kissed me softly like we were back at the start, like this night could go on forever.

I wondered if her words were true, if Sadie had actually thought of me as a sexy girl at her bar, if she'd ever thought of this and wanted it, too. But I could feel that I was getting into my head again, and that was the last place I wanted to be. Instead I kissed Sadie back, let the kisses melt into one another as I reminded myself that I was the person who'd walked into Johnny's and made the big move.

Sadie hitched her leg up and over my hip, and I grabbed her ass and let my hand drift down the curve of the back of her thigh, where her soft skin turned to goosebumps under my fingertips. We were still kissing, as if tonight we'd been the first two people to discover kissing and needed to chart a lot of new ground. Our hands, though, were restless, and I loved the push-pull we'd found, how I'd caress her side, the small of her back, her breasts once I'd unclasped her bra and eagerly tossed it aside, and then wordlessly it was Sadie's turn as her fingertips traced lines down my chest, my side, under the waistband of my briefs but not an inch further. There were so many reasons I was thrilled we were going slow right now, not least of which were the two orgasms that had already rocketed through my body, but deep down I knew that I wanted to savor this. I didn't know what tomorrow held for us; tonight needed to last.

"Max," Sadie murmured into my ear, shifting slightly so that I was on top of her. It was a mind-blowing move for a girl to use on me, as I felt every inch of my body pressed up against Sadie's bare skin. "Will you fuck me?"

"Yes, of course," I said, and she snorted at that.

"So polite," she said, pressing a soft kiss against my neck. "That's what I look for in this situation. Manners."

"That's like the only thing I can promise, Sadie," I said, and tried to keep my thoughts on track and not flown off to in-my-head world where the writing on the wall seemed to read that I'd always let girls down. And this was *Sadie*.

But, also, it was *Sadie*. The woman who listened to me and wanted to show me LA and believed I'd already succeeded despite plenty of evidence to the contrary. And I'd fantasized about this, of course, Sadie underneath me in my bed. I was ready for this, and tired of running scenarios in my head when it was time to live them instead.

I still wanted to savor everything, though, so I took my time, tracing lines across the low curve of her ass, right under the edge of her boy shorts. Her hips rocked up, seeking me, but I continued exploring. I licked down one collarbone, then the other, and as I kissed a trail from the base of her neck to her bellybutton, the only sounds in the entire world were Sadie's tiny moans of impatience. Me, I thought, finally stroking my fingers between her legs, over her damp underwear, as she groaned out something that sounded like *please*. I was the one she was ready—beyond ready—for.

I hooked my fingers through the sides of her underwear, playing with the elastic as I eased her underwear down, taking my time still. Her breath was ragged and, as I positioned myself on top of her again, urgent against my neck. I slipped my hand between her legs, overwhelmed by the intensity of her heat. Sadie eagerly wrapped her thighs around my hips, opening up to me, and I stroked her gently as her hips rolled with the rhythm of my hand, my arm, my breath. As our pace quickened, I nudged a finger into her entrance, warm and wet and velvet soft as I slid inside her. There was little I'd experienced in life that filled me with the gratitude and awe of making love to a woman. Even before, when it had been awkward, I'd still felt something sacred in it. Tonight, though, it was beyond divine.

Sadie shifted one of her thighs, moaning into my ear for *more*. I eased another finger inside of her, deeper at this new angle, and thumbed her clit as I thrust. While I was eager to make her come, I loved every single moment. I loved her hips grinding against mine, I loved her soft inner thighs pressed against my hips, and I loved her hands tugging my hair.

"I'm close," she said.

"Good," I said while maintaining my rhythm like I was an extremely cocky person who gave girls orgasms constantly. "I can't wait to watch you come, Sadie."

"Oh, *fuck*," she said, as her hips rocked up and she tightened around my fingers. "That was so hot, Max, jesus. I wasn't ready."

I marveled at what we'd just done together. If *kissing* seemed like something we'd just discovered tonight, this felt like a new invention altogether.

"Come here," she said, and soon I was lying next to her again. "What else do you want to do?"

"I'm really not great at talking about any of this," I told her. In my fantasies, we'd always just known what to do next. "Which I'm sure is something I should work on."

"Yeah, absolutely," Sadie said, grinning. "What about right now? Tell me what you want, Max."

"Oh, um, whatever you want to do is good with me," I said, as she slipped her hand into my briefs. "Like . . . this is great."

Sadie laughed. "Sure. I'd also like to go down on you, if that's something you'd be into."

I nodded so quickly that she laughed even harder.

"Tell me, then," she said, like a dare. *Be bold*, I thought, and nearly laughed at all the advice from You Point Oh that could double as advice in bed.

"Sadie, I would very much love for you to go down on me."

We worked together to get my underwear off as quickly as possible, and then Sadie's mouth was between my legs and my knees were thrown over her shoulders. And it turned out that asking for what I wanted had never turned out so good.

Chapter 20

Depleted Electrolytes & Other Effects

I woke up early the next morning and glanced over to see Sadie asleep beside me. It should have still felt unreal and other-worldly, but last night had been too good to write off as fantasy. Maybe that didn't make any sense, but I'd never had a fantasy as good as last night, the two of us in my bed. It was real, and it was *ours*.

Sadie stirred, and grinned before her eyes were even open. "Hey."

"Hi," I said.

I waited to feel something more—I wasn't sure exactly what. I'd finally had earth-shatteringly good sex. I'd fallen asleep naked wrapped in someone's arms. I felt safe and cozy and bound-to-reality in the best way possible. So why did I still feel exactly the same otherwise? Why did I still feel like I was supposed to make a big move?

"I should probably go," Sadie said. "Let you get to work and everything."

"It's Saturday," I said, which I hadn't meant as an invitation until I saw that Sadie took it as one. Before I knew it, I was under the covers with my hands on Sadie's breasts and my tongue tracing designs between her legs.

After Sadie insisted on reciprocity, we heard Chelsey making noise in the kitchen, and it seemed like a good time for Sadie to head out. I stayed in bed as Sadie got dressed in last night's clothes, and even though I was freshly post-orgasm again, I still felt the same. Shouldn't this have felt . . . I don't know, bigger? Different? *Something?*

"I guess we already fulfilled our off-the-grid activity for today," Sadie said with a grin. "I'll see you soon, Max."

"See you soon," I said, and it was as she let herself out of my bedroom that I felt just how wrong I'd been. The big move hadn't been *this*. The big move wasn't about mutual orgasms or fantasy scenarios come true and then some. The big move was supposed to be the truth: that I'd fallen hard for Sadie and wanted something real with her. That no matter what she thought about herself, I believed in her and everything I knew she was capable of. That even though other people disregarded me, I could feel how she never had. We were good for each other, because we saw what others couldn't. We could never fulfill our off-the-grid activities or finish exploring LA together, because all I wanted was more and more with her.

But I hadn't said any of that at all. I'd only said *see you soon.*

When I eventually slipped out of my bedroom, Chelsey looked up from her spot on the living room sofa and let out a squeal.

I jumped back. "Oh my god, *what happened?*"

"What do you mean, *what happened?*" Chelsey leapt to her feet. "You finally hooked up with the hot bartender!"

"Her name is Sadie," I said.

"Max! You did it! You made the big move!"

"Sure," I said, instead of, *No, I actually wimped out like anyone who's known me for more than this month could have guessed.*

"Huge success story," she said. "The team will be thrilled."

"I didn't do it for *the team*," I snapped.

"No, I'm sorry, of course you didn't," she said. "I didn't mean it specifically. I only meant that in thirty days, you did everything you set out to do. That's *amazing*."

"I need coffee and then I should probably get some fresh air," I said.

"Be sure to replenish your electrolytes," Chelsey said, settling back in on the sofa. "From what I overheard, yours are probably severely depleted."

"That's a weirdly dirty thing to tell your roommate," I said, and we both cracked up. "Can you look at my résumé for me when I get back? Joyce recommended me for this junior manager position, and I don't know if I want it, but—"

"Of course! And that's exciting. I heard managers have more fun than agents anyway."

I shrugged. "I mean, I'm not doing it to *have fun*."

"Sweet little Max, did you know you're allowed to want a job that you're good at *and* that's fun?"

I rolled my eyes, but maybe there was a small part of me that hadn't fully considered that possibility.

"You're going to nail this new job process," Chelsey continued. "Just as well as you nailed—"

"That is way more than enough from you," I said, but by the time I was off on my walk with my thermos of hot coffee, I felt a little less like a wimp. What did it matter if I hadn't told Sadie yet? I had plenty of time. You Point Oh didn't own me. I could make my big move whenever I wanted.

BBQ—who by now I knew was named Marisol, but BBQ had just really stuck—texted the team for another backyard hangout, and so after I spent the afternoon catching up on script coverage and switching outfits so I could film several days' worth of content for Chelsey, I headed over. BBQ and her wife Kristina had a cozy house tucked into the wild hills of Mount Washington, and when I walked up the driveway toward the sounds of conversation and Harry Styles, I gave myself a little moment to wonder if I could ever have something like this. There was something about last night and my potential career momentum that made a little house, someone to share it with, and a big loud group of queers to invite over on the weekend a little less impossible than it would have been before.

Our catcher, Val, aka The Wall, walked up from the opposite direction as I did, dressed in black joggers and a bright green crop top with their curly black hair free of the ponytail they wore for games and practices. Val wasn't much taller than I was, and it felt like magic seeing them in practice and in games playing such an important position. Sure, it was a noncompetitive league, so most of us were not really *athlete*-athletes, but I still appreciated every single aspect in which I was just ordinary here. I guess that was part of community I'd never even considered before.

"I heard from Paige and Megan you're doing some kind of influencer campaign," Val said as we walked around the side of the house to the back patio. "My day job is like a super boring digital marketing gig, so I'm really interested in how that's going."

I shrugged. "My roommate's the one doing all the deals and influencing. I guess I'm just benefiting. And like airing all my weird feelings for hundreds of thousands of people, something I probably should have considered way more before saying yes."

Maybe I should have changed how I discussed You Point Oh. After all, my thirty days were up, and I had a potential new job, new teammates-possibly-someday-friends, enough clothes that I could stop wearing my most faded shirts to work, and one perfect night with Sadie—with hopefully many more to follow. How embarrassing could it be to reveal my feelings in front of hundreds of thousands of followers when everything was going so well?

"Are y'all talking about Max's whole influencer thing?" Megan called to us in lieu of a greeting as we reached the patio. "Yeah, I need to hear as much as possible about it."

"I'm not sure it's that exciting," I said, even if—of course!— it was to me. I assumed my teammates knew how to advocate for themselves already, how to find community and noncompetitive sports, how to ask dream girls to go home with them. This stuff was big for me, but out of context I wasn't sure if it was the same.

"It's more exciting than hearing more about if Val is getting back together *again* with their ex or not," Tonya said, and it seemed like everyone—even Val—burst into laughter at the exact same moment. It wasn't only that perhaps it was true, it felt so shocking to hear Tonya being shady instead of bellowing motivational sayings about teamwork.

So I popped open a La Croix and managed to talk about You Point Oh and Chelsey without revealing too much about myself; and because conversation moved fast in this group, by the time BBQ was serving fancy Icelandic sausages off the grill, we'd already moved on to our chances for the playoffs (low) and Megan and her wife's chances of finding a sperm donor with all the criteria they were in search of (also low).

I knew there were scripts I could be reading, and I still hadn't really researched historic preservation as much as I should have, but it was tougher juggling this kind of life that I wanted than I'd expected. Still, as it felt like our afternoon hang was winding to a close, Tonya strongly suggested we should reconvene at a bar and, instead of saying goodbye, I very quickly advocated that that bar should be Johnny's.

As soon as I was driving over, though, I tried to figure out why I'd thought that was a good idea. Yes, obviously I couldn't

stop thinking about the night before, and any excuse to see
Sadie as soon as possible was an excuse I was going to take. But
I didn't even know what Sadie thought, and I had not helped
matters by first wimping out and then distracting myself with
Icelandic sausages and potential friendships instead of coming
up with what I'd say when I actually made the big move with
Sadie. And instead of doing something like making plans to
get coffee or take a walk or anything private, I was showing up
with teammates I didn't even know that well, probably also in
front of Billy, who seemed mildly suspicious of my intentions
on a good day. And he was right to be! My intentions were
more than worthy of suspicion.

Billy gave me a nod as I walked in. "Good to see you, Maxine. The usual?"

"Sure," I said, trying to glance around subtly.

"She's in the back," he said.

"Oh, I wasn't . . ." I waved as Paige and Tonya walked in and
tried to look nonchalant. "Just trying to figure out where to sit
because some people are joining me."

Billy shrugged and gestured toward the booths like *where
else.* I waited for my drink while Tonya examined the menu, if
you could even call it that, and raised their eyebrows.

"You sent us to a Comic Sans bar?"

"No, I've been here before," Paige said with a smile. "The
drinks are solid, despite the font choice."

As a few more of our teammates walked in, Sadie emerged
from the back carrying a rack of tumblers, and I felt my entire
group see her at the exact same time.

"I guess this is my favorite bar now too," Val muttered, and
everyone laughed, including me, until I made eye contact with
Sadie.

"Hey," she greeted me, her usual self, no sign at all that mere
hours ago she'd been in my bed. "I see Billy's got you handled.
Who else from the Kickballers needs a drink?"

"Wait, are we famous?" BBQ asked, which made us all laugh again. "I'm gonna say that sounds unlikely."

"Sadie was at our game the other week," I said instead of introducing anyone officially. It wasn't the right time to make some kind of big deal over anything. Not until I talked to Sadie one-on-one. Which I could do literally anytime! After the bar closed tonight, or tomorrow before practice, or tomorrow after practice. The future where Sadie understood exactly how I felt was so near. Maybe next time I brought the whole team by Johnny's I could introduce Sadie as my—well, we'd figure that out. *Girlfriend* seemed so serious, but it wasn't as if I wasn't serious. When it came to Sadie, I was serious as hell.

Once we had drinks, we crowded in and around the largest booth here, and I thought about Sadie's plans for this place and how it could become a much easier bar to hang out in if her dreams became reality.

"So what's going on there?" Paige asked me with a nod to Sadie. The rest of the group was discussing an episode of a podcast I didn't listen to, and I could feel that Paige had waited for a moment like this to start the conversation.

"Um," I said, and then didn't know where to go with it, so that was all I said.

"It's fine, you know, you and I went on *one date*," Paige said with a laugh.

"Oh, no, it's not because of that," I said. "Maybe it should have been, would that have been more polite? I only mean that I don't know, and it's complicated, and also it involves me getting up the nerve to say all my feelings, which is not always my forte."

"What about all that saying yes and being bold?" Paige asked, and we both laughed.

"Right? That's how I got here. I guess literally. There's still a lot left, though." I watched Sadie waiting on a guy around Billy's age who was sitting alone and could tell even without hearing them how engaged they were in conversation. I loved that about her, the way anyone could feel welcomed by her presence.

"Saying things is hard," Paige said, and I looked back to her and laughed. "What? It *is*. Like I said, there's a reason all your videos with Chelsey are so relatable, Max. You think you're the only one who doesn't know how to say the right things to girls? Come *on*."

"You're way less awkward than I am," I said, and she covered her face.

"Let me tell you about my conversations with the cute person who works the desk in the lobby of my office building and you can tell me if you actually still think I'm less awkward," she said.

By the time Paige had finished her tales and I was halfway-ish through the Sadie Saga, we were both out of drinks, so I slipped out of the booth and headed back up to the bar. Sadie was organizing everything on the counter, but she nodded to Billy as I walked up and headed to the back. I guess I had more awkwardness to report to Paige, like breaking news.

"Maxine, another?" he asked, and I nodded. "And for your lovely companion over there?"

"She's more like my lovely teammate, but, a Negroni." I looked back toward Paige and then spun around as if I could see into the back room if I only stared hard enough. "Billy, can you make sure Sadie knows that's my teammate, not my— never mind, ignore me."

"I never ignore a regular customer," he said, and I could see that a smile was fighting its best to shine through as he mixed the two cocktails. "But I've always done my best to stay out of other people's business. When I was younger I had enough of my own to contend with, and now I enjoy having none of it at all to worry about."

"That sounds ideal," I said, and he chuckled.

"Enjoy it while you've got it, Maxine. Even when it's hard, it goes really fast." He set our drinks on the counter and started walking away. "Take 'em on the house."

"Wait, really?" I asked.

"Yeah, don't make too big of a deal about it," he said, "or I'll change my mind."

I grinned as I carried my drinks back, and tried to quietly fill in Paige even more on whatever was happening, but I guess the rest of the team was finished talking about *Normal Gossip* or *To L and Back* and were now trying to listen in.

"Do you want my advice?" asked Tonya, who'd only heard the last sentence or two, which was greeted immediately by a boothful of laughter.

"Your confidence is always something to be admired," BBQ said. "Y'all, this has been great, and as much as I want to dive in more on the disastrous love lives of all the single people on the team, I should probably get back to my wife and help clean up from this afternoon."

It was like the seal was broken, and most of the team headed out behind Tonya. I hugged everyone goodbye but lingered near the bar. Sadie was busy with a few regulars I recognized, so I tried to look casual, even though I remembered that Paige once said I wasn't capable of holding a neutral expression.

My phone buzzed, and I glanced down at it. A new message from *Sadie Bartender*, who'd disappeared into the back again.

billy and i r both here until closing tonight. what r u doing afterward?

I felt my face flush before I fully even thought it, and I started typing before I dwelled on it for too long. **You?**

It took a while for a response to come through, and I reminded myself that it was apparently labor-intensive to text on a flip phone. Plus there were no texting dots letting me know it was happening. I really didn't understand how people hooked up before iPhones.

great answer. c u l8r.

It was embarrassing that *l8r* was now, apparently, something that could turn me on.

Sadie arrived later than I expected, and I'd dozed off before hearing the *ping* of my watch and phone letting me know she'd messaged. I tried to play it off when I ran down to let her in, but she eyed me as we walked into my room and I closed the door behind us.

"You were sleeping," she said.

"I'm up now," I said, sliding my arms around her waist, finding that perfect gap between her T-shirt and jeans so I could touch her silky skin.

"The reality of a bartender's schedule is terrible, I know," she said with a sigh, and I pulled her even closer.

"Nothing about you is terrible," I said. "Don't put words in my mouth."

"Yeah? What about . . ." Sadie leaned down to press her lips against mine, and I felt dizzy as the kiss went on, deepened, pulled me into some kind of orbit alongside her.

"Even with the height difference," Sadie said, grabbing me by my hips and slowly turning me so that she was pressed up against me from behind, "maybe we were too fast to rule out standing last night."

"Don't come at me if you get some kind of neck cramp," I said, and Sadie chuckled as she slid a hand into my shirt.

"I'll take my chances," she said, and dragged her lips down my neck as her other hand worked at unbuttoning my jeans. Sadie had *moves* and I loved that, even if I myself had no moves to speak of. What did I need moves for if she had them all?

Her fingertips dipped lower. I gasped and arched back into

her as she stroked me slowly. Her other hand was still on my breast, and her lips found their way back to my neck as she kept up a slow rhythm.

"Sadie," I said, reaching back to grasp her shoulder as my knees, I realized, literally felt weak. "I'm not—if I don't—"

"I've got you," she murmured, though we stayed right there, waves threatening to knock me over as Sadie's hand moved faster and I pressed back against her. Everything felt near collapse as my hips rolled with her movement and nothing short of an electrical current built within me. Somehow I was still standing when the charge blew, and I collapsed back against Sadie even as I still shook from the force of my orgasm.

"Told you I had you," she said, kissing my cheek gently. "You good?"

"I'm like literally seeing stars." I realized I hadn't fully caught my breath yet. "Oh my *god*. I've never . . ."

"God, I love watching you," she murmured, and I couldn't figure out what I liked more, that she felt that way or her use of the word *love*. "You're so determined not to give up control and then—"

"I'm not determined," I said. "Just bad at it, maybe."

"—it takes you over anyway."

"*You* take me over," I said, and worried for a split second it was too much, too intimate, but Sadie gently took my shoulders and pulled me so that we were facing each other again.

"It seems pretty mutual to me," she said, and I kissed her before she'd even finished talking, kissed her for saying exactly what I needed to hear, kissed her because I loved the person she was.

"I'd like to return the favor," I told her, "keep it completely mutual and all, but I need a minute first."

"No problem, I can wait," Sadie said, walking toward my bed while she pulled her T-shirt off over her head. I watched as she stepped out of her jeans, and for just a split second it was

like a scene from a dream and not my real life. The last thirty or
so days felt a little like I'd started writing fanfic about myself.

"What are you thinking?" Sadie asked, reaching both arms
behind her back to unclasp her bra, then letting it go.

"That you're like a dream," I admitted.

She raised an eyebrow. "Want me to pinch you?"

I stepped toward her and pushed her back on my bed. "I had
something else in mind."

Chapter 21

Going, Going, Gone (Viral)

It hit me when I woke up on Sunday morning that I'd forgotten again to actually talk to Sadie, because it turned out that sex was very distracting. And very fun. And very mind-blowing. Before, the word that came to mind about all of my sexual experience would have been *fumbling*, but now—

I still fumbled, was the thing. It just didn't feel like a test now. Not that I'd thought of it that way before, not exactly, but I'd always noticed the moments that hadn't felt smooth, suave, skilled. Last night, when Sadie asked, with purpose in her voice, about the strap-on she'd spotted in my nightstand drawer, I flashed back to an awkward night with Daniela, not long before she broke up with me, the purchase freshly arrived from the internet but my confidence wavering. My first reaction had been to convince Sadie she'd imagined it. *Really*, she'd said with a laugh, *you're telling me I imagined a dick in your drawer.* And then before long she was in my lap facing me, swiveling her hips in a slow figure-eight as I watched in grateful awe.

Sex being—well, *great* was obviously something plenty of people knew. But everything felt new with Sadie. Actually, everything felt *expected*—like I'd always hoped for, the way songs and steamy romance novels and fanfic made it all seem. Brand-new and wishes-granted at the same time.

"Good morning," Sadie murmured. "Is it Sunday? You're off work?"

"I like how you're so off-the-grid you don't know what day it is," I said. "Yeah, it's Sunday. I have practice in a while but that's it."

"We could walk down to All Day Baby for biscuits," Sadie said. "I mean, if you wanted. Low pressure suggestion."

I picked up my phone to keep myself from shouting *yes!* too quickly, but that impulse faded immediately. My screen was a mess of notifications, the way it only was once a year, on my birthday. Was it my birthday? Could sex distract you from that? No, my birthday was eight months away.

"Everything OK over there?" Sadie asked, running her fingertips down my arm. I wanted to throw my phone aside and focus only on her, but panic pulsed within my heartbeat that something bad had happened. There was nothing good that could account for that lit-up screen.

OMG FINALLY read a text from Nina. **Drinks and details soon?**

I knew something was up, Tonya had texted. **There are no secrets in the world of noncompetitive kickball, Weapon.**

I even had a work Slack notification, a new DM from Javier. **Here I was worrying your big move was somehow going to swoop in and steal the next promotion opportunity away from me, when you were just trying to nail some girl. Well-played, Van Doren.**

"So I guess that's a no to biscuits?" Sadie asked, a note of edge in her voice.

"I just—" I stopped myself because I didn't know how to finish the sentence I'd started. *I just need a minute to figure out how apparently everyone knows we slept together?*

"Got it," she said, standing up and picking up her clothes from the floor. I desperately wanted to stop her; a post-Saturday-night-sex Sunday morning of brunch with Sadie was the kind of thing I'd dreamt about. Relationship behavior. The future I wanted with her.

"No, I just have to—"

My phone buzzed three more times in my hand, and I could tell that Sadie could tell.

"All right," Sadie said, checking herself in my mirror. "Get back to it. I'll see you soon?"

"Yeah," I said, just wanting to see who the newest messages were from, but when I looked back up, she was already gone.

I was hardly relieved—in fact, I was the exact opposite of *relieved*—but there was a certain freedom without Sadie in the room. With the full ability to browse all of my apps, it didn't take long to find the source.

"Hi, y'all," Chelsey addressed the internet in a new video she'd uploaded this morning but had clearly, based on her outfit, filmed yesterday. "As you know, I've been loving these new Good Smoorning smoothies from Smoothie Moves, so I got super excited when I found out they were adding mango and dragon fruit versions. I thought I'd try out dragon fruit for y'all today, so let's find out—"

As Chelsey had reached for the patented Smoothie Moves biodegradable pouch, Sadie was clearly visible through the doorway over Chelsey's shoulder for more than a split second before she walked out of the apartment. I cursed the filmmaking standards of the latest iPhone, because the image was plainly clear that it was Sadie.

On the screen, Chelsey glanced back. A huge grin spread across her face as she turned back to camera. "We're all aware Max received the *MAKE THE BIG MOVE* task yesterday." Her grin intensified into something I might associate with *villain origin story*. "As Max's roommate, I know that she's been fixated on hooking up with this bartender, so I'm glad to see that—thanks to You Point Oh—that goal has finally been achieved. Way to make the big move, Max."

I started to charge out my door, but I was still naked and did not feel that would be the best way to confront anyone. But by the time I was in my sweats and down the hallway, I realized Chelsey was nowhere to be found. Which was probably lucky because while I'd never thought of myself as a violent person, at the moment I felt a little like dabbling in some light murder.

Where are you??? I texted. You know I wanted to keep the specifics of my actual life private. I cannot believe you posted that video and said what you said. I need you to delete ASAP!!!

I stared at my phone, willing Chelsey to respond, waiting desperately for the three dots to appear. But there was nothing.

I ignored every message I'd received and finally hopped in the shower to force myself away from my phone. If staring at it yielded results, after all, Chelsey would have already responded. The video would already be down. A watched pot, etc.

By the time I was out of the shower, dried off and dressed in my clothes for practice, Chelsey had texted back.

OK hear me out. I knew you would initially freak out, but I thought about this, and how the very best thing about the You Point Oh campaign has been how relatable you are. And what's more relatable than pining after some girl? So here you are GETTING THE GIRL! Perfect ending. Who wouldn't sign up for the app after seeing that? You should feel good about this, Max! Between this and the new job you're going to land any day now, this has been a way bigger success story than probably anyone dreamed! The client is going to be so thrilled.

A chill shook through me, as a sort of amorphous blob of dread sharpened into something more specific. It had been gen-uinely *great* to spend so much more time with Chelsey this past month. I liked her, and I liked her and Ava together, and I liked her group of friends who, sure, were objectively cooler than me but had never gone out of their way to actually make me feel like it. But like most of this past month, it had all had the tinge of *too good to be true*.

The client?? I texted. You know I didn't want it to get too personal. This was SUPER PERSONAL, Chelsey.

Yeah, exactly! Personal = relatable

I couldn't believe that I'd gotten sucked into it. Why had I been so sure about who Chelsey was and then so ready to throw that whole idea away once this You Point Oh thing was underway? She wasn't my friend, I was just the loser she could manipulate for her client, and it had been embarrassingly foolish for me to think otherwise.

Chelsey, I am serious. I need you to take it down. I have done enough for you and the client. You don't get Sadie, too.

Every single moment that passed contained the potential for countless more people to see it. My friends, my teammates, my coworkers. Thank god for Sadie and her flip phone, though I knew she wasn't actually fully off-the-grid. She had friends, she had a computer, she was hardly cut off from society. And the longer she was available on people's screens, leaving my bedroom, the bigger the chances were that she'd see it.

I really think you're overreacting and missing the whole point, but, fine. It's down. I'm at Loupiotte for brunch btw if you wanna join!

I thanked her for deleting, declined the brunch offer, and realized I had no idea what I was supposed to do next. The damage, luckily, couldn't spread further, but there was no doubt that it had happened. Kickball had become something steady and good in my life that didn't hinge on work or romance—even when things had been awkward with Paige—but the group chat was light on practice chat and extremely heavy on chat about *me*.

Yes, I'd actually dreamed of having a group of friends where we discussed our love lives and gossiped—politely—about each other. The Kickballers were turning into something I'd wanted for a very long time. But I'd never wanted it like this—out of my control and without the knowledge of the other person involved.

I could have been out, right now, across from Sadie, devouring breakfast and confessing my feelings. No, I didn't know how she'd react, but it would have been a move forward; it would have been all the things You Point Oh asked of me.

My stomach clenched, though, thinking about the app. While it had been fun to be a part of something—and obviously I'd needed help—I hated that I'd fallen under Chelsey's spell. Even if my goals had been deeply personal, I should have worked harder to set up boundaries. I should have remembered that Chelsey was an influencer first, a roommate second, and potentially a friend not-at-all.

Still, I made myself a stupid smoothie because I genuinely liked them, brewed a fancy cup of coffee because of course it tasted better, and tried to calm down before I left for practice. As soon as I walked toward my team gathered at the park in our usual spot, though, I felt their eyes on me only seconds before I heard their cheers and applause.

"Can we . . . not?" I asked.

"I told everyone yesterday something was up with you two," Tonya said.

"Oh yeah, it took a real detective to crack that case," Megan said with a laugh.

"Seriously," I said, and the stress was making my voice squeak more than usual. I imagined a tiny mouse negotiating her own privacy and didn't particularly find her convincing. "There are things about my life that are private, even if my roommate doesn't understand that."

"Got it," Paige said in a tone so stern that even Tonya looked chastised. "You OK, Max?"

I shrugged. "Can we just run drills or whatever? Whatever's most distracting?"

"You heard her," Tonya said. "BBQ, what's our most distracting drill?"

I turned to Paige as BBQ and Tonya debated the medicine ball pass versus intervals. "Thank you."

"Your roommate seems chaotic," she said. "It made me very glad to live alone where no one can film people leaving my bedroom."

I raised an eyebrow, and we both burst into laughter.

"There's not that many people! Maybe that's the more embarrassing part, the lack of exit traffic down the hallway."

"I think it's all embarrassing," I said. "I mean, not *embarrassing*. Just *private*."

Tonya yelled at us to start running intervals, and I let the physical activity take over. By the time we were in modified formation to play on two teams of five, I could feel that my panic hadn't just gotten buried amidst drills and conversation. If I could get my teammates off my back as easily as things had gone this morning with them, all things considered, I knew that the rest shouldn't be too difficult. Javier would get in a few more shady DMs, Nina would beg for more details but ultimately be kind and respectful, and then . . . that was really it. With the video down, I felt less and less that Sadie seeing it was some kind of real possibility. Even if someone she knew had caught a glimpse of it, there was no longer proof it had actually happened.

The team was heading to Little Barn for brunch, but today it sounded better to say goodbye and head back home alone. Paige walked with me to my car and nodded toward the rest of the team. "Everyone means well. They're just happy for you, in their own very loud and not-private ways."

"No, totally, I get it."

"If you want company, we could just grab a cheap lunch somewhere and talk. There's at least seven embarrassing details about Sloan I didn't tell you yesterday."

"Wait, their name is Sloan? That sounds really hot, honestly." I laughed and shook my head. "I'm OK. I think I need introvert time or whatever."

"Got it. Text me if you change your mind. I'm just going to be working on a craft project and catching up on my podcast listening."

My phone, which had quieted down *substantially* since Chelsey took down the video, buzzed in my hand. If it had been anyone else but Paige, I would have tried to hide it, but I trusted she'd be quiet even upon seeing *Sadie Bartender*.

"Do you not know her last name?" Paige asked. "Or is she, like, of the New England Bartenders?"

"See, every time you think you're going to out-awkward me, I always win." I tapped on her message. **I know ur busy 2day but can u stop by Johnnys**

"Everything OK?" Paige asked lightly.

"Um, maybe? I have no idea. But thank you for checking, and being nice, and everything else."

"We're friends, Max, what else would I do?" She grinned and punched me lightly on the shoulder like we were actually athletes and not adults playing a child's game. "Talk soon."

I drove home with my loudest playlist blaring and walked right to Johnny's even though they weren't open for hours and I was still wearing my sweaty kickball gear. It was easy to worry that this was about the video, but wouldn't Sadie have just asked about that? Or would she? The flip phone, I knew, wasn't conducive to nuanced conversations.

This morning hadn't been *good*, though. The memory settled on me that Sadie had asked for more time together and I'd stared at my phone instead of being honored and grateful for the offer. After all her talk about getting me off-the-grid, I couldn't believe I'd behaved that way. After the nights we'd shared together and the intimacy of everything that had happened in my bedroom, I didn't understand how I hadn't prioritized her even with a phone full of messages. The goal had been to lay out all my feelings for her, and instead I'd acted like—

I didn't want to dwell on how I'd acted. I wanted to be there for anything Sadie needed, and then finally have that conversation so that I couldn't screw up again. I was finally ready.

Just as I was about to get out my phone to text Sadie that I was there, the door opened.

"Hey," Sadie greeted me. She was still in her clothes from last night, faded black jeans and a heather-gray muscle shirt. Perfect classic Sadie.

"Hi," I said, wondering if we were at the stage where, as long as we were alone, I could kiss her as a greeting. From Sadie's expression, the answer was *no*.

"Come on in." She stepped aside and then locked the door behind me. "Max, what do you think we're doing?"

"Um . . ." I searched her face as if the right answer was hidden there. Her eyes, which normally looked back at me with so much openness and curiosity, seemed as closed off as Johnny's was right now.

"I know we haven't defined anything, and I know . . ." Sadie shrugged. "I'm messy. I do messy shit. I told you we shouldn't be anything other than friends when we both knew I was full of shit. I'm acknowledging all of that so that I don't seem like a hypocrite when I tell you that whatever you're doing is *fucked up*."

"You saw the video," I said.

"Yeah, I saw the video." She crossed her arms over her chest. "Apparently everyone I know follows your roommate on Tik-Tok or whatever."

"She's annoyingly successful," I said. "But—"

"You know, I don't actually care that people know I spent the night with a hot girl," Sadie said, and I knew that it was inappropriate within this moment but I felt buoyed by *a hot girl*. "Not like I love sharing my business with everyone, but, whatever. I'd get over it."

"But I should have told you," I said. "I'm sorry. I got all these notifications and—my brain jammed or something. I just didn't want to explain about Chelsey and her whole deal and—I should have just told you the truth which was that I wanted to get biscuit sandwiches with you at All Day Baby and also—"

"I don't give a shit about biscuit sandwiches," Sadie said. "And I don't give a shit about the video. Here's where I am, Max. I thought I had become friends with someone I liked on this level . . . fuck! I liked you so much. I liked how you listened to me and were really encouraging, even though you were so much further along in life. You never made me feel like shit about all the stuff people tended to make me feel like shit about. And I was good at ignoring how attracted I was to you, until you knocked that all down and—god, I just feel really stupid now. Because this whole time you were, what? Doing some app challenge? Like get ten-thousand steps and fuck a bartender?"

"Sadie, *no*," I said, as a chill enveloped me. "It wasn't like that at all."

"Then tell me what it was like, Max. Because from where I'm standing, it looks really fucking bad."

"I *liked* you," I said, rushing to make all the points from the speech I should have already given. "I've had a crush on you since the first time I came to Johnny's. And the more I get to know you—Sadie, you're like my dream girl. You're so good with people and how you make everyone feel welcome here. And I know people have been terrible to you in the past but I don't get it because you're *great* as you are and you've got so much to offer and—Sadie, being in LA, it hasn't felt like home to me, not how I thought it would. But when I'm here, when I'm around you—"

Her arms were still crossed, and her eyes were still cold. It was as if all the things I loved about Sadie were locked away from me.

"Don't," Sadie said.

"But it's true," I said. "I'm sorry, I'm bad at saying things, and this weekend—"

"I mean it," she said, her voice sharper than I'd ever heard it. "*Don't.* I feel like an idiot that I thought that maybe you *weren't* like the other girls. Like, yeah, they only believed in me up to a point, couldn't imagine settling down with someone who hadn't gone to college or law school like she'd originally planned a million years ago. But you just pretended, which is so much worse. At least they were upfront that I wasn't good enough for them."

"Sadie," I said, bursting into tears, "what are you *talking* about? You're one of the most incredible people I've ever met. I should have said sooner what I felt, which is that I think I'm in love with you, and I want to be your girlfriend and help you achieve all of your goals. Ever since I met you . . ."

"Ever since you met me, *what*?" She wiped her eyes with the back of her hand. "I should have known this wasn't real. All the time you've spent here, swiping through apps, hitting on other girls right in front of me. I spent all this time thinking you weren't interested, and then—"

"But I was. I *am*." I cried harder because I couldn't have felt more stupid, and I thought about the dating coach telling me not to treat dating apps like Candy Crush, and how if I'd gotten that advice sooner—well, it wouldn't fully have helped me here, but maybe I wouldn't seem like such a thoughtless asshole. "For so long I thought you were so out of my league, that you were cute and nice to me because you're good at your job. I didn't want to be like one of those gross men who think all waitresses are into them."

"I don't know how you could say something like that after the time we've spent together," she said, turning away from me, though of course I could tell she was crying more by now. All I wanted to do was wrap my arms around her until she felt better, which was the dumbest thought possible.

"I'm bad at stuff, Sadie, but you have to believe me that—"

"I don't *have to* do anything," she said. "Get on with your whole high-achiever life, Max. I'm sure there's someone out there with an MBA who's already all self-actualized you can check off your serious girlfriend app goal list."

"I don't want a girlfriend with an MBA," I said. "I want you. The thing with the app—the whole thing was that I was supposed to get serious about who and what I actually wanted. And even though I got all this advice on how to use dating apps or whatever, the only thing that kept coming to mind was you. Also I'm not a high-achiever or whatever you think! I'm an assistant who barely makes enough money to live here and I'm only starting to have friends and a life and—"

"I get that you have an excuse for everything," Sadie said. "It's just fucking hard to believe you."

I felt myself reel back from that, because there was plenty I didn't like about myself, and there was plenty more that others counted as strikes against me. A timid, weak-willed mouse who'd never be taken seriously. My honesty and integrity, though—those had never come into question.

Sadie stepped past me and opened the door. "You should go."

"I really think if we could just talk more and—"

"You had so many chances to talk to me, Max," she said softly. "It's way too late to start now."

I walked past her and waited outside for a moment, then two, and then ten. But she didn't change her mind and come after me. The door stayed locked between us.

Chapter 22

A Canine Double Date

I was never so happy to get to work early as I was the next morning after lying awake all night. Here, at least, I had something to do other than replay yesterday's conversation with Sadie over and over and over again. Here there was an infinitely refreshing inbox and a boss with calls to roll including a request to *Get that guy with the terrible glasses who works at that new streamer startup* and an office lunch to have catered. Aidy wanted help knowing which "bougie candle" (her phrasing and not mine) to send to a *Euphoria* actress her boss was determined to steal from CAA. Javier DM'd me about You Point Oh and Sadie.

And, even without sleep, I did it all. I maintained my inbox zero-email management. I connected every call Joyce asked for including Len Morrow at Waffle Watches (whose neon orange glasses were fine in my opinion). I ordered a selection from Wally's and got myself a salad as Joyce offered (and I hoped by lunchtime tomorrow I'd be in a salad mood). I knew the bougie candle answer for people under thirty was usually the D.S. & Durga Big Sur After Rain candle (though I wasn't sure that alone was enough to make anyone reconsider her representation). I got Javier's messages off my screen (by uploading a dump of extremely stupid memes I'd saved on my phone until his questions were far enough back I'd have to scroll up to see them).

That was all stuff I could handle. There were right answers and I had them all. During a brief moment of afternoon downtime, I skipped lunch and instead finalized my résumé revision and sent it along to Riley Howe along with what I was certain was a very strong cover letter. Right now I felt like I had very little left except work and the possibility of a bigger career path.

Not that I felt *great* as I hit *send* on that email. Sadie misunderstood, obviously. I didn't want her to be anything she wasn't—but I knew my ambitions were impossible to ignore, not after You Point Oh at least. Now I had Aidy and Javier showing up early to compete with me, a boss who was letting me in on more, and of course a potential new job a couple of rungs up the career ladder. That was all for *me*, though. I wanted my dumb Hollywood job and I wanted Sadie running Johnny's exactly as she wanted. And I wanted kickball and friends and a bunch of things that had nothing to do with money or careers. I wanted to travel to places that weren't Kentucky or here and I wanted someone to see those places with me. I wanted coming home at the end of the night to be the best part, and I wanted to be coming home to someone.

And of course I wanted that someone to be Sadie.

I could know all of that, though, and still hate what Sadie thought and why she thought it. It couldn't be worse timing to try to make some career power move after Sadie's accusations. But Chelsey—who'd been at Ava's since yesterday—and her stupid video had screwed that up for me.

Something rattled around in me that Chelsey was not purely to blame, but without her video, I could have gotten it together. I would have gone to breakfast with Sadie and I would have said something, and today we'd—well, now it seemed silly and too-easy that we'd be in a relationship, that she'd be my girl-friend and me hers, but—

Joyce's line rang, and I grabbed it quickly when I saw that it was Tess. Those calls usually went in the other direction and were often coordinated by assistants and managers, so I was on high alert on the rare occasions it happened.

"Joyce Harris's office, Max speaking," I answered.

"Max, hi, how are you? It's Tess Gardner," she added, even though of course she knew that I already knew it was her. Joyce was savvy about only working with non-asshole clients, so we didn't get much *don't you know who I am*-ing—at least from the talent. (Executives, et al, were another story.)

"Hi," I said. I had not yet decided if it was more appropriate to call her Tess or Ms. Gardner so leaving out her name entirely seemed like the wisest move. "Let me connect you with Joyce."

"Wonderful. By the way, I wanted to send along my appreciation to you. Joyce told me that you two talked out the whole *The Westinghouse Gambit* versus *The Only One* situation, and I was really glad to know you'd been part of that talk. I'm only about a thousand years old—"

I knew that Tess was only eight years older than I was.

"—and so is most of my team. So it's good knowing someone your age has weighed in. The decision was definitely tougher for me than I know Joyce thinks that it should have been, so it was just really helpful knowing your input was involved."

"Oh, I'm really glad to hear that," I said. "I just thought *The Only One* was such a beautiful script. I read so many and, like, lots of things are good, but I thought it was *great*. It moved me so much."

"Yes," Tess said. "I thought so too."

"*The Westinghouse Gambit* is a cool opportunity, I know," I continued, even though I should have just put Tess through to Joyce. It was so rare I got to have conversations like this, and I knew that if I got the Spring Hope job I'd be having so many more of them—though probably not at this A-list level. "*The

Only One is just so fresh and modern. Sorry, I'm rambling. I turn into such a nerd over projects I'm excited about."

"Oh, please," Tess said. "I'm exactly the same way. Once a theater kid, always a theater kid."

"I know people think Sorensen is really good," I said. "I guess I just feel like his time is . . ."

"Already passed?" Tess asked, a smile in her voice. "Yes, I know what you mean. I won't make you say it. I really appreciate your candor, Max. It can be hard to come by in this business."

"Oh yeah, of course!" I said. "Let me put you through to Joyce. It was nice chatting with you."

I let Joyce know that Tess was on the line and got back to my inbox. My mood was, sadly, slightly lifted by a few minutes on the phone with a beautiful actress. I got back to work and had just about everything filed when my intercom buzzed.

"Max, could you please come here?"

Joyce's tone sounded sharp, but I was also running on no sleep and a pile of heartbreak, so I told myself that I was imagining it and forced myself to walk calmly to her office.

Joyce's eyes were on her computer monitor, and she didn't look up as I stepped in. "Close the door behind you."

Yikes.

"Max," she said, as soon as the door was shut, in the calmest of tones, "did you tell Tess Gardner that Eric Sorensen's work is passé?"

"Not . . . exactly." I wasn't seated, and it felt strange having this conversation sort of hovering. Not that I thought it was a good moment to sit down across from Joyce. "Tess said—"

"I understand that you're looking to make some kind of move here or elsewhere," Joyce said, her tone still chillingly calm. "And I know that you had strong feelings for the other script. But I cannot imagine what got into you that you thought you should say such a thing directly to the talent."

"I didn't," I said, as my heart beat so quickly I wondered if I was having some kind of attack. "Joyce, I *wouldn't.*"

"Are you suggesting that Tess lied?"

"No, definitely not, Tess is one of the nicest clients here and—what I mean is, Tess thanked me for sharing my feelings about the two scripts with you, which she said you passed on. So I thought she already knew."

Joyce sighed loudly. "No, Max, I did not tell one of my highest grossing clients that my assistant thought she should take the lower profile script that'll make her substantially less income. Tess has this idea that she needed the POV of a younger person on her team, so I said that you and I had talked out the pros and cons of both scripts. And I stressed that, despite the obvious strengths of *The Only One*, it made the most sense to move forward with the Sorensen script."

"Oh," I said, feeling heat in my face, the back of my neck, my chest. "Joyce, I'm so sorry, I misunderstood what she meant. I promise that I *never* would have said something otherwise."

"You're normally so cautious," Joyce said. "It's something I've always valued in your work and your outlook here. And, again, I understand that you're gunning for a promotion, but this isn't how to do it."

"I swear it wasn't about that," I said. "I just thought that Tess already knew."

She sighed again. "Well, regardless, this puts us all in a tough position. We've already started the process for signing for this film, and now Tess seems ready to pull out. Which won't look great for anyone."

"No," I said softly. "I really am sorry. If there's anything I can do—"

"I think you've done enough on this matter as it is," Joyce said.

I wanted to ask if I was about to be fired, but I also was afraid to put the idea in Joyce's head, if she wasn't already thinking it. Also it seemed statistically improbable that my roommate could humiliate me on social media, my whatever-Sadie-was could end things with me before they were fully started, *and* my boss could fire me, in about forty-eight hours. But maybe that's what was happening. Everything awful all at once.

Back at my desk I kept focused on all my tasks and tried not to think of all the worst possibilities. My watch dinged a few times, and I assumed something else embarrassing or private had somehow gone viral. It was only Paige and Nina, both checking in on me. Despite—well, *everything*—a warm feeling swirled in me, that this was what it was like to have friends. Which was a silly thing, maybe, to be twenty-six and just realizing it, but before recently it just hadn't worked out that way for me. Honestly, it was good timing that now it was.

Nina asked if I wanted to go out for drinks after work, and considering my other option was to go home and wait to yell at Chelsey, I decided going out was a better option. *Anywhere but Johnny's, but yes!*

So after work—where I miraculously still had a job, at least for now—I headed to Bar Stella, which was only a few blocks from my place—and Johnny's, of course—but it basically existed in another stratosphere. I knew from scheduling drinks meetings for Joyce that this was a place that talent—even A-list names—could drink in peace. It wasn't just the inherent understanding of Los Angeles to leave its best and brightest stars alone. This was a place where extremely attractive people hung out, and the talent just . . . kind of blended in.

Nina had texted me that she was out on the patio, so I walked directly there upon entering. She jumped up to hug me, and it hit me how much I needed a hug today.

"How's everything?" she asked, settling back into her chair. Her brown hair looked freshly blown-out, and her emerald-green dress made her brown eyes glow.

I took a deep breath. There was so much to cover, and it was all the worst! "Oh, actually it's—"

"I'm so sorry, I have a surprise for you, and she's here earlier than I expected," Nina said, and I watched as Ari Fox, walking a brown and white dog, walked over to us and pulled me out of my seat before I could react to any of it.

"Hey, Max," she said, giving me a tight hug. "It's been way too long."

Ari wasn't just Nina's girlfriend; she was one of Joyce's clients. It was a little embarrassing to look back on it now, but when I'd first started working for Joyce, I'd considered it a good omen when I saw Ari's name on her roster. Ari had been out her entire career, playing gay onscreen when I was still scared to play gay in real life. She was the most famous person at that time who looked how I wanted to look someday—I mean, way hotter, but still. Back when I was desperate for an adulthood when I could truly be myself, Ari Fox had been some kind of guiding light.

And now she was a friend's girlfriend. Because it turned out that was what Hollywood was actually like, a very small town in the second-biggest city in the country.

"Why aren't you reacting?" Nina asked. "We got a dog!"

"Nina Rice," Ari said, her tone somewhere between adoring and exasperated.

"I'm sorry I didn't acknowledge your dog," I said. "So the app finally worked out?"

"Actually, no," Ari said, kneeling down to pet the dog, who looked like some kind of border collie mix. "Our friend owns a dog grooming shop and has all this access to dog stuff in LA. She found out about this girl who needed a home and texted us right away."

"She's really cute," I said, as the dog stepped forward and licked my face. "Wait, sitting down am I the same height as a dog?"

"Is that bad?" Ari asked, and we all cracked up. "Let me get everyone drinks. Max, what's your poison?"

I loved that extremely hot people could say things like *what's your poison* and it was charming instead of cringe-inducing. "I don't know, I'm in a weird place. Something like a Paloma but not a Paloma?"

"Got it," Ari said as if that was a standard request. "Babe, should I surprise you?"

Nina beamed. "Please. And Max, go with Ari to help carry the drinks, and also because the hot bartender's working tonight. Give me Cristina's leash."

"I think I've had enough of hot bartenders—wait, your dog is named Cristina?"

"Yeah, her full name is Dr. Cristina Yang," Ari said, and we were all laughing again. I couldn't believe my life could be *this bad* right now and yet I could still feel so safe here on this hot-person patio with my friend and her Academy Award–winning girlfriend. "Well, Dr. Cristina Yang Fox-Rice. Nina convinced me to name her after the greatest *Grey's Anatomy* character, and so now I'm going to dog parks screaming *Cristina!*"

I followed Ari inside, and she passed me a cocktail menu as we waited for the—OK, fine, very attractive—bartender to mix drinks for a couple of industry-looking guys. She was tall and angular, and her hair was a little wild and untamed, and on another night I definitely would have spent time hypothesizing about what it would feel like to run my fingers through it.

"How's work?" Ari asked. "How's Joyce?"

I accidentally made a sound that literally sounded like *argh*, and Ari's eyes lit up. "Why do you look happy at that?"

"I dunno, I enjoy my fair share of industry gossip. Give me the scoop."

I gave Ari a very anonymized version of the story, and she nodded attentively as I explained. The bartender stopped by, and Ari pushed me up to the counter and repeated my *Paloma but not a Paloma*, which made the bartender nod thoughtfully and begin mixing.

"I know Joyce probably has me on some list of clients who are practically more trouble than they're worth," Ari said.

"I mean, not since you won the Oscar."

She cracked up. "Sure. I'm saying my opinion may not be the right one to get. But I think it's badass you told the truth to whoever this client is. Even inadvertently. This whole industry's full of people afraid to say it, and probably even deep-down Joyce feels the same way. Not that she will ever admit that to you."

"So do you think I'm getting fired?" I asked, not sure I wanted the answer from someone who valued truth so much.

"Nah, I think you'll get through it OK," she said, as the bartender set our drinks on the counter. "I think Joyce'll be chilly for a bit and make you prove yourself again, and then it'll blow over. And if I'm wrong, text me, I'll find you something else, promise."

I thanked her as we walked back outside to rejoin Nina. Cristina the dog sat politely next to me as Ari squeezed in next to Nina. I felt like we were on a double date and I was paired with a dog. It didn't necessarily feel like the best of omens for my romantic future.

"I know that you probably think I only made plans with you to get the dirt on whatever's up with you and your bartender," Nina said, and I felt my stomach clench. "And there'll be plenty of time for that later. But I was going to make plans with you anyway, because I—well, we have really good news and I wanted to tell you in person."

"Oh, cool, good news," I said, which miraculously made Nina and Ari laugh, even though I was being a huge jerk. It seemed to be a proven fact that I was genuinely incapable of sarcasm.

"Nina has graciously accepted my proposal of marriage," Ari said with a grin, and I felt so many things at once. Truly, all I wanted for people I liked and cared about was happiness, but—did that happiness have to happen now? While I was heartbroken and potentially soon-to-be-jobless and on a double date with a dog?

"Congratulations," I said, and I felt myself tearing up as Nina showed me the glittering diamond on her ring finger that I couldn't believe I hadn't noticed yet. It was ridiculous because I managed never to cry at my dumb Hollywood job. There, on the surface, at least, I had emotions of steel. Here, I had a dog licking my face again.

To be fair, I had been on way worse dates.

I tried to pay attention while Nina and Ari gushed about each other and the house they were thinking about making an offer on near the reservoir and how Dr. Cristina Yang the dog had already learned four commands since they'd adopted her one week ago. I was happy for all of it, truly, and not just because I cared a lot about the two of them. I wanted queer people getting happy endings, period.

It just felt terrible that maybe I would never be one of them.

Chapter 23
Proper Form

"Finally," Chelsey said when I got home from my drinks that turned into dinner at The Kitchen. She'd texted me multiple times today and, for various reasons, I'd ignored all of them. Now, standing in the living room wearing a bright pink maxi dress with white platform Docs, she was tougher to ignore.

"I'm really tired and should have probably just come straight home to go to bed," I said. "So whatever you want, can you just bother me tomorrow?"

Chelsey stepped back from me, and if I didn't know better, I'd swear a look of hurt flashed in her eyes. But that was the Chelsey I'd invented, the one who was my actual friend and cared about me and didn't just see me as a pathetic loser through the dollar signs in her eyes.

"We still need some content to close out the campaign," she said. "All the good news that happened because of You Point Oh. All the ways you've self-actualized. Can you get up early tomorrow so we can film before you go to work?"

"Are you serious?" I stared at her, waiting for her to do an *I'm kidding* face or something, but this seemed to be an actual request. "Chelsey, I'm not filming anything else for you after what you did. I'm completely done with You Point Oh."

"I know you're pissed about the video I posted, but—"

"But nothing! I cannot believe you thought that was OK to share. I feel like such an idiot that I thought you saw me—and Sadie—as people with feelings and privacy and boundaries or whatever. Just because you live your whole life that way doesn't mean the rest of us want to."

"OK," Chelsey said, nodding, "that's fair. If I could, though—"

"I'm not here to, like, *negotiate* with you about this! You're barely even a real person, your whole life is for the people who follow you, and it's *humiliating* to me that I thought you actually wanted to be my friend. Guess you're just that good at your whole influencer thing."

"Max," she said in an infuriatingly pleasant tone, "I know you're pissed about the video, but—"

"But nothing. I'm going to bed."

I didn't, though. Despite how long I'd been up at this point, when I crawled under my quilt my eyes wouldn't close and my brain refused to shut off. Chelsey, I knew, would be waiting when I left my room tomorrow, would corner me with multiple ring lights and her iPhone on a tripod. And what was I supposed to say? That I'd done every single thing You Point Oh had asked of me, but it didn't matter because—

I wasn't even sure how I wanted to end that sentence. Because I accidentally screwed up at work and maybe it was a little because I was feeling bolder and getting more opportunities? That I'd ruined all my chances with Sadie because Chelsey didn't understand boundaries and I had forgotten to understand how much actually separated me from my roommate?

It was embarrassing, I knew, that I'd needed You Point Oh at all. I hadn't known to just freaking *say yes* on my own. I wouldn't have thought to google for queer kickball leagues. And even though my job prospects with Riley Howe's company were now probably doomed, I needed that appointment with the career counselor to put together my résumé as well as I had. And, sure, I had also blown any chances of moving up at Exemplar, but it was also thanks to You Point Oh that I got to try in the first place. Why couldn't I have just gotten my own shit together? Was I pathetic or was life actually kind of hard? Sometimes it felt like other people didn't struggle as much as I did. Sometimes I felt uniquely bad at everything.

I got out my laptop and looked up You Point Oh. There was nothing I was in search of; I didn't actually blame them for any of it. Chelsey was the one who'd posted the video. Chelsey was the one who acted like we had some kind of friendship when I was only part of a sponsored content deal. Chelsey had presented my motivations as deviously ambitious and hurt Sadie in the process. You Point Oh was just an innocent app that had merely been the one to get sucked into all of this. Just like me.

I didn't know what I was expecting, but thankfully there weren't any images of me on the You Point Oh homepage. There was nothing terrible at all, just a diverse group of cool Gen Z-type people captured in photos where they appeared to be getting self-actualized. And they probably actually were! I couldn't deny that in many ways, I was better off than thirty days ago.

Just not the one that mattered most.

I clicked over to the membership information, because the truth was that, especially now, I should probably think about subscribing on my own. If I was jobless and hated my roommate with a burning fiery passion and had inadvertently ruined things with the woman I loved, I probably couldn't count myself as self-actualized yet. And then I literally *choked on my own spit* when I saw the monthly subscription fee—and that was before realizing that things like my appointments with Judy Wax and Isabella Morales and my sessions with Landon at All Bodies were all *add-ons*. Oh my god, plus all the free clothes people had sent me because they knew I'd wear them on camera for a half-million people! I was drinking rich-people smoothies and coffee. My teeth were getting polished by a dumb expensive toothbrush.

My life had not gotten better because of You Point Oh. My life had gotten better because I was reaping rich-person benefits. I could have told anyone all along that I would have solved plenty if I were making more money! Not that You Point Oh hadn't made it easy—they'd made it so easy! But if I had that much extra expendable income, I was pretty sure I could also make it really easy, on my own.

I shut my laptop and tried again to fall asleep. It didn't even seem physically possible I was still awake. I guessed that righteous anger was even more powerful than caffeine, because even the thought of sleep sounded like science fiction.

The lights in the hallway were out, so I tiptoed out of my room and down the hallway to find that everything was already set up in the kitchen for whatever content Chelsey thought she'd squeeze out of me in the morning. Talk about science fiction.

I set up my phone on the tripod, tapped to my Instagram account, and went live before I thought about it for any longer.

"Hey, everyone, this is Max, posting from my own account for once. Thanks to everyone who's been following my progress or whatever with You Point Oh. I know you're all expecting some kind of grand conclusion where I reveal how self-actualized I am, but the truth is that doing this actually messed up my life, and I'm really mad and wish I could take it all back.

"I thought I was learning all about self-actualization, and honestly a lot of it helped. There were a lot of things that went better with my job, and I've made some new friends and found community—just so many things I was hoping for. But—and I know I should have realized this from the start—this app is *stupid expensive*. Like, if you watched Chelsey's content about me and were impressed my life got better, I promise you that if anyone got an influx of cash to get custom coaching sessions and higher-quality super gay shirts, you would also be excelling more.

"I feel like a jerk, actually, because I was talking to y'all like anyone could do this, but I myself *never* could have done this if not for the whole sponcon thing. And now I feel kind of like I tricked all of you, making it seem so doable even as an assistant who hardly makes any money and barely can afford her bills as it is. If I had enough money for You Point Oh, I'd already have talked to a career coach and joined a cool inclusive gym!

"Anyway, I'm sorry, I'm genuinely sorry," I said. "Trust me, I will never do sponcon again, it's not my thing—though I really did love all the companies and people I was connected with and I want to make sure I say it, Good Smoorning smoothies are one of my favorite things in life now. But if I could do all of this over, I would have looked into the app first and seen how prohibitively expensive it was and just . . . not done any of this. Or told y'all this was rich-people shit."

Chelsey appeared in the doorway, holding up her phone and pointing to it. My livestream was running on mute on her screen.

"Influencers can make you believe a lot of things," I continued. "And some of them are even true. But that makes it even harder to tell when you're being lied to. So these are all my truths. I feel like I owe y'all that much.

"I guess that's all I have to say. Wait, no, I still have the most important thing to go. Someone I care about a lot got hurt during all of this, and even though I know she'll never see this, I wanted to apologize anyway. I would love a chance to explain myself better, if you'd be willing to hear it."

I clenched my jaw so I didn't start crying and managed a weak *Good night, y'all* before turning off the livestream.

"Max—"

"There," I said, grabbing my phone and walking past her down the hall. "There's your content to close out the campaign. Now we're really done."

I kept my session with Landon after work the next evening, even though I was still running low on sleep and coming to the realization that my days working out here were numbered. Hopefully there wasn't anything inherently hypocritical in attending our sessions. Last week I'd finally added ten-pound weights to my squats, and I was determined to add even more this week or next.

"Hey, Max, how's it going?" Landon greeted me after I'd locked up my stuff in the locker room and met them over by the weight racks.

"Oh no, you sound like you're sad, is it obvious I'm semi-falling-apart?" I asked, and they laughed.

"Not at all. I don't have to pretend I don't follow you and your roommate on social, though, do I? I know you're not feeling great about stuff right now."

"Oh, yeah, I don't know why I keep forgetting that my social media isn't private," I said. "I mean, I accept that the public or whoever sees it. It's weirder that people I know in real life do, too."

"Yeah, I completely get it," they said. "Want to start warming up?"

I nodded and grabbed the empty bar. Facing the mirror, I started a set of squats.

"Your form is really improving," Landon said. "I'm glad you're here. I've gotta tell you, I've powered through lots of shitty days by giving my all to lifting. It can really channel some frustration or aggression or whatever's going on in there."

"Here's hoping," I said, pausing between sets to add slightly more weight. "Almost everything in my life feels like a mess right now. Sorry, I shouldn't be whining to you. This is the gym, not therapy."

"Eh," Landon said, and I found myself laughing along with them. "Your video actually really made me think more about—well, accessibility, I guess. So I wanted to let you know that I'm going to figure something out so that when our time from the app runs out—if you want to, that is—we can find a way for you to keep working out here. You and other people in similar financial situations."

"I'd like that a lot." I worked through the remaining sets before switching to presses. Even at my extremely-new-to-this level, I always felt a little like a badass lifting above my head. The closest I'd come to a badass, at least.

"Move your hips forward," Landon said, demonstrating. "You'll be able to find more strength that way."

"I mean, only so much," I said with a laugh. Badass in the mirror or not, I knew I only had so far I could probably go with this.

"I mean it," Landon said. "I hear from you that you've been telling yourself that you're weak, and that you buy into this narrative. And, look, I get it—you're small and I'm sure you've spent lots of your life being underestimated."

"This really does feel like therapy," I said.

"Seriously, though, what if you tried not assuming you couldn't do something?" Landon asked. "I can feel how you use your perceived weakness as an out. Can you feel that? Your form was legit off. Not because you're weak. It's easier to go with that than work on your form, but, Max, *work on your form*. You have all the strength you need *right now* to perfect that."

"I wasn't trying to get out of anything, really," I said.

"I know," they said gently. "It's automatic for you, because you're still learning to believe in yourself here. So I'm gonna remind you that you've gotta do both: believe in yourself *and* put in the work."

I tried the lift again, and Landon nodded enthusiastically.

"Yeah, so much better. Can you feel how you're using your power more strategically this way?"

I nodded back at Landon and tried again. The more I concentrated on my form and nothing else, the easier it was to let everything else go. It almost felt a little like cheating, but maybe Landon was right about powering through. By the time I was in my car on the way home, I was sweaty and tired but no longer feeling powered by a constant buzzing resentment. After a long hot shower and two episodes of *Frasier*, I slept the best I had all week.

And then my alarm went off the next morning and I thought of how it felt waking up next to Sadie. Even though it had only been two mornings together, it was going to take a lot more to get over how huge my full-size bed felt now.

Still, I kept getting up alone. No more Sadie, no more Good Smoornings, no more quick videos filmed with Chelsey on my way out the door. It was like the last month had magically vanished.

That wasn't actually true, of course. A month ago, I spent at least a few nights every week on my usual barstool at Johnny's. This week without it felt emptier, even if I had my sessions with Landon and a very disappointing kickball game in which we lost to the worse-ranked Lydia Társ, but at least went out for margaritas and snacks afterward at Casita del Campo. Obviously I wouldn't have had these new—and really objectively good—things in my life without my campaign with Chelsey, but that didn't mean it wasn't a mistake. Or was it? Life was getting harder for me to work out in my head.

When Saturday morning rolled around without an off-the-grid activity, I wondered if she was also lying in bed wishing she had a walk to take or tokens to buy to trade for Thai food. I picked up my phone to think about texting her, but got distracted because I had a notification of a direct message—from *Tess Gardner*.

Tell me you've seen the news! You must be basking in validation-type feelings.

I had no idea what it meant, but I knew—based on annoyance from Joyce and the rest of her team that Tess wouldn't hand over the reins of her social media to one of them entirely—that this message was absolutely directly from her.

I haven't, I replied. **What's up?** It was the most casual I'd ever been with talent, outside of Ari Fox of course.

Enjoy the schadenfreude! Tess sent along with a link to a story in *Deadline*. "Eric Sorensen Speaks Out on WGA Panel: It's 'Ridiculous' to Suggest Marginalized Writers Should Be the Ones to Tell Their Own Stories."

"Yikes," I said, then laughed, then clicked to read the full story. Maybe his full quote wasn't as bad as the headline appeared, but, no, it was just another aging straight cis white guy who didn't understand why he wasn't always the right choice to pen stories about women, people of color, and queer people. "If someone like me is objectively a more skilled writer, I don't know what some less experienced woman is going to bring to a project," he literally said *to a female journalist . . .* in front of *a room full of people.*

OMG, I messaged back to Tess. **But is there actually schadenfreude? People'll talk shit about him on Twitter for a while but it's not like the studio isn't going to support The Westinghouse Gambit.**

Well, let a girl dream! LOL

I took a screenshot because even though I was absolutely a professional, one day I knew I'd want to show someone else that Tess Gardner was the type to message "LOL."

Seriously, I'm glad to have something substantial to point to when someone asks why I turned down that film to make what Joyce has referred to on multiple occasions as "relative pennies" because before it was just a hunch that it didn't actually feel like the right fit for me. Thanks for your honesty. It can be really hard to find in this industry. If you ever need a favor returned, just say the word!

I hesitated for a moment, but despite how I felt about You Point Oh, I did like the advice. And if this wasn't a time to be bold, when would it be? **Actually . . . if you're serious, there is something that would mean a lot to me.**

I didn't feel like actually waiting around to see if nearing-A-list celebrity Tess Gardner would do me a personal favor, so I got up and showered and dressed as if I were a person with plans. And even though I wasn't, I left the apartment because I didn't want to risk crossing paths with Chelsey, who I'd managed to all but completely avoid this week. Outside with the sun on my face, I thought back to growing up in Kentucky and how at least the weather could manage to match my bad moods. Here, though, there might be a metaphorical storm cloud hanging over me, but LA was going to LA anyway.

I got into my car and blasted a record I'd loved in college, when every single day I felt moody and misunderstood and ready for a change. Back then I'd drive backroads around home, jump on the freeway, see where my mood took me because it didn't stand for sitting still. I decided to do the same today, and ended up at the Lake Hollywood Reservoir. Maybe it was because it reminded me of Sadie, maybe because I knew my signal would drop out on the walk and disconnecting wasn't the worst idea in the world, maybe I just needed a walk.

Three and a third miles were a while to be left completely alone with your feelings, but there really wasn't a better place for it. I couldn't believe I'd never known about this beautiful loop of green, and I felt a wave of gratitude wash over me that Sadie had taken me here. It hit me that I'd gotten distracted by Tess earlier and forgotten to text Sadie, but now I was glad I waited. I snapped a photo of the lake and sent it with my message. **I wish you were here with me and I'm really grateful you took me here. I would really love to talk. Maybe it's weird I miss you so much because it hasn't even been a week since I saw you but I miss you so much.**

The message immediately failed because there was no service back here, but once I had made it all the way around and back to my car, I tried again. She didn't respond, but I was still glad I'd sent it. It felt like time to take whatever good pieces I could harvest from the You Point Oh experience, which meant I was finished not speaking up or trying new things or making the moves I wanted to make.

It would have been nice to realize all of that *and* get Sadie back, but on my ride back through Hollywood, I ended up switching off the old favorite album for a newer playlist that Megan had shared with the team on our group chat. It wasn't that my taste in music had changed—it absolutely had not—but the angsty lyrics and heavy guitars were the soundtrack to a different life, I realized. Hearing them now made it very hard not to realize just how different things were.

It wasn't that everything was great. Things were kind of laughably *not great* at the moment. But even though I was heartbroken, back then I hadn't even experienced enough to know what heartbreak felt like. I mean, it *sucked*, but it sucked because I knew what it felt like to actually fall for someone, to spend time with a girl who thought I was interesting and funny, a girl who knew how to make people feel seen and welcome. If she never talked to me again, which unfortunately seemed really likely, I still felt honored that at one point she'd looked at me like I was the only other girl in the world.

Back in college, back during the year that felt shipwrecked in between graduation and moving here, no girl had ever looked at me like that. And the only person I ever went out with was Mom! Here I had friends and at least a tenuous career path in front of me, and I lived in the greatest city in the world. Somehow, I realized, I'd managed to grow up a little, enough at least that I could look back on my younger self as someone who I used to be but wasn't anymore.

Landon's words from the other night echoed in my head, and while I knew that they'd been talking specifically about my form doing presses, the words felt bigger now. *You've been telling yourself that you're weak, and that you buy into this narrative. I can feel how you use your perceived weakness as an out.* It had been so easy to see myself as small and not taken seriously. That let me off the hook and made it all other people's problems. Maybe the reason that so much had changed after thirty days of mostly pretty generic advice from an overpriced app was that there were other capabilities I'd ignored, too.

At home I wrote up a new list of goals for myself. They weren't for You Point Oh or Chelsey, though; they were just mine.

Max's Non–You Point Oh Goals

#1. Think about what went wrong with Sadie that you can't blame on Chelsey and see if you can fix it.

#2. Follow up later next week about the Junior Manager job at Spring Hope. Don't be afraid to look ambitious— YOU ARE.

#3. Make sure that Nina and Ari know you are actually happy for them and not just a jealous immature wet blanket.

#4. In general find ways to be a better friend, even if it's kind of embarrassing that having so many people in your life is new to you.

#5. Improve your form—literally and metaphorically speaking.

Chapter 24
Thank-You Memes

My cell buzzed with an unknown 213 number while I was at work on Monday. Since it was relatively quiet—and also because I guessed I secretly hoped that Sadie might be calling from some random number to tell me she'd rethought everything and understood my POV now—I answered it.

"Max Van Doren?"

"This is Max," I said, trying not to sound disappointed that it wasn't Sadie. Since that meant it was probably a random scam call though, my politeness wasn't really an issue.

"This is Riley Howe at Spring Hope Talent Management. Is now a good moment to talk for a few minutes?"

I coughed on *nothing*, which I had no idea was a reaction someone could have to flat-out shock.

"Max? Are you all right?"

"Oh, yes, I'm very good, thank you. Just a moment." I typed frantically into my Slack window to Javier. *WATCH JOYCE'S LINES? PLEASE??* I barely waited for him to agree before dashing into the smallest meeting room that executives never booked.

"OK, I'm sorry about that, just relocating for the call."

"It's no problem at all," Riley Howe said. "I should have gotten something on your calendar, I know, but sometimes an impromptu phone call can be so much more *human*, you know?"

"Sure," I said, pacing the tiny carpeted room. Though could Riley Howe tell I was pacing? I stopped myself so abruptly that I fell backward onto a stiff business sofa.

"As I'm sure you know, Joyce Harris talked you up quite a bit when I mentioned the opening for the junior manager role here," she said.

"That was really kind of Joyce," I said, even though I knew that had Riley and Joyce run into each other even a week later that my name would have never come up relative to this job. I probably actually had Tess, who had enthusiastically agreed to put in a good word with Riley for me when I'd DM'd, to thank for today. "And, yes. Joyce told me a little about the role, and I looked into Spring Hope, and I'm genuinely really excited about the opportunity."

"Let's not get ahead of ourselves," Riley said, and I felt myself flinch. "After all, you're at perhaps the top talent agency in the country, and we are—let's just say *smaller*. And Joyce let me know you were very much interested in continuing down the agency path, so I definitely want to chat with you about what you'd be getting into before we go any further."

"Oh—of course. But I've spent some time thinking about it, and it does seem like management might be a better fit for me. Though I guess that's something I would like to discuss more with you. And small doesn't scare me. I'm only five-foot, I feel like small things get underestimated all the time and it's fun when people are wrong about it."

I couldn't believe I blurted that out and decided that lying on this terrible sofa was probably not keeping me in a very businesslike mode, so I sat up. But then Riley *laughed*.

"That's a great way to look at it. I usually feel the exact same way. Do you have a moment to hear a little more about the company and the role?"

I wasn't really sure that I did, but I said yes anyway.

"First of all, I started out as an agency assistant, too, and I moved up through the ranks fairly quickly. It's a hard life, though, and not in the ways that were fun to me. I wanted to find time for my friends, and I wanted to get married and have kids someday, and given my schedule I couldn't figure out how I was going to do any of that, much less all of it, and not half-assedly at that! A friend steered me in the direction of management, and—well, spoiler alert, that was twelve years ago and now I have most of the same friends, plus a wife and two kids and a high-needs cat, and they all basically get enough time from me. Well, the cat's never happy, but everyone else seems to be doing well."

"Yeah, that's like my dream," I said. "Including the cat."

She laughed. "I also get to be a little more creative here, and I've gotten to produce, which is no guarantee but definitely something you could explore with the right clients and projects when you're a little further along in your career. I get the feeling you're ultimately looking to do more than negotiate and close deals."

"Yeah, I think maybe that's true," I said. "Sorry, I should probably make that a stronger statement, but the truth is I'm still figuring things out. I love working for Joyce and I do think I could do the kind of work she's doing. I'd never even considered being a manager until she brought it up. But everything you're saying just makes sense to me. So I'm being honest and saying I hadn't thought about it before, but when I think about it now it seems like a good fit."

"I'm glad to hear that. Can I pass you over to my assistant to schedule some time for you to come in, see the office, chat in person?"

I managed to calmly say yes and make the appointment for later in the week. Once I finally made it back to my desk and tapped out a thank-you to Javier, followed by three stupid *THANK YOU!* memes, I got right back up to head to Joyce's office. It felt a little bonkers to be walking in here any more than I absolutely had to, but even if my self-actualization *campaign* had been a disaster, I still wanted to—well, *self-actualize* was a bit dramatic, but risking Joyce's ire was worth it to keep my career moving forward.

Joyce glanced up as I leaned into the doorway. Her hair was in its very tallest form, an elaborate topknot, which wasn't helping my intimidation factor or nerves. "Yes?"

"Do you have a minute?" I asked, and when she nodded I forced myself to sit down right away like this was any ol' business meeting between peers.

"I just got a call from Riley Howe," I said, and Joyce *smiled.* "Wait, didn't you decide you couldn't recommend me? I'm sorry, it's absolutely your right not to, but—honestly, I'm just really confused right now."

Joyce's laugh pealed out. "Max, I could have murdered you last week. It was so unlike you to be so careless in client communications. But then—"

"Eric Sorensen did that panel where he said white men could do anything best, including the POV of women?"

She cracked up. "That certainly didn't hurt your cause! No, even though what you did would have been a fireable offense in some cases, I obviously believed that it had been a genuine misunderstanding. And, to be honest, even if it hadn't been, I didn't think you were acting purely from your own opinion. I knew that Tess had reservations, too, and she wanted me to confirm or deny them. I wanted that big paycheck and guaranteed awards season for her, but I couldn't stop wondering if you'd zeroed in on what she actually wanted. Or maybe you did just act impulsively and unprofessionally. In this business, sometimes it's hard to tell. I did tell Riley the events of last week. Let her make her own mind up if you were someone she might want to mentor."

"Oh. That's super fair." I thought about the phone call. "I guess she didn't think it was too terrible? The call was more her selling me on management than having me sell myself for the position."

"She's nervous you're too used to the perks here," Joyce said. "And the office is in some ugly building downtown."

"Do you know how much closer downtown is to my apartment?" I asked. "I don't care how ugly it is."

Joyce laughed. "Then I hope it all works out for you, though it really is extremely ugly. And I'm already irritated thinking about training a new assistant."

"Please don't jinx anything, Joyce! It still feels like a long shot."

"I think it's more likely than that," she said with a smile. "But I'll respect your jinxing beliefs."

I dialed Mom as I navigated my way onto Wilshire Boulevard after work that night.

"Hi, honey, big day in Hollywood?"

"Kind of, actually, yeah. I'm interviewing for a junior manager role at another company. Or I guess I already interviewed? It's not a guarantee, but it feels like it might work out."

"That's great," Mom said, and I heard the warmth in her voice. "And, of course, if it doesn't—"

"Mom, please don't say it. I love you, and I know you mean well, but every time you tell me I can just move home it reminds me how you don't believe I can do this. And I know that a lot of people think that about me, but you're *my mom*. I need you to at least pretend you think I can succeed."

"I wasn't going to say you could move home," Mom said. "I was going to say that if this opportunity didn't work out, I'm sure there are others out there, too."

I felt a pang of guilt hit, but—"OK, you weren't going to say it *right now*, but you understand that you say it a lot, right? And that you're keeping my bedroom as like a Max Van Doren museum exhibit so I can like slip right back in? And I'm realizing I probably sell myself short a lot but . . . I don't know. Whenever you say that, it feels like you don't believe in me either."

Mom sighed loudly. "Max, of course I believe in you. I guess it's just that I can't relate to the kind of life you're living out there."

I opened my mouth to respond but Mom was still going.

"And, no, I don't mean because you're gay. I mean because you have these big goals and dreams for yourself. All I wanted was to finish college and get married and have a family. And I was very happy, you know. I had everything I wanted, until your father . . ."

I wiped at my eyes. "Yeah, me too. Do you think it's weird I couldn't just stay there and meet some girl and get married and have goals that were like more realistic?"

"Absolutely I do! It seems so hard out there and you're my little girl and I just want you nearby where—oh, I don't know. You're an adult, I realize this. I just want your life to be as easy as possible. And that's not the path you chose."

"No," I said. "Sometimes it actually feels like I'm doing everything possible for my life to *not* be easy."

"Your dad would be so proud of you," she said. "He'd brag to everyone he knew about his daughter's big Hollywood job. And he'd convince me to worry less about you. He'd remind me that if you were doing something that required bravery, that didn't mean I was supposed to be scared. It meant I should be proud at how brave you were."

I tried to imagine it, phone calls with both of my parents on speaker. It was funny how something could make you cry more and warm your heart, all at once. "I promise to call you more and give you more updates about—well, everything. If you can take Dad's hypothetical advice and worry about me less. It's not that I'm brave, either, I'm just kind of stubborn about all the stuff I want."

"Deal," she said. "Though some people might see that as bravery."

"Agree to disagree," I said.

"Sure. So have you made up with that cute bartender yet?"

"No, I think I messed up too badly and in such a specific way that's against everything she believes in to—wait, how do you know about that? Wait, Mom, are you on TikTok? The other month you didn't even know what Venmo was."

"I still don't know what Venmo is! TikTok is easy, though. One of the neighbor kids set it up for me."

"That," I said, "is horrifying."

When I arrived home, I heard the familiar sounds of Chelsey setting up her gear in the kitchen and was relieved I could make it into my room without any potential interactions. I'd gotten very good at listening for where she was in the apartment. Once I sat on my bed, though, I kept hearing Mom saying *brave* in her really-inaccurate Dad voice, and there was nothing that seemed brave about gnawing on a Kind bar I'd squirreled away from one of Joyce's leftover swag bags while watching *Frasier*.

I slammed my laptop shut with an *ugh* and trudged to the kitchen, where Chelsey was setting up lights around an un-opened meal-prep-branded box.

"Yes?" she asked coolly.

"You're obviously busy right now but I just wanted to say— I acted like a real jerk, and I'm sorry. Half the things I said, I didn't even mean and—"

"Stop," Chelsey said, holding up her hand. "I can't believe you're apologizing. Well, no, I guess you should, but also, I can't believe I did that."

I laughed. "I mean, fair. It was *terrible*."

"In my defense, I've seen how thirsty you've been for that bartender—"

"Her name is Sadie."

"For *Sadie*. It was just too good. The big move! That story-teller part of me couldn't resist it."

I couldn't help it; I cracked up. "The *storyteller* part of you? I felt like it was way more the influencer part who wanted views and likes and going viral."

"Yeah," she said. "That's fair. But, honestly, I really was in it for the whole love story of it. Which in retrospect—trust me. I knew I should have stopped the video or ignored Sadie or deleted it as soon as you asked—basically, any of the things I chose not to do."

I sat down at one of the barstools at the counter. "Yeah. You should have. But I *may* have gone overboard calling you out on it. And You Point Oh. Neither of you is completely terrible."

Chelsey shrugged. "I've been thinking about it so much since you posted your video. While you might have been a teeny bit dramatic, your point stands. I actually have a call set up next week with the marketing team to discuss some of my concerns. Which started out as your concerns. They're at least telling me they're open to some free and sliding-scale rate options."

"That would be great," I said. "I actually think it could be a really good app. Like, despite everything I said, it helped me. I can't imagine how long it would have taken me to talk to my boss about moving up if not for this program. And maybe I should be embarrassed about this, but I *did* make the big move or whatever with Sadie because of the app. I mean, I tried to."

Chelsey grimaced. "Sorry about that. Really."

"No, it was—look, you didn't help—but it was me," I said, realizing it as I said it. "I had multiple chances to tell her how much she means to me and that I want to have a real relation-ship with her and that I completely believe in her and all her plans, and I just *didn't*. I managed to mess all that up on my own."

"Well, she's not dead, far as I know," Chelsey said with a grin. "Why not tell her now?"

"Oh, trust me," I said. "I tried. It . . . did not go well."

I caught Chelsey up on the whole chain of events. It took so long that she turned off all her lighting and retrieved a couple of Taiwanese beers from the fridge for us.

"Remember the night we had these last?" I asked. "I thought you wanted to hang out, but you were just buttering me up to ask about You Point Oh."

"What do you mean?" Chelsey, I had to admit, looked believably confused. "Yes, I wanted to ask about You Point Oh, but I also wanted to hang out. The buttering-up was so you'd hang out with me!"

"Oh, please." I rolled my eyes. "I'm your awkward nerdy roommate who only fit your brand when it required someone un-self-actualized."

"OK, Max, I get that's the story you've told yourself, but have you not noticed I've been trying to befriend you since you moved in? And you almost *always* blow me off! If anyone feels like the awkward nerdy roommate, girl, it's me."

I focused on peeling the label off my beer bottle. "Chelsey, it was really obvious I didn't fit into your whole beautiful influencer life. You invited me to stuff so you didn't seem like a jerk, not because you actually wanted me to go with you."

She rolled her eyes. "I have no idea how I could have been *more obvious* than inviting you even though you kept saying no."

I didn't know how to respond, because it had always seemed clear as day that I wasn't part of Chelsey's world, not outside of the room I rented from her. Chelsey was confidence, success, beauty—literally all the things I wasn't.

"I just think that maybe someone like you could never understand being someone like me," I said gently. "I'm not someone who, like, automatically fits in places. All this stuff is really hard for me."

"Max." Chelsey set down her beer with a *thud*. "I'm a fat queer girl from Kentucky. Where are these mystical places where I've automatically fit in?"

"Um . . . here?"

She burst into laughter. "OK, that's a little fair. Moving to LA was actually really easy for me. I made some friends and then my, like, third date here was with Ava and so her friends became my friends too. But mostly I've had to fight my way into every space I've been part of. Including, apparently, with my impressively stubborn roommate."

I drank silently for a few moments, trying to put it all together in my head.

"I always actually felt more comfortable around you in a lot of ways," Chelsey said, "even when you were working so hard to avoid me. So many people out here are like, *Oh, it's so great our generation doesn't have to deal with being scared to come out or dealing with homophobia*, and it's like, *Congratulations for growing up in a blue state in a progressive family, queers, some of us were not going through the same life experiences*."

"Yeah, I thought I'd get out here and it would all sort of snap into place," I said. "Not that I'd still feel like an out-of-place weirdo. But I really had no idea you felt that way. You and your life seem perfect to me. Seemed? I don't know. It's hard to imagine hot blond girls with hot genius girlfriends don't always have it easy."

"That's very flattering," Chelsey said with a laugh. "Ava says people confuse me with the Chelsey I am online, too, which is—well, it's *me*, but it's like a highly curated me. A me who only has adorably relatable bad days. And if you believed that was the real version of me . . ."

"I mean, I get that Ava knows you better, but I freaking live with you and you seem pretty identical to the Chelsey you are online," I said. "In my defense."

"The truth is," she said, "it's hard to be a person. And not to sound like the *Friends* theme song but gay, but being in my twenties and figuring out life is way less defined than I expected."

"Oh my god, right? I was just talking about this with someone the other week. I thought by the time I was twenty-six I'd have it all figured out. Which—I mean, *why*?"

Chelsey clinked her bottle against mine. "Truth."

"You seem to have more figured out than me," I pointed out.

"Maybe I'm just good at faking it," she said. "Max, I am terrible at emotional intimacy, I have an amazing girlfriend I keep delaying moving in with, I tell all my feelings to the world on social because saying things one-on-one is so scary. Honestly, this conversation right now?" She pretended to shiver. "Terrifying."

"Oh, good, it's not just me."

We both laughed, and Chelsey sat down at the stool next to me. "First, let's order in dinner. Yes, with one of my many delivery-app gift cards. No, I am not trying to bribe you. Except maybe into actual friendship, is it working?"

"Depends on the size of the gift card," I said, and she burst into laughter. "OK, if that's first, what's second? I can tell you have some kind of plan. Do you want me to shoot a video where I say that You Point Oh is fine and as long as they make a cheaper version I'll stop being a jerk about it?"

Chelsey waved her hand. "Let's find out what they actually tell me in my meeting next week. No, second on the agenda is figuring out how you're going to win back your bartender."

"She's not mine," I said. "Can we focus on something less hopeless?"

"Sure, what do you have?"

"Anything is less hopeless than the state of things with Sadie."

As we put in an order for Thai, I told her about my upcoming interview at Spring Hope, and she told me about some nonprofit work she was thinking about taking on. I asked for advice about being a better friend, and Chelsey unearthed a promo code for a free flower arrangement so that I could congratulate Nina and Ari properly.

Ava stopped by, and for once I didn't clear out to my room, but stayed on my barstool while Chelsey gave her the highlights of the evening so far. I noticed how they watched each other, like they were each other's very biggest fans, and it hit me how much I wanted that feeling—and how terrible I'd been at making it happen with Sadie. For all that I said I believed in her, I'd let everything else distract me from actually helping her.

And even if she was done with me, I didn't want her dream to die. Once Chelsey, Ava, and I had eaten way too much Thai food, I said goodnight and headed back to my room to start researching for real. And then I changed my mind and turned around.

"Fine," I said. "I need help."

"Ooh, with Sadie?" Chelsey asked. "Aren't you proud of me for saying her name?"

"Sadly, yes," I said, as Ava burst into laughter. "And . . . not exactly. I need to figure out how to help Sadie save Johnny's."

"Of course, but you get that I'm better at cute girl advice than, like, historical designation bureaucracy advice, right?"

"Ooh, bureaucracy," Ava said, leaning forward. "Just tell me where to start."

Chapter 25

Appointment with a Boomer

I called ahead, because I knew a boomer would appreciate no mode of communication more, but even so it was vaguely terrifying to show up at Johnny's the next week with still no word from Sadie. Sadie, though, as promised, wasn't there. It was just Billy and me.

"I can't remember the last time someone scheduled an appointment with me," Billy said, unlocking the door to let me in. "It was too strange to refuse."

"That's my goal," I said. "You're sure that Sadie's—"

"Yeah, she won't be in until we're open," he said. "Though that doesn't make a lot of sense to me. Didn't think you ever came here for any other reason."

I felt myself blush. "Yeah, I try not to be such an obvious mess, but I know I'm super obvious."

"A lot of obvious girls in here over the years," he said. "But you probably win the prize for most obvious."

"Yeah, that feels right," I said, and he laughed. "Sadie thinks that's all there is, though, and I—my intentions are real. I don't know why I'm telling you this, I came to talk about the bar and not . . ."

Billy, as usual, wasn't smiling, but there was a twinkle of something in his eyes. ". . . your intentions?"

"First of all, I know that lots of this is none of my business, so at any point you should just tell me to shut up and get out," I said. "But I'm hoping you won't, because—"

"Your intentions are noble or what have you?"

I grinned. "Exactly. So as you know, Sadie wants to buy the bar by the time she's thirty, which is like—"

"Next week," he said.

"Yeah," I said with a sigh. "Soon. And she doesn't actually have the money yet and she's terrified you'll have to sell the bar then, so you can go retire in Fresno."

"You don't have to use that tone when you say *Fresno*, you know," Billy said, and we both laughed. "Look, Maxine, I'd hand over the title to this place to Sadie today, if I . . ."

"Had the cash?"

Billy shook his head, looking serious again. "Don't let anyone tell you that Billy Thomas can't afford to retire in Fresno. *No.* This place is barely hanging in there. I've done what I could, but—I don't know. If Johnny were still around, maybe it would be different. But it feels like this place was part of something old, and maybe its time has passed. And sometimes I wonder if I should have done what I did, you know. It felt so important to keep this place going after Johnny died, but maybe I should have let it go with him instead of running it for another nine hundred years or however long it's seemed. I had this whole life, Maxine, believe it or not, and then in a flash all I had left was this bar that he loved. The last thing I want to do is saddle Sadie with it, the way I did to myself. She's still just a kid and she's given up her whole life for this dumb dream I had, to keep this place going."

"It's not a dumb dream," I said. "I love this place. And don't say it's because I'm an obvious girl and Sadie's very—*I love this place.* Moving to LA was a lot harder than I thought it would be, but this bar is just one of those spaces that makes everyone feel like they're home."

"That's sweet of you," he said. "But it's beside the point. I don't want to take every last cent from Sadie because she thinks she has to do this. You know her, kid could do anything she set her mind to. Staying here—"

"She wants this, though," I said. "She's told you about her ideas for the bar, right?"

"Her whole thing how it should be better lit?"

I cracked up again. "Oh my god, *no*. I mean, yes, obviously, but so much more. She wants to make Johnny's feel new again, and still give queer people a community space. People have made her feel really terrible about her goals, and I can tell she's maybe afraid to want it too much, but she wants it."

"Hmmm," is all Billy said, but I could tell he was still listening.

"I've done all this research about historic preservation," I said, because in the last week, much of my—and Ava's—downtime had gone toward it, like it should have from the moment Sadie had originally asked. I'd been busier than ever, but now I felt like there was no excuse for not prioritizing her at least a little more than I had. "People act like LA is constantly just knocking things over and putting up Erewhons, but they actually have the oldest historic preservation society around, which I think is really cool."

Billy's expression told me he did not enjoy that factoid as much as I did, so I kept it moving.

"Given how old this place is, and that it's special to the LGBTQ+ community, this building is completely eligible to be designated as a historic place," I said. "And once that's underway, no one can knock it down and turn it into a parking lot or a store that sells twenty-dollar smoothies. Which I feel like could take the pressure off of Sadie *and* honor everything Johnny wanted for this bar. Also, anyone is allowed to nominate places and get the ball rolling, so I could handle the whole thing if it makes your life easier."

Billy made a sound I couldn't quite categorize, so I figured I might as well finish my spiel.

"Also my roommate is this pretty popular queer social media influencer and she wants to launch a campaign to help Sadie fundraise. We think this bar—especially if more people knew about its history—means a lot to the community, and it would be amazing if the community got a chance to help."

"That part," he said, "is really not up to me."

"No, totally, it's all up to the two of you to discuss, but she doesn't want to talk to me, and I didn't want this place getting lost to time because I promised to help her and didn't. Even if she never forgives me, I owe her that much."

He was silent for a long moment, but I'd said everything I set out to, so I tried to be comfortable in the silence. Or at least fake it.

"What'd you do?" he asked.

"What do you mean?"

Billy raised an eyebrow. "Why do you need to be forgiven?"

"Oh my god, no. It's all too stupid and thoughtless and—I just made her feel like she wasn't special, and that she didn't matter to me. When that is the exact opposite of how I feel."

"This all go down about a couple weeks ago?" he asked, and I nodded. "Yeah, she's been in a rotten mood."

"Yeah, I screwed up a lot," I said, hating that I could hurt someone enough that others would notice. "So, anyway—"

"So why don't you go fix it?" he asked. "When you're lucky, Maxine, life is long, and you get time to fix stuff later on. What I learned though is that there's not always a later on. So if there's something you feel—your noble intentions and all—you should say it."

"I don't think she wants to hear from me," I said. "I tried texting her and—I don't know. I don't want to follow up being a thoughtless jerk by being a pushy jerk."

He chuckled. "You *are* an odd mix of noble intentions and pushiness. But you're a good kid. So let's do it my way, OK?"

"Wait, what does that mean?"

"You come by, tell Sadie all of this, and I follow up with

a real discussion with her about changing hands here. I don't know why I believe you so much that Sadie actually wants this place, but . . ." He shrugged.

"It's because I'm weirdly honest and incapable of lying," I said. "Which has caused some issues for me, as I'm sure you can imagine."

He laughed again. "What are you doing tomorrow? Six or seven? I'll make sure Sadie's working in the back room, you come in and talk to her privately. Sound good?"

"Um, no, I need time to—" I shook my head. Why was I delaying this second chance with Sadie that I thought I'd never have? "No, tomorrow's fine, Monday nights at six or seven are super unromantic but I'll make that work to my advantage somehow. Though I have a million questions to ask you first, if that's OK."

His expression was immediately suspicious. "What kind of questions?"

"To start, can you tell me about Johnny opening the bar? And what it was like back then?"

He sighed and shook his head, and I worried that this was it and I'd lost him. He turned away, while I wondered if I could patch together a loose history without his help. And then I realized he was making me a drink.

"Yeah," he said. "I'll tell you what it was like back then."

"Thank you," I said as he set the Paloma in front of me. "I can't wait to hear it."

I calmly said goodbye to Billy about an hour later as the bar was opening for the evening, then ran all the way home to tell Chelsey and Ava everything. If I was going to write up a beautiful essay and then give some big speech tomorrow, I was going to need their help again.

"No," Chelsey said.

"Rude," I said, which made Ava laugh.

"You're always trying to get out of content," she said. "Even when it's partially your idea. We shoot, then Ava and I will help you plan a beautiful romantic speech that'll make Sadie forgive you and also see how perfect you two are for each other. Deal?"

I complained only a little but let Chelsey blot my shiny face with powder and then stood next to her in front of her iPhone, just like old times.

"Hey, y'all, it's me with a very special guest," Chelsey said.

"You probably thought you saw the last of me," I said, which made Chelsey burst into laughter.

"No way, Max, your brand of low-key high drama is exactly what people expect here," she said. "So I'm very glad you're back. As I'm sure all of you are as well. If you saw Max's video, you probably have some questions about our campaign with You Point Oh. I actually *know* you saw it and have questions, because my DMs are always open and *I sure heard from y'all.* So first of all, I just want to say that I was a real monster for divulging things about Max's personal life that were not mine to share. I actually care a lot about being a good friend and roommate, plus just generally a decent person, and I absolutely neglected all three of those aims in one fell swoop. So, Max, I'm sorry. Sadie, if you're watching, which Max says you aren't because you're off-the-grid or whatever, so more like Sadie's friends, please tell Sadie that I'm sorry."

"I'm also sending out an *I'm sorry* to Sadie," I said. "For her to get third-party or whatever. Sadie, I'm really sorry."

"Great, now that we've got the person without a phone covered, let's get down to the other matter at hand. Yes, You Point Oh is expensive. I didn't think much about that because it seemed so exciting, and—look, y'all. I get a lot of offers from apps and other startups where it's clear they're letting tech bros run wild with power but no actual heart. You Point Oh was nothing like that. Their team is incredible, and I genuinely felt like I watched Max learn and grow and realize how amazing she's always been. So I didn't focus much on the financial aspect, and ultimately now that seems super disingenuous of me. Like Max said, if we were all rich, we'd need way less help in a lot of these areas."

"I mean, I'd still screw up my love life," I said.

"Oh, same," Chelsey said. "My disastrous tendencies are finance-neutral."

We heard Ava cackle from the next room, which set us both off again.

"Anyway, there will be official things to announce later, but you can rest assured that You Point Oh has heard all of us broke masses, and are soon releasing free and low-cost subscription models. And . . ." Chelsey nudged me.

"And I am, unbelievably, going to try out the free version in front of the entire world again, for some reason," I said. "I still have a lot I'm working on, and apparently it actually helped people to watch me flail and semi figure it out."

"You barely flailed at all," Chelsey said.

"Well, not on camera."

"We're going to kick everything off in a week or two, so check back here and on Max's account. You excited, Max? Or just terrified again?"

"Yeah, believe it or not," I said, "I'm only ten percent terrified. The rest is pure excitement."

Chapter 26
A Piece of Paper

Chelsey and Ava were in the living room when I headed out the next evening to—well, to say the things I should have said before. And then some.

"What do you think?" I ask. "Do I look grand-gesture-worthy?"

I was wearing the suit from the night I'd thought I'd made my big move over one of my most comfortable T-shirts and my Docs. A mix of my old and new, just the way I liked things these days.

Chelsey frowned slightly. "Oh, what about the new button-down and—"

"You look *great*," Ava said sharply, with a look to Chelsey, and the three of us cracked up. "Go get your girl."

"She's not my girl," I said.

"Yet!" they said in unison, and I felt so empowered by their energy that I waved and let myself out.

"Get in, loser," I whispered to myself. "We're going to save the day."

I walked into Johnny's with the email printout clutched in

my hand. Watching it roll off the printer at work earlier today, it had felt embarrassingly low-res for a bold declaration, but I reminded myself that this was Sadie. The printout itself didn't matter, anyway. It was, hopefully, everything that went along with it.

Even though we'd planned it this way, I hated walking in again and not seeing her. I hated the time I'd spent away—even if it was what she'd wanted. Now that I was back here, during business hours, feeling the warm buzz of the small crowd, I remembered why I'd felt so welcome at Johnny's from the beginning. This was my *home*, and I hoped I'd never have to give it up again.

"You're right on time," Billy said to me with a nod. "I can only invent so many backroom duties for her, you know."

"Billy, you've been doing this job for—according to you—nine hundred years. You probably have a million fake jobs for her."

He grumbled but I saw the smile in his eyes.

"Thank you," I said, hoping my voice wasn't too shaky to sound sincere.

"Thank *you*, Maxine," he said. "Your weird optimism about this place is nice to have around."

"Well, fingers crossed," I said.

"Nah, I've gotta good feeling," he said. "Which is rare enough it probably means something."

I smiled. "I hope you're right."

He cocked his head toward the back. "I thought I told you to hurry and stop dillydallying up here."

"I definitely would have remembered you saying *dillydallying*," I said with a smile, but I walked past him and through the swinging doors into the back room. Sadie's back was to me, and I watched for a moment as she pulled pint glasses out of the dishwasher. I loved how she moved with so much purpose, like even a small job was worth doing well.

"Are you going to stand there or give me a hand?" she asked, and my heart sped up. It was now or never.

"It's me," I said. "It's Max."

Sadie spun around. "I thought you were—"

"Well, yeah, obviously, but it's me. Though I'll give you a hand, if you want."

"I'm good," she said coolly. I hoped I'd never have to get used to that unfamiliar tone from her. "Billy let you back here?"

"Yeah, Sadie, I have something to say, and I really hope you'll listen." I longed for her to respond with something, *anything*. She was silent, though her hazel eyes met mine. Her gaze, at least, felt like an invitation to keep going.

"I should have said it the other week, the morning after we— or maybe the night before. The next day after that. I should have already said it, Sadie, and I hate that I didn't."

She was still silent, though I didn't know what I was expecting.

"Sadie, you make my whole life better. You listen to me and take me seriously, even when it seems like no one else does. You make this place feel like home for so many people—and your dream is to make it feel that way for even more people! You, like, build community. And me, a person who felt like she'd never had one, I love that so much about you."

"I have an impossible and embarrassing dream to buy a bar," Sadie said. "I wouldn't call that *building community*."

"Well, I would. And I wouldn't say anything was impossible or embarrassing either. You're really capable and I think you can make this dream come true. But it's not even the point—the point is that I should have said this sooner. I should have told you I was crazy about you instead of asking you to come home with me."

She grinned, and a wave of relief washed over me seeing that crooked smile. "Not that I minded that."

"I should have done both. And I should have told you about

You Point Oh to begin with. I just felt like you were this awesome off-the-grid person who didn't suffer foolishness like apps and influencers, and I wanted you to respect me."

She was still smiling, so it made sense to keep talking.

"I only did the whole self-actualization app thing with Chelsey in the first place because I felt like I had to. I'd moved out here with this whole idea of what my life would be like, but none of it seemed to come true. And I guess that would have been OK, but it just kept feeling like—well, no one *expected* things to come true for me. No one took me seriously, you know? At least it felt that way."

Sadie was still watching me, but she didn't look like she was fighting off a smile anymore.

"But not with you," I continued, and I was rushing and my tone was probably a little squeaky and panicky. In my fantasies if I were to declare my love for somebody, I'd sound cool and less like a dog toy. But, I realized, it was OK that I didn't. It was more than OK that I was just me. *"Never* with you, Sadie."

She wiped her eyes with the back of her hand. "You either, Max. You've got to know that, yeah? To everyone else I felt like such a fuckup, even though I felt lucky to like the life I actually had. But you . . . I thought you were the person who could see all that."

"I actually think we were both a little wrong, maybe," I said. "Maybe more people believed in me than I knew. I had created this whole narrative, you know, nothing was my fault because no one took me seriously and so it sort of became self-fulfilling. Following just like the most basic advice from this app unlocked a lot of things for me, and I can see now that it's because I'd been the one locking it all away. So I'm doing all the things that You Point Oh told me to, because honestly they're all good things. I'm saying yes, and I'm being bold, and I'm making the big move."

It hit me that Sadie would have no idea what I was talking

about and it probably sounded like I was just spouting random aphorisms that could be embroidered on pillows. "Oh, sorry, those were the things the app—"

"I'm aware," Sadie said, and slid something out of her back pocket. Something shiny and rectangular.

I actually gasped. "Did you steal that iPhone from someone?"

She burst into laughter. "You know, it turns out that staying off the grid to avoid your old problems and the social media accounts of your exes and your more successful friends and such is not necessarily the healthiest move. Emotionally speaking and all. Anyway. I watched all of your videos, Max."

My head spun at that. "Wait—you did?"

"You know, I felt like I knew you really well," Sadie said. "I saw you so often here, and even when your head was buried in your scripts or you were taking calls on your robot watch or whatever, I still felt like I was getting to know you. And talking with you was like . . . I dunno, Max. It was so easy. I loved how smart and ambitious you seemed, like the girls I always fell for, but . . . I don't know. Kinder. More open to the idea of other people. And so I had this idea of who you were and . . ."

I waited, but she only trailed off. "And?"

"And for the person I thought you were—and what happened between us—Max, it didn't make any sense to me. When I saw that video of your roommate, I felt really fucking betrayed. No matter how well I thought I'd known you, all I kept thinking afterward was that you'd done this whole scheme on me."

"I mean, I kind of did do a whole scheme on you," I said. "I know it doesn't make any sense when I say it aloud, but it was easier to tell the whole world I was ready to fall in love for real than to just tell you that I was—"

I caught myself, because even if this was my big gesture, was it time to say it? Movies didn't explain the whole logistics of the big gesture very well.

"You were what?" Sadie asked, smiling right at me. God, that smile could still take me completely apart.

"Falling in love with you," I said. "And instead I made you think I was checking you off of some kind of list."

"I liked you too much to see you clearly," Sadie said. "It seemed nuts to me that you struggled for respect at work when you were clearly such a freakishly talented little badass. I assumed you were moving on up whatever corporate ladder you were on. That's how I would have seen it, at least, until I watched your whole series with your roommate."

"I actually love the way you saw me," I said. "It's why I fell for you. I mean, I also have a thing for hot bartenders but you're not just like *any* hot bartender. And I should have found a way to say all of this sooner."

"Yeah, well, I don't think I'd win any awards for direct communications either," Sadie said. "So I'll say that one of my favorite parts of my day was knowing you'd probably be at your usual spot at the bar. Look, girls do hit on me all the time, it's part of the job, but when you talked to me, it never felt like you were only trying to get into my pants."

"To be clear, Sadie, I care a lot about what you think and what your dreams are and also I was absolutely trying to get into your pants."

"Yeah, understood," she said with a grin. "You were just . . . the exact kind of person I always fell for, but you made me feel like I was good enough as I was. And maybe that sounds like a low bar to clear, but . . . it felt big."

"I think that maybe connecting with someone who sees you as you are and thinks that's more than enough *is* big," I said.

"Maybe so," she said softly. "So what's next?"

"What do you mean?"

"You're the one who marched in here with some paper acting like you were giving some big speech. I feel like you're the one running whatever this is."

"OK, well, my goals were threefold," I said, and Sadie laughed again. "First, my real apology. I'm sorry I ever made you feel like something checked off my list. I'm sorry I didn't tell you sooner how amazing I think you are. I'm sorry I didn't just tell you about Chelsey's video and then take you out for biscuit sandwiches like you deserved. Second, I'd love a second chance to see what it's like if we actually try this for real and not just leave it all unsaid. Third, no matter what, even if you never want to speak to me again after today, I wanted to help this place stick around. Also I want you to get to take over and make it even more amazing. So I talked to Billy and . . . honestly, the two of you need to have a real conversation."

"We'll see," she said.

"No, please, if you can take any lesson from me and my You Point Oh misadventures, stepping up and actually going for things is the right move. Anyway, one of my big regrets with you is that I didn't jump in and help with all the historical preservation stuff right away. I was still getting used to having extracurriculars and a social life, and—anyway, it's no excuse. I finally sat down and began researching historical preservation for you."

"Max," she said, her voice warm. "I didn't expect you to actually do that. I liked having an excuse to talk to you about something."

"Well, too bad, I'm very goal-oriented," I said. "And even if you never wanted to speak to me again, I wanted to help save Johnny's. This place means something, Sadie, and not just because it's where I get to spend time with you."

Sadie nodded. "Sure. But I'm accepting that might not ever happen, and—"

"No, shut up," I said, shaking the piece of paper at her. Why didn't I frame it or make it look more impressive? I was just a girl, standing in front of a girl, shaking an email printout at her.

"Do you know what I found out? Well, Ava found out and got me up to speed. Anyway, it turns out that buildings don't have to be nominated by their owners. Buildings in LA can be nominated by anyone who's willing to write up what the building means to this city and why it should be deemed historic. And there are even special designations for places that are important to the LGBTQ+ community."

Sadie stared at me, and all the blush and smiles she'd been only moments earlier were completely gone. "Max, what did you do?"

"This is the confirmation of the submission I sent," I said, my heart in my throat and my hands sweaty enough to make the paper wilt even more. "And, don't worry. I talked to Billy before I actually applied. But there's no reason Johnny's won't be accepted, and then once the whole thing is in progress and the Cultural Heritage Commission is making their decision—which, by the way, could take months or even years—the building has to be basically left alone."

Sadie's eyes were still wide and right on me. I couldn't read her at all.

"So, no condos," she said.

"No condos. No parking structures. Time for you to work out a deal with Billy. Again, it's not really my place, Sadie, but there's a deal to be made, you know? Plus, with your permission of course, Chelsey and Ava and I were talking, and there are so many ways to make this happen. Chelsey has a million followers—I mean, not literally, but close, and Ava is really skilled at community fundraising, and—I don't know. It sounds fun to try, if you'll let me. If you'll let *us*."

Sadie chuckled. "You understand I obviously thought it would be easier saving up a down payment big enough for the real estate market in this ridiculously overpriced city than to have some big talk about this with Billy, right?"

"I feel like if you can buy a giant new phone, you can do

anything," I said, and all of a sudden she was closer, right in front of me.

"You make me feel like I can do anything," she whispered, and I felt my whole body lean in to her in response. "Not so fast. I want to hear it. Your submission."

I stared up at her, ready for her lips against mine. Desperate for her arms around me. "Right now?"

"Right now."

I shuffled my papers. Sadie, maddeningly, stayed just as close to me. I could feel her breath on my face, and I wanted it everywhere. Instead, though, I found my place and I started to read.

"Johnny's Bar in Silver Lake opened in 1977, helmed by Johnny McDaniel. While it was a quieter spot than the Black Cat down the street, it was still opened with a sense of welcome for the LGBTQ+ community before society—and Los Angeles, specifically—were as accepting as they are today.

"People, of course, drank at Johnny's—he was known for his perfect Tom Collins. But they also connected. They networked when leading an open life could be dangerous. They made friends and chosen family. And, of course, they fell in love.

"Johnny fell in love, too. He met his partner, Billy Thomas, at the bar. Billy had a successful career at the Downtown LA law firm Safi & Romanoff, and he was known for knocking out a large majority of billable hours sitting on the stool at the far end of the bar. In the days long before cell phones, his colleagues and coworkers knew he was as reachable there as his office direct line.

"In the 1980s, Johnny's became a different kind of community space. As HIV and AIDS ravaged through the population, people found a safe place to gather, grieve, and give comfort and advice, even as so many longtime regulars were lost.

"Times changed. Silver Lake gentrified greatly, and the area became less of an LGBTQ+-specific neighborhood. Johnny's

still had their crowd of regulars, but things were different. And then Johnny, who'd done what seemed like the impossible and survived his HIV diagnosis, died of a sudden heart attack."

Sadie swallowed hard, which I only knew because of how close we were still standing. I took a chance and took her hand in mine. She didn't pull away.

"*The community, much smaller by then, was bereft. Not only had they lived through an era of indescribable loss, without Johnny they worried they would lose their community space as well. But something extraordinary happened: Billy left his job at Safi & Romanoff and took over Johnny's. Johnny's niece, Sadie McDaniel, who he'd helped raise after her parents died, joined the staff as well.*

"*I've talked so much about Johnny's as a community gathering place, so I don't want to neglect that it's also just a great bar. Billy and Sadie take their drinks seriously and make a wide variety of regulars and one-off customers alike feel welcome. With all of the new and trendy bars in this incredibly gentrified neighborhood, there is something unique about a place that's held onto the aspects that made it special from Day One.*

"*An unexpected development from the welcome shift in LGBTQ+ rights and representation is that safe spaces like Johnny's feel, in some ways, of another time. This building, its construction overseen by Johnny himself, was a haven, and now in this day and age some see havens as unnecessary.*

"*Communities, though, still need spaces to gather and to feel connected. I know personally that Sadie's plans for Johnny's are to revitalize the bar into a more modern space that nonetheless serves the LA Eastside's queer community in the same spirit that Johnny's set out with, back in 1977. And so it's not only because of this historic significance to Los Angeles, but its future in which it remains a welcoming and comfortable space for this community to gather, I nominate Johnny's Bar as a Historic Place.*"

We were still standing so close, and even though we were holding hands, I had no idea what to think.

"You made it sound magical," Sadie said. "Not just a bar that would have died off long ago if Billy weren't so stubborn."

"Yeah, isn't that part of the magic, though?" I asked, and I took a chance. I stood on my tiptoes and found her mouth with mine.

There was no hesitation, thank god. Sadie's lips moved against mine, like a whisper and a prayer at the same time. I wrapped my arms around her shoulders, holding myself steady at her level, as hers circled my waist and pulled me tightly against her.

"Wait, I should say something," I told her, and she laughed.

"Is there something more pressing than this?" she asked.

"Sadie, I love you. I love the community you're building, I love how you listen to people and make them feel special, and I love that you believe in people who no one else seems to understand. I love how you treat me like I'm special. I love that when I think of the different kinds of futures I could want, you're in every single version."

She leaned in and kissed me with an urgency I'd never experienced, like a shockwave jolting us somewhere new, together. Sadie, always so damn cool and collected, was a force of nature.

"I don't have a long list," she said, "but I love you too, Max. Sometimes I feel like I've loved you since whenever it was you first walked into my bar and ordered a Paloma. The way you looked at me—"

"Oh my god, I'm sure I seemed embarrassingly thirsty!"

"You seemed like you wanted to get to know me," she said. "And when a cute girl wants to get to know me, it could make me pretty weak in the knees. *You* made me pretty weak in the knees."

This time it was me kissing her with everything I had. Me, Max Van Doren, who'd been so afraid of so many things, and yet here I was with everything out on the table to the person I loved. To Sadie.

"I really hate doing this right now," Sadie said. "But I should get back to work. Can you hang around a while?"

"Sadie, I can hang around as long as you want."

Epilogue
One Year Later

"This was a terrible idea and I can't believe I let you talk me into it."

I calmly sipped my cocktail. "First of all, it was Chelsey who talked us all into this opening-night party. Secondly, it wasn't a terrible idea. Third—"

"Why are you so chill?" Sadie asked, narrowing her eyes. "It's suspicious."

I was anything but, but I'd gotten even better at keeping emotions to myself when I needed to. And tonight, the grand reopening of Johnny's after months of planning and weeks closed for renovations, was no night for my panic. Sadie had that much covered on her own.

Not that I was nervous about the bar itself. Sadie had collaborated with a designer whose queer daughter had seen Chelsey's series about Johnny's and begged her dad to offer his services at a sizeable discount. Now new lights gave the room a warm glow, and sleek tables fit in perfectly between the bar and the booths lining the wall, which now led out to a twinkle-lights-lined patio big enough for a DJ and a tiny dance floor. It was funny how much hadn't actually been changed at all, though. For one thing, the historic preservation process with LA Conservancy meant that too many updates couldn't be made. But it also turned out that restoring the beautiful hardwood flooring, redoing the walls in a mix of muted tones and bold wallpaper panels, and adding art by local queer artists made the whole place somehow look new and like it was always supposed to look this way, all at once.

"It's perfect," I said. "You know that, right?"

"Yeah, I just hope people show up," she said, shoving her hair back from her face.

I leaned over the bar to kiss her and pretend that I wasn't at least a little nervous about the exact same thing. "People are going to show up."

Luz, one of the bartenders Sadie had hired for the reopening, walked out of the back room with a stack of papers. "I forgot to bring these up earlier."

"I'm second-guessing these now," Sadie said, and passed me one. It was the new Johnny's menu, printed in bold ink on heavy cream-colored paper. And it was still in Comic Sans.

"But it was his favorite font," I said, and we both laughed. I'd learned a lot more about Johnny from both Sadie and Billy in the last year, and I knew enough to feel how much he would love all of this—both the upgrades as well as the devotion to honoring history.

"I might be less sentimental about font choices next time I have these printed," Sadie said, as someone banged loudly on the door. I glanced over the menu as she ran over to look out the window and grinned when I saw that Johnny's signature Tom Collins was at the top of the menu, now named after him. There was an overly fussy martini named after Billy, and then—

"Oh my god," I murmured as Sadie returned with Chelsey, Ava, and celebrity DJ Hadley Six, who had volunteered to spin this evening. The third drink on the list was the modified Paloma that Sadie had invented for me, mezcal instead of tequila and a low-heat spicy rim, but now it had a name. The Secret Weapon.

"You named a drink after me," I said to her as she walked behind me.

"The least I could do." She kissed my cheek and continued through the room, as the DJ got set up outside and Chelsey and Ava sat on either side of me at the bar. I'd always loved watching Sadie work, but now that it was in this place that she owned—not literally, she was renting from Billy until she'd saved up the rest—there was a new level to her purpose and ease in her movements. It was like she'd always been meant to do exactly this.

"I'm second-guessing this, too," Sadie said, walking up to us and pulling at her shirt. It was her vintage Los Angeles T-shirt, the softest one in her collection, and I loved how it hugged just slightly at her curves. "Should there be a dress code? Should I make people dress like this is a gay speakeasy or something?"

"Ooh—" Chelsey said, and Ava and I both glared at her.

"Sadie, with no disrespect implied to your girlfriend or mine," Ava said, "you look extremely hot. Leave the gay speakeasy to someone else."

"No disrespect to the gay speakeasy either," I said, and even Sadie laughed. "It's going to be great."

"I think it's time to open, boss," Luz said with a nod to the door. "Want me to?"

"Nah, I've got it," Sadie said, and we watched her walk to the door and flip the latch. It would have been a bigger moment if people would have started flooding in, but it was five p.m. on a Thursday, and for the next five minutes we were the only people there.

But the DJ started up, and Chelsey started posting on her Instagram stories, and Sadie and Luz got us drinks, and before long, the door opened and a small group none of us knew

walked in, followed by a couple of regulars who eyed the updated space before grabbing their usual spots around the bar
from mine.

"So glad y'all could make it tonight," Sadie said, casually
passing out the new menus like she'd been doing this her whole
life. "Drinks are on the front, and the Los Tacos menu's on the
back—they'll deliver here and you can order through us."

Sadie had struck the deal with Los Tacos recently. They
were so thrilled that another small business was determined to
stay on the block that they were happy to work out a deal with
Sadie that profited both of them. I couldn't believe that the very
queso that I'd once accidentally flung onto Sadie's ass was part
of our happily-ever-after, but somehow it felt right.

Before long, Nina and Ari arrived, and they grabbed a back
booth while Chelsey and Ava headed to the patio to get the
dance floor started.

"Looks like it's just you," Sadie said with a grin. "Like the
old days, except you don't have a pile of scripts and contracts
with you."

Riley Howe had been right that my life had a little more
time to breathe now that I was on the management side, though
I still brought plenty of scripts to Johnny's. Sadie planned to
figure out a better work-life balance as well, when Luz and
others could manage the bar without her. For now, though, Sadie was here on most nights and that meant when I had work,
I tended to do it from my usual spot here at the bar. As close as
my old apartment was from Johnny's, now all I had to do when
it was time to call it a night was cut through the backroom and
head upstairs. Moving in with Sadie had set off a chain reaction that led directly to Chelsey finally asking Ava to move
in with her. (The room that had been my bedroom was now
Chelsey's full-time content studio, which meant I still more-
than-occasionally spent time there, talking into Chelsey's
iPhone about topics including You Point Oh and local fashion
companies who specialized in extremely cute button-downs.)

"I like watching you work," I told Sadie, as more people flooded in and she kept at it. The Kickballers gradually rolled in, wearing our new sponsored-by-Johnny's jerseys even though the season had just ended and we'd done very poorly in the playoffs yet again. I got pulled into conversations about Tonya's terrible boss and Paige's latest crush and the chicken coop BBQ's wife was trying to convince her to build in their backyard, but I always managed to look over just in time to catch Sadie's gaze.

Riley, her wife, and some of my coworkers showed up right before a small group of Exemplar and former-Exemplar assistants arrived. I tried to introduce everyone, even though I still felt fairly new at managing multiple social groups at once, though it was getting easier—or at least more familiar. My friends had started taking it for granted that they could find me, most nights, at Johnny's, which meant it was becoming more of a normal thing to juggle people from different parts of my life at once. Tonight, though, felt like that on steroids.

Everyone raved about the flooring and the new art and the custom neon JOHNNY'S sign that glowed behind the counter (Chelsey had, of course, worked out a deal with a custom neon sign shop), and I felt already how this place was built to last.

"Max, it's so good to see you," a familiar voice said, and I looked over to see that Joyce had joined Riley and her whole group. I hadn't seen her in the year since I left Exemplar, though we both occasionally liked each other's photos on Instagram.

"You too," I said, getting up from my seat to give her a very Hollywood-style hug, no tight squeezing or actual emotions displayed. "I didn't think you'd actually come, I know you hate driving to the Eastside."

"Oh, Riley put some pressure on me, and then Ari did the same, and I heard rumors of all the assistants showing up, and next thing I knew I was headed east." She beamed at me. "Plus, you knew I was invested in your whole bartender saga. Felt like I owed it to myself to see how that finally worked out."

"Oh my god, please don't tell Sadie my crush was so out of control *my boss knew about it*," I said, and we both burst into laughter. Joyce was so much more fun when I didn't have to be terrified of her.

"You really do look great," Joyce said. "I know assistant life is rough. It's clear you've thrived now that you're on the other side of things."

"Thank you. It turned out I kept thinking I needed people to believe in me to—I don't know. Grow up or whatever, but—" I cut myself off when it hit me that I was going full-on self-actualization app mode with one of the most powerful behind-the-scenes players in Hollywood, who still, if I was very honest, terrified me a little.

"But?" Joyce asked with a smile.

"Yeah, I guess I had to believe in myself," I said. "Which is embarrassing and annoying, I know."

"Your secret's safe with me. Now tell me what I should order."

"Well, there's a drink named after me, but don't feel any pressure," I told her, as Ari and Nina made their way over to greet Joyce. Sadie caught my eye, and I pulled her over to introduce her to Joyce, and then everyone else from my life that she hadn't met yet. I was looking forward to the time ahead of us when she'd have more time off and we'd have more plans together, but this part was great too, where almost all of the people I cared about in the world were together and getting to see the girl I loved doing what she was best at.

The bar kept filling up, and eventually I ended up on the dance floor surrounded by my friends and teammates and former coworkers in the crisp LA night air. I wished I could send video of this moment back to younger me—not just the kid who felt alone and too scared to come out in her red-state high school, but the girl who'd moved to LA expecting it to open up for her and give her everything she wanted. *You're going to have it all,* I wished I could tell her. *You've just got to be the one doing the opening!*

I slipped back into my spot at the bar—there was now an extra little ledge so that people as short as me could sit on the barstools without any awkward jumping or hoisting—and made eye contact with Sadie as she finished up with a customer. I saw her say something to Luz and then head off toward me.

"Sorry, I feel like I've hardly seen you tonight at all," she said, leaning over the bar to kiss me. "I know business won't stay at this level, but still. It's pretty good, right?"

"*Pretty good,*" I said, nudging her. "More like amazing."

"Look at this," she said, taking her phone out of her pocket and handing it to me. She'd texted a photo of the crowded bar to Billy, and he'd responded with **Why is it so bright in there?**

"I like how reliable he is," I said. "Just sitting up in Fresno thinking about dark places or whatever."

"He said he'd drive down soon," she said. "I told him to come the weekend your mom visits, but that might have broken the rule where Billy and I pretend we're not family to one another, so maybe I'll take back that invitation."

"No, don't, I've told way too many Billy stories to Mom, she'll kill us if we don't make it happen." Mom had a long list of demands for her first trip to LA, but I was excited to show her my home here. I had demands too; she was bringing along an extra suitcase filled with some of my things I'd left behind. Now we both knew that my old bedroom didn't need to stay empty, waiting for my return. Now we both knew that my home was here.

Mom was also bringing me her old engagement ring, not that I planned on doing anything with it immediately. But I liked the thought of it tucked away with my things, ready and waiting for the right time. I loved that, even if it was still years away, I knew that there would be a right time.

"I know I have to let you get back to actually working," I

said, "but I just hope you can see how amazing this all is, because of you. You totally did it, Sadie."

She waved me off. "Everything's only this good now because you helped me get here. Without you I'd still be roommates with Billy and begging him to turn on another light in the bar."

"And using a flip phone!" I laughed and shook my head. "Seriously, though. I'm so proud of you. I love what you built here."

I loved how she ducked her head, the way her cheeks flushed at my words. I knew that it was the closest she came to actually accepting a compliment. The bar buzzed around me, louder than nights at Johnny's used to be, and I thought about how many people I cared about who were here tonight. I ended up crowded into a booth with some of my friends, laughing about an incredibly stupid meme we'd all shared, before I got pulled back outside onto the patio to dance, before I ended up back inside splitting an order of queso with my old coworkers. I'd put together this whole life for myself, and even if hardly any of it had gone how I'd expected, I somehow had everything I needed in this moment.

Except another drink. So I elbowed my way up to the bar and my usual stool, and Sadie grinned her crooked smile right at me.

"The usual, Max?"

"The usual, Sadie."

Acknowledgments

Thank you so much to my kind, enthusiastic, and supportive editor, Norma Perez-Hernandez. I feel so lucky that we get to work together! Thank you to Kate Testerman, the best agent I could have, for everything.

Thanks to the entire team at Kensington, including Jane Nutter, Michelle Addo, Lauren Jernigan, Kait Johnson, Matt Johnson, and anyone I forgot to mention! Thanks to Kristin Dwyer and Molly Mitchell of LEO PR.

So many people helped me with so many aspects of this book. Thanks to all of my friends, of course, as always, but specifically: thank you to Samantha Powell for knowing exactly which bar the hot and/or famous would frequent. Thanks to Maret Orliss for all of the information about lifting. Thank you to Aysha Wax for all of your wisdom about dating coaching. Thanks to Adam Grosswirth for talking about fictional cocktails with me. Thank you to Christie Baugher and Jessica Morgan for naming fake movies and even faker screenwriters. Thanks to Robyn Schneider for introducing me to Wat Thai Temple. Thanks to Morgan Matson for naming You Point Oh.

Thank you to everyone who talked to me about agent, management, and Hollywood assistant life, especially Charlotte Huang, Rochelle Hartson, Tom Harrison, and Scott Wexler.

Thanks to everyone who helped me name kickball teams, especially Riley Silverman and Laser Webber.

Thank you so much to Erik Van Breene for all of your knowledge and guidance about historical protections and preservation in Los Angeles.

Thanks to my mother, Pat Spalding.

Thanks to every single queer bar that's created community for people. My regular queer spot was actually Mokabe's, a coffeeshop that was open bar hours during the 1990s and gave young people a safe space to congregate. I'm so glad it's still around. In a time where hateful laws and public figures target the most vulnerable members of the LGBTQ+ community, I'm extra grateful for queer spaces where community can still be found.

Visit our website at
KensingtonBooks.com
to sign up for our newsletters, read
more from your favorite authors, see
books by series, view reading group
guides, and more!

BOOK **CLUB**

BETWEEN THE CHAPTERS

Become a Part of Our
Between the Chapters Book Club
Community and Join the Conversation

Betweenthechapters.net